SALEM STREET

SALEM STREET

Anna Jacobs

St. Martin's Press
New York

Library of Congress Cataloging-in-Publication Data

Jacobs, Anna.
Salem Street / Anna Jacobs.
p.   cm.
"A Thomas Dunne book."
ISBN 0-312-11884-8
I. Title.
PR9619.3.J24S25   1995
823—dc20   94-41107   CIP

First published in Great Britain by Hodder & Stoughton

First U.S. Edition: February 1995
10 9 8 7 6 5 4 3 2 1

With love to my parents, Lucy and Derrick Sheridan, to whom I owe a great deal.

CONTENTS

Annie Gibson was born on the fifteenth of May 1820, in the front bedroom of her parents' new house in Salem Street, one of eight narrow terraced houses built for the operatives at Hallam's Mill. You had to be tough to survive in those mean little streets and squalid alleys. More than half the babies born in Bilsden did not live to see their fifth birthday. Annie did. But then, Annie Gibson was a survivor.

Part One

1

Salem Street: 1820 to 1830

The handcart creaked and groaned as it trundled slowly along Florida Terrace and the man pushing it laughed aloud as he guided it on its erratic course. "Nearly there now, love," he said encouragingly to the woman walking by his side.

"I'm all right, John," she insisted, but her face was white and sweat beaded her forehead. She held one hand protectively over her belly, as if to keep her unborn child safe. As he slowed down, she added sharply, "Nay, get a move on, will you! We'll not be there till after dark at this rate." This was a gross exaggeration, for they were only moving a few streets, although it seemed like a different world here, away from the stinking yards and alleys of Claters End.

John Gibson knew better than to argue with his wife. Lucy was not well, but she hated anyone to fuss over her, so she got a bit sharp occasionally. He had begged her to stop work and take things easy, for the baby's sake, but she wouldn't. If she went on at Hallam's Mill, they could buy a few more things for their new home and anyway, she'd have plenty of time to rest once the baby was born.

When he had met her after work today, he had noticed how haggard she was looking, her red hair faded and brittle, her skin sallow and her body over-thin, except for the curve of her swollen belly. Only her eyes were alive, green and alert. She had lovely eyes, did his Lucy. If anything happened to her . . . He banished the thought, as he banished all unpleasant thoughts. Nothing was going to happen to her. He wouldn't allow anything to happen to her!

As they slowed down to turn the corner into Boston Street, he let the cart run to a halt against the wall. "Heavy work," he said. "Mind if I rest a bit?"

Lucy looked at his face, pale from the long hours inside the mill, and thought how much she loved this rough lad of hers. When he leaned against the wall and put his arm round her, she sagged against him gratefully, feeling his bristly chin next to her cheek, for he was not much taller than she was. John had been a bit of a favourite with the women before she met him. Perhaps it was his curly brown hair and wide grin that had attracted them. He'd not looked at another woman in that way since they'd got wed, though. She wouldn't have stood for it, any more than she'd have stood for him drinking himself stupid on Saturday nights and getting into fights, like he used to.

"Eh, what a day this is!" he said and gave her a hug, his pulse quickening as always at the touch of her body. It was worth working hard for a wife like her and he was proud of his record as a provider. He was always one of the last to be put on to short time in the mill nowadays and he reckoned he'd be in line for the chargehand's job in a year or two, when old Ben got past it. All they needed now to complete their happiness was a live baby, not a limp little corpse like the last one. He pushed that sad memory away quickly.

After a few moments, Lucy nudged him. "Come on, my lazy lad! I shan't feel right till we're settled in."

By the time they were halfway along Boston Street, Lucy

was panting again from her exertions. She forgot her tiredness, however, as she looked at the houses they were passing. How envious she used to feel of the lucky people who lived here, for they not only had whole houses of their own, but private back yards behind them! Well, there was no longer any need to feel envious, for soon she too would have a house and yard of her own – and not just any house, either. She and John had been lucky enough to get one of the brand new houses in Salem Street. It was kind of young Mr Frederick to speak up for them, though he wouldn't have done so if John hadn't been such a good worker. He was sharp as they came, Mr Frederick, for all he was only seventeen, and would make a hard master for the mill when old Mr Hallam died. They were all hard, were the cotton masters, and didn't she know it, for she'd been working in the spinning mills herself for over eleven years now, ever since she was a child of ten.

They passed the water tap, with its little queue of women and children. The water was turned on all the time in Boston Street. That'd be grand, that would. No need to skimp when you could get a clean bucketful at any time of the day or night. Lucy smiled at John, a radiant smile, weary as she was, for they were almost there. Salem Street was just around the corner.

It had been touch and go whether the new row of eight houses would be finished in time for Lucy Gibson to have her child there, or whether she'd have to bear it in the damp room where she had already lost one baby. But the builder was more interested in making money than in doing a good job, and Thomas Hallam was desperate for more accommodation for his operatives, so work on the little terrace went on apace. And if the timber could have been more carefully jointed or the bricks more evenly laid, who was going to complain? Certainly not the lucky families waiting to move in! Specially chosen, they were, for it was one of the best terraces in the Rows, a single-sided street facing the mill wall, with a good big private yard behind each house and a shared patch of dirt in front.

As they turned the corner into her new street, Lucy let out a long exhalation of pure happiness. "We'll do better here, love, I know we will." She paused for a moment to look possessively at the houses and to enjoy the feel of the weak April sunlight on her face after working in the noise and clatter of the mill.

"We've not done that badly so far, lass," said John, surprised.

"Aye, I know, but I want us to do better still," Lucy insisted, both hands on her belly, because the baby had started kicking vigorously. "Eh, but he's lively today! Takes after his father, he does." She threw John a look of complicity.

He grinned back at her. "His mother can be a bit lively at times, too!"

The cart was a tight fit at the corner, where the two privies barred part of the entrance to Salem Street, for its wheels pulled to the right and it wasn't easy to manoeuvre, but a bit of tugging and they were through.

"I wouldn't like to live in this end house," commented Lucy, "right next door to the privies like that. Still, it'll be nice to have two privies, won't it? Not so much queuin' up, eh?" Without waiting for John, she hurried towards Number Three, her weariness forgotten in her pleasure at taking possession of their new home.

The door was slightly ajar and she stopped to take a deep breath before pushing it open and stepping inside reverently, as if she were treading on holy ground. It was a good house, all of twelve feet wide with bigger windows than usual. The front door opened straight into the largest of the four rooms, which had a nice level floor paved with two-foot-square flagstones. "I'll soon have that floor clean and my rag mats down," she said aloud.

John followed her in, carrying one of their bundles and she turned towards him, her eyes filled with tears. "Eh, John!" she said huskily.

He put the bundle down and held out his hand. "Come on, my lass, let's 'ave a good look round before we start. There's no rent agent breathin' over our shoulders this time."

Between the front room and the kitchen at the rear a flight of steep wooden steps led up to the two bedrooms. The stairwell was cramped and dark, but the house seemed the height of luxury to two people who were more used to sharing a room with several others than having four rooms all to themselves. After they'd walked proudly round their new domain, Lucy left John to bring the rest of the things in and stood gloating over the kitchen. The fire grate was nice and wide, with a brick ledge at each side to stand things on and a good strong metal bar across the middle, about two feet above the hearthstone, to hang the pot hooks on. The triangular space under the stairs would make a fine cupboard to keep her things in. It was a good job John had some tools and knew how to use them. He'd soon build her a set of shelves.

Hearing voices outside, Lucy went to see who John was talking to and found him with another young couple whose children were rushing up and down the narrow front yard, shrieking and tumbling around like a litter of puppies. The mill wall had already cast its shadow over the sour earth and the broken glass in the top of it was glinting in the late sunlight.

"This is Mick and Bridie O'Connor, love, who're movin' into Number Five."

Irish, thought Lucy, as she nodded at the couple. How had they got a house? She looked at them searchingly, for the Irish were not well thought of and what your neighbours were like could make a huge difference to your life, when walls were thin and houses small. She liked what she saw, however.

Bridie O'Connor was a short, stocky woman, with dark hair and a broad smile. As she got to know her, Lucy was often to marvel at Bridie's energy, for nothing seemed to get her down. Mick was tall, with a ruddy complexion and bright blue eyes. It soon became obvious that for all his great size, his wife ruled him with a rod of iron and her children, too, though Danny, the eldest, was a handful, always into mischief.

It was not long before Lucy learned their story. The O'Connors had been brought over from Ireland a few years previously, when the owners of the new mills were so short of operatives that they were bringing in workers from anywhere they could find them. That made a bond between them, for Lucy herself had been brought in as a terrified child of ten, when her parents died and she was left on the parish in a distant village. She would rarely discuss that time, even with John, for the mill-owners had been far less tender with their child apprentices in the early days than they were now. She had survived, she said, and that was enough. But she would never, she always added, let her own children go into the mill.

"Let my Mick give you a hand with those things, Mr Gibson. You'll not want your wife doin' any heavy liftin' in her condition." Bridie smiled at Lucy, for she too was expecting a child, though she did not look to be very far on yet. "Is it your first?" she asked, more to make conversation than anything else.

"Sort of. We lost one last year," said Lucy.

Bridie squeezed her hand in quick sympathy. "Ah, 'tis hard on a woman. I lost one meself three years back. She only lived a few hours, God rest her poor little soul!"

They turned in common accord to watch the men carry the Gibsons' few bits and pieces of furniture inside, and Bridie shooed away her children when they tried to follow. "Little devils!" she said fondly. "We'll be movin' in ourselves later today. Charlie's lendin' us his handcart. We've just come over to pick it up."

"Charlie?"

"Aye, Charlie Ashworth, him as was injured in that accident afore Easter, God bless him. The poor fellow's been given the end house, Number Eight. They didn't think he'd survive, but he's comin' along nicely now. A doctor came and sewed up his wounds with a needle and thread, just think of that, will ye! D'ye know Charlie?"

"No, but I heard about the accident." Lucy shuddered. There were dreadful accidents sometimes in the mills. A girl had been killed right next to Lucy, years ago, caught by her hair in the machinery and scalped within seconds. Lucy had had nightmares about it for months. Charlie Ashworth's accident had also been horrendous, but it was the men who shuddered as they spoke of it, for it was every man's worst nightmare. It was a miracle he was still alive. If anything ever happened to her John . . . She banished the thought quickly.

Over the next day or two the other houses were taken possession of, the last people arriving on the Tuesday, when Lucy was at work. She was too tired when she got home that night to do more than nod at them and exchange a few words with Bridie, standing on her doorstep watching the children play and waiting for Mick to come home.

By the end of the following week, Lucy could no longer work with her usual efficiency, and the chargehand sent her home. Her wages were paid meticulously, right up to the hour she'd been summoned to the office, and she was told she'd be welcome back when she'd weaned the child, for old Tom Hallam knew the worth of all his workers.

When John came hurrying home that night, worried because she'd had no one to look after her, his meal of cabbage and potatoes with a little fat bacon was bubbling in a pan and Lucy was sitting with her feet up in front of the fire. The most she would admit to was that she did feel 'a bit peaky-like' and was glad to stop work. During the next few days she pottered about the house, trying to get everything straight before the baby arrived. She found it comforting to have Bridie only two doors away and they soon became firm friends.

Bridie, never one to be reticent about herself, told Lucy all the details of how she and Mick had left their village in Ireland, because the new owner wanted the land for other uses and his agent was starting to evict people. It was Bridie who had forced Mick to look further afield than the next village for a job, and the big, gentle chap, who loved to feel the sun and wind on his face, found himself putting his cross on an agreement to go and work in a cotton mill in Lancashire. All they knew was that this place was across the sea in England and that the mills spun cotton wool into thread and yarn. At that time they'd not been long married and had only the one child. They'd thought they were living in luxury in Bilsden, what with the regular work, always something to eat and a clean room to themselves.

Mick had gradually grown used to the work and found himself a niche tending the dray horses and doing odd jobs round the mill, but he never grew used to living in a town or working indoors. He tried to take his pleasure from seeing how well his Bridie was and how his children were thriving on the regular wages. "Sure, we'd have lost more of 'em if we'd stayed there," Bridie would say, crossing herself, and he would nod. But just occasionally Mick would turn gloomy and bad-tempered for no obvious reason, and then he would vanish without a word for the whole of the next Sunday, to tramp the moors and "breathe in some daicent air that don't choke a man".

When Lucy went into labour, it was Bridie who came in to sit with her, leaving her own children with Alice Butterworth in Number One. It was Bridie who sent her Danny for the local midwife and shooed John out to work, for what man would dare to lose a day, just because his wife was having a baby?

And after all, it was not until the middle of the afternoon that an exhausted Lucy at last produced the child, to her disappointment only a girl and not very big.

"An' what're ye lookin' so glum about, woman?" asked Bridie softly once the midwife had gone. "'Tis a fine, healthy daughter you've got there!"

"I wanted a son," admitted Lucy, in a tired voice.

"More fool you! It's best to have a girl first, as I should know havin' had three boys in a row. That way, she can help you look after the others. That Danny of mine is a little devil, so he is, and I can't trust him to look after any of 'em, not even for a minute."

Lucy couldn't help smiling. Bridie could always cheer her up.

"Now what'll you be callin' the little darlin'?"

"Annie, after my mam," said Lucy, leaning back tiredly. She fell into a light doze and Bridie, keeping an anxious eye on her, was pleased to see some of her colour returning. Lucy dozed on and off for the rest of the afternoon, waking occasionally with a start to check that the tiny creature in the box next to her bed was still alive. Reassured by the baby's soft, snuffling breaths, she would drift off to sleep again, relieved that her ordeal was safely over.

John came rushing home from work at seven that night and Bridie only just managed to grab his arm and stop him from pounding up the stairs.

"Whisht now, do ye want to wake them up?"

"Them?"

She smiled warmly. "Aye, them. Your wife an' daughter."

He gulped and swallowed hard. "Lucy – she's all right?"

"Sure, she's fine. They both are."

"Thank God!" His eyes were bright with tears. He sniffed and swallowed again. "A daughter, you said?"

"Aye. Pretty as a flower, she is, with red hair like her mam." Bridie frowned at him. "Now, ye won't be after upsettin' Lucy because it's not a son, will ye? She's tired out, poor thing." Doesn't give birth easily, she thought to herself. I'm glad I'm not that way. Sure, it's a cruel hard world for us women!

"It's my Lucy as I care for," said John. "So long as she's all right, I'm not mithered whether it's a boy or a girl, though I'd like to have a son one day." He pulled away from her and moved purposefully towards the stairs.

Annie Gibson was the first child to be born in Salem Street. Bridie's fourth son followed her into the world three months later and after that the babies came thick and fast.

Lucy never did go back to work in the mill. Before Annie was even weaned, she found herself pregnant again, though she lost that baby in the fourth month. Another pregnancy, hard on its heels, produced the lusty son she'd longed for, but somehow it was Annie who remained her favourite. By the time Annie was ten, there had been two further miscarriages and one more living daughter. And Annie, young as she was, had become her mother's right hand.

* * *

Twenty-five years before, the town of Bilsden had been a small village, nestling in a narrow Pennine valley to the north-east of Manchester. In the early days, small mills had been built along the river, their machinery driven by its rushing waters. Then steam power freed the cotton men from so close a dependence upon the whims of nature and they bought up nearby farmland to build larger and larger mills.

As the mills proliferated, housing had to be built for the operatives and the village developed into a town that grew bigger each year and soon swallowed up half the neighbouring farms. Within a decade, the Rows had crept out across the valley floor like living scars. Before its former inhabitants knew where they were, Bilsden was a bustling town, its streets teeming with the stunted bodies of those who served the Great God Cotton.

Fine new houses were built on the slopes above the town by those upon whom the Great God had smiled, for the moors around Bilsden were beautiful still, in their own stark way. But the valley of the Bil grew steadily filthier, the river polluted by the effluent from the processing and dyeing of cotton, and most of the greenery stamped out of existence. Now, day after day, the steam engines burnt up offerings of best coal and covered everything around them with a pall of black smoke and smuts, all in the name of Cotton. And not even the rich could escape from this dark rain.

Old Tom Hallam boasted in his declining years about the part he had played in such progress. He had been the first man to build a cotton mill in the district, in the days when Bilsden was only a cluster of farm workers' cottages around the parish church of St Mark. Folks had thought him mad with his great water wheel and had counselled him against the venture, but he'd proved them wrong, by George! In the library of his large new mansion on the very top of the hill they called the Ridge Tom had a window specially built to look out over the valley for, unlike his wife, he loved its smoky bustle. He did not enjoy the view from the windows which looked out across the grey-green stretches of moorland or across his well-tended gardens, but he saw that his family was protected from the cold moorland winds above and the unpleasant sights below by high stone walls topped with broken glass to keep out intruders.

By 1830, Tom Hallam was dead and the houses in Salem Street were showing distinct signs of wear and tear, though its inhabitants still considered it a cut above most other streets in the Rows. Only seven out of the eight houses were occupied in March, for Grandpa Burley at Number Seven had died suddenly the previous week and his wife had gone to live with her eldest daughter over in Rochdale. The house wouldn't stay empty for more than a day or two, though. There were many families living in one or two rooms down at Claters End who'd give their eye-teeth to move in, if only Mr Frederick Hallam's hard-eyed rent agent would let them.

Annie Gibson, skipping solemnly up and down the paved pathway in front of the houses with a piece of rope her dad had brought home for her, made a game of counting the number of people who lived in the street. Her thick red plaits bobbed against her back and her skirt flew up and down in time to her jumping, showing a pair of thin legs covered with coarse black stocking that her mam had knitted for her. Five people in Number One, she said to herself, five Butterworths. She wrinkled her nose distastefully at the proximity of the privies. Six people in Number

Two – George and Polly Dykes and their three young children, and now Grandpa Dykes as well. She didn't like George and Polly, who often kept the whole street awake on Saturdays with their drunken singing and shouting. Her mam didn't like them either. She said Polly was a slattern and should be able to manage on George's wages, instead of spending half her time at the pawnshop.

Annie waved to her mam as she passed Number Three and nodded at Widow Clegg who was coming out of Number Four, because her mam always told them to be polite to the neighbours. Widow Clegg was at least a hundred years old. She was tall, with a bony face and straight black hair dragged back in a tight bun. She took in lodgers and she also laid out dead people and helped women who were having babies. She'd helped Annie's mam when Lizzie was born. Annie wished she hadn't bothered, for their Lizzie was the bane of her life. She was for ever making a nuisance of herself and tagging along when she wasn't wanted.

The children of the Rows were in a constant state of feud, with territory strictly marked out between the different groups, which were usually based on the streets in which they lived. The Salemites and the Bosties had clear lines of demarcation along the ginnel between their two rows of backyards. You were allowed to walk along your side of the ginnel to get to your own house, but if you crossed over, you were in for trouble.

Lizzie was always transgressing such rules, and then Annie or Tom would have to rescue her, because you couldn't let anyone bash your little sister, however much she deserved it. Tom was only eight, but he was a good fighter, able to beat lads older and bigger than himself. He couldn't play out much with Annie, though, because he had to go to Sergeant Brown's day school. John and Lucy wanted to make sure that their only son had a better start in life than themselves.

Annie had begged to be allowed to go to school, too, but her dad said it wasn't worth it for a girl, because she'd only go and get herself married. Besides, she was needed at home. The schooling caused a lot of bickering between Annie and Tom, though not in front of her dad. He wouldn't stand for any quarrelling in the house, her dad wouldn't.

As she came to Number Five, Annie stopped frowning and smiled. The O'Connors lived here, a whole house full of them. Her lips moved as she counted them up, still skipping in time to the numbers. Danny was nearly twenty now, a man grown. She liked Danny, who always had a cheerful word for everyone. Most folk as old as him were married and too busy to talk to their neighbour's children, but Danny had told her that marriage was not for him. He was going to make something of himself and he didn't want a wife and children keeping him poor. He was taking lessons in reading and writing from the priest and, until he saw his way forward, he was working at Hallam's. She knew that he'd been fined the previous week for arguing with the overseer, because she'd heard her dad telling her mam about it in bed one night. Mr Frederick himself had said that it was not to happen again, or else Danny would be out. Her dad said Danny wouldn't last much longer if he didn't mind his step.

When the new baby came, there would be thirteen O'Connors in the little house. Annie had asked Bridie if she hadn't got enough children now, but Bridie had just laughed and said that babies were the Lord's will. Annie's mam was expecting another baby, too. Women were always having babies. Annie just hoped that the Lord wouldn't send them another girl. One sister like Lizzie was enough for anyone!

She skipped quickly past Number Six, because she wasn't supposed to play in front of that house. Her mam said Sally Smith wasn't respectable and when Annie had pressed for an explanation, she said that it was because of Sally's gentleman friend, who came to see her every Tuesday and Thursday. Annie would have liked to press for further explanation of this, because the gentleman friend had a nice smile and so did Sally, but her father had said that was enough of that, thank you, just remember to keep away from Number Six.

Number Seven was empty now. Poor house! It looked sad. Poor Grandpa Burley, too! What did it feel like to be dead?

In Number Eight lived Barmy Charlie, only her dad said they had to call him Mr Ashworth, which wasn't fair because no one else did. And he *was* barmy! He had funny turns. He talked to himself as well, and sometimes he even started singing at the top of his voice as he walked down the street. You couldn't help laughing at him then. His clothes were funny, too. He liked to dress in bright colours and he wore the daftest things! Annie had seen him once with a red and yellow woman's shawl wrapped round his shoulders.

Charlie traded in junk of all sorts, and he had the biggest yard in the street, over twice the size of Annie's back yard. Charlie's was piled high with things and he'd built a lean-to along one wall. There were clothes, pieces of broken furniture, papers, rags – he collected just about anything. When folks got wed, they often bought stuff off him for their houses. She'd love to have a good look round his yard, but he didn't allow children inside it and he had a big dog that barked at you and showed its teeth if you went too near. Every now and then, Charlie would take a pile of stuff away on his handcart to sell, but it didn't seem to make much difference to the piles in the yard.

On his bad days he stayed home and drank, mourning his lost manhood, he said, lost in that damned mill. On such days the women kept their children away from that end of the street and everyone tried to ignore Charlie's drunken singing, crying and shouting. Sometimes he sang all day, till his voice was hoarse and all that came out was a croak. It made Annie's throat ache even to think of it. She'd asked her dad what lost manhood meant and been told to mind her own business. It wasn't fair. No one ever explained anything interesting!

So, she said to herself as she skipped back down the street in a complicated pattern of movements, that made thirty-one people living in Salem Street, with three more babies on the way. And she knew all of them. Hers was a nice street. She'd hate to live somewhere like Claters End, where whole families were crowded into one room and rough drunken men shoved you aside as they walked past. In Salem Street each family had a proper house and its own yard. It was the best street in the Rows, her dad said, and she didn't want to live anywhere else.

2

Brighton: 1826 to 1830

Jeremy Lewis stared listlessly out of the window of the lodgings he had just taken in Bedford Square, Brighton. The attack of influenza had left him so weak that the five-hour coach journey down from London had exhausted him.

"Time for the dining-room ordeal," he said aloud and began to straighten his cravat and tidy his short light brown hair. As he looked in the mirror, he laughed and said, "Physician, heal thyself!"

At the door, he paused, then his eyes widened. Sitting at the large central table was a young woman, not strictly beautiful, but exquisitely dressed and coiffed. She was flanked by a plump elderly woman in black, to whom she was listening with an appearance of interest, but when her eyes met his across the room, she gave him just the tiniest of smiles. Encouraged by that, he went across to join them.

"Is this seat taken?"

Mrs Graham, the proprietor, bustled over to introduce them. "Mrs Parton, Miss Parton – Dr Jeremy Lewis. Pray take a seat, sir. We stand on no ceremony here."

When she heard that Jeremy was a doctor, the old lady brightened up and began to favour him with a dissertation upon the state of her health and to enumerate the reasons her daughter had insisted upon their coming to Brighton. "Though 'tis so late in the summer that it is often too cold for me to take the air, and I'm not one for meeting strangers. It does me no good, no good at all."

"I've come here to recuperate from the influenza," volunteered Jeremy, trying to stem the complaining flow. "The fresh sea air of Brighton was strongly recommended by one of my medical colleagues."

"Well, it's not done me any good, especially when Annabelle goes out walking on her own, which I cannot approve of in a strange town, and leaves me to sit and worry about her. And why people should want to come here when the weather is so cold, I don't know, but there's no accounting for taste." She sighed and looked around the room with a disparaging expression. "I still think we might just as well have remained safe at home."

"Now, you know that your health has improved greatly here, Mama," Miss Parton interrupted in a soft voice which Jeremy found a pleasure to listen to. "And I've come to no harm on my little outings, have I?"

"I should be happy to escort you for a walk around the town tomorrow, Miss Parton," Jeremy said. "If your mother will give her permission. Indeed, you would be doing me a favour, for I have only just arrived and I don't know where anything is."

"That would be most pleasant." Miss Parton inclined her head. "Would it not, Mama? You cannot object to my walking out if I have a gentleman to escort me."

Mrs Parton pressed her lips together, caught her daughter's eye and mumbled something which could have been assent.

It became plain as the meal progressed that Mrs Parton objected to many things about Brighton, and Jeremy admired the patient way her daughter bore with her grumblings. He very much liked Annabelle Parton's restrained, ladylike air, and the smooth dark blond hair that looked so silky and soft.

"In the morning, then, Dr Lewis," she said, as they rose to leave the table.

"I shall look forward to that, Miss Parton." He was by now feeling utterly exhausted and so he sought his bed, to sleep better than he had in weeks.

There was a heated argument in Mrs Parton's sitting-room before either lady retired that night.

"What do you want to encourage that young fellow for, Annabelle?"

"I think he's very pleasant and gentlemanly."

"You think anything in trousers pleasant since James Westby died! Ain't this one a bit young for you?"

"Mama, Dr Lewis has only offered his escort for a walk along the sea front. In such circumstances, his age is irrelevant."

"Well, I don't approve of it. Doctors aren't gentlemen and never will be, whether they've learned to ape their betters or not! And we know nothing about him, nothing at all! I said no good would come of this visit. What's to become of me if you find yourself a husband? I'm not leaving the village, whatever you do. I was born there and I intend to die there. And if I had my way, we'd go back there right now!"

Annabelle's soft white hands turned suddenly into bloodless claws that clutched at her mother's arm, and her voice became harsh. "If you force us to go back, I shall be very upset and you might regret it later, Mama! And if you do *anything* to spoil this chance for me to further my acquaintance with a gentleman who is possibly eligible, then I will guarantee to make your life extremely uncomfortable!"

Mrs Parton gasped, and when her daughter let go, took refuge in her bedroom. She made no further protests and was very quiet from then on when Dr Lewis was around. She knew Annabelle too well to think these were idle threats.

Jeremy enjoyed several strolls round Brighton with Annabelle. They chatted about books and music and exchanged reminiscences of their childhoods. She was a charming companion and so lovely to look at with her fine blond hair ruffled by the sea breezes and her cheeks rosy from the fresh air and exercise. She had, she told him, never felt as well in her life, and he could feel his postinfluenza lethargy improving daily.

Three days later, Jeremy invited Annabelle and her mother to join him in a carriage ride to Chalybeate Spring at the Wick, Hove, and the old lady made a silent third to their outing. Another day, he and Annabelle went on their own to the German Spa in Queen's Park to drink the waters and grimace at their taste. Already he was feeling in much better health than he had for a long time and, as he had been very lonely since the death of his parents, he was enjoying Annabelle's company.

Within a week, they had become Jeremy and Annabelle, and were spending most of their time together, unchaperoned, thanks to an Indian summer that tempted even old Mrs Parton to sit outside and doze or watch the ocean.

Annabelle was no great beauty, which was a good thing, for that would have frightened Jeremy away, but she was slim, elegant and possessed of a great deal of charm, when she bothered to exert it. She was well read and showed a flattering interest in his chosen career. For her part, she found Jeremy fairly ordinary in looks, very tall and over-thin for her taste. His hair was an undistinguished light brown, his eyes were blue-grey and his complexion was pale. His only real beauty was his hands, which had long tapering fingers and were always clean and well-kept. They were wasted on a man, she thought idly, as she creamed her own one night.

Within two weeks, Jeremy had decided to propose, which he duly did one night as they took the air after their evening meal.

Annabelle clasped her hands together. "Oh, I didn't expect – it's so soon! Indeed, I don't know what to say, Jeremy."

"Say yes!"

"I should greatly like to, but, forgive me, are you in a position to support a wife, you being so newly qualified?" Her eyelashes fluttered upon her cheeks and a slight flush only enhanced her attractiveness. "Oh, I feel so embarrassed asking this, but since I have no father or brother to speak for me, I must be practical. Mama and I were not left well situated after Father's death, I'm afraid, and I shall bring my husband very little."

"I have a private income of five hundred pounds per annum, savings to the tune of two thousand more and my parents' furniture waiting in storage. And I shall start earning a living as soon as I find somewhere to put up my brass plate. I'm not a rich man, my dear, but we shall be comfortable, I promise you."

Her grey eyes, veiled in those long dark lashes, gave him no clue as to her feelings. He reached out to clasp her hand and she allowed this, but he heard her sigh.

"What is it, my dearest?"

"I'm a little worried about the difference in our ages, Jeremy. I'm nearly twenty-eight, you know, and you're only twenty-four."

He laughed aloud. "And are these your only objections?"

"I have no real objections," she said in a low voice. "I'm

just trying to be – to be practical and honest with you. Give me a moment or two to think as we stroll on."

She thought furiously as they walked. Her first engagement had ended several years previously with the sudden death of her fiancé. She had been annoyed about this, rather than heartbroken, because by that time all the other good catches in the neighbourhood had been snapped up. Her hopes had been raised again only two years ago by a gentleman visiting the district, a man rather older than herself, but with a comfortable fortune. The untimely death of her father and her mother's insistence upon a year of strict mourning and sequestration had nipped that affair in the bud. Moreover, to Annabelle's chagrin, it had been found that her father had left them less well provided for than they had expected and her suitor had never returned. They had been obliged to move to a smaller house, give up their carriage and live very quietly.

She had hoped to marry someone of a higher status than a mere doctor, but she could no longer afford to be choosy. As Jeremy had some money of his own, they would not just be dependent upon his earnings and would be able to live in what she considered a reasonable style. And if anything happened to him, that same money would mean security for her.

"What about your mother?" He felt it his duty to ask, though he did not like the prospect of Mrs Parton living with them.

"I think she would be much happier in her own home, in the village she has lived in all her life." Annabelle hid a smile as Jeremy sighed with relief.

He had intended to look for a practice in a small country town, but Annabelle found out that a local doctor was seeking a partner and persuaded him to try Brighton, with which she had fallen in love. Jeremy found Dr Elmswood to be a very pleasant fellow and at that stage, he could refuse his new wife nothing.

It took only six months of married life to disillusion Jeremy. In the beginning, Annabelle had kept her temper and tongue carefully under control. The first time he saw her in a rage, he was horrified at the vicious way she berated a hapless maidservant who had spilled tea upon her mistress's skirt. Seeing his shock, Annabelle explained her temper away quickly, saying she had a dreadful headache, and took more care for a while. The servants could have told him a few tales, but he saw nothing untoward.

Annabelle was an excellent, not to say parsimonious, manager and enjoyed from the first being mistress of her own house. The physical side of marriage came as an unpleasant shock to her, but she did her duty and counted it a price well paid for the pleasure of being a married lady and independent of her mother's whims and vagaries. Jeremy, a warm and loving man, was disappointed at her lack of response to his careful love-making, but as his other encounters had been with women of the lower orders, he put Annabelle's reactions down to her delicate breeding and tried not to force his attentions upon her too often. However, the near abstinence fretted him and made him irritable at times.

At the end of six months Annabelle found herself to be pregnant. She did not mind the idea of a baby, because the world always pitied a woman without children. She was, however, very sickly, vomiting morning, noon and night, and she soon came to resent her condition most bitterly. No more cosy little tea parties with her lady friends, no more leisurely morning calls, no more elegant little soirées. Even before her condition began to show, her body could not be trusted not to disgrace her.

25

All peace was at an end for Jeremy. She moved him out to another bedroom, and treated him and the servants to displays of temper and peevishness that gradually dispelled all his sympathy and sickened him. She made the servants' lives a misery and twice dismissed maids for the merest trifles.

A few weeks after the second dismissal, Jeremy saw the girl, destitute and offering her body for sale, when he was returning home one night after a late call.

"Mary! What are you doing here?"

Mary burst into tears and tried to run away, but he caught hold of her arm.

"Can you find no other work?" he asked gently.

"No, sir. And I did try, truly I did! But the mistress wouldn't give me a reference an' no one would take me on without."

"Oh." He saw how white and thin she had become. "Are you hungry?"

She nodded.

"Do you know where we could buy you something to eat?"

"Oh, sir!" She sobbed so bitterly that he put his arm round her to comfort her.

Within a week, Jeremy had set Mary up as his mistress in a pleasant little room in a back street. He went through agonies of guilt at this, his first infidelity, but he was young and could not deny his sexual needs. And there was more to it than that. Mary's simple warmth and frank enjoyment of their love-making was the only peace he found during Annabelle's pregnancy. Without the release of that relationship, he soon realised, he could not have maintained the calm and kindly façade that he showed to Annabelle for the sake of the unborn child which he, at least, desperately wanted.

26

During this period he became more and more dissatisfied with his job. Dr Elmswood ran a fashionable Brighton practice and it was tacitly understood that Jeremy was to take it over eventually. But the rich hypochondriacs and elderly attention-seekers who formed a large part of the clientele only irritated Dr Lewis and he longed to offer his skills to people who really needed them. He suggested setting up a free clinic for the needy, but Dr Elmswood instantly vetoed this. Such a thing would harm the practice! Rich patients did not like to think that their doctor had come straight to them from the filth and diseases of the poor.

Fifteen months after their marriage, Annabelle was delivered, with much screaming and protesting, of a tiny daughter. To Jeremy's disgust she insisted on hiring a wet-nurse and would have little to do with her infant. When the baby was two months old she was christened Marianne Louise at an elaborate ceremony, which heralded Annabelle's re-entry into polite society. After the guests had left, seeing his wife in a good mood for once, Jeremy put his arm round her. "Perhaps we could now begin to share a bedroom again, my dear?"

She turned on him like a she-wolf, throwing his arm off and moving quickly behind a small table in case he tried to paw her again. "No! Never again! I'll run your house for you, I'll entertain your friends and I'll bring up your child, but if you so much as lay a finger on me in that way, I'll scream and fight every inch of the way!" Her tone was calm, yet vicious, as she added, "You wouldn't like that, Jeremy, I know you! And I'd make sure that everyone heard about it, too."

He bowed his head, knowing that she had gauged his weaknesses correctly. He could never have taken a woman by force and even less could he have borne to have it known that he had to force his attentions on his own wife.

"I was very ill when I was carrying the child," went on that hard voice, "and the birth was a painful and degrading experience. I do not intend to repeat it."

Apart from the nausea, she had been reasonably well and had produced a healthy child, but if she wished to hide behind that pretence, he was not the man to stop her. "Very well. As you choose." It was not the denying of her bed which hurt him, but the denying of other children.

For another eighteen months Jeremy Lewis continued to work in Brighton, sustained by the thought of Marianne, the little daughter whom he adored and for whom nothing was too good. There was also Mary and even the occasional patient who was genuinely ill. At the end of that time Dr Elmswood took him into his study and told him frankly that he would not do in such a practice.

"Your heart's not in it, man! And the clients can tell. Oh, they respect your medical expertise, but they don't enjoy your visits." He looked at Jeremy across the desk. "And they want to enjoy their doctor's attentions. They pay very highly for that privilege."

"They're fakes!" said Jeremy, glad now that matters had been brought to a head.

"But fakes who pay well. Fakes upon whom our living depends. And if I'm to retire on a part share in this practice, then I wish the practice to go on thriving." He sighed, for he had no desire to hurt his young colleague. "Jeremy, you're a good doctor, very good. You've a lot to offer humanity. Find yourself a real practice, somewhere where you'll be needed and where you can enjoy your work. Never mind that wife of yours! Think of yourself for a change."

"You're asking me to leave?"

"Yes. I'm afraid so. I'll repay your partnership fees. I can

easily find someone else to buy in. There's no hurry. Take your time. Look around. Find something that really suits you. You'll be grateful to me for this one day."

Jeremy sat there for a few minutes, his eyes on the floor. His first feelings of rejection and failure were giving way to a sense of elation. To find a really worthwhile job! To do what he was trained for! He couldn't believe that this was at last possible. Annabelle would be furious, but even she could do nothing about it if Dr Elmswood asked him to leave. He took a deep breath. "You won't change your mind?"

"No. No chance of it. I didn't think you'd want me to!"

"I don't! But Annabelle will take some convincing."

"You can rely on me to make the facts very plain to her," said the older man sympathetically. Neither he nor his wife could stand Mrs Lewis, with her airs and graces and her sly wheedling ways, and he thought it a pity that Jeremy had saddled himself with her.

"Then I'll admit that you're right," Jeremy told him. "This is not the right place for me. And – thank you for putting it so nicely."

"I told you. You're a good doctor. You're wasted here."

To say that Annabelle would be furious had been a gross underestimation of her reaction to the news. She ran the whole gamut of rage, hysterics, bitter accusations and threats of retribution. She also managed to rouse Jeremy to an equal fury for the first time in their married life, to the surprise of them both.

In the end he slapped her face to bring her out of the hysterics, then sat her down forcibly in a chair. "For three years I've tried it your way!" he shouted, wagging his finger in her face. "Three years of hating my work, hating the fat, self-satisfied fools who waste my time with their imaginary illnesses! Now we'll try it my way. I'm going to find myself a real practice and we're going to leave Brighton and live there, wherever it is!"

She opened her mouth to protest.

"Not another word!" he roared in her face. "I haven't finished yet! We should never have got married. I've known that for a long time. Presumably you married me for the security, but I married you in the mistaken belief that we loved one another, and it's been a bitter disappointment to me that you seem unfamiliar with that emotion. Well, we're stuck with each other now, for better, for worse, and we have no one to blame for it but ourselves."

He stared at her so inimically that she flinched. "I'll do my best to give you the sort of life you want, Annabelle, and I'll leave your precious body alone – and that will be no penance, for you've little joy to offer to a man – *but . . .*" he paused and scowled down at her, "I intend to choose my own practice this time. If that doesn't suit you, you can go back to live with your mother and I'll not prevent you, though Marianne stays with me, of course. And that, madam, is my final word!" He turned and strode out of the room, slamming the door behind him to emphasise his point.

Annabelle sank back into the armchair and gave herself up to a hearty bout of sobbing. She couldn't bear the thought of leaving her elegant little terraced house and carefully-chosen circle of friends. She loved everything about Brighton, the visitors who brought life and variety, the beauty of the sea, the drives along the coast. She knew she could never be happy anywhere else.

During the next few days she tried several less direct approaches to Jeremy, exerting every ounce of charm, short of allowing him back into her bed, to make him change his mind. But he remained adamant. Weak he might be in some ways, but when driven into a corner, he could be a very stubborn man. In desperation she even went to call on Dr Elmswood, to beg him to make Jeremy see sense, but although he was as polite to her as ever, the senior partner was not to be moved.

During the next two months Jeremy made several journeys across the country to inspect practices that were for sale. He tried at first to find somewhere near Brighton, for Annabelle's sake, but soon realised the futility of that. The area was already over-supplied with doctors. It was by sheer chance that he met a businessman from Bilsden at a hotel in London. It seemed that the Lancashire town, which he'd never even heard of before, completely lacked a modern, well-trained doctor. As he questioned Frederick Hallam further, Bilsden began to seem a distinct possibility and one, moreover, where he would not have to buy into an established practice but could just put up his shingle and start practising.

Jeremy travelled up to Lancashire the following week and Frederick introduced him to some of the more influential citizens, who were equally encouraging about the prospects in Bilsden and who readily promised their future patronage. The only one to whom he did not take was the parson, an old-fashioned gentleman named Kenderby, who had no sympathy for the poorer members of his flock and who displayed a dogmatic arrogance even when talking with his peers.

In between meeting people, Jeremy wandered round the streets and marvelled at the squalor that lived cheek by jowl with wealth in the town. Claters End was as bad as anything he'd seen in Edinburgh during his training, and although the Rows were a little better, the people who lived there seemed pale and stunted in growth. But they had a friendliness and directness about them that he found very taking.

Behind the High Street, on a gently rising slope, stood several commodious villas and some terraces of larger houses, each with its own narrow strip of garden, before and behind, for people of the better sort. Here, he thought, he might make his home, near enough to those who needed him most, but not too close to the unhealthy crowding of the Rows, for he had Marianne to think about. Annabelle, he knew, would prefer to live up on top of the Ridge, where people like his patron, Frederick Hallam, lived in great mansions, but she would be disappointed. He must be nearer to his work than that and besides, he would never be a rich enough man to build a mansion.

Yes, he thought, as he packed his things on the last night, by most people's standards Bilsden was ugly, dominated as it was by tall chimneys belching black smoke, and consisting mainly of terraces of mean huddled houses. But to him, Bilsden was beautiful, because the people needed him, needed him badly. He could not wait to start work there.

Before he left he set in motion the purchase of a largish house near a newly-created park, recently gifted to the town by Frederick Hallam in memory of his father. The price of the house seemed ridiculously low after Brighton prices and there was a builder in nearby Rochdale who would be delighted to erect a new wing for him, where he could have a proper dispensary and receive his patients without disturbing Annabelle. He even found time to order brass plates to be made for the wall outside: Dr Jeremy Lewis, Surgeon and Physician.

Annabelle, surly and shrewish, took to her bed at the news and informed her husband that she was too ill to move at present.

"Then the servants shall pack for us," Jeremy retorted, "for I've given notice and we must be out of this house by

the end of the month." He had regained his good humour now that he had a purpose in life and he refused to be shaken from it by anything Annabelle said or did. For him, the month could not pass quickly enough. He tried to be as kind to her as he could, but he was unable to hide his excitement and happiness about the move, and that galled her.

Annabelle burst into angry tears at her first sight of Bilsden. Looking down from the moors she thought it like the black pit of hell after Brighton. It was a long thin valley full of smoke and filth, with a river threading its greasy way among the mills and terraces. She loathed the town on sight and complained vociferously about the house he had bought without even consulting her. It was ugly, had no style, the rooms were not large enough, the builder's noise was driving her to distraction! Why, in heaven's name, could he not have found somewhere for them to rent, instead of sinking good money into this hovel? And how much would it cost them for window tax at over eight shillings a window, not to mention heating in the winter? Nothing could be less like their cosy terrace in Brighton. Just think about the extra servants they would need!

Jeremy's smile was serene, and her complaints made no impression on his happiness. It galled her still further that she seemed to have lost her ability to hurt him and her voice tailed away, as she stared at him.

"I sank good money into this house, Annabelle, because I knew that I should like living in Bilsden," he said, as calmly as if they were discussing the weather. "There's real work for me to do and I expect to spend the rest of my life here. This house was just what I wanted, large enough for our needs, yet close to the people whom I shall be serving. It was for sale, not for rent, so I bought it. And I like it very much! Look at that view over the park. And look at the size of the garden for Marianne to play in. There's nothing wrong with the situation, surely! I think we shall do very well here, once you have got over your tantrums."

The only regret he felt was a mild one at leaving Mary, but she had not wanted to move to the north, away from her family and friends. In any case, it would not have been good policy to bring along his mistress to a town where he was trying to establish a name for himself. That would be no way to gain people's confidence! He gave Mary a tidy sum and left her happily setting up a little sweet shop. After all, Bilsden was quite near to Manchester. Jeremy was sure that he would be able to go and assuage his physical needs there from time to time.

He turned away from his wife's sour pinched face to stare possessively at his house. Soon he would be able to start being a real doctor. He was impatient to begin helping people, to start his new life in Bilsden. He had tried fitting in with Annabelle's desires and failed; now she would have to fit in with his.

3

Bilsden: March to May 1830

Annie Gibson never forgot the day that the new family
moved into Number Seven, because that was the first time
she saw Matthew Peters. She didn't usually like boys; they
played too roughly and they were scornful of girls. This
boy, however, was different. He was tall and well-built,
and she was surprised when she found out that he was only
twelve. Most of the older boys she knew were pale and thin,
with dull hair and tired faces, for they worked long hours in
the mills or in workshops and rarely saw the sunlight.
Matthew Peters was an attractive lad, with shiny brown
hair and a fresh complexion, and although he too was soon
swallowed up by the mill, he somehow managed to retain
his air of health and vitality.

Annie was getting a bucket of water for her mother from
the tap when she saw a small procession turn the corner into
Boston Street. The man who led it was pushing Barmy
Charlie's handcart, which Charlie loaned out at sixpence
a time. The woman was carrying a knotted blanket full
of lumpy shapes, and the boy and three girls were all
carrying tattered bundles. The two eldest girls each held
a very young child by the hand. Annie guessed at once
that they must be moving into Number Seven. She hastily
finished filling her bucket at the tap, then dragged a

protesting Lizzie back home at top speed, turning into Salem Street well ahead of the slow-moving group with the handcart.

"Mam, they're moving in!" she announced breathlessly, setting the bucket down on the kitchen floor so that the water slopped over the edge.

"Mind what you're doin', our Annie!" Lucy said sharply. Then the words registered. "Who's moving in?"

"A family. Into Number Seven. Come an' see!" Annie pulled her mother up from the rocking chair near the kitchen fire and dragged her into the front room to peer out of the window. "See! There they are! I saw 'em turn into Boston Street an' guessed where they were comin' to."

Lucy forgot her heavy body for a moment or two. "They look all right," she said, her eyes weighing up their baggage and noting their clean, if ragged clothes. "They 'aven't got much stuff, though, 'ave they? I wonder what they're called."

"They look nice," said Annie, feeling possessive about the newcomers because she'd been the first to see them.

"There's a girl who looks about your age, love," Lucy pointed to a curly-haired girl with the same rosy cheeks as her brother.

"Mmm." Annie stared at the girl. "She might be all right." It occurred to her suddenly that if she made friends with the girl, she'd be bound to see something of the boy. "She's got nice hair," she conceded.

Lucy laughed and hugged her daughter. She didn't know what she'd have done without Annie in the past few months. "Get on wi' you! Who're you to pick an' choose?"

A sudden clatter and a wail of dismay from the kitchen at the back sent them both hurrying in, to find Lizzie sitting howling in a puddle of water next to the overturned bucket.

Annie flew across the room and clouted her sister on the ear. "I'd only just fetched that water!" she shouted, and followed up the clout by giving the little girl a good shake. "*Will* you leave things alone, our Lizzie!" Then she saw her mother standing in the doorway, looking wearily at the wet floor. She hastily swallowed her anger and pushed Lizzie out of the way. "It's all right, Mam. I'll mop it up. Won't take me a minute." She took the floor rag from the cupboard under the stairs and set to work to clear up the mess. The looks she cast at Lizzie from time to time boded no good for the little girl, but she knew that any more shouting would upset her mother, so she held her tongue.

"Why don't you go an' have a bit of a lie down, Mam?" she suggested. "I'll get some more water an' see to Dad's tea."

Lucy hesitated, swaying on her feet. "I think I will, love, if you c'n manage. Eh, I don't know what's wrong wi' me today! Must've got out of bed on the wrong side!"

The fiction was maintained at all times that the ill-health was a temporary thing. Every afternoon Lucy took a nap so as to look her best when John came home from the mill. Only Annie realised how ill she really was, much worse than she'd been with the other babies. Tom was out all day at school and Lizzie noticed only herself.

Annie finished mopping up the puddle and picked up the bucket. She hesitated for a moment, then sighed and yanked her sister to her feet. Lizzie at once let out a wail of protest at this rough treatment. "Shut up!" hissed Annie. "You're comin' wi' me. I'm not havin' you wakin' Mam up. She's tired." She sighed again. If only she didn't have to look after Lizzie all the time, or if only her sister had a bit more sense! Neither Tom nor Lizzie was of much help around the house. And anyway her brother was not often there. His schooling always rankled with Annie, for he would not share his knowledge with her.

As she was running a fresh bucket of water, Annie was joined by the boy she'd seen moving into Number Seven. What a bit of luck! When the bucket was full, she hesitated for a moment, then addressed him breathlessly, afraid of a rebuff.

"I'm Annie Gibson an' I live in Salem Street as well, Number Three. I saw you move into Number Seven just now. This is our Lizzie." She waited. Would he speak to her or would he ignore her? You could never tell with boys.

He nodded and smiled down at her eager face. "I'm Matthew Peters. They call me Matt."

His bucket was soon full and they turned by common consent to carry the water back home. He didn't seem to mind being seen talking to a girl. She tried desperately to think of something interesting to say to him. She wished Lizzie weren't trailing along behind them with her snotty nose, which she never bothered to blow unless someone reminded her. What would he think of her with a sister like that?

"I've got a sister about your age," he said abruptly. "Ellie, she's called."

"I've got a brother who's eight," she volunteered. "Our Tom. Can your sister play hopscotch?"

"Yes, she can. She likes playing out."

"She can play with me sometime, if she wants."

"I'll tell her. She'll like that. Thanks." They turned the corner into Salem Street.

"Our dad works in t'mill. He's a chargehand," she boasted.

"I'm startin' there on Monday." His dad hated the idea, hated the big new mills altogether and said they were abominations, but his mam said they needed the money.

The two children arrived at Number Three. Annie

wished it had been a longer walk. Matt was nice to talk to. She nodded shyly. "I'll 'ave to go in, then. 'Bye!" Once inside, she put the bucket down carefully in a corner and threatened to murder Lizzie if she went anywhere near it. Then she got some more coal in. Lizzie curled up on the rag mat in front of the fire and fell asleep.

Annie went out again and got the washing in, careful not to let it touch the floor. She set it to air round the fire on the wooden clothes-horse her dad had made, resisting the temptation to shove Lizzie out of the way with her foot. When it grew dark, she lit a candle and started getting the tea ready for her dad. He got mad if his tea wasn't on the table when he came in. He said it made you famished working in the mill all day.

She put the breadboard on the table and got out the loaf and the sharp knife. Putting the frying-pan ready near the fire, she carefully shaved six pieces of bacon off the piece that her mother had bought two days ago. It had to last for a while. In some families only those bringing in money got any meat or cheese, and the others thought themselves lucky if they had dripping or gravy on their bread. But her dad said that little 'uns needed good food to grow on, so they all got a share of the bacon, or an egg occasionally. He was a lovely man, her dad was, though he'd been a bit edgy lately.

Annie met Ellie Peters the very next day on the way back from the privies. The two girls were of much the same height, in spite of Ellie being a few months younger. They stopped and stared at each other, Ellie with a hopeful expression on her face. Matt had told her that there was a girl of her own age in the street, who looked nice and who had said she could play with them.

Ellie was agonisingly shy when she first met people, but Matt had made her promise to speak if she met a girl with red hair. She swallowed nervously. "H-hello." Her face was a bright peony-red by this time.

Annie nodded. "Hello," she said confidently. No one could ever accuse her of being shy. "You're Ellie Peters." It was a statement, not a question.

"Yes."

"I'm Annie Gibson. I met your brother Matt."

"Yes. He said."

"Do you want to play with us?"

"Yes. If that's all right."

"I have to help Mam now. She's not so well. But I can play out later. When t'one o'clock siren goes at the mill. That's when I allus play out."

"I – I'll ask my mam."

"Right," said Annie, brisk and businesslike. "I'll meet you back here, then." She turned and went into her house. For the rest of the morning as she bustled about helping her mother, she speculated aloud about Ellie Peters until Lucy had to laugh at her.

"Go on, do, our Annie!"

"Yes, but, Mam – don't you think she looks nice? She's got such lovely hair." Annie held up a red braid scornfully in her thin, work-reddened hand. "I wish I had long, black hair."

"You've got lovely hair."

Annie pulled a face. "I'd rather've had black," she insisted. "An' Ellie's got lovely rosy cheeks, too!" She sighed and reached down the twelve-inch square of speckled mirror that stood on the mantelshelf for John to shave by. She scowled as she peered into it. "Look at me face, Mam! Just look at it! Dead white, it is!" Her reflection stared back at her solemnly, its clear pale skin flawless by most standards, but in Salem Street and the Rows, you had to have rosy cheeks to be considered a beauty.

40

Lucy hugged her again. "I think you're lovely," she said. "I couldn't wish for a better daughter. When I'm better I'll make it up to you for all this."

"I like to help you, Mam." Annie nestled against her for a moment. "Now, shall I start sewing that shirt for our Tom?" Lucy had passed her sewing skills on to her daughter and they were working on a new pair of shirts for Tom, who had grown again. The Gibson children often had new clothes, thanks to Lucy, except for Lizzie, who had to wear Annie's cast-offs and already resented it. Not many of the women in the Rows had any skill with a needle, so Lucy, with Annie's help, occasionally made or altered clothes for others, for a small payment. More often altered, for there was a thriving trade in cast-offs and little spare money for new things.

When they'd all had their noon slice of bread and dripping, Lucy sent Annie out to play. For once she made the effort to look after Lizzie herself; for once Annie, lost in dreams of friendship with the Peters, didn't urge her mam to rest.

Ellie was waiting outside, her hands clasped nervously in front of her. It was a cold day and she had a matted, much-washed shawl pinned round her faded dress.

"Hello," she said, still nervous.

"Come on," said Annie. "I'll show you the places where we play."

Ellie tagged along meekly, her heart bursting with anxiety to please. When they had lived down in Claters End, she had been forbidden to play with the other children, who were not only lousy, but light-fingered and foul-mouthed, her mam said. And before that, the Peters family had made so many moves, even in Ellie's short lifetime, that no friendship had been more than transient. *This* time, her mam said, they were here to stay, if she had to cut out their father's tongue herself, to stop him getting turned off from his job again. Her father had looked angry at that, but he knew that even Elizabeth's monumental patience had at last worn out.

Salem Street was a step up again in the world for the Peters family, a step nearer to what Elizabeth had known before she got married. They'd recently been reduced to living in one attic room down Claters End, because yet again Sam's incurable honesty and blunt speech had cost him his new job in Bilsden.

Sam Peters was a slow, painstaking man, who had learned to read late in life by courtesy of the Methodist Church. He was now not only a staunch Methodist, but a firm believer in the rights of the common man to literacy and a vote, a dangerous combination, this, to most employers. A few weeks ago, however, Sam had got a job with the new doctor, who had set up near the park and who was even willing to tend the poor. Sam had met him quite by chance after a street accident, when some bales had fallen off an overloaded dray. Being Sam, he had automatically gone to help the victim, regardless of possible damage to his one and only decent set of clothes.

The doctor, noting his gentleness with the injured woman and the way he didn't flinch at the sight of blood, had asked him abruptly how he was employed. When Sam had admitted that he was seeking work, the doctor had offered him a job as a kind of general helper. He would have to drive the gig, tend the pony on the yard boy's day off, learn to mix simple medicines and roll pills, and help with the patients, especially the poorer ones. Sam had accepted the offer on the spot, without even asking about the wages, for it was a job after his own heart. Master and man were so pleased with each other after a few weeks, that the family had dared to move to Salem Street, to a house

42

the doctor had found for them. Now, Ellie was hoping to make and keep a friend, and she was desperately hoping that it would be Annie Gibson.

The two little girls wandered around the streets, exchanging information about their families and the things they liked to do. It was to be the beginning of a life-long friendship. Annie soon forgot that she had seen Ellie as a way of getting to know Matthew and came to love her for her own sake. They played together when Annie could get away and occasionally Ellie came into the house. They both had to take their younger sisters with them much of the time and this, too, formed a bond. Ellie understood and sympathised when Lizzie was naughty, and Annie showed a similar understanding when Patty and Addy became unbearable.

It was a few weeks before Annie was invited back into Ellie's home. In a burst of confidence one day, Ellie explained that this was because they had not yet got much furniture.

"You see," she said, scuffed boot drawing careful patterns in the dust, "our dad, well, he can't help speakin' his mind when summat upsets him an' – an' sometimes the masters don't like it an' – an' then he loses his job." She shivered at the memory, then brightened, "But he's suited now. He says Dr Lewis is the best master he's ever had. An' our Matt's doin' all right in the mill, so our mam says we c'n begin to get a few things together again. On'y – well, we haven't got much yet."

"Nobody has much round 'ere," said Annie, as one who knew. "Your mam doesn't have to bother about that. An' you're one of the cleanest families in the Rows, my mam says."

Ellie blushed pink with pleasure at this compliment and later passed it on to her mother.

When Annie was at last allowed to go into the Peters' house, she sat shyly in front of the fire and listened to Sam reading the Bible aloud to his family, which he did every evening and twice on Sundays. She didn't understand a lot of the words, but she liked the way it sounded.

One evening, she confided in Sam her burning desire to learn to read, like her brother Tom.

"That's a fine thing to wish for, lass," he told her seriously. "Don't you let anyone stop you. There's allus a way, if you look for it. You'll get your wish one day."

"Aye, but when?" she answered, practical as ever. "Our Tom goes to Sergeant Brown's for schoolin' an' he won't show me anythin' he learns! He's a mean pig! He's not doin' so good hisself, I reckon." She brooded for a moment on the injustice of life, then burst out, "It's not fair! I'm older'n he is an' I'm cleverer, too! I bet I could learn to read twice as quick as him!"

"I know me letters," Matt volunteered. "I'll learn you them, if you like. But I'm not so quick at readin', though."

Annie blinked at him, uncertain whether he meant it or not. He smiled across at her. He had a lovely smile, did Matt, she thought. It made her feel all warm inside. "D'you mean that?" she asked at last, very hesitantly, hardly daring to believe her ears.

"Aye, 'course I do. An' our Ellie can learn her letters with you. It's time she learned, isn't it, Dad?"

The two little girls squeezed each other's hands in mutual excitement.

"When?" demanded Ellie.

"Next Sunday."

Annie walked home on a cloud that day, her expression so blissful that even her father forgot his worries and asked her if she'd found a sovereign.

"Better'n that," she assured him. "Matt Peters is goin' to

teach me an' their Ellie our letters. An' Mr Peters is goin' to help us, an' all. An' I bet I learn to read better'n you, our Tom, so there!" She stuck her tongue out at him for emphasis.

"You won't, neither! You're only a girl." Tom gave her a shove and she spilled some water over her dress.

She shoved him back at once. "You watch what you're doin', you daft lump!"

"Stop that, Annie!" Lucy intervened, as she so often had to. "An' you give over too, our Tom!"

The two children subsided, for neither parent would tolerate any disobedience.

"When're you goin' t'start your lessons, love?" Lucy asked diplomatically.

"Sunday." Annie beamed at her mother, restored to good humour at the mere thought of learning the magic that enabled you to make sense of the lines of black marks in books.

"I daresay we could run to a slate for her, couldn't we, John?" Lucy reached out to hold her husband's hand and smile at him. She could always bring peace to her family. "She'll need to practise her letters."

"I daresay we could," he agreed. "If she's been a good girl."

"She's allus a good girl, our Annie is. I don't know how I'd have managed without her lately."

"Good lass," said John, but his eyes were on his wife and they held anxiety behind the smile.

Annie flushed with pleasure, both at the rare compliment and at the thought of getting a slate of her own. She had few personal possessions. None of them did. Even a chargehand's wages did not allow many extras, though Lucy always tried to put a bit aside for a rainy day, which was what she called it when the mills were on short time.

Annie had long envied Tom his slate, which he would not even allow her to touch.

The lessons began on the very next Sunday afternoon, with the rain pelting down the windowpanes and the children sitting cross-legged on pieces of sacking in front of the Peters' fire. Annie knew her alphabet within the week, drawing Ellie along with her in her burning enthusiasm to learn to read. Matt found himself enjoying giving the lessons to such willing pupils and his own reading improved rapidly in the process.

Sam was pleased to see the children working to better themselves, and began to ponder yet again how he could help set up a Methodist chapel here in Bilsden. If he could only manage to do that, they'd be able to run a proper Sunday School for the children – yes, and have evening classes for the adults, too. At present all he'd managed was a twice-weekly prayer meeting with a few other staunch souls, but he ached to spread the gospel more widely and to help bring others to salvation, as he himself had been brought into the fold years ago by a visiting preacher.

Bilsden had grown so rapidly from a hamlet to a mill town that it lacked many facilities. It had only two places of worship, the parish church, St Mark's, and the brand new Catholic church, St Anne's, which had caused a lot of fuss when it was built. Papists were barely tolerated, but the mill-owners knew that they wouldn't keep their Irish labour if there weren't a church for them to go to, and a priest to christen, marry and bury them.

When he first moved to the town, Sam had tried going to the parish church, but had found its welcome cold. Its parson was unwilling to listen to the views of an impertinent labouring man who didn't know his place in society, and Mr Kenderby was outraged when that same man dared to question what his betters told him. Sam, deprived of the theological discussions which were his favourite form of entertainment, now tried to console himself with the thought that at least he had found himself a good job and was free to scheme for his chapel. He had come to respect Dr Lewis greatly and to admire the good he was doing among the Rows. If he'd been born rich, Sam sometimes thought wistfully, he'd have become a doctor – or a minister. But ifs didn't build castles, he told himself firmly. Be thankful to the Lord for what you *have* got, Sam Peters!

Jeremy Lewis was equally satisfied with his new man. It would have been more normal to employ an apprentice, but Annabelle refused point-blank to have one living in her house, and he was reluctant to expose any lad to her temper and malicious whims. He had a boy come in daily to tend the pony and the garden, but young Bill was not over-bright and had neither the time nor the aptitude to help the doctor.

Sam was invaluable in dealing with the poor, who seemed to trust him on sight, and he was absolutely reliable when it came to mixing standard draughts and rolling pills, for with no apothecary in the town, Jeremy had to make his own medicaments.

Jeremy Lewis wanted very much to help the suffering he saw all around him. It gave a meaning to his life that tending the rich did not, filling a need Annabelle would never understand.

He smiled grimly at the thought of Annabelle. She was not capable of being any man's wife or even a good mother to Marianne, although she was settling down a bit now in Bilsden. It had cheered her up a little to buy some new furniture in Mr Watts' Manchester Bazaar in Deansgate, and to be given free reign to furbish up the house. Her temper had also improved when she'd met and been accepted by a few of the local dignitaries and their wives.

The industrial gentry had fewer reservations about the social eligibility of doctors than the landed gentry had. It must have been sheer desperation, he mused, that had driven Annabelle to snare a young doctor of moderate means, but nothing like the desperation he felt now, four years later, about their sham of a marriage.

4

Early June 1830

In the first week of June, Lucy Gibson had to take to her bed. She'd been feeling poorly all through the pregnancy, but things had got much worse during the last week or two and she now felt dizzy and breathless if she stood up, while her legs were swollen to twice their normal size. Even her fingers were puffy.

Annie, very self-important, took over the housekeeping, helped occasionally by Bridie or one of the other women in the street. And she coped well, in spite of Lizzie, who whined constantly and kept getting in her way. For once, Tom fetched coal and water without complaint and refrained from teasing Annie. He had realised at last how ill his mother really was.

Lucy's pains started during the night, but by morning they didn't seem very far advanced, so John went off to work, a little anxious, but knowing that his Lucy was never quick to give birth. He went to say goodbye to her and Lucy summoned up a wavery smile to speed him on his way, then she abandoned herself to the ministrations of Widow Clegg.

When John hurried home that night, the baby had still not been born and Lucy was very weak and only semi-conscious. Elizabeth Peters had taken Lizzie and Tom round to her house, but Annie had refused point-blank to go with them. Widow Clegg told John bluntly that things were going badly and that there was little more she could do to help Lucy, who was exhausted. Neither of them noticed the little girl crouched by the fire, her hand pressed to her mouth and her eyes filled with terror.

"Tha'd better go an' fetch that there new doctor," the widow wound up. "Perhaps he'll be able to do summat."

John fought down a rising panic and asked hoarsely which doctor.

"That new 'un," she said impatiently. "Doctor Lewis, they call him."

"Doctor Lewis," John echoed blankly, his mind still not functioning properly.

"Aye. Lewis. The one as Sam Peters works for. He lives in that big corner house near t'park. There's a bell round t'side that you 'ave to ring when you want the doctor."

"Will he come out for such as us?"

"Aye. He'll come for anyone, that one will. He come to a woman down Claters End last month as lived in a cellar. Given 'er up, I had. But he saved 'er. No better'n a pigsty, that cellar was, but he didn't seem to notice. No, an' he never asked her to pay, neither!"

"We can pay!" said John sharply. "We've allus paid our way!" He looked despairingly up towards the bedrooms, then rushed out. He ran most of the way, till the breath was sobbing in his throat, not even seeing the people who got out of his way. He pounded past Hallam's Mill, along by the Bilsden Permanent Dye Works and across the corner of the new park they were still working on, arriving at last at the better end of town.

When he arrived at the doctor's house, he leaned against the wall, panting, and tugged on the bell pull. Within seconds, he pulled it again, so that the maidservant who answered it spoke sharply to him. He didn't even notice her annoyance. Chest heaving, he gasped out why he needed the doctor.

She pursed her lips in disapproval, showed him into the empty waiting-room, and then went off to fetch her master. Her mistress was not going to like this and then the servants would suffer, as they always did from Annabelle Lewis's bad moods.

The doctor and his wife were holding a dinner party that evening. Annabelle still sneered at the Bilsden gentry behind their backs and bemoaned her days in civilised Brighton, but she had decided to make the best of a bad job and now wished to make a stir in local social circles. Now the house was in immaculate order, two dinner parties had been planned for that week to impress the leading citizens of Bilsden and show them that their new doctor was a cut above the average medical practitioner and most definitely a gentleman. She had driven the servants hard for days with her preparations. Her elegantly-furnished parlour shone and sparkled in the light of the graceful lamps she had found in the Manchester Bazaar, and her dining-table was a masterpiece of floral art and gleaming napery.

Annabelle was as much a work of art as her rooms and table. She was superbly gowned in self-striped pale green silk, which had a close-fitting and décolletée bodice with darker ribbon bows all down the front. Her short beret sleeves were the largest ever seen in Bilsden and her female guests wondered how she got them to stay so puffed out. Her hair was swept up from a central parting into a tightly plaited chignon on the crown of her head, the forehead softened by small curls. Around her neck were her mother's pearls, borrowed for her wedding and never returned.

The parlourmaid served a brandywine punch to the assembled guests – no gooseberry wine in Annabelle's house, thank you, however popular it might be with those who knew no better! The hostess was just congratulating herself on how well everything was going, when the chambermaid, who always came down to help at such functions, entered the room and whispered something in her master's ear. Jeremy rose at once, excused himself to his guests and followed the girl out. He spoke to John Gibson, then returned to apologise to everyone before going to collect his medical bag. He was about to leave the house when Annabelle swept into the surgery and demanded in a far from polite tone to know why he was doing this to her.

"I'm not doing anything to *you*; I'm going to attend that man's wife, who is having a difficult confinement," Jeremy replied curtly.

"But we're in the middle of a dinner party! It's my first proper function in Bilsden! You can't leave me now! Go and see her later!"

"She needs me now," said Jeremy, unmoved. "She's been in labour since early this morning. You'll manage perfectly well without me, Annabelle. You always do."

She bit back an angry retort. Jeremy was becoming harder and harder to manage since he'd dragged her to this wretched town. But she would find some way to get back at him for this, she vowed, as she watched him leave. She always did, usually through their daughter, with whom he was besotted. Forcing a smile to her lips, she returned to her guests. "I'm afraid my husband can never refuse the call of a sick person. He's *so* devoted to his work."

"A good fault in a doctor," said the man next to her, raising his glass to admire it and wondering how much it had cost.

"Yes, isn't it?" Annabelle had trouble maintaining her smile as she said this, however. "So, if you will please excuse my deficiencies, I shall do my best to act as both host *and* hostess." She bowed her head modestly, as they assured her that they were already impressed with her hospitality. Later, she had at least the satisfaction of knowing that the evening had been an unqualified success, even though Jeremy had not returned at all.

Oblivious to his wife's anger, Jeremy hurried across the town with John, not bothering to get his pony and trap out for a visit to the Rows, for he'd have nowhere to leave it safely. As they walked, he questioned the man about his wife, her pregnancy and her previous confinements. He did not like the sound of things. Why did poor people only call in a doctor when it was too late? It didn't occur to him that he was still in his good clothes and that people were staring at him as he strode along next to John. The ruin of his best brown evening coat and new buff trousers was yet another piece of fuel to Annabelle's anger the following day.

Jeremy Lewis worked all night on Lucy Gibson. He had the baby out within two hours. It was a little boy, perfectly formed, but a bluish white in colour and it never breathed. At first, it seemed that he was going to save the mother and he won Widow Clegg's deepest admiration for the skill he showed. But about dawn, Lucy had a massive haemorrhage and died a few minutes later, before they could even call her husband up to her side.

Jeremy sat there for a moment, staring bitterly at her dead body. There should be some way to help women like her. If only more were known about the dangers of pregnancy! But few doctors that he had met cared for that field of study. It was neither fashionable nor lucrative nor, to most of them, of much importance. Women had always died in childbirth and always would. Unlike most doctors,

Jeremy took Lucy's death as a personal failure. He stood up and nodded to Widow Clegg to tidy things up, then went down to inform John himself. He never left that job to others.

When John was told that Lucy was dead, he went mad, hurling everything off the table and cursing the doctor, God and finally himself. The rage was soon succeeded by loud and bitter grief and he stumbled upstairs and flung himself upon Lucy's body, sobbing dementedly and begging her to come back to him. The doctor did not notice the white-faced child curled up in the corner behind the rocking-chair, but Annie noticed him, noticed the ruin of his lovely clothes, noticed the angry way he brushed away a tear.

After he had gone, Widow Clegg came down for some water and found Annie still in the corner, curled into a tight ball, weeping quietly.

"Does ta want to go up an' see thy mother?"

Annie blinked the tears away and shivered. "No!"

"Where's t'water?"

"It's all gone."

"Then tha'll 'ave to go an' get some more, for I need to wash thy mother's body." She didn't wait for an answer, but turned and went back upstairs.

With the sound of her father's sobbing echoing in her ears, Annie took hold of the empty bucket and went out of the house. The sun was just coming up now and people were beginning to stir. At the tap she met Matt Peters.

"Tom an' Lizzie are both asleep," he told her. "How's your mam?"

She could not speak, only sob and collapse against him like a little rag doll. He held her for a moment or two, then turned her gently around, "You come home to us, Annie. I'll get the water for you."

"I can't!" she wept. "I hafta get the water. She's got to wash me mam's body! Mam allus likes things to be clean."

"I told you, I'd get it for you. See, I can easy carry two buckets."

A woman came up to the street tap. "Shame on thee, a great lump of a lad, teasin' a little lass like that!"

"I haven't been teasin' her!" he answered indignantly. "Her mam's just died."

The woman peered more closely at Annie.

"Isn't that John Gibson's lass?" she asked. "Well, I never! I used to work with Lucy when we were little 'uns. Eeeh, poor Lucy!"

They left her at the tap, still muttering about the news, and went back to Salem Street. Annie was calmer now, comforted by Matt's fussing. She refused to go home with him and insisted on taking the bucket of water inside the house herself. It seemed important that she do this last service for her mam. As she was opening the door, Sally Smith's gentleman friend came out of Number Six and made his way swiftly along the street, and Bridie O'Connor poked her head out of the door and shouted along, "How's Lucy? Has she had it yet?"

Annie burst into tears again and rushed into the house, and it was left to Matt to spread the news to the shocked neighbours that Lucy Gibson was dead.

Widow Clegg finished laying out the body. John wouldn't leave the bedroom but sat by his Lucy, locked in grief. He cursed Annie when she went upstairs, laid a hand on his shoulder to get his attention and asked if he'd like a cup of tea. He cursed Widow Clegg when she asked him what he wanted to do about the funeral. She just shrugged her shoulders and left him to it. She had her lodgers to see to and this was not the first grief-stricken husband she'd dealt with. He'd have found himself a new wife within a month or two, she thought cynically. Men couldn't manage on their own.

When she came back later, she found Annie huddled in the corner of a neat and tidy kitchen and no sign of John. "Is he still up there?" she asked.

"Yes."

"Go an fetch thy brother an' sister back. Happen he'll pull himself together a bit when he sees th'other childer."

Annie went slowly along the street, passing Michael O'Connor and his three sons, on their way to the mill.

"It's a tragedy about your mam," Michael said to her, crossing himself. "A lovely woman, she was. Will I be telling them at work that your da'll not be in today?"

"Yes, please, Mr O'Connor."

When Annie arrived at Number Seven, Matt was just leaving for work and patted her encouragingly on the shoulder as he walked past. Elizabeth tried to take the little girl in her arms, but Annie wriggled out of her grasp. She stood there, "like a woman grown, that pale an' stiff you'd never imagine her only ten," Elizabeth later told Polly Dykes. "'I've come for my brother and sister, please, she said, an' thank you for having them.' Eh, she spoke as if they'd only been round here to play with my lot."

The sight of his three motherless children in no way brought John Gibson to his senses. In fact, he roared at them to get out of the bedroom. If it wasn't for them, Lucy would still be alive! Children were a curse!

Widow Clegg waited till they'd clattered back down the narrow stairs, then asked John for her money. She waited again until he'd finished cursing and then repeated that she wasn't moving a step until she got paid. She'd had too much experience with bereaved families to wait until after the funeral, when they'd likely be owing money all round. In the end he threw some coins at her. She picked up the three florins she thought were her due and left the others lying on the floor. When she went down, she told Annie to keep out of her dad's way till he came to his senses.

The three children spent the morning as quietly as they could and, for once, Lizzie and Tom gave Annie no trouble. About ten o'clock Elizabeth Peters came to the door to see if she could help in any way, but John, still up in the front bedroom with his wife's body, yelled down to Annie to send that woman away. He wasn't having any neighbours coming prying into his affairs!

Elizabeth, who had heard every word, shrugged and whispered through the door, "You just send along if I can do anythin' to help, lass. An' our Ellie sends her love to you."

Annie smiled wanly. "Thank you, Mrs Peters." She didn't really like Matt's mother, but she was grateful for any attempt at kindness, because she felt very alone and frightened that day. What would she do without her mam? What would they all do?

A little later, Bridie O'Connor also knocked on the door. This time John came storming down the stairs. "Go away and see to your own family, you nosey bitch! Bloody well leave me an' mine alone! There's nothin' you or anyone else can do now but leave us to our grief!" Slam went the door.

John appeared briefly in the kitchen. "Bloody nosey-parkering, that's all it is! Don't you answer that door again, our Annie, do you hear me – or I'll take me belt to you!" He went out and relieved himself in the yard, a thing Lucy had never allowed, then climbed the stairs again. The three children huddled together in a corner of the kitchen till he was gone. They'd never seen their father like this and were terrified of the stranger he'd become. Five-year-old Lizzie whimpered, but softly, for fear of him hearing, and Annie cuddled her. Even eight-year-old Tom's hand crept into Annie's for comfort.

In the early afternoon John came downstairs. "Remember what I said an' don't let anyone in!" he growled at the three children. He then went up the street to arrange to borrow Barmy Charlie's handcart the following day and to ask Charlie to find him a coffin. Charlie always knew somebody who could provide things, never mind what you needed. He wasn't too barmy for that.

After that, John walked round to Parson Kenderby's house to arrange for the funeral. He wasn't allowed to see the parson himself, of course, who dealt only with the gentry, but the curate agreed to hold a short service for Mrs Gibson the next day. On his way home John passed a gin shop and, dreading returning to a house without Lucy, he called in and had one or two drinks to calm his nerves. It didn't seem to do much good, and the bright lights hurt his eyes, so after a while he left. He met Sam Peters at the corner of the street.

"Do you want any help with the funeral, John?"

"No!" said John harshly. "You can all keep your bloody noses out o' my business! She's my wife an' I'll see to 'er. An' tell your wife to keep away, too!"

Sam's mouth dropped open in amazement at this rude response to a perfectly civil question. "Now, then, John . . ." he began, but John had already moved on.

They buried Lucy the next afternoon. John accepted Charlie's help in carrying the coffin out to the handcart, then took the three children along with him to the brief ceremony, where the grave-digger helped him lower the coffin into the ground and the curate gabbled a few prayers.

The main thing Annie remembered from that day was the brightness of the sun, which hurt her swollen red eyes, and the buzzing of the insects which matched the ache in her head. It seemed wrong for the weather to be so beautiful on such a day. She saw another fresh grave nearby with flowers on it and wished she'd had time to go and pick some flowers for her mam. She decided that she would come back sometime and bring some flowers herself. Sometime when her dad was at work, so that he couldn't stop her.

John stood stony-faced as earth was shovelled into the hole, then sent his children home again, threatening to murder them if they didn't go straight back or if they so much as poked their faces outside the door after they got there. He cursed anyone who spoke to him in the street and cut short their expressions of sympathy, telling them to mind their own business and leave him to do the same. There was no comfort anyone could offer; all he wanted was oblivion from the pain of losing Lucy. And the only oblivion he could think of was in the gin shop. Maybe he hadn't had enough to drink the day before.

He spent the rest of the day in the gin shop, sitting huddled over his pot in the darkest corner, growling at anyone who came near him and getting steadily drunker. But nothing seemed to dull the anguish of a world without Lucy.

In the end his money ran out and they refused to give him any more gin, so he staggered home to Salem Street. It took him a while to get the door opened, but at last he managed to crash it back on its hinges. He stood there swaying on the threshold. It made everything worse to go into *her* house. He closed his eyes for a moment and when he opened them, Annie was standing there, asking if he wanted anything. She had a look of her mother, the same green eyes and red hair, and he couldn't stand it. He shoved her out of the way and stumbled up the stairs, sobbing hoarsely.

Annie sat and sobbed too as she rubbed her bruised face, for her dad had never hit any of them like that before. After a while, she crept up to bed.

The next day John made no attempt to go to work, though it would likely cost him his job. Mr Hallam was a good Christian employer and allowed his operatives two days off, without pay of course, for a close bereavement, but no more than two, or they might try to take advantage. Death was not, as he was fond of saying, to be made an excuse for a holiday.

John got up late, his head throbbing from the unaccustomed drinking. He came downstairs, cursed the children and wolfed down the last of the bread and bacon. Then he sat sprawling in a chair in the front room until the afternoon. The children stayed in the back room, afraid to make a noise. Annie, who was having trouble keeping Lizzie quiet, went in at last and asked if they might go out for a bit of a walk in the fresh air.

"Out! Go out! Shows what you thought of your mother, that does, wanting to go out an' play! No, you bloody can't go out! You can stay in th'house an' show some respect for t'dead!"

Lizzie, who had crept in after her sister, started to cry, frightened by his harsh voice, and he slapped her face. "Shut up your caterwauling!" he said with a viciousness the children had never seen in him before. Lizzie fled back to the kitchen to hide under the table and Annie followed her, tears rolling down her face.

Later in the afternoon John got up and began to fumble around in the kitchen.

"Where is it?" he demanded. "Where's t'money? Where'd she keep the pot, damn you?"

"On the shelf, Dad," Annie answered nervously, staying well out of reach of his hands, "behind the mirror. But it's

nearly all gone – an' there's nothin' left in the house for us to eat."

"*She* won't never eat no more. See how you like it for a bit!" he told her indifferently, shoving the last few coins into his pocket and reaching for his cap. He turned round at the door. "An' no playin' out!" He raised his voice so that the whole street could hear him. "An' don't you answer t'door, neither! Bunch o' bloody nosey-parkers, that's all they are in this street. Can't leave a man alone with 'is grief. Well, they'd better not come sniffin' around *my* house!" And he stamped off to the gin shop.

Bridie, Elizabeth and Polly Dykes met later that day to discuss John Gibson's strange behaviour.

"He's gone mad," said Polly. "Should've 'eard what he called me yesterday – an' all because I said I were sorry about Lucy."

"He's takin' it hard," said Elizabeth. "But it's the children I'm worried about. He won't let them out of the house. What's happenin' to them? My Ellie's that upset about Annie, she's just mopin' about. An' my Sam says the doctor were upset, too. Says he don't like his patients dyin'."

"It's a bad business, so it is," said Bridie, her hand on her own distended belly. "I heard Lucy cryin' out when she was in her labour. She always had a hard time, poor thing, God rest her soul!"

But although they chatted for a good half-hour, they could think of nothing to do about the Gibson children, and they dared not go into Number Three. A man was the master in his own house and had a right to do what he wanted with his own children.

Not until ten o'clock that night did John stagger home again, and he was even drunker than the previous day.

When he'd fumbled his way into the house and was standing swaying in the front room, Tom went up to him.

"Dad!"

"Eh? What?"

"Dad, we're hungry. We haven't had nothin' to eat."

He waited for a moment, but there was no reply from his father, so he tried again. "Dad, we're hungry . . ."

That was as far as he got. John's arm shot out and smashed the irritating noise to one side. Tom's shrill scream of fright cut off abruptly as his head hit the brass fender with a thump. There was a moment's complete silence in the room, while John blinked and tried to bring the scene into focus. What had happened? What had he done?

Annie darted across to her brother, fear for him conquering her fear of her father. "You've killed him! You've killed our Tom!" she shrieked, dropping to her knees and cradling her brother's head against her thin chest. Lizzie burst into terrified sobs and ran back to her refuge under the table in the kitchen, calling out hoarsely for her mam.

And for the first time since Lucy's death, John Gibson really looked at his children and realised what he was doing to them.

"Oh, my God!" he muttered thickly and dropped into a chair, partly sobered by the shock, but still muzzy-headed and feeling sick now. "Oh, Lucy!" he moaned to himself. "Lucy! What 'ave I done?"

Annie was desperately trying to staunch the blood which was pumping from the gash on Tom's forehead. Tears streamed unheeded down her face, leaving runnels in the dirt. The bruise that John had given her when he clouted her the day before stood out lividly on one cheekbone.

The boy hadn't moved since he fell. His breathing was

stertorous and his face chalk-white. John made a big effort to conquer his nausea and went across to his son. Annie hunched over her brother protectively.

"Nay, lass," said John slowly, the words coming out thick and slurred, but making sense at last. "Nay, I'll not hurt you again. I'm over that." He knelt by his son. "Oh, my God!" he moaned as he saw that the boy was unconscious. "What have I done? What would Lucy say?" Then he pulled himself together and tried to think what to do. "Go an' get the doctor, our Annie, the one as came to your mam. He's a good man. He'll come an' see to our Tom."

Annie stared at him blankly for a moment.

"Dr Lewis!" said John again. "Near t'park. That big house wi' the wall round it. Go an' fetch him for our Tom."

She rushed out of the house and almost collided with a woman passing by.

"Hold on a minute, young Annie Gibson! What's the matter with you?"

Annie blinked up at Sally Smith. "It's our Tom," she gasped. "He's banged his head. Me dad says I've to fetch t'doctor." She tore her arm from Sally's grasp and darted off, running as John had run a few days earlier, along the dark streets and across the new park.

Sally looked after her, hesitated for a moment, then went into Number Three through the half-open door. People didn't usually invite her into their houses, but this seemed like an emergency. She found John still crouching on the floor, holding Tom in his arms.

"I hope you don't mind me coming in, Mr Gibson, but the door was open. Annie said Tom was hurt, so I wondered if I could do anythin' to help."

John looked at her owlishly for a moment and she realised that he was dead drunk. She moved over to look at the boy.

"It's his head," said John, speaking slowly and in a slurred voice. "I didn't mean it! Oh, God, I didn't mean it!"

"I'm sure you didn't. No, don't try to move him. Head wounds is dangerous. Just lie him down carefully where he is. Here, let me!" She lifted Tom gently out of his father's arms and laid him flat on the floor, injured side uppermost.

"You come an' sit down over here, John Gibson," she said and coaxed him into a chair. "You've had a shock. What you need is a hot drink. Have you got any tea in the 'ouse?"

He just sat and looked at her uncomprehendingly, so she walked through to the kitchen to look for herself. There she found Lizzie whimpering under the table.

"Eh, lass, come on out of there!"

Lizzie peered at her suspiciously with a face made unlovely by snot and tears. Sally plumped down on her knees beside the child.

"Don't you remember me? I'm Sally Smith from Number Six."

A flicker of comprehension came into the puffy red eyes.

"I'm just goin' t'make yer dad a cup o' tea. D'you want one too?"

Lizzie's mouth opened and shut, and she nodded, but she said nothing.

"I've got some bread an' cheese in my house. Are you hungry, love?"

Lizzie nodded again and smeared the snot away from her nose with her sleeve.

"Right, then. You come with me and we'll make summat to eat for you an' yer dad."

Lizzie crawled out from under the table and put one hand trustingly in Sally's. They went through the front room, Sally talking cheerfully all the time. John was still huddled in a chair and Tom was on the floor. They were back five

64

minutes later with a tray of tea and sandwiches. Sally persuaded John to drink a cup of hot, sweet tea, but he wouldn't eat anything. He just sat watching his son, listening for the doctor and muttering every now and then that he hadn't meant it.

Annie found the doctor's house easily enough, for it was lit up brightly in the dark street, but she did not know about the special doctor's bell at the side and she went right to the front door. A lady in a black dress, with a frilly white apron and cap opened it. She looked so fine that Annie couldn't speak for a moment, then she managed to blurt out, "Our Tom's hurt. He's cut his head open. Please, can t'doctor come to see him?"

The lady's lip curled scornfully. "This is the house," she said loftily, outraged that a dirty child had dared to knock on the front door.

"Don't the new doctor live here?" asked Annie, bewildered.

"He lives here, but he doesn't see people here. You have to go to his rooms for that. Round the side. But he's closed now." She looked down at the child, but could see that her words hadn't penetrated. "Come back tomorrow," she said loudly and slowly, and turned away, adding under her breath, "The cheek of it! Fancy knocking on the front door!"

Annie burst into tears. She hadn't understood what the lady meant and she was nearly ready to collapse. "Please, missus, tell the doctor! He's got to come! Our Tom'll die!" she sobbed, clutching at the frilly apron.

The altercation reached the ears of those in the drawing-room. Annabelle excused herself gracefully, came out into the hallway and stared incredulously at the filthy, tear-stained child who was making so much noise. "Get rid of her!" she hissed at the maid.

Before the maid could push Annie out, Jeremy had joined them, having guessed by now that someone else must need his services.

Annie recognised the doctor, eluded the maid's hands and fairly threw herself at him. "Dr Lewis! It's our Tom! He's cut his head open an' it's bleedin' all over t'floor. He won't wake up. Me dad said to fetch you." She tugged at his hand. "Oh, please, you've got to come an' save him!"

Ignoring the amusement of his guests and the quivering indignation of his wife, as her social life was ruined for the second time that week, Jeremy led the child, who looked to be in a bad way herself, across to the nearest chair and made her sit down.

"Just sit down there for a moment," he said kindly but firmly. "We aren't going anywhere until you've calmed down and told me properly what's wrong." He looked round. "Ah, Hallam! Could you get me a glass of brandy, please? This child is suffering from shock."

Annabelle made an inarticulate noise of protest in her throat, but Frederick Hallam, who had wined and dined well, said jovially, "Certainly!" and did as he was asked. His nostrils wrinkled a little at the smell of the child, but Jeremy didn't appear to have noticed anything wrong.

"Shall we retire to the drawing-room and leave Jeremy to his – er – ministrations?" asked Annabelle, trying to retrieve the jovial mood of the evening. She shepherded the Hallams and the Purbrights, who owned one of the smaller mills in town, out of the hallway, saying archly, "You'll have to get used to Jeremy, I'm afraid. He can never say no to a patient."

"I admire him," said Mary Purbright frankly. "It must be wonderful to have the skill to help people like he does. I'm really glad that this town has acquired a new doctor with proper modern training."

"A devoted doctor's the best sort," said Frederick, patting his hostess's arm soothingly, "but it's a bit hard on the doctor's wife, eh?"

Annabelle fluttered her eyelashes at him gratefully. "Not if one has understanding friends," she cooed.

"I'm sure we all appreciate your problems," said Christine Hallam, taking her husband's arm and smiling tightly at her hostess. She hoped Frederick wasn't going to set up another of his flirtations with this hard-eyed woman. When he shook her arm off, Christine crept back to her chair and sat smiling vacuously at nothing, her usual defence against awkward situations. Mary Purbright tactfully started to talk to her.

In the hallway, Jeremy made the child drink a little brandy and then a glass of milk, which the maid had reluctantly brought. He watched with satisfaction as a little colour returned to Annie's cheeks. As he encouraged her to talk, he learned that their dad had hit Tom, who had fallen and hit his head on the fender and that she was afraid he'd die, like her mother had.

"Is he unconscious?" asked Jeremy.

"What?"

"Is he – er – knocked out?"

"Oh, aye. An' he's breathin' funny, too." She imitated Tom's stertorous breathing as best she could.

"That's a good girl. I need to know exactly what's happened. Now, I'll just go and get my bag and then we'll be off. You wait for me here and," he made a quick foray into the dining-room, "eat this." He thrust a piece of cake into her hands. As he turned, he saw that Henry Purbright had come out of the drawing-room.

"Mary thought – maybe you'd like to take our carriage. It'll be quicker. We left it waiting outside on a balmy night like this."

"Thank you. It could drop us off at the end of Boston Street. You can't get a carriage into Salem Street, where this poor child lives. I'm very grateful to you, Henry. She's absolutely exhausted. Now, if you'll excuse me, I'll go and get my things."

"Oh, yes. Certainly." Henry looked at the scrawny child sitting on one of Mrs Lewis's velvet-covered chairs, stuffing cake into her grimy mouth and his lips twitched in amusement. It hadn't taken him long to get Annabelle's measure. Thank God his own Mary was a sensible woman, and compassionate, too. No airs and graces from her! It was a mystery to him why some people got married in the first place, for they seemed to have nothing in common. This doctor and his fine lady wife barely looked at one another and didn't speak to each other unless it was absolutely necessary. Frederick and Christine Hallam were another funny pair, 'the tiger and the mouse', Mary called them. Poor Christine was frightened to open her mouth in company. Hell, she had a lot to put up with, for Frederick's womanising was a byword in the town. And he was a man who liked his own way in everything, so she couldn't call her soul her own.

Annie hardly heard what the two men were saying because, now that the brandy had relaxed her and she had some food in her stomach, she was sitting goggling at what she could see of the doctor's house. How bright it was! Fancy using all those lamps and candles at once! And the furniture so smooth and shiny! Furtively she stroked the side of the chair she was sitting on. It was beautiful. But most beautiful of all had been the doctor's wife. She'd never seen a lady dressed up as fine as that. Just like the princess in Matt's story book.

Annabelle was wearing that evening a new and very becoming dress of soft blue watered silk, cut very low and swirling out over no less than eight layers of frilled and padded petticoats. It was embellished with soft blond lace and made a wonderful rustling sound as she moved. Annabelle always dressed well, changing for dinner, even when they had no company, because she considered it to be the 'proper' thing to do, and also because it kept her occupied for an hour or more beforehand.

She grew so bored at times! She didn't really care for reading, had no talent for sketching and kept her embroidery, which was exquisite, mainly for showing off in company, because to do it by candlelight tired her eyes and she didn't want to encourage wrinkles. Jeremy humoured her fancies, spent as much time as he could during the day with his little daughter Marianne and often escaped to his dispensary in the evenings, leaving a furious Annabelle to her own resources.

When the doctor and Annie got back to Salem Street, they found that Tom was no worse, at least. He was lying unconscious on a rag rug on the floor, covered with a blanket. John had sobered up somewhat, thanks to Sally's ministrations, and Lizzie was asleep upstairs, thumb in her mouth and belly full of bread and cheese.

Jeremy took immediate charge, as he had learned to do in the homes of his poorer patients. The father was, he noted angrily, still too drunk to be of much use, but the neighbour turned out to be a sensible woman and Annie too made a useful assistant. She watched with deep interest as the doctor stitched up the cut on her brother's head.

"I didn't know you could sew people up like that," she said. "Won't he look funny with stitches sticking out of his head?"

"Oh, we'll take the stitches out in a few days, when the cut's healed," said Jeremy, smiling at the solemn-eyed slip of a girl to whom he had rather taken a fancy. She might be dirty, but she seemed an intelligent little thing, with her sparkling green eyes.

"Can I watch you do it?"

"Of course you can! And help me, too."

She nodded happily, then her eyes slid round to the remaining sandwiches.

"You eat 'em up, love," said Sally easily. "I've fed your Lizzie an' she's in bed asleep now." She turned to the doctor and whispered, "I don't think the children've had much to eat since their mam died. He's taken it badly."

Jeremy finished with Tom and carried him upstairs, then came down to confront John Gibson. "Are you sober enough to talk sensibly now?" he asked coldly.

John struggled to his feet and stood there swaying. "Aye, sir. I didn't mean to do it, though!"

"I'll slip off home now," said Sally quickly. "I'll pop round again in the morning, Mr Gibson, and see if there's anythin' I can do. You get off to bed when you've eaten those sandwiches, Annie."

"Have you been back to work since your wife died?" Jeremy asked, taking in John's unkempt appearance and the reek of gin that still clung to him.

"No, sir." John's voice was so low that Jeremy could barely tell what he was saying.

"Speak up, man! Where did you work?"

"Hallam's. I was a chargehand." A touch of pride lifted John's head for a moment, then it faded and his eyes fell. "But I'll have lost me job now. Mr Hallam don't allow more than two days off for a death in the family – and someone'll 'ave told him I were drinking."

"Have you finished your drinking now? And your beating of innocent children?" The doctor's voice was stern. "What would your wife have said about that?"

Tears were rolling down John's face. "She'd have gone

70

for me with a stick, she would. She didn't like drinkin' – just a glass of ale now and then is all I used to have, all I used to need after I'd met her. It were just – it were losin' her, sir. I couldn't bear things without 'er!" He broke down completely.

Jeremy waited for a moment or two, then said briskly, "Right then, pull yourself together now. I know Mr Hallam. He's at my house at this moment. I think he might give you your job back if I asked him. You're sure you've done with the drinking?"

John shuddered. "Oh, yes, sir. Never again."

"Then turn up for work tomorrow as usual."

John stared at him, half-blinded by tears, hope fighting the despair in his face. "I – you – you'll not regret it, sir, I promise you. I won't let you down. An' I'll look after the childer from now on."

"See that you do!" Jeremy began to gather his things together. "You're all they've got now."

When he arrived home, the guests were just on the point of leaving, but he had time to persuade Hallam to give John Gibson a second chance. Then, when everyone had gone, he had to face the inevitable scene with Annabelle.

"Bringing filthy children into my house!" she stormed. "I won't have it! Just look at that chair! It'll have to be re-covered. And that's the second time this week you've got your clothes messed up!"

Jeremy picked up his medical bag and looked at her wearily. "In an emergency," he said, trying to speak calmly, "one doesn't worry about chair covers – or clothes: one just tries to save lives. That little girl was in a desperate state. Her mother had died two days previously; she hadn't eaten properly since; and her father had just knocked her brother senseless."

Annabelle's lip curled scornfully. "Please spare me the

sordid details," she said coldly. "Just keep such creatures out of my house in future!" She sought for a way to make him squirm. "Oh, and I'd be grateful if you'd also make sure that you keep your womanising quiet while we're living in Bilsden. This is a small town."

"What?"

"Your womanising. Creatures like Mary."

"You knew about her?"

"Of course I knew! She was a maid of mine once, after all!"

"I never went near her till you threw her out into the street," he said quickly, shocked that Annabelle had even mentioned it.

"She deserved to be dismissed. She was a clumsy fool."

"She didn't deserve to starve!"

"Well, you saw that she didn't starve, didn't you? And if she hadn't found you, she'd have no doubt found someone else."

"You don't seem to mind about her all that much."

"As long as you keep out of my bed and keep your whoring quiet, I don't care who you lie with!"

"I'll do my best to meet your conditions. Keeping out of your bed, Annabelle, will be very easy indeed." He turned and went up to his room, even more sickened than usual by her coldness and callousness. Whatever had made him imagine himself in love with a woman like her? If he hadn't been still convalescing from the influenza and still missing his parents, he would probably have seen through her wiles in time to avoid the altar. At least, he hoped he would.

And he and Annabelle could have made something of their marriage, even then, even without real affection, if she were not frigid in bed, if she did not refuse to bear him any more children. It was bitter gall to him to deliver so many babies to other women, women who often didn't

72

want any more children, and then to come home to a house where Marianne was alone in the nursery.

It was ironical that the work he loved so much should so heavily emphasise the lacks in his own life. But he had married Annabelle for better for worse and would just have to endure the emptiness at home as best he could. And at least he had one child; at least he had Marianne.

5

June 1830 to 1832

With the doctor's help, John Gibson got his job back at Hallam's, though not, of course, as chargehand. Frederick Hallam did not put drunkards in authority over others.

Young as she was, Annie shouldered the burden of running a home and did her best to be a mother to Tom and Lizzie. It was hard going, but she never complained. She knew her mam would have wanted her to look after the others. She wished her dad would talk about their mam sometimes. It would have been a comfort. When she could, she went to the churchyard and put some flowers on her mam's grave and that made her feel better. And even Lizzie behaved herself on those outings.

Tom's head healed slowly, and he was fretful and difficult to manage for weeks. Lizzie had never been an easy child and now she seemed to Annie to whine all the time. The other women in the street came in occasionally to help, especially Bridie, but most of them had their own families and troubles, and John's glum face was enough to drive anyone away, though he was nothing but polite and had apologised to everyone for his rudeness.

Annie rarely had time to play out with Ellie now, but Ellie came into Number Three and helped with the chores whenever her mother would let her, which was only when John was out. Mrs Peters seemed to have taken against John Gibson for some reason, even though she sometimes allowed the Gibson children to come round to Number Seven.

The high spot of the week for Annie was the Sunday afternoon reading lesson there, for on that day John would look after Tom and Lizzie, and send Annie along to the Peters' house with her precious slate.

At first Sally Smith, who was lonely, tried to go on helping the Gibsons, but the other women she met there made it plain she wasn't welcome and she stopped coming. Annie went round to Sally's house one day and demanded to know why.

"Oh, I – I think the other women – er – don't like me comin' to your house, love," said Sally.

"Why don't they like you?" asked Annie, not to be put off with half-tales. "My mam didn't explain it proper when I asked 'er."

"Because – because I'm not married."

"That's silly," said Annie scornfully. "You've been a good friend to us and you helped us when we needed you."

"I know, love, but – but I'm not respectable."

Annie's eyes were puzzled. "Because of your Harry?"

"Yes. Because he keeps me here when we're not married. That's not respectable."

"I don't see how Polly Dykes can be respectable an' you not," said Annie stubbornly. "She's dirty an' she gets drunk every Saturday an' she's allus down at the pawn shop. Them kids of hers are lucky to get a piece of stale bread an' scrape." Annie, in her own eyes, was no longer a child, and spoke as one woman to another.

Sally sighed. "Well, that's how the world is, love. Take my word for it. You have to stay respectable, else folk don't want to speak to you, let alone invite you into their houses."

"Well, I don't care about that. I like you. An' if you won't come to see me, then I'll come round to see you. So there!" Annie set her hands on her vestigial hips and nodded to emphasise her words, just as her mother had used to do.

"Look, I'll tell you what," said Sally, tempted, but trying to do the right thing by the child. "You ask your dad. If he says it's all right, then you can come round sometimes. I'd like that, I must admit. It does get a bit lonely when my Harry's not here. Maybe you could have tea with me, eh? Bring your Lizzie too, if you like."

"I'd have to bring *her*. If I leave her on her own, she breaks things." Annie thought bitterly of the mischief Lizzie could create within minutes if the mood took her.

John, when applied to for permission to visit Sally, at first demurred. He knew how the other women ostracised her and he didn't want his own children to get at outs with their neighbours. Within seconds, he found himself faced with a raging fury, half the size of his Lucy, but so like her that it unnerved him. He capitulated almost instantly and later wept into his bedclothes at the memory of his wife.

From then on, every Monday and Friday, Annie and Lizzie scrubbed their hands and faces and went to take tea in some state with Sally. Ellie would have been welcome too, but was not allowed by her mother to go. Annie always gave Ellie a faithful account of everything they had to eat and what they talked about, for Sally made the occasion a treat each time and even Lizzie looked forward to going there.

Elizabeth Peters, her conscience pricking her at the thought of the motherless child consorting with a loose woman, even one as well-behaved as the tenant of Number

77

Six, tried to have a talk with Annie. She was not a tactful woman, being more in the habit of ordering her own children around than of reasoning with them, and she put up Annie's back within seconds of broaching the subject. Like John, she found herself faced with a miniature virago, for the child hotly defended her friend and would not listen to a word against her.

"That Annie Gibson's a stubborn young madam, and she'd be all the better for a good spanking," she said crossly to Sam when she got back. "I don't think we should let our Ellie play with her any more."

"You'd break Ellie's heart if you tried to separate her from her best friend!" said Matt indignantly.

Sam signalled to his son to be quiet and put his arm round his wife. "Nay, Elizabeth, we can't do that to the child. You know how shy she is at makin' friends. An' besides, she thinks the world of Annie."

"Oh, you never see any harm in anyone, Sam Peters!" Elizabeth saw that he'd got his stubborn expression on and abandoned the attempt, but she was the sort of woman who could hold a grudge for years, and she never felt the same about Annie after that encounter.

Annie had another new acquaintance too, in the person of Dr Lewis. He came to the house several times, ostensibly to see Tom, but in fact to check up that the family was all right. He let Annie help to take the stitches out of Tom's head, as he'd promised, and was touched by her intent face as she bent over her brother.

He also stopped to talk to her a time or two in the street and even, on one wonderful occasion, bought her and Lizzie a gingerbread man each from a street vendor. How they'd enjoyed eating those! They'd nibbled delicately at the feet and made them last as long as possible. Annie saved some of hers for Ellie, who didn't get many treats from a mother who preferred to spend her money on soap than titbits. Lizzie ate every bit of hers, to Tom's loudly expressed annoyance.

Once John was back in work, Annie insisted that they pay the doctor, though he'd never asked them for money. John felt guilty. He should have remembered this himself, but since Lucy's death he had felt a bit vague at times, as if he were only half-alive. Annie consulted Sally Smith, then presented Jeremy with two shillings, which, after a slight hesitation, he gravely accepted. He knew, even if his wife didn't, that two shillings represented a considerable sum to most people in the Rows, but those shillings also represented self-respect to Annie and her family, so he could not refuse them.

By now, Jeremy was starting to make a name for himself in Bilsden, among both rich and poor, as a fine and dedicated doctor. Annabelle, though she continued to complain about the town, enjoyed basking in the reflected glory. During the next few months, Jeremy set a broken arm for the Purbrights' youngest boy and it healed as good as new; he attended the confinement of another mill-owner's wife, a difficult breech birth, and saved both mother and child; and when he was summoned to Hallam's mill after an accident, he earned even Frederick's reluctant admiration by the rapidity with which he sewed up gashes and set broken limbs, helped by that quiet-speaking man of his.

There were a lot of poor people who also had cause to be grateful to Dr Lewis. It might be a matter of indifference to his wife, but it was soon known all over the Rows that you could trust Dr Lewis to look after you, whether you could pay him or not. He wasn't frightened of the bullies in Florida Terrace or Claters End, either, and would scold them vigorously as he bandaged them up after their fights.

They chose to be amused by this and spread the word to leave the new doctor alone, so that he was safe wherever he went, whatever the hour of day or night.

Sam Peters, seeing that John Gibson was just drifting along since his wife's death, introduced him to a few fellow-Methodists, who met every Sunday and sometimes mid-week as well, to pray and to read the Bible. John couldn't read, but he listened avidly and was soon a fervent convert, eventually being saved and reborn in the Lord. He found some comfort for the still-aching gap Lucy's death had left in his life in the idea that he would be reunited with her in heaven, if he set to and earned his way into the Kingdom of God. He never had the slightest doubt that she would be waiting for him there. Pure gold she had been, his Lucy, pure gold.

The little group of Methodists was labouring hard to raise funds to build a chapel. About a year after John joined them, they were left a few acres of land by an old spinster, whom Sam had met through his job with the doctor. With no thought of gain, he had gone regularly to see the lonely old woman and had talked to her, without realising what he was doing, of his hopes and plans. As well as the land, she left fifty pounds towards the building of the chapel, not enough, but a wonderful start.

Jeremy, who had been made responsible for dispensing this money, recounted this tale to Frederick Hallam and some other men one night after dinner and, to his surprise, Frederick grew thoughtful. "It might be worth lending them a hand," he said, rubbing his nose.

The other three men at the table shouted with laughter.

"*You*, helping the bloody Methodists, Hallam! That's rich!" spluttered one of them, choking on a mouthful of port.

"You'll have to give this up," said another, brandishing

the decanter and slopping the rich ruby liquid on to Annabelle's best damask tablecloth. "It's affecting your brain!" More paroxysms of mirth.

Frederick banged on the table to get their attention. "You lot can't see further than the ends of your own noses. You all know the problem we have with the operatives and their drinking. I get some damned careless work on Mondays. And they throw stones and break the windows of the mill at nights when they're drunk. I have to employ a watchman, and a fat lot of good he is! It'd take an army to police my properties properly."

"And you think the bloody Methodists can stop the damage? You've had a bit too much port, old chap!"

"Not stop it," said Hallam, smiling to himself, "but I was talking to an owner from over Oldham way last week and he reckons it cuts down the drunkenness *and . . .*" he paused and waved a cigar at them, "the Methodists also teach the children to read and write, and the women to look after their families better."

Jeremy's interest was fairly caught. "Go on, Frederick!" He sipped a little port and nodded encouragingly. He was not a drinker himself, but acting as host at her parties was one of the few things he was prepared to do to keep Annabelle happy. He'd learned to make one glass of wine spin out for a long time and occasionally enjoyed the conversation.

"If you teach 'em to read, you're asking for trouble," the man with the decanter declared, banging it down on the table. "I prefer 'em ignorant, myself."

"You're short-sighted, Jonas Dawton," said Hallam, "and you always have been! Look, man, the machinery's getting more and more complicated. We're going to need operatives with a bit of sense in their heads to work it and service it, men who can read and write, and who can follow

81

instructions and diagrams. Peter Dodson, over in Oldham, reckons he gets his best overseers and chargehands from the Methodists. Not counting his first steam engine, he says giving them a bit of land for their chapel was the best investment he ever made."

He sat there for a moment, then slammed his hand down on the table. "I'll do it! I'll put up some money towards their chapel! It'll be fifty pounds well spent, I reckon. They can have that pile of lumber behind my mill, as well. It wasn't strong enough for my flooring, but it'll do well enough for roofing their chapel. And if you have any sense, you'll all do the same. These Nonconformists not only educate themselves, they also look after those who're in trouble. And that keeps those damned poor rates down."

There was a chorus of amazement, for Frederick Hallam was not noted for his philanthropy or for his generosity, and few of them believed his explanation for his gesture. Educating the lower classes only led to trouble.

"Your man's a Methodist, isn't he?" Frederick asked Jeremy.

"Yes. He's very committed. One of the leaders, you might call him, though he'd deny that."

"Send him over to the mill to see me when you can spare him for an hour. And now, that's enough about chapels, gentlemen. Let's return to the lovely ladies!"

The scheme, born in a moment of drunken conviviality, gained enough support in the town to furnish funds for a small, very plain red-brick chapel. Under the wing of the circuit committee in Manchester and a local steering committee, chaired by a farmer from Clough Knowle, with the thirty-two-year-old unmarried daughter of the town's leading grocer as secretary and Sam in charge of the practical details of the building, the chapel was funded, designed and built in record time.

It was finished just before Annie's twelfth birthday. From then onwards, Annie, Tom, Lizzie and the Peters children found their Sunday activities seriously curtailed, for there was chapel in the morning and Sunday School in the afternoon. Annie was not overly taken with chapel, for she was tone deaf, and had to mime the words to the hymns or else people stared at her. And the sermons were far too long, in her opinion. Her dad got angry if she let Lizzie fidget, but it was hard to keep a small girl still for so long.

Tom hated going to chapel from the start, for he always loathed being penned up indoors, but he didn't dare say so to his father, who had found a new meaning to life in Methodism. The Peters children accepted it more philosophically, for they were used to a lot of praying at home, as well as Sunday readings of the Bible. Matt Peters actually enjoyed the sermons and would discuss them at length with his father on the way home.

Annie's devotion to Matt had increased rather than decreased over the two years she had known him. She didn't realise that the whole street knew her 'secret', for she had confided only in her friend Ellie. Annie longed to grow up, to keep up with Matt, who was now so large and manly. She was terrified that he would meet another girl and start walking out with her.

Matt himself was aware of Annie's devotion, though not of the depths of it, and always tried to be kind to her, assuming that it was merely a childish infatuation. In the meantime, she was Ellie's friend, she was a nice lass and he didn't mind her tagging along.

There were few changes in the street in those two years. The Butterworths moved out and a young couple moved into Number One. Fred and Carol Peck had one child and another on the way. Carol's aunt came to live with them shortly afterwards and they got on very well with everyone in the street, except George and Polly Dykes in Number Two. Polly drank as much as George now, and had done ever since her little son had died of the measles the previous year. Even the new baby, another boy, didn't seem to ease her loss. Well, women always did take the first loss of a child hard, Bridie O'Connor said, and tried to be kind to poor Polly.

She knew about that sort of thing, Bridie thought bitterly. She'd lost a few children herself, in more ways than one. Her two eldest sons had recently moved out. Peter had got married to a feckless girl from down Claters End and Danny, the eldest, had got fed up of working in the mill and had just gone off on the tramp one day. The last they'd heard of him, he'd gone for a navvy and was helping to build a pit railway near Sheffield. He was earning good money, Bridie told everyone proudly, and had written to the good father about it, but she could not help fretting for him. He'd always been her favourite, in spite of his wilfulness. There was no one who could make you laugh like her Danny could. No, nor a finer looking young man anywhere.

The first minister to be appointed to the brand new Todmorden Road Methodist Chapel was Saul Hinchcliffe. This was his first full-time appointment and he was burning to spread the Lord's word. He was the only son of a well-to-do farmer from Knutsford, in Cheshire, and had been called to salvation at a prayer meeting when he was only fifteen.

One of the causes dearest to Saul's heart was the education of the young. Bilsden, the mushroom growth of the industrial age, had no grammar school and its little day school was a disgrace. Sergeant Brown had gone suddenly to join his Maker at the beginning of 1832, and the man who

had taken over his school was an ill-educated bully. Saul knew that it would take years to find a proper solution to this problem of educating the young of the poorer citizens, but in the meantime, he made it his business to set up a proper Sunday School, where the children could at least be taught their letters. He even wheedled slates and primers out of Frederick Hallam, having quickly realised that that gentleman's interest lay not in Methodism, but in ways of obtaining sober, better-educated workers.

Matt, Annie, Ellie and any other children old enough to attend were drilled in their reading by using the Bible and various religious tracts, written especially for children and provided free by a group of charitable ladies in Manchester. These ladies visited the chapel once a year and listened to the best scholars read, but the children of the Rows mostly found their little lectures incomprehensible.

Saul himself taught the top class, which contained the older or the more promising students, among them Annie. He was a firm believer in the education of women and entirely applauded the saying that 'the hand that rocks the cradle rules the world'. He left the younger children, who were just beginning their letters and with whom he had not much patience, to his helpers. He also ran a men's Bible Group on Thursday nights, ostensibly to study the word of the Lord, but in fact to teach the grown men to read. John attended this for a while and learned to write and to read simple texts, but he soon found other things to occupy himself with.

The main outcome for the Gibsons of John's involvement with Methodism was his growing friendship with one Emily Taylor, a widow with one child. She made a meagre living by taking in lodgers and washing, and it was one of these who brought her to the chapel one Sunday. Her husband had died two years previously, leaving her with a

85

young daughter and another baby on the way. Fortunately for her practical needs, she'd miscarried. Once she'd recovered from that, she found herself some lodgers, took in washing and managed to scrape a living. She was a thin woman, with a bumpy nose and mouse-coloured hair, screwed back into a tight bun, as different from Lucy as chalk from cheese.

John gradually grew used to Emily. He didn't fall in love with her, as he had once fallen in love with Lucy, but he asked her advice sometimes about his children and found her to be a sensible woman, not realising that she was just echoing his own thoughts. He drifted into a courtship, as much for practical reasons as anything. He wasn't the sort of man to live for ever without a woman.

Annie had met Emily Taylor at chapel, of course, for in a small congregation everyone knew everyone else. It was a while before she realised what was happening and when she did, being Annie, she confronted her father immediately. "Dad – if you don't watch out, people will think you're courting Emily Taylor."

He flushed and concentrated on his pipe.

"Dad – you're not!"

"Well, a man needs a woman t'look after him."

"But I do the house! We don't *need* anyone else!"

"Aye, an' you do it very well, lass. But it's a heavy burden on one so young. Em'ly says . . ."

"I don't *care* what Emily says. I *hate* her! She's stupid!" Tears were streaming down Annie's thin face. "Dad, you can't! Not after Mam!"

John grew angry. "You mind your manners when you're talkin' about your elders!" he shouted. "I'm not askin' you, I'm tellin' you! Me an' Em'ly's goin' to be wed, an' that's all there is to it."

Annie's sobs redoubled.

"An' what's more, she's comin' round to dinner after morning service on Sunday, so I want everythin' nice here. You mind what I say, our Annie!"

Everything was immaculate in the little house on the Sunday. Annie had debated leaving things in a mess, to put Emily Taylor off them, but had then come round to Ellie's view that she owed it to herself and her dead mother to show what she could do.

The visit was not a success. Emily already counted Annie as a cross she would have to bear in her second marriage. Tom was a normal enough boy, if a bit rough, and Lizzie was still young enough to be moulded in Emily's ways, but that Annie was a cheeky young madam. Emily also resented Annie's efficiency as a housekeeper, for she knew she could not match it.

In October 1832, John Gibson and Emily Taylor were married. First they fulfilled their legal obligations by a brief ceremony in the parish church of St Mark, conducted in a cursory manner by a bored curate. Parson Kenderby acknowledged that it was his legal duty to marry even those who were not members of the congregation, but he did not trouble to hide his disapproval of those damned impertinent Dissenters and Nonconformists, and he mainly left them to the curate. John and Emily, supported by their children and witnesses, all of whom felt as uncomfortable as they did amid the gaudy trappings of the Established Church, breathed a sigh of relief when it was over and they were free to walk down to their own bare chapel. There, they went through what they felt to be the real wedding ceremony.

Afterwards the family went back to Salem Street and Emily took possession of Number Three. She immediately reorganised the furniture, putting her own pieces into prominence and putting Annie's back up in a dozen different ways. John and his new wife had the front bedroom and Tom, who had been sleeping with his father, was relegated to a mattress in a corner of the front room downstairs, because Emily said he was too old to sleep with his sisters now and anyway, May wasn't his sister. Annie found six-year-old May's presence in the bedroom irritating, not only because she told her mother everything that Annie said or did, but because Lizzie struck up a friendship with May that left the older girl out.

After a few weeks, Emily broached the idea of finding Annie a job.

John was startled. "Nay, there's no rush!" he said. "Is she – is she givin' you any trouble? I won't have her upsettin' you."

"No, no! It's not that," replied Emily, who knew better than to admit that she just couldn't stand the girl to a father as fond of his children as John. "It were all right when she stayed home to look after you, but," she added coyly, "you've got me to do that now."

"You're a good woman, Em'ly." He refused to let himself think of Lucy as he said this. There had only been one Lucy.

"Well, love, your Annie's turned twelve. We have to think of her future, you know. Most girls of her age are out at work, bringin' a bit in and savin' up to get wed."

"I suppose so."

"That Ellie Peters is goin' into t'mill."

"Is she? I didn't think Sam wanted her to. I wouldn't let my Annie go there. It's all right for boys like Tom, but I don't want it for my girls. Their mother was dead set against it."

"Well, there's not much else girls can do round here if they don't go in t'mill. But," Emily brought the conversation firmly back to the point, "I wouldn't want your

Annie to feel she'd been done badly to. When I made my promises to you before the Lord, I promised meself that I'd be a second mother to your children."

"Aye. I knew I could rely on you, Em'ly."

"But the thing is, John, a girl of her age needs to be kept busy. The devil finds mischief for idle hands, you know."

"I suppose so." John felt out of his depth. What did he know about the needs of twelve-year-old girls? "What did you have in mind, then?"

"Well, she's a clever lass, Annie is. She could do better for 'erself than t'mill."

John squeezed her hand, grateful for this thoughtfulness.

"So I thought about puttin' her into service." She didn't tell him that the most appealing thing about putting Annie into service was the fact that she would have to live at her employer's house and would thus be out of Emily's way. "It's a respectable life for a girl, an' there's prospects. An' your Annie's that clever, she'd be bound to do well. I – er – I've already asked Mr Hinchcliffe if he knows anyone as is lookin' for some help an' he thinks he'll be able to find Annie a place. He says folk in the country are allus lookin' for help, so he's goin' to write to his family."

"Y're a good woman, Em'ly." John was a happier and more relaxed man nowadays. A man needed a wife. He'd loved Lucy, but it was hard to sleep alone. He didn't love Emily in the same way and she could be a bit sharp at times, but she was a good woman too and would be a mother to his children. Look at the way she'd sorted young Lizzie out! No more tantrums and waywardness. It needed a grown woman to care for a child of that age. And now, all this thought for Annie, wanting to do the best for her. He was a lucky man and he thanked the Lord for leading him along the path to salvation.

Annie, told of the fine plans Emily had made, burst into

tears and begged her father not to send her away. He dried her tears and told her of the rosy future she had in store, but she remained unconvinced.

"What about our Tom and our Lizzie?" she sobbed. "I've allus looked after them. I know *you* don't need me any more, but they do!"

Her pleading was to no avail. At first John tried to reason with her, then he grew angry and thumped the table. He wasn't having disobedience from one of his children. She would do as she was told and that was that!

Emily, ostensibly busy cooking a meal, cast Annie a flickering glance of triumph from behind John's back and Annie realised that there was nothing she could do.

The next day she went off on her own, making her way up towards the moors, not caring that she would be in trouble when she got back home.

Jeremy Lewis, driving his gig back from a case at one of the farms, recognised the little figure sitting hunched up by a brook and pulled up. "Hey, isn't that young Annie Gibson?" he shouted. He tied the pony's reins to one of the stunted moorland trees and walked across to join her. "Not often we see you out here on the moors, Annie."

She raised a tear-stained face towards him. "H-hello, Dr Lewis."

"Now, what's the matter with you, lass?"

"They're sendin' me away," she blurted out, sniffing and wiping a tear away on her sleeve.

"Who are?" he asked gently, disturbed to see this normally brave little girl so upset.

"*She* is! She's the one who wants to send me away! She's got round me dad."

He pulled his handkerchief out and wiped her eyes, astonished at how beautiful they were, of an unusually bright green, with hidden gleams in them like the facets of a jewel, and fringed in long dark lashes. "Who's 'she', Annie?"

"Me dad's new wife. He's got wed again."

"Yes. I heard."

"An' – an' she says I've to go into service – to leave home - leave Tom an' our dad." She scrubbed her eyes fiercely with his handkerchief. "She says it's because she's thinkin' of me future, but I know it's because she wants to get rid of me!"

"That's a hard thing to face."

She looked up, startled that he wasn't trying to persuade her that it was all for her own good, as even Sally had tried to do. "I was happy," she said brokenly. "We didn't need her. I did the house an' everythin'. An' I did it better than *her*! Why, she can't even sew properly! Me mam would have a fit at what she does to the clothes. Oh, why did me dad 'ave to marry her?"

"Sometimes a man needs the company of a woman," he said gravely.

"You mean he wanted a woman to sleep with," she said savagely. "I know about that. Sally Smith told me why he needed a wife. Oh, aye, me dad's happy enough. But why do *I* have to go so far away? Ellie's gone to work in t'mill. Why couldn't I go into t'mill too?"

Heaven forbid! he thought. Not this bright-eyed child. He put his arm round her. "Maybe you won't have to go too far away."

"Oh, yes, I will! She's asked Mr Hinchcliffe to – to recommend," she brought out the long word triumphantly, "me to a family an' his mother knows someone in Cheshire." It might have been the moon, from the way she said it. "I'd never get to see M . . ." she was going to say Matt, but changed it to, "me friends if I worked in Cheshire."

"That'd be terrible," he agreed. "I'll tell you what – I'll ask my wife if she knows anyone who is looking for a maid in Bilsden. How about that?"

"Oh, Dr Lewis – would you?"

He took the problem to Annabelle the same evening, telling the story casually, asking if there was any chance of finding the girl a place in Bilsden.

"Oh, you and your slum children!" she scoffed. "She won't find a place with a good family. They're too ignorant and stupid, those girls from the Rows!"

"This one's an exception, I think. She's very intelligent, for a start, and she's been running the family home for two years, ever since her mother died, and running it well, too, by all accounts."

"Is she clean?"

He thought back to the morning, to Annie's pale clear skin. "Yes, I think so. Cleaner than most, anyway. She lives near Sam Peters in Salem Street. One of the more respectable streets, that."

Annabelle pulled a face. To her, none of the mill streets was respectable. Still, the last girl she'd had, who had come to her highly recommended from a farm family, had been slow and stupid, absolutely unteachable. And she'd be able to get this girl cheap. And what was more, it wouldn't hurt to have Jeremy grateful to her, in case she needed a favour. "I'd have to see her first," she said warningly. "*And* her stepmother. I like to know where my girls come from."

His face brightened. "You mean, we need someone ourselves? Why, that's marvellous!"

"Tell them to come and see me tomorrow, at eleven thirty sharp," she said, already bored with the subject. "Now, about this party on Saturday. I've got some new people coming . . ."

* * *

Annie and her stepmother presented themselves at the back door of Park House at eleven twenty-five the next day, having waited near the church clock to be sure of not being late. Mrs Gibson was dressed in her wedding clothes, a dress in an unflattering shade of dark blue and a skimpy bonnet, which looked silly, Annie thought, perched on her stepmother's narrow head. They had done their best to turn Annie out presentably, but there had been great consternation when Emily realised how the child had grown out of her Sunday clothes. Her boots stuck out clumsily below the dress which Lucy had bought for her second-hand just before she died, and which could no longer be let down.

When Annie and Mrs Gibson were shown into the back parlour, Annabelle closed her eyes for a moment in dismay. Really! How could Jeremy expect her to take on a girl like this? Then she remembered the maid she'd just dismissed and the desperate need to find a replacement. She ran a tight house and the other servants could not be expected to cope with the extra work for longer than was absolutely necessary. Only this morning, Cook had been hinting that they needed another pair of hands and saying that she was 'fair wore out' doing everything herself.

She studied the girl and woman more closely. Yes, Jeremy was right. Considering where they came from, they were surprisingly clean. What a frightful bonnet the woman was wearing, though!

"You're Mrs Gibson," she said coldly, "and this is Annie."

"Yes, ma'am." Annie bobbed a curtsey, having been coached by Mr Peters on how to address Mrs Lewis.

"Come over here to the window and let me have a proper look at you, girl."

Annie stepped forward and the lady eyed her as if she were a worm crawled from under a stone, as Annie later told Ellie. "An' she flicked at me with her fingertip, as if I was too mangy to touch."

"I need a girl to help with the general housework," the cold voice continued. Annabelle's pale eyes were focused on Emily now.

"Annie's a good little worker. She ran the house for two year when her mother died – ran it well, too."

Annie blinked in surprise at this praise from her stepmother.

"And can she obtain references as to her character?" continued Annabelle, determined to maintain some standards.

Sam Peters had told them about the references too.

"Mr Hinchcliffe, the minister at the chapel, said he'd speak for her." Emily was just as intimidated as Annie by Mrs Lewis. "She's in his Sunday School class."

"I see. You can read, then, girl?"

"Yes, ma'am."

That'd be an improvement on her predecessor, who might have been taught her letters, but who couldn't string the words together well enough to make any sense. "Read this aloud, please." Annabelle held out a card.

Annie took it from her in one trembling hand. "It says, Mrs Jeremy Lewis r-requests the pleasure of the company of – of . . ."

"Thank you. That will do."

Annabelle turned to the mother. "I will give your stepdaughter a month's trial. Were she not exceptionally well recommended by my husband, I would not have considered employing a girl from the Rows. In the circumstances, she will have to work particularly hard to earn my trust."

Mrs Gibson flushed a dull red at this and Ellie later

shared Annie's indignation that anyone should think that Salem Street was anything but respectable.

"Has she got an outfit?"

"A – a what, ma'am?" Sam had not told them about this.

"An outfit. It is customary for a girl, when she gets her first place in service, to provide her own uniform, which is then replaced by the mistress as necessary. That is termed an outfit."

The red deepened in Emily's cheeks. "I – what would she need, please, ma'am?"

Annabelle reeled off a list of clothing.

Emily swallowed. "We – we could get some of it . . ."

Annabelle debated on withdrawing her offer of employment, then decided to be generous – or to let Jeremy be generous. She never told him how much she was managing to save from her housekeeping allowance, and she was putting together a tidy little nest-egg for a rainy day. "Very well then, Mrs Gibson. Supply what you can and I will provide the rest." After all, she had plenty of old clothes in the attic that could be cut down and she would deduct their cost from Annie's wages, which would mean a further saving.

"Thank you, ma'am."

"She may as well start immediately. Go home and get your things, girl. I need you today."

6

November 1832 to May 1834

The first few weeks at Park House were lonely and difficult for Annie. The other servants laughed at the way she spoke and at the clothes she wore. She had to share a room and bed with Bet, the parlourmaid, and Bet made it very plain from the first that she considered herself a cut above the newcomer. And then, there was so much to learn! Annie had thought she knew how to run a house till she went to work for Mrs Lewis, but she found out immediately that she knew very little. The furniture, the clothes people wore, the food they ate and even the way they spoke – everything bewildered her at first. It was like another world.

She had to rise at five in the morning and get the kitchen fire drawing, and though the early rising was no hardship, the kitchen range soon became the bane of her life. Then she had to clean the grate and light a fire in the nursery before sweeping and dusting that room out. Meantime, it was Bet's duty to go down, do the grates and light the fires in the downstairs rooms. Then they both washed and had breakfast with the other servants.

There were five servants in all, Mrs Cosden, the cook, Mabel, the chambermaid, who also acted as lady's maid to the mistress, and Katy, the nursemaid, as well as Bet and

Annie. There was also Mrs Wilkes, who came in to do the washing and ironing once a fortnight, on a Wednesday and Thursday. Annie had to fetch and carry for her, running to and fro between the kitchen and the washhouse, and then she had to put away the finished piles of neatly-folded linen after it had been ironed on the following day. From Mrs Wilkes, Annie learned about the care of materials and the removal of stains.

Mrs Lewis ran a very economical household, for one of her station and high social aspirations. She kept a watchful eye on everything the servants did, as well as what they ate, and her suspicious attitude seemed to have communicated itself to the women who worked for her. They too kept a jealous eye on each other and were less than co-operative with the newcomer. Many times in those first few weeks Annie sobbed herself quietly to sleep, taking care not to wake Bet.

Used to the rough friendliness of Salem Street, where people were always ready to lend a hand if you were in trouble, Annie couldn't believe it the first time Mabel blamed her for something Mabel herself had forgotten to do. If it hadn't been for Dr Lewis, she believed she might have run back home. But he had got her this job as a special favour, and she couldn't let him down. And somehow, the way the doctor winked at her when he passed her on the stairs and asked how she was getting on made her even more reluctant to give in to the petty persecutions and spitefulness she had to suffer in those early days. Besides, if she went home, they'd only send her away to Cheshire, which would be even worse. At least this way, she would still be able to see Matt every now and then.

She had one Sunday off a month, though it was not really a whole Sunday, because she couldn't get away until nearly ten o'clock. The first free day came just as Annie thought she could bear Park House no longer. She walked home towards Salem Street very slowly, savouring her freedom. It all seemed part of the wonder of the day when she met Matt at the water tap and lingered to talk to him and stroll back with him. He asked about her new job and told her that Ellie had missed her and was dying to see her.

Salem Street seemed very cramped and the houses smaller than she had remembered, but little had changed inside Number Three. To Annie's surprise, even her stepmother appeared glad to see her. All the family questioned her eagerly about Park House and she was conscious of a feeling of superiority as she answered their questions and told them how the rich lived. Both John and Emily shook their heads at some of the extravagances practised by Dr and Mrs Lewis. John quoted the Bible to show how wrong it was that some folks should have so much while others were in want, but that didn't stop him from listening to her tales and asking more questions.

Then they all suddenly realised that it was time to leave for chapel and there was a rush to get ready. Annie had to attend the parish church on the other Sundays with the rest of Mrs Lewis's staff, and she secretly thought the service there a lot more interesting and the church, with its flowers and ornaments, much prettier than the chapel – but of course she didn't say so to her father, to whom religion now meant a great deal.

After the midday meal, Annie met Ellie, and this, apart from seeing Matt again, was the high spot of her day. Since it was a fine, though dull day, they walked out of town towards the moors, talking nineteen to the dozen about themselves and their new jobs. Only to Ellie did Annie admit that she was having a bad time at Park House; only to Annie did Ellie admit how much she hated and feared the mill. The noise of the spinning machinery made her head ache and the cotton fluff got into everything, even her mouth, till her throat was clagged with it and you either coughed it up or swallowed it.

"But at least you get every Sunday off," Annie pointed out, trying to be of comfort.

"It's not worth it," said Ellie glumly. "It only makes it seem worse of a Monday."

"And you get paid more than I do."

"I'd rather get less money and stay out of that place," said Ellie, shuddering. "And besides, Mam takes all me money. I have to ask for a penny and tell her what for, and half the time she says no. Eh, Annie, love, you don't know how lucky you are!"

When Annie got back, she was summoned to see the mistress.

Annabelle stared at the child, who was already looking better for the more varied diet at the doctor's home. She would be pretty when she grew up, with that colouring, and they would have to keep a careful eye on her. She cleared her throat. "I'm pleased to tell you, Annie, that you have not done too badly, considering your background."

Annie bobbed a curtsey. "Thank you, ma'am." Mrs Cosden had already hinted that she was likely to stay.

"You may therefore consider yourself engaged in a permanent capacity. Katy will make over some old clothes into a proper uniform for you, and the cost will be deducted from your wages."

Annie's eyes lit up at the thought of some decent clothes. She had felt her shabbiness very strongly, for Mabel and Bet had commented on it almost daily. "Oh, thank you, ma'am! I'm that grateful."

"*Very* grateful, or *so* grateful. For goodness sake, try to learn to speak proper English! Listen to how the doctor and I speak, and do your best to imitate us. I can't possibly live

100

with that flat ugly accent in my ears."

"No, ma'am. I mean, yes, ma'am." Another curtsey was safest, Annie reckoned.

Before she had been at Park House for two months, Christmas was upon them. If life had seemed lavish before, it seemed sinfully extravagant now. Mrs Cosden grumbled and complained, but produced several superb dinners for Mrs Lewis's friends. She even unbent enough to give Annie tastes of the wonderful things she was making. In the general conviviality, Annie somehow found herself accepted by the other servants and treated more kindly, though you always had to watch Mabel and you had to tread lightly if Mrs Cosden had one of her heads.

On Christmas morning, Annabelle distributed presents to the servants, though only because Jeremy insisted on it. Annie found herself the stunned possessor of a length of stout white cotton suitable for a petticoat. Annabelle played Lady Bountiful at a little ceremony for the benefit of the visitors, her mother and Barbara Dwight, an old friend from Brighton, who were both staying with her for the festive season. Although Mrs Parton was not much impressed by the idea of giving presents to servants who got paid perfectly good wages, Barbara was, or pretended to be. She later recounted the touching scene at great length to a room full of guests, to Annabelle's prettily-assumed embarrassment.

Annabelle greatly envied Barbara, who was a widow of some years' standing, with a comfortable private income. How pleasant it must be to have one's independence and to be able to do as one pleased at all times! When Barbara invited her to come for a return visit to Brighton, she accepted eagerly – though it later led to a quarrel with Jeremy, who felt that her place was at home with her daughter. Annabelle was determined to go, however. She needed quite desperately to get away from Bilsden for a time, and from Jeremy, who was for ever boring on about his stupid patients.

Christmas in Salem Street was celebrated on a much less lavish scale. The Gibsons and the Peters went to chapel twice; the O'Connors went to their Catholic church at midnight on Christmas Eve; and no one else bothered with the observance of any religious formalities.

By the end of the day, the Dykes were drunk enough to have another fight and break a window, which made Emily mad as fire, and Barmy Charlie was singing away to himself down at Number Eight. Even Sally, after a solitary Christmas dinner, because Harry couldn't get away from his family at such a time, allowed herself a few generous measures of gin to dull the edge of her loneliness.

In almost no time, it seemed, Annie had been at Park House for a year. Even Mrs Lewis now conceded to Mrs Cosden, the cook, that Annie was "coming along" and "not as bad as the last one" which, for her, was high praise indeed. At the end of the year she presented Annie, who had grown considerably, with some lengths of material and told her to make herself some more clothes as quickly as possible.

Annie asked Bet's advice, for she had no idea of how to cut out a dress. She was now on good enough terms to be the recipient of confidences about the butcher's boy, with whom Bet was walking out. Bet sent her up to talk to Katy, who was noted for her skill as a needlewoman. In return for some extra help in the nursery, Katy agreed to help Annie cut out and make up some new dresses.

"My mam taught me to sew," said Annie wistfully, fingering one of Miss Marianne's new aprons, on to which Katy was sewing a lace trim, "but not the fancy stuff or embroidery, and I haven't learned to cut out."

"You'll never get on if you can't sew well, young Annie," Katy said patronisingly, with all the superior knowledge of one who had spent fifteen years in service to the gentry. "They always expect you to make your own clothes, even if they buy the material, and to mend their clothes, too."

Annie, who liked Katy best of all the other servants and who greatly respected her hard-working, no-nonsense attitude, meekly agreed.

"If you want, I could give you a few lessons."

"Oh, yes, please, Katy. I'd be ever so grateful!"

"All right, then. You're a good kid, not like that Bet."

Annie goggled at this criticism of Bet, who knew so much more than she did.

"She'll come to a bad end, will that Bet," prophesied Katy. "Man-mad, she is, and always has been. Men is the ruin of us maids – or can be, if we let 'em have their way. You watch out you don't get taken in by a man, young Annie."

"No, Katy." Annie giggled a little at the mere idea of a man taking an interest in her. She was still as angular and undeveloped as a boy and was bitterly disappointed that she hadn't yet started to get her figure, like her friend Ellie. Bet, at eighteen, was the proud possessor of lush curves and rosy cheeks. Annie was sometimes sunk in despair about her own body, her pale complexion and most of all about her red hair – though there were some signs that its harsh tint was toning down to a more acceptable auburn. But this was not happening fast enough for Annie, with Mabel jeering "Carrots!" whenever she was in a bad mood. Mr Hinchcliffe might preach about the perils of the flesh and the sin of vanity, but Annie always included in her prayers a humble request for just a few curves and some colour in her cheeks, if God didn't mind, please.

When the new clothes were finished, even Mrs Lewis deigned to compliment Annie on the improvement in her appearance and to suggest a new way of doing her hair. Annie had such a mass of it that it could not just be tied back and left hanging down her back. Really, Annabelle thought, watching Annie bob a curtsey and leave, that child has turned out surprisingly well! And she might be ignorant about the finer points of living, but I've never had to speak to her for laziness. I've never before allowed Jeremy to foist one of his waifs and strays on to me, but for once he was right.

If only Jeremy would show more sense in other matters, she thought, staring out of the window at the grey town she hated! He was getting far too interested in that research of his and even talked about it at dinner parties sometimes. Ugh! As if anyone wanted to hear about the problems of childbirth! The Purbrights were the only ones who seemed to enjoy such talk, heaven knew why! You'd think people who owned a big mill would have had enough of the operatives and their problems during the day. She and Frederick Hallam, who was really a most cultured man, had to smile at each other sometimes across a dinner-table or drawing-room, when the others went on about the living conditions of the poor, or other rubbish of the same sort. As if the poor didn't deserve all they got!

It had taken Frederick Hallam several months to win over Annabelle Lewis. He had realised almost from the beginning that she was a cold fish, and would probably be useless in bed, but he'd been intrigued by the challenge of captivating her. And, by George, he had done it! It was Frederick and Annabelle now, and cosy chats in corners and alcoves, not to mention the occasional meeting in Manchester. He didn't know why he bothered, really, because she certainly was not going to give him anything except her company, but he enjoyed watching her affected mannerisms almost as much as he enjoyed seeing his silly fool of a wife squirm when he talked to other women.

Jeremy Lewis, though, didn't even seem interested in the fact that his wife was flirting with another man, and servants' gossip said they had separate bedrooms. If Frederick had not seen the good doctor going into a certain house of assignation in Manchester one day, he might have believed that Jeremy was as cold a fish as his wife. It just went to show that you never could tell.

Just after Annie's second Christmas at Park House, Bet was discovered to be pregnant and was summarily dismissed by Mrs Lewis, after a shrill harangue on immorality that was audible even in the kitchen. Bet's sobs could be heard all over the house and none of the servants was allowed near her. She was turned out of the house within an hour of Mrs Lewis finding out about her condition and the mistress seemed to take the matter as a personal affront.

It put Mrs Cosden in a bad mood straight away, losing Bet's services in the kitchen. It also gave Annie a great deal of extra work.

Annabelle, afraid that the moral infection might have spread, summoned her maids one by one to her boudoir. "Ah, come in, Annie. I should like to speak to you."

"Yes, ma'am." Annie bobbed a curtsey, clasped her hands together over her apron, because Mrs Lewis couldn't stand servants who fidgeted when she was speaking to them, and fixed a clear, unblinking gaze upon her mistress.

"Are you aware of why Bet was dismissed?"

Annie nodded her head. "Yes, ma'am. Because she's goin' to 'ave - I mean, have a baby."

"Yes. And are you aware of how wrong she was to behave in such a manner?"

105

"Oh, yes, ma'am!"

"It is the duty of every female, whatever her station in life, to keep herself pure. If, and only if, one gets married, are relations with a man permissible. I trust I make myself clear, Annie?"

"Yes, ma'am. Like they tell us in church, ma'am." Annie mouthed the phrases which would satisfy her mistress. It had taken her a while to understand what the parson of Mrs Lewis's church meant by fornication and adultery. Even Mr Hinchcliffe went on about it sometimes, but he used milder language. She and Ellie had giggled about one such sermon afterwards, but Matt had overheard them and had scolded them for making light of important matters.

Matt was doing well at the mill. Because he could read and write so well, Mr Hallam had told the foreman to keep an eye on him and teach him as much as he could. Sam used to tell Annie about his son's progress sometimes, when they had a minute to spare after she'd cleaned the doctor's rooms.

Sam and Elizabeth were very proud of their son; it was only Ellie who worried Sam. She still hated working at the mill, and was getting very thin and peaky, in spite of working hours being reduced to twelve a day for children her age by the new Factory Act. Sam thought that she ought to stop working there, but her mother wouldn't hear of it, which had caused a few rows between them, Ellie said.

Ellie's mother, Annie thought, got grumpier as she got older, and more penny-pinching, too. She herself had heard Mrs Peters scolding Ellie about her silly notions and fussy ways. "You should learn to accept what life brings you," Mrs Peters had shouted, "because what it brings in the main is trouble, an' you can't afford to be finicky."

Annie thought privately that it was just Ellie's money her mother wanted. Mrs Peters had been a bit funny ever since the death of Lily from the fever and the new baby, Samuel, hadn't made much difference. Mrs Peters had nearly driven her family mad lately, fussing about keeping the house clean. Annie didn't enjoy going there any more. You were frightened to touch anything.

Annie realised that Mrs Lewis was still speaking and dragged her attention back reluctantly.

"Of course, I realise that Bet's leaving like this will give you a lot of extra work. You can be assured that as soon as I find a suitable girl, I shall engage her. Mabel and Katy will give you some extra help, and you will take over Bet's duties. Although you're young, you're doing very well, but don't let this praise go to your head. You still have a lot to learn. You will receive six pounds a year – er – from the next quarter."

"Yes, ma'am. Thank you, ma'am." Annie suddenly had a wonderful idea and stood hesitating by the door. Dare she make a suggestion to the mistress?

"Please, ma'am . . ."

"Yes. What is it?" Mrs Lewis was already thinking about something else.

"Please, ma'am, if you're looking for another girl, well, I know one as would . . ."

"*Who* would!"

"Sorry, ma'am, *who* would like to find a job in service. Beggin' your pardon, ma'am, an' I don't mean to be cheeky."

Annabelle looked at Annie thoughtfully. It wasn't her normal custom to take on girls recommended by fellow servants. On the other hand, Annie had made the request politely and this was only a position as a general skivvy. "Oh, yes? I might be interested. Who is this girl?"

"It's Ellie Peters, ma'am, the daughter of Mr Peters, the doctor's assistant."

That was a point in the girl's favour, at least. Sam had been with Dr Lewis for over three years now and even Mrs Lewis was aware that he was a solid, respectable sort of man, considering his lowly background.

"And how old is your friend?"

"She's thirteen, ma'am. She's been working in the mill . . ."

Mrs Lewis pulled a face.

". . . but she hates it, ma'am!" Annie finished desperately. "She'd give anything to get out, to find a job like mine."

Annabelle sighed. Servants! What a nuisance they were! Just as soon as you'd trained one, she left or did something that forced you to dismiss her. "Is she clean and hardworking?"

Annie smiled visibly at that. "Mrs Peters, her mother, is the cleanest person I've ever met," she said frankly.

"Can she read and write?"

"Yes, ma'am. We both went to the same classes at Sunday School, ma'am."

"Mmm. Well, you may tell Mr Peters to bring his daughter to see me tomorrow at ten. If she appears suitable, I'll give her a trial." She nodded dismissal and Annie scurried out, bumping into the doctor in the hallway.

"Ooops! I'm sorry, sir!"

He laughed. "That's all right, young Annie. You look happy."

"I am, sir. Mrs Lewis is goin' to see my friend Ellie Peters about a place here, now that Bet's left." She stopped and her hand flew up to her mouth. There she was, chattering on again. Would she never learn to hold her tongue? "Sorry, sir."

"Why? For being happy? It's nice to see a smiling face. Sam's in the dispensary at the moment, rolling pills. Why don't you go and tell him of Mrs Lewis's offer?"

"Oh, yes, sir. Thank you, sir." It was funny how he rarely said 'my wife', just Mrs Lewis. In fact, he rarely spoke to the mistress at all when there weren't other folks around. Probably too busy thinking about his patients.

Ellie was taken on, in spite of her mother's objections to losing some income. Sam put his foot down, for once. They were not that short of money! He didn't know why Elizabeth was so hard on the girl. Hadn't she noticed how sickly Ellie had been looking lately? Didn't she know that some girls became ill and died, from working in all that fluff? And besides, it was about time Ellie had a bit of money of her own. Let the lass keep her wages, like others did. Let her have a bit of fun. The hard times would come soon enough once she settled down and had a family of her own.

Elizabeth was furious, but Sam remained adamant.

Annie's life suddenly became twice an enjoyable as before and it only took a few weeks for Ellie to become her old rosy self again. Unlike Annie, she had a relatively easy induction into a general maid's duties. Annie helped her over the first few difficult days, shielding her alike from Mrs Cosden's sharp tongue and from the mistress's sharp eyes. And Ellie was so gentle and willing to learn, so little resentful when scolded, that even Mabel said she would maybe scrape through.

As for Miss Marianne, who was now five, she took a great fancy to Ellie and it had to be Ellie who carried up her tray and Ellie who brought up her hot water morning and evening, not Annie. Miss Marianne was growing up into a real charmer, the servants said to each other, with her father's kindness and warmth, and the same charm as her mother could turn on when they had guests – only with Miss Marianne, it was genuine.

The little girl went every day now to share lessons with the Purbrights' daughters, who had a governess to teach them their letters and the accomplishments necessary to a lady. Later on, Annabelle told Jeremy, Marianne would need a governess of her own, but for the moment Katy looked after her well enough and was considerably cheaper, at only twelve pounds a year. Besides, it was better for Marianne to have the chance to play with other children.

As Marianne seemed very happy with the arrangement, Jeremy didn't interfere. He didn't want a governess coming between himself and his daughter. The time he spent playing with her, or taking her for a walk was the highlight of his day. Apart from his work and his child, Jeremy's life was empty, and he often felt angry about that.

7

1834 to 1837

During the next three years Emily presented John Gibson with two children, both boys, and Annie felt a distance grow between herself and her family. Tom was going through that stage common to lads, where he hated girls and wanted nothing to do with his sisters. He had shown little aptitude for his studies and when Sergeant Brown's successor died, John took him away from school and for lack of any other opportunities put him into the mill.

There, Tom mixed with a set of rough lads, of whom his father disapproved, and got into more fights than other lads in the street did. To his disgust, he now had to have some schooling at work, because the new inspectors came to the mill and said all those under fourteen had to attend classes for two hours a day.

Mr Hallam hired a schoolmaster and put some benches and desks into one of the outhouses. At first, the lads played up and made the little lasses, sitting at the other side of the classroom, cry, but Mr Hallam came out in person and told them they'd have money docked out of their wages if they didn't behave, and if they didn't like schooling, they could always find themselves another job. That threat was enough to improve behaviour immediately. Hallam's was the best mill to work in and they all knew it. Within a few weeks, Mr Hallam had found another stricter schoolmaster and bought him a big leather strap, which clinched matters.

"You want to do your best at them classes, our Tom," John said one night. "Eh, we should've thought oursen in heaven if we'd been let off work to do lessons like that."

"Well, I don't call a draughty old outhouse heaven, when the sun's shining outside, and it'll be worse in there come the winter," Tom replied sulkily. "Besides, I can't see what good these questions and answers do." He pulled a face and declaimed in a loud voice, "'What is the nature of the heavens?' Who cares what's up in the sky? I mean, Dad, what use is that ever goin' to be to me?"

"What else do you have to learn?" asked John, unable to answer that one.

"Verses from the Bible."

John's face cleared. "Why, that's wonderful, lad. The Scriptures are sent to guide us through this vale of trouble."

"I don't see how they can guide us when we can't understand them stupid long words!" muttered Tom, but out of his father's hearing.

Everyone in the town, rich and poor alike, was surprised that Frederick Hallam insisted on strict attendance at his little school, when he could have got away with a pretend schoolroom like Jonas Dawton and only filled it when the inspectors were in town. Hallam's school was a nine-day wonder, then folk began to get used to it, and some of Dawton's workers actually complained because their children weren't getting any schooling.

When he was thirteen, and as tall as his father, Tom refused to go any more to Sunday School classes, saying that he had had enough schooling. He got his way on that, but he didn't dare refuse to attend chapel in the morning. Tom knew his father would never have stood for that, so he didn't even try. Like his father, Tom was solidly built, with curly brown hair, but he was already harder than John had ever been, and more ready to take advantage of those around him.

When Annie was at home on her days off, the two of them often exchanged sharp words. Tom didn't like the way she talked and he called her Miss Mincy-Mouth to her face. She didn't like his coarse language and dirty ways, and had no hesitation in saying so. She got on no better with Lizzie, who was fat, dull-eyed and sly, clinging to her stepmother when Annie was around, as if to emphasise the fact that although Annie didn't belong in the family now, she did.

Annie felt duty-bound to call at home on her Sundays off, for her dad's sake, but took to spending more time with Sally Smith, or with the O'Connors, or even just walking alone on the tops, as everyone called the moors. It was lovely up there on a summer's day, with the tiny streams trickling through the tussocky grass and the wind sighing around you. Anything to get her away from Number Three and from Salem Street, which she had grown to hate. If she had her way, she would never go back there, even for a visit.

Matt was overjoyed when Annie got Ellie the job at Park House, and it seemed to bring the three of them closer together. He often walked home from chapel with the Gibsons, and talked to Annie about Hallam's and the books he was reading, which the overseer had lent him. There was nothing lover-like in the way Matt treated her, no sign that he had noticed that she was growing up into a young woman, but at least he was still her friend, and at least he had not started walking out with any other girl!

In May 1836 Annie celebrated her sixteenth birthday with a cake furnished by Mrs Cosden on the doctor's orders. With Katy's help she had made herself a new dress, which she wore for the first time the following Sunday. Of course, its neckline was high, and its cut demure, because a maidservant wouldn't be allowed to wear anything else, but it did, Annie felt, nicely show off the curves of her figure, thanks to Katy's lessons in how to cut out a dress. Thank goodness, she said to Ellie, twisting to and fro in front of the mirror, she was now beginning to look like a woman and not a broom handle. The dress was of a green checked cotton, the checks very faint, more to Annie's taste than the bright ginghams now in vogue among those in service. Under Katy's supervision, she had carefully worked a collar and cuffs in fine white lawn, with picot edging. She'd have preferred muslin, but it didn't wash as well.

Even Mrs Lewis had deigned to admire the dress and compliment her on her taste. The only time the mistress became half-amiable was when talking about clothes, and she even took an interest in what her servants wore. Mrs Lewis had exquisite taste, Annie thought, comparing her to other visitors to the house. You could learn a lot from what the mistress did or did not do. Of course, Annie's dress was very impractical for anything but walking out (as Emily didn't fail to point out), with its full skirts over three frilled petticoats and its paleness, but it made a good foil for Annie's auburn hair, which had darkened considerably over the past two years. She knew she had never looked as good.

Ellie, who was growing rather plump, looked at her enviously when she was all dressed up and ready to go home for her Sunday off. "If he doesn't fall for you looking like that, he never will!" she said. "I wish I was slim like you, Annie, love."

"Do you think he will – notice me as a woman, I mean?" Annie asked nervously. They both knew who the only 'he' was in her life. She felt that she had loved Matt since she first saw him and that if he didn't show some sign soon that he regarded her as more than just another sister, then she would die of despair. There was only one thing she wanted out of life, one overriding ambition she'd had since she was ten years old, and that was to become Matt Peters's wife, to live with him and look after him and have his children. Everything she learned so willingly at Park House she learned because it would make her into a better wife for Matt, who was obviously going to rise in the world.

There had been some bad years for the cotton trade in the last decade, and sometimes Hallam's had to lay off workers, or put them on short time. Annie was glad she didn't work in the mill, which was a very chancy way of earning a living, it seemed to her. There were weeks when her dad had no work at all and when the Gibsons had to pawn things to buy food. And not all the things pledged were redeemed. Emily was a terrible manager and spent lavishly when she got John's wages, but had nothing left by the end of the week. She even tried to get money out of Annie sometimes, but Annie pretended that she had spent all her wages and Emily was too afraid of Mrs Lewis to go to the house and ask for Annie's wages to be paid to her parents. Besides, Annie's dad wouldn't have let Emily do that. Annie's dad, like Mr Peters, said that the money she earned was her own.

Matt was different from everyone else in Salem Street. Mr Hallam kept him on when others were lacking work. The overseer, Mr Benworth, was now giving Matt a good all-round training, with an eye to making him an assistant overseer one day. Overseers earned three or four pounds a week, more than Annie earned in a quarter, and they were never laid off, not at Hallam's, anyway. They could afford to live in the good, stone-built houses in the older part of the town, pretty houses with a bit of garden, not filthy little red-brick terraces like the Rows. Salem Street seemed smaller and dirtier every time she went back there.

Eyes glazed over with daydreams, her thoughts miles away, Annie walked slowly home. She was brought rudely down to earth by a hand grabbing her arm and swinging her round.

"My, look what the cat brought in!" said a deep voice, and she was pulled into a beery embrace.

Annie cried out and tried to break free, but it was no use. The man had hands like iron. He was broadly built and his body smelled sour and long-unwashed. Even when she kicked him, he only threw back his head and laughed. A woman walking past stopped and cried out, "Shame!" but scurried away when the man swore at her. No one else came forward to help the struggling girl. The man pulled her to him again and she screamed, fighting desperately to get free.

Abruptly the hands let her go and she staggered backwards, nearly falling. The man uttered a curse and swung his fist at his assailant, but he was too drunk to aim straight. Matt laughed and dodged it easily.

"She's my girl, Fred Coxton," he said. "And if you touch her again, I'll smash your face in!"

There was a moment when it all hung in the balance as to whether there'd be a fight, then Fred muttered something and lumbered off.

Matt turned to Annie. "Are you all right?" he asked gently.

"Yes. Now I am." She shuddered and looked so white that he put his arm around her shoulders.

"I'll see that he doesn't touch you again."

She took a deep breath, trying to regain her self-control, but she couldn't stop trembling.

"Look, let's go and walk round the park till you feel better," he suggested.

She nodded and he led her through the new wrought-iron gates. It was still early enough for there to be few people around.

"I thought – I thought no one was going to help me," she said shakily. "He was so s-strong. I couldn't get away."

It was so unlike Annie to tremble and be upset, that a wave of tenderness swept through Matt, taking him by surprise. After staring at her in astonishment for a minute or two, he succumbed to temptation, pulled her towards him and kissed her gently on the cheek. "It's a good job I saw you, then." He smiled down at her. He was nearly six feet tall and she was small enough to nestle in the curve of his arm. He kept his arms round her, enjoying the feel of her soft warm body against his.

"Matt?" she asked shyly. "Did you – did you mean what you said to him, that – that I'm your girl?"

He didn't look at her. "Would you mind if I did?" he asked, rashly committing himself, though he knew his mother would go mad if he started walking out with Annie, or anyone else.

"Oh, Matt, you know I wouldn't!"

Bashfully, for he had had no dealings with girls before, had avoided them after chapel and taken no part in the horseplay and furtive confidences of his peers, he took Annie's hand in his. "Aye. I didn't know how I felt till I saw him attacking you, but then I realised. You *are* my girl, an' I wanted to kill him for hurting you, for darin' to lay his filthy hands on you." He laughed shamefacedly. "Not a very Christian way to feel, is it, love?"

"I don't mind. I like you to feel that way about me. I – I'd like to be your girl."

His finger traced the curve of her cheek. "You've grown

up lately, Annie Gibson. That's a new dress, isn't it? You look very pretty today."

"Do I?" She felt so happy she was sure he would hear her heart beating.

He daringly pressed a kiss on her soft lips. "So – you're my girl now, eh?" Just let the other men tease him again about being afraid of women! Just wait till they saw him with this new, grown-up Annie on his arm!

"Yes. Oh, yes!" She looked radiant. "Oh, Matt, it's the best birthday present I've ever had."

They walked slowly back to Salem Street, hand in hand, neither of them paying much attention to their surroundings. When they arrived at Number Three, they stood outside the door chatting.

At last Annie said reluctantly, "I suppose I'd better go in."

"Yes. Me, too. Are you goin' to chapel?"

"Yes. We always do."

He flushed and swallowed hard. "Right, then. Don't go with your family. I'll walk you there." It was tantamount to a marriage proposal. It meant he wanted to show the world that Annie and he were courting.

She floated through the rest of the day in a dream, oblivious to the knowing glances of the rest of the congregation. She was conscious only of Matt, walking by her side, sharing a hymn book, repeating the prayers in his deep voice.

When he returned home for his midday meal, Elizabeth Peters greeted her son with a scowl and a sharp, "What do you think you're doing, then, our Matt?"

He looked at her warily. "What do you mean?"

"What do I mean?" she shrilled. "You know very well what I mean! I mean what are you doing with that Annie Gibson?"

"We're walking out together."

"You're too young!"

"I'm eighteen. You were wed at eighteen."

"Yes, and look where it got me."

"Mam, I—"

"So much for you gettin' on in the world, then!" Elizabeth went on scornfully. "Once you get wed an' the babies start comin', there'll be no gettin' on for you, my lad! I thought you knew better than to get mixed up with a girl for years yet, let alone a girl from the Rows. I thought *you* at least had enough sense for that!"

"Now, Elizabeth . . ." began Sam.

"It has to be said and since you're too soft to do it, I must!"

Sam rolled his eyes to heaven, but said nothing. The more you opposed her, the worse Elizabeth got.

Matt stared at his mother, shocked by her vehemence. He had expected her to be displeased, but she looked furious, with hectic red spots on her cheekbones and her mouth a grim bloodless line. He realised suddenly that she didn't want him to get mixed up with any girl, that she hated the idea of his marrying. He tried to speak to her gently. "I'm not stupid, Mam. We shan't be gettin' wed for a few years yet. An' she'll make me a good wife, will Annie."

"She'll drag you down!" Elizabeth said viciously. "Have you seen what her family's like? They'll never be off your doorstep. I want better for you than a girl like her!"

"Now that's enough!" said Sam sternly, as amazed as his son by the way she was spitting the venom at Matt. He spoke softly, trying to coax her into a better humour. "You're bein' unfair to the lad, Elizabeth. It's up to him what he does with his life, not you, now that he's a man grown. An' you're bein' unfair to Annie Gibson, too. She takes after her mother, not after Emily. Lucy Gibson was a fine woman, a good wife and mother, and near as house-proud as you are. Annie's a right nice lass, hard-working and bright as a button. It's given her a bit of style, working for Mrs Lewis has. You've only got to listen to her talk, or look at how she moves." He turned to Matt. "I like her, son, and I think she'll make you a good wife – though I do agree with your mother that you shouldn't rush into marriage."

Matt nodded and looked pleadingly at his mother, whose favourite he had always been. "Mam?"

She shrugged. "I haven't changed my mind. And I shan't. I'd hoped for better things for you, our Matt, than marriage. As for how all this turns out, well, we'll just have to see, won't we?"

Annie received no such hostile reception at Number Three. When Tom started taunting her about her young man, John turned on him and told him sharply to mind what he was saying.

"I'm very glad for you, lass," he said gently to Annie. "You've allus liked Matt, haven't you?"

"Yes. Yes, I have." She smiled blissfully.

"How long's it been goin' on?" asked Emily curiously. She could have sworn there was nothing between the two of them.

"Oh, just today. I mean, we just decided today. I – we haven't made any plans or anything yet. Well, we couldn't for ages, could we?" She didn't really want to talk about it to anyone; she just wanted to hug her happiness to herself.

"Well, he's not a bad catch," said Emily grudgingly. As long as Annie didn't have to come back to live with them, she'd be glad to see her well set up. It never hurt to have children who could help you in your old age. And they said that Matt Peters would be an overseer one day. A man in that position wouldn't let his in-laws be put into the union workhouse, which was Emily's biggest dread in life.

Matt walked Annie back to Park House and planted another of his shy kisses on her cheek under a tree in the park. "Next time we'll talk properly, make plans," he told her. "We – we can't do anything for years yet. You know that, don't you?"

"Yes. I know that. We need to wait an' save some money." She would have liked him to say a few more-loverlike things, but he talked instead about his work and his prospects there.

Ellie fell on her neck the minute she walked into their bedroom. "It's happened! I can see it's happened!" she cried. "It shows in your face!"

Annie blushed and admitted that she and Matt were now walking out together officially. Ellie squealed so loudly that Mabel banged on the wall and told her to be quiet, after which they had to discuss everything in whispers.

The next year passed in a blissful dream for Annie. She did her work as efficiently as ever, but her real life, she felt, was lived on her Sundays off, which she spent mainly with Matt.

At the end of that year, Katy astonished everyone at Park House by leaving to marry a farmer, from a family she'd known for years. His wife had died a few months previously and there were three children from that marriage, but she said they were nice kids. All the bitterness, all the antagonism towards men dropped suddenly out of her and she blossomed into a comely woman.

Mrs Lewis was furious. She always took it as a personal affront when servants left. To her it was a step down in the world for them to get married. They would have done better to have stayed on in service and enjoyed what she considered to be an easy life. They would only wind up with large families and small purses if they got married, and so she always told them. But did they listen to advice from their betters? No, they didn't! They just went ahead and ruined themselves.

Ellie was the one to benefit from the resulting rearrangement of staff. Dr Lewis insisted that a governess now be hired for Marianne. Her mother spent far too little time with her and the child needed to spend time with a more educated woman than Katy, with a lady, in fact. Watching how Annabelle neglected her only child, he often wondered what madness had driven him into her arms? The only things that interested her were herself, her social life, money and her clothes. The only things she read were books of etiquette, or fashion magazines, such as the *World of Fashion* or *The Court Magazine and Belle Assemblée*. She would pore over their illustrations for hours on end and take all their pretentious advice to heart, even when it conflicted with good sense. It quite sickened him.

No, he told her firmly, when she protested about the expense, their daughter now needed a governess and Annabelle must recognise that fact. She was furious. The last thing she wanted was another lady living with them. Apart from the expense, it would mean that there was always someone observing what she was doing, possibly trying to interfere. And you couldn't treat a governess like a servant. She would expect better food and accommodation than them.

Jeremy proved very stubborn and unmanageable, and the servants had a bad few days until Mrs Lewis had grown accustomed to the idea of the governess in her house. A chance remark from Mary Purbright made her realise just how much employing a governess for Marianne would enhance her social status, and she therefore began to recover her temper, though she still grudged the expense.

Ellie was promoted to nursery maid and was to earn eight pounds a year, as much as Annie. She was delighted with this arrangement, because she had grown very fond of Miss Marianne.

"I don't think I shall ever want to get married," she told Annie, when they were discussing her and Matt's plans. "This job suits me fine. You can never tell what'll happen with a husband. Look at what my mam had to put up with when Dad was out of work. And look at what it's done to her! She's as sour as a lemon and getting sourer all the time."

She smiled and added, "Though my dad's a lovely man."

Annie laughed indulgently, secure in the knowledge of her own happiness with Matt. "You'll change when you meet somebody," she said. "It's lovely to know that someone loves you! You'll *want* to marry then, see if you don't."

"But it's not lovely to have a family to feed and clothe," retorted Ellie, who had never forgotten the bad times.

"Me an' Matt aren't rushing into things, are we?" protested Annie. "It's people who rush into marriage who suffer. You have to save up and buy your furniture and have a bit put by before you get wed. And besides, Matt's got a lot to learn before he can become an overseer. Mr Hallam's going to send him to Liverpool next year, to study the raw cotton trade. An' Mrs Cosden is teachin' me to cook. I'll want to be able to do things properly when we have our own house. She says I have a very nice touch with sponges an' my pastry's nearly as good as hers now."

The new general maid in the house was a twelve-year-old girl called Susan Marker, daughter of a smallholder over Bacup way. As she was one of the eight children who had survived out of fourteen births, she told Annie and Ellie earnestly that she'd have to make her own way in the world, so her mam had said she'd best go into service. Katy had shared an attic bedroom with Mabel, but Mabel flatly refused to share with a twelve-year-old skivvy and threatened to give notice if forced to do so. And since Mabel liked to make herself useful acting as lady's maid, as well as performing her other duties, Annabelle did not wish to dispense with her services. Annie and Ellie did not want to be separated, either, so Cook persuaded Mrs Lewis to let them clear out one of the little boxrooms for Susan.

After a lot of fuss and bother, and sheer bad temper from Mrs Lewis, a governess was hired for Miss Marianne. She was found through an agency in Manchester and was the third one that Mrs Lewis had interviewed. Annabelle had very definite views on the sort of woman she wanted to bring up her daughter. "She must be ladylike, but not pretty, and she must speak properly, for really, Marianne is beginning to talk as broadly as the servants!"

"Then you should talk to her more yourself," said Jeremy.

"You know how busy I am. It's just like you to interrupt me all the time! We were talking about governesses. The one we appoint must be able to teach her French, embroidery, the piano and sketching."

"What about reading and writing – or aren't they important?"

"Of course they are. But Marianne is already a good little reader and too much knowledge is fatal for a female's chances. Men don't like bluestockings for wives."

The devil was in him that night. "Oh, some of us would like our wives to be better educated, to be able to discuss what's happening in the world. We don't all live for gossip, Annabelle."

The look she threw him spoke volumes, but he just smiled lazily at her. "And she mustn't cost more than twenty-five guineas a year," Annabelle continued. "Any more than that would be a criminal waste, for one child."

"Let's have a few more, then, in the interests of domestic economy," he jeered, and she left the room as quickly as was consonant with her dignity.

In the end, most of these criteria were satisfied by a Miss Richards, daughter of a deceased clergyman – of the Established Church, of course. Annabelle considered Dissenters common and unfit to teach her daughter.

Jeremy was not overly taken by the colourless Miss Richards, but agreed to give her a trial. And he had to admit that Marianne's accent and general deportment did begin to improve and that she took a surprising fancy to the unprepossessing Miss Richards, as did Ellie, so he began to revise his opinion of the woman.

In fact, the servants all approved of the new governess. She didn't expect miracles of service from them and only put on a starchy act when the mistress was around. Miss Richards dined with the family when they were not entertaining, but had to dine in the nursery when there were guests, which made more work for the people below stairs, but her trays, which Annie took up to her, were very generously supplied and were carried up promptly and willingly, while the food was hot.

Best of all, to Annie, was the way Miss Richards encouraged her and Ellie to read Miss Marianne's books. The governess believed, she said, that everyone should be educated, whatever their station in life, though, she added hastily, she did not, of course, support the Chartists, whose demands were very unrealistic. Annie had heard much the same thing from Matt, though she knew that Sam Peters was very much in favour of universal suffrage for men and resented not having a vote. Annie didn't have time to think about such things. She was too busy learning everything she could about gracious living and the ways of the gentry, not to mention sewing things for her bottom drawer.

The only cloud on Annie's horizon, and that a very minor one, was Fred Coxton, who had followed her along the street once or twice when she'd gone on errands for Mrs Lewis, though he'd made no attempt to do more than leer at her or make suggestive remarks. The sight of Fred, usually half-drunk, was starting to make her feel very nervous. He was a revolting man, dirty and hairy and strong as an ox. She did not mention these episodes to Matt, not wanting to cause any more trouble between the two men, who both worked for Hallam's, but she still had occasional nightmares about the way Fred had grabbed her that day and the fact that none of the bystanders had come to her rescue.

Matt told her, just before her seventeenth birthday, that Coxton had been fired for being drunk, so even that cloud disappeared from her horizon. Matt didn't tell her that he was the one who had reported the man and that Fred had threatened to get even with him for it. He was, he decided, strong enough to be able to stand up for himself. No need to worry Annie about men's affairs. But he worried about it sometimes himself.

If Annie had known about Fred, she would have been terrified. Every time she went out she worried about meeting him. Somehow she could not get him out of her mind. He was such a horrible man.

8

June to August 1837

In June of the following year, just after Annie's seventeenth birthday, Mrs Lewis decided to go and visit her mother. She might, she said casually, also pay another little visit to her friend Barbara in Brighton.

"I've been feeling a little down lately," she told Jeremy. "I'm sure the sea air will do me good."

"Oh, yes?" He knew better than anyone that her health was always excellent.

"Yes. Poor Barbara does get lonely, living on her own. She's for ever begging me to stay with her again." Annabelle fiddled around with her knife and fork, not meeting his eyes.

"You must do as you see fit," he told her. "You'll be leaving Marianne here, I take it?"

"Oh, yes. Miss Richards is most competent. And the child is rather young for all that travelling, don't you think?"

"Yes, she is!" he said firmly. "Besides, I should miss her."

"But you won't miss me," she said. "Oh, don't bother to deny it, Jeremy. It's been a long time since we even talked together."

The calm way she spoke showed how little she cared

about this and stung him to say, "If we're being honest for once, then I'd like to know why you ever married me in the first place. I've often wondered."

"Oh, the usual reasons," she said lightly. "I thought I would be happy as the wife of a rising young doctor."

"And I didn't rise – at least not in the way you expected," he said thoughtfully. "I'm sorry for disappointing you in that."

"I believe you are." Her voice was cool and impersonal, but at least it was not hostile.

"I hope you enjoy your visit to Brighton, Annabelle. There's no reason why you shouldn't have an occasional trip, now that we have Miss Richards, whether you're going to see your mother or not. I'll let you have some extra money, of course." A gleam of humour lit his eyes briefly. "I may not have risen to the top of my profession, but I do earn a reasonable living here in Bilsden." He hesitated, then added, "Annabelle, is it too late to mend our relationship?"

She was instantly on guard, her expression hostile. "If by that you mean that you wish to share my bed again, then my original threat still stands."

"Don't you want other children? We need only – well, cater for that. I wouldn't disturb you at other times."

"No! I won't willingly ever share any man's bed again! Nor will I have other children. You may have forgotten how ill I was when I was carrying Marianne. I never have. It's the most painful, undignified process and I *won't* go through it again. I thought I'd made that more than plain."

"Yet you're still my wife, and I'd have the right to force you."

Her eyes narrowed and an ugly look came on to her face. "I would fight you every inch of the way and make sure that people knew what a monster you were."

He looked at her. She had lost any semblance of the soft femininity she normally cultivated and her innate shrewishness was very obvious. "It's all right," he said wearily. "I don't find you *that* tempting! And I have no taste for rape." That was the last time he ever tried to effect a reconciliation between them. "Go away and enjoy your holiday, Annabelle. Stay as long as you wish. Polite little tea-parties, strolls along the promenade – that's all you're fit for. You have ice in your veins, Annabelle!"

She shrugged and bit her tongue, not wishing to antagonise him further for fear he might withdraw the offer of extra money. "I'll plan to leave next week, then."

She watched him leave and heaved a sigh of relief as he closed the door of the room she insisted on calling her boudoir behind him. She hadn't told him of her savings, the money she slipped away every week from the housekeeping allowance. Jeremy considered her indifferent towards him, but in reality she had much stronger feelings. She'd come to loathe him, both for exiling her from Brighton and for his silly obsession about helping the poor – at his family's expense, she always felt. She knew very well that he did not charge those who couldn't afford it, and that he gave away medicines free.

Even Jeremy's gentle voice irritated her nowadays. She liked a man to be more positive and masculine. Like Frederick Hallam, for instance. What wouldn't she have done with a husband like that? He'd made a brilliant success of his life, building on his father's achievements till he was a very wealthy man. But poor Frederick was, like her, hampered by his spouse. They had a lot in common, but not so much that he would persuade her to become his mistress. She was not that stupid.

She had watched with interest the way Frederick had made himself the leading figure in the town, not just because he was a successful businessman, but also by sheer force of his personality. He was now a member of the town's newly-formed corporation and was confidently spoken of as a future mayor. She wished Jeremy took a more positive interest in his civic duties, instead of for ever complaining about things like the water supply.

When Jeremy did take part in a wider world, it was a world she could not share in any way. He made regular trips into Manchester, where a group of doctors indulged in the, to her, filthy practice of cutting up dead bodies. Why the Government had ever made that activity legal Annabelle could not understand. Jeremy insisted that he needed to know exactly what people were like inside if he were to treat them effectively when they were ill or had accidents, but Annabelle could not bear to have him even touch her with hands that did that sort of thing, however well scrubbed they were afterwards.

Jeremy was also spending far too much money on equipment, like his new stethoscope Fancy listening to the vulgar noises bodies made inside! She had had to speak to him very sharply about encouraging Marianne to listen to other people's hearts beating with the thing. Did he want the girl to turn into an unnatural ghoul whom no man would marry? And as for the packet of the new Congreves, for which he had paid the outrageous sum of one shilling, why, pray, did anyone need equipment to generate fire when there was always a fire burning in the kitchen or scullery grate? He was always buying such things. Toys, they were, expensive toys for idiots like Jeremy to waste good money on! Who knew what he would come home with next?

Annabelle often sat in her boudoir and brooded over her future. She had no intention of enduring this exile from civilisation for ever. One day, when her mother was dead, she would have some money to come. With what she had saved from the housekeeping, it should be enough to allow her to leave Jeremy, leave Bilsden, leave all these dreary people. She would not say she was separated from her husband, of course, for that would seriously curtail her social life. Estranged wives were not well received in polite society. She would say that she had to live in Brighton for her health, that only in the sea air was she ever well. She had it all planned out and had already started dropping hints to her acquaintances in Bilsden. She doubted that Jeremy would ever contradict her about that.

Unfortunately, Annabelle's holiday plans were delayed a few weeks by the death of King William. She felt that it would show a lack of respect to travel for pleasure so soon after his death, and there was also the question of whether she should wear a black armband, or carry a black-edged handkerchief, not to mention whether national mourning would affect her shopping trip to London. Annabelle thought that it indicated a lack of regard for royal dignity to die sitting in a chair in the middle of the night, while as for a young girl of eighteen sitting on the throne of England, that, too, seemed absolutely wrong. And such an un-royal name, Victoria, so ugly. Her other name, Alexandrina, was much prettier.

Three days before Mrs Lewis was due to leave, Mabel, who had been going to accompany her as a lady's maid, fell and broke her arm when carrying some newly-laundered linen upstairs. The doctor set the arm and told her she was lucky; it was a clean break and should mend as good as new. Annabelle was furious. How on earth was she to manage without a maid? She couldn't possibly travel on her own and she had no intention of looking after her own clothes. The other servants, recognising the danger signs, trod warily. It didn't do to cross the mistress when she was in one

131

of her rages. Poor Mabel was in hourly expectation of dismissal.

When the bell rang for Annie in the kitchen the next morning, she cast a despairing glance at the cook. "Oh, Mrs Cosden! Whatever do you s'pose she wants?"

"I don't know, but it'll make her worse if you keep her waiting. Here, give me that dirty apron and get a clean one off the hook. And tidy your hair, do!"

"I haven't done anything wrong, I'm sure I haven't!" Annie worried as she changed her apron and smoothed her hair in the narrow mirror on the wall by the door.

"Well, whoever said you had? Mercy me, stop talkin' an' get up them stairs! She'll likely just want something fetching from the shops."

Annie dashed up the stairs, slowing down only as she approached the mistress's boudoir.

Mrs Lewis looked up from her writing desk as the maid entered. "Come over here, Annie," she ordered coldly. "Stop! Turn round! Slowly! Let me look at you!"

Puzzled, Annie obeyed. At least Mrs Lewis didn't seem angry with her!

"That dress won't do! Haven't you any better ones?"

"Yes, ma'am, but I don't change into them until the afternoons." What was the mistress on about?

"I'll have to see them. And your other dress, the one you wear on your days off. Oh, and your outer garments. I can't possibly travel to Brighton with a badly-dressed maid!"

Annie's heart skipped a beat. "I – I beg your pardon, ma'am?"

"Oh, yes, I should have explained. You are to accompany me to Brighton and act as my personal maid. I cannot possibly travel alone, and I shall need someone to look after my clothes and do my hair. I've seen for myself that you're very quick to learn and Mabel assures me that

132

she can show you how to arrange some of the simpler hairstyles before we leave. Really! As if I hadn't enough to do. It's most inconvenient of Mabel to break her arm like this!"

It didn't occur to her to ask whether Annie wanted to become a lady's maid and go to Brighton, any more than it occurred to Annie to question her orders.

"Go and tell Cook that she must manage today with a bit of extra help from Ellie and Susan, then go and lay your clothes out on your bed. I shall be up to inspect them in ten minutes."

Head spinning, Annie dropped a curtsey and sped off to inform Mrs Cosden of the arrangements. On the way back up from the kitchen she bumped into the doctor. "Oh, sir, I'm sorry! I didn't see you!"

"You were miles away. What's the matter?"

"Mrs Lewis is taking me to Brighton with her!" Annie gasped, still overwhelmed by the prospect.

"My goodness! That's an honour! You'll be able to see the sea and travel by mail."

"Yes, sir."

Jeremy smiled. "It'll do you good. Travelling is good for people. Broadens the mind. Teaches them things."

"I had expected to find you ready upstairs by now, Annie." Mrs Lewis's voice interrupted them, chill with disapproval.

"I'm sorry, ma'am." Annie dropped a curtsey and fled.

"I do wish you wouldn't gossip with the servants like that, Jeremy," said Annabelle, once Annie was out of earshot. "They can't spare the time, even if you can."

Jeremy's lips tightened. "I stand rebuked. In future, I will content myself with merely paying their wages." He went back to his surgery and banged the door behind him.

Annie stood anxiously by the bed as Mrs Lewis examined

her clothes. "You keep them very clean, I must admit," she was told graciously, for Annabelle never vented her ill-temper on those from whom she needed a special effort. "The room, too. I like my servants to take a pride in themselves."

"Thank you, ma'am."

"However, you'll need other clothes, if you are to be seen in my company. Put these away and come down to my dressing-room."

In the dressing-room Mabel, her face drawn with pain and one arm in a sling, was awkwardly pulling some clothes from the back of a cupboard.

"It's lucky that I'm a hoarder," said Annabelle complacently. "I believe some of these can easily be altered to fit you. It's a good thing you're not as fat as Mabel." She laid before the bemused Annie a black silk gown, old-fashioned in style, but with few signs of wear, and followed it by three other dark gowns, a petticoat or two and a travelling cloak.

"We must call in the sewing-woman immediately," she told Mabel. "She can alter these for Annie." She turned to the girl. "You may keep the dresses afterwards if you prove satisfactory." That would be more than enough reward, she thought, happy not to have to spend any of her precious money on recompensing Annie for the extra duties. Even the sewing-woman would charge only a few shillings for the alterations. "Now, we have to show you what I require. You may stay and help Mabel for the rest of the day and I shall come up early to dress for dinner – half an hour early, Mabel – so that you may practise doing my hair, Annie. I shall go downstairs now to tell Mrs Cosden and then to receive my callers."

Left alone with Mabel, Annie let out her breath in a long whoosh. "Oh, Mabel, I'll never do it!"

"You'd better! She won't keep you on at all if you don't. She can be a right bitch. Doctor said I was to rest, but she says there isn't time."

Annie was shocked by this disrespect towards the mistress. Then she noticed that Mabel was swaying on her feet and looking as white as chalk. "Look, you sit down an' tell me what to do. You look awful!"

"I feel awful," Mabel admitted. "The doctor said I should stay in bed for a day or two, but *she* said the least I could do was to train you as a replacement, and I could rest once she'd gone. You'd think I done it on purpose! You'll have to watch your step with her, I can tell you. She likes everything just so, does the mistress. I'm used to her nasty little ways, but you're going to have trouble if you don't keep on your toes."

As Annie cleared up and prepared Mrs Lewis's room and clothes under Mabel's direction, they discussed her duties. There were so many things to learn that Annie's head was soon spinning and she quickly became convinced that she would never remember half her instructions.

In the afternoon the sewing-woman came and Annie had to try on the dresses whilst Mrs Lewis and the woman discussed what alterations would be necessary. Annie was greatly embarrassed at having to undress in front of her mistress and a stranger, and blushed furiously. She kept her eyes on the floor and let the discussion about how the ornamentation on the dresses should be reduced in keeping with her station flow over her head.

"You're the lucky one!" Mabel said enviously when it was all over and the woman had taken the dresses away.

"What do you mean?"

"Gettin' all them dresses. She must want to make a good impression on that friend of hers. A real old skinflint, *she* is! Not that it's costin' her much to give you the things. She's got cupboards full of old stuff like that. Never parts with anything till it falls to pieces, she don't!"

"I can't believe that they'll be mine," Annie confessed, still in a state of shock.

"You'll earn 'em," said Mabel cynically. "She'll make sure of that."

"If she's so bad, why do you stay with her?"

Mabel shrugged. "I dunno. I've learned a lot from her. Maybe one day I'll be able to get a job as a lady's maid. You've got to give the devil his due – *her* due, I should say – she teaches you to do things proper an' she's got style."

They both fell silent as footsteps were heard on the stairs. Mrs Lewis swept back in. "Shoes," she announced. "And gloves." She allowed her calm façade to crack and her impatience to show as both maids looked at her in puzzlement.

"Oh, don't stand there like a pair of idiots! There's so *much* to do! Show me your shoes, Annie!"

Annie lifted her skirts and looked down at her feet, encased in the soft felt-soled slippers all the servants wore about the house.

"Not those! Are you quite stupid? Get out your outdoor shoes! And be quick about it!"

Resentfully Annie obeyed and stood there fuming while Annabelle scornfully examined her footwear, all of which had been repaired many times.

"Terrible! You can't possibly be seen in those things! They're more suitable for a farm labourer. Fetch a pair of my old shoes, Mabel. The child's feet don't look too big, unlike yours."

Annie was presented with a pair of Mrs Lewis's old shoes and two pairs of real leather indoor slippers. She hadn't realised how alike she and her mistress were in size. It made her hold her head higher and helped her to put up with the acid remarks aimed at her later by Mabel, when even Mrs Lewis's old gloves fitted her perfectly.

"I hope you realise what a lucky girl you are," Annabelle told Annie. "And don't let these new things go to your head! You're only getting them because I can't be seen with a maid dressed like a skivvy!"

The worst thing about becoming Mrs Lewis's maid was giving her a bath. Annie didn't believe it at first when Mabel told her she would have to wash the mistress's back and hold her towel and help her to dry herself.

"It's not decent!" she gasped. "I can't do it! I'll *die* of embarrassment!"

"Get on with you," said Mabel. "She's only a woman, same as you an' me. But take care you don't stare at her. An' be sure the towel is properly warmed."

The ordeal took place at five o'clock in the afternoon, with Mrs Lewis sitting in a hip-bath in front of the bedroom fire. A red-faced Annie tried to remember all Mabel's instructions and, apart from dropping the soap, she didn't do too badly. It seemed wrong, somehow, seeing the mistress mother naked, but, as Mabel had said, she was only a woman, wasn't she? It was the first time Annie had really realised that employers were not a different species.

Annie's fingers were trembling when first she started to do Mrs Lewis's hair, but that too went off better than she'd expected. Really, if you forgot it was the mistress, it wasn't much different from doing Ellie's hair. Her fingers gradually grew steadier and she managed to achieve the desired effect. She even had time to wish Matt could see her now. He'd be that proud of how she was coping!

At last the interminable day was over and Annie was free to collapse into bed next to Ellie and discuss her news.

"Aren't you scared?" Ellie asked. "I would be. She fair terrifies me!"

"She does me, too," admitted Annie, "but it's a big chance, isn't it? We'll be travelling most of the way by mail-coach. We get off to stop the night in Leicester, because she says it isn't ladylike to travel by night in the company of strange gentlemen."

"What she means is that she wants a proper night's sleep," said Ellie cynically, and they both giggled.

"Just think of it, though! I've never even been to Manchester and now I'll be seeing both London *and* Brighton."

"They say you go faster than the wind on that mail-coach," said Ellie. "Up to sixteen miles an hour. It doesn't sound safe to me."

"Oh, it must be, because *she* would never risk it if it wasn't." They both giggled again. "Dr Lewis said I'd be seeing the sea, too," Annie went on. "Just fancy!" Years later she was to marvel at her own seventeen-year-old ignorance; now it was all new and exciting, though frightening too.

"Oooh, you are lucky!" Ellie sighed. "I'd give anything to see the sea."

"I'll tell you all about it when I come back."

"I'll miss you!"

"I'll miss you, too, Ellie."

They squeezed each other's hands across the bed. Living and working together had only strengthened the bond between them.

"Will you – will you tell Matt for me an' give him a letter?" whispered Annie. "I shan't be able to see him before I go. I daren't ask *her* for time off. She'd throw a fit."

"Of course I'll tell him."

"Thanks. I knew you would." Annie yawned hugely. "I'll have to get to sleep now. I'm that tired and there are so many things to do tomorrow."

She fell asleep and dreamed of the adventure to come, of travelling on a mail-coach, going to London, then far away from Bilsden to the seaside. Would the sea look like the pictures the doctor had shown her in one of his books? Would she really be able to touch it?

9

August to September 1837

The journey south, though it was exciting, was also exhausting. Annie travelled inside the coach, because Mrs Lewis said she'd be no use to anyone if she caught her death of cold riding outside. When Annie saw how high up the roof of the coach was, and how precariously the passengers were perched there, she was grateful for this concern. Even with the night spent in Leicester, she found the journey very wearing. White-faced, her head aching and her stomach churning from the jolting, she struggled to do all that her mistress demanded when they stopped and when they arrived in London. She was determined to give satisfaction.

Annabelle, shrewdly watching her new maid and seeing more than Annie realised, decided that the girl would just possibly do. She had a long way to go, of course, and a lot to learn, but she was quick and deft, far better than Mabel had been at first. And she looked so much better now she was properly dressed, quite respectable, in fact. What a difference clothes made! It might even be worth training her to be solely a lady's maid, for Annabelle had decided that she needed a servant of her very own, whatever it cost. Mabel was very willing, of course, but she was slow, painfully slow, and she looked so common, with that big red face of hers and that awful frizzy hair.

To Annie, London was like another world. She got lost in the nether regions of the hotel and she was outraged by the familiarities attempted by the young male servants she encountered, though not too outraged to slap the face of one fellow, who dared to lay his hands on her.

"'Ere, what did you do that for?" he demanded, in genuine surprise, nursing a stinging cheek.

"What did I do that for? What do you think? To teach you to keep your hands to yourself, that's what!"

"Only 'avin' a bit of fun," he grumbled.

"Well, you'd better save your fun next time for someone who appreciates it, hadn't you?" she told him, nose in the air.

"Bleedin' right, I will! I wouldn't be seen dead with a red-'eaded scrag like you!"

Best of all were the London shops. Annie was expected to accompany her mistress everywhere to carry the parcels. They did a lot of walking, but they sometimes took one of the new hansom cabs. Annie wondered if they were safe the first time she saw one, with only two wheels and the driver perched up high behind the passengers, and she felt embarrassed to be sitting so close to Mrs Lewis, but she soon got used to everything.

The fashionable hours for shopping, Mrs Lewis informed her, were from two to four in the afternoon, and, of course, Mrs Lewis made a point of spending those hours in fashionable places, such as Regent Street. She might have no acquaintances among the ton, she said to Annie, but one could learn a great deal about how things were done by simply looking and listening. However, Mrs Lewis's real shopping was done at other times of the day, when the fashionable people were not present, and she knew a surprising number of unfashionable shops where you could get things at more reasonable prices.

After their outings, Mrs Lewis came home and made sketches of gowns or mantles or bonnet trimmings which had appealed to her particularly. No detail was too small for her serious attention. Annie, whom she kept with her at all times for company, watched wistfully and admired the drawings with such whole-hearted enthusiasm that her mistress's amazing good-humour continued. Mrs Lewis shopping in London, Annie found, was a very different person from Mrs Lewis fretting in Bilsden.

The first modiste's they visited astonished Annie so much that Annabelle had to hiss at her to stop gaping and to mind where she was going.

"Sorry, ma'am!" Annie tried to make herself as unobtrusive as possible behind a large potted fern on a stand while she watched her mistress being attended to. It was hard to believe you were in a shop at all, for no goods were on display. Soft carpets and a few pieces of elegant furniture made it look more like a lady's drawing-room.

And the person attending to Mrs Lewis's needs seemed more like a lady than a shopkeeper or seamstress. After a few moments of discreet conversation, the modiste rang a little silver bell and a young woman glided into the room. A whispered command and she glided out again, to return a few minutes later, accompanied by another young woman, both of them reverently carrying several partly-completed gowns. These were spread out for Annabelle's inspection. Two she rejected instantly and they were whisked away. The others she examined more closely. Eventually she chose two and was led into a small dressing-room to try them on.

143

Annie was summoned to help her out of her clothes and stood in a corner ready to help while Mrs Lewis twisted and turned before a large gilt-framed mirror, before eventually deciding to purchase one of the gowns. Then she had to have it fitted properly, for some of the seams were only tacked together. Annie watched everything open-mouthed. The assistants drifted in and out, bringing more gowns, bolts of material and selections of braid and trimmings. It was nearly an hour before Annabelle emerged again, followed obsequiously by the owner.

"I'll have the blue gown sent round to your hotel by tomorrow afternoon, madam. And the other will be ready for fitting the day after."

"See that you keep to that!" said Annabelle sharply. "I'll want the gown finished and sent down to Brighton by the end of the week."

"Oh, certainly, madam."

Annie hadn't realised that they were to spend so long in London, but Annabelle was in her element and making the most of every hour. The next two days were a blur of visits to shops and warehouses. Little was purchased in the elegant, expensive shops, but much was inspected. In the process both Annabelle and her maid were brought completely up to date on all the latest fashions and Annabelle succumbed to a delightful new parasol, which was jointed to fold up small when not required, and to a babet cap whose frills framed her face most becomingly, did Annie not think? Again, Annie's enthusiasm was in no way feigned and Annabelle purred beneath the admiration of her maid. After visiting the more expensive shops, they would visit the bargain bazaars and purchase cheaper imitations of high fashion.

At one such bazaar, Annie plucked up the courage to ask if she might please buy a length of ribbon to trim up her own best dress and Annabelle, sated with her orgy of purchasing, unbent enough to offer advice and explain why a certain shade would be preferable to bring out the best in Annie's dress and hair.

"I remember the dress you mean," she said graciously. "An excellent choice for someone with your colouring. In fact, for a servant, your taste is remarkable, unlike your friend Ellie, who seems to have a lamentable penchant for trimming her garments with red, regardless of their basic colour."

Annie couldn't help smiling. "Ellie does like to brighten things up, ma'am."

"So I have noticed. Who makes your best clothes, Annie?"

"I do, ma'am. My mother taught me to sew. I like sewing."

"You do a good job." Another point in Annie's favour. A maid who was good with her needle could save her mistress a lot of money.

Four days later they left London. The journey to Brighton was shorter and much less tiring than the journey from the north, for the coach was well-sprung and the roads well-maintained. Annie couldn't believe the amount of traffic they met on the way, private carriages, sporting vehicles driven by dashing young men, farm carts, drays and men on horseback. The journey only took just over five hours, with a short cab ride at the end of it.

When they saw the sea, Annie gasped aloud at its vastness. "Oh, I'm sorry, ma'am! Only I didn't know it would be so big!"

Annabelle laughed indulgently, relaxed and happy to be back in her beloved Brighton. She'd stood the journey and the gruelling days of shopping much better than Annie had, amazingly well, Annie thought, for a woman who made such a great play of her delicate health. "That's all right. It *is* the first time you've seen it, after all. And dear Brighton cannot fail to please!"

Mrs Dwight's house was a bit of a disappointment to Annie after the London hotel. She'd been expecting something far grander and certainly not a house in a terrace. To her, rich people always lived in separate houses; terraces and rows were for poorer people, those who had to work for a living. Mind, this wasn't like the terraces she knew. It was a great sweeping curve of houses, built of stone and three full storeys high, with half basements below that and attic bedrooms crammed above under the roofs.

Perhaps things were done differently in the south, she thought. They certainly looked different. Everything was so clean! Even the air you breathed tasted fresher. And it was nice not to have tall mill chimneys wherever you looked, pouring out their black smoke. Maybe when she and Matt were wed, they could live a bit out of the town. Anywhere but Salem Street and the Rows!

"Come along, girl! What's the matter with you? This is no time to daydream!"

Annie followed her mistress into the house, clutching the travelling bag which contained necessities for the journey. Mrs Lewis, after embracing her dear Barbara, was swept away into the sitting-room. She tossed back a casual command to Annie to see that the luggage was taken upstairs and to start the unpacking.

Annie eyed the elegant parlourmaid they'd left her with and waited for her to speak.

"I'll send the boy to help the cab driver with the luggage." She looked down her nose at Annie and moved towards a flight of steps.

Annoyed by her tone, Annie put her chin up. "Are there

signposts, or do I have to guess which is Mrs Lewis's room?"

"I'll send the chambermaid up to show you the way."

"Thank you *so* much!"

The chambermaid came panting up the kitchen stairs almost immediately, followed by a boy, who stared at Annie, pulled a face at her and then vanished out of the front door.

"I'm Patsy," said the girl, smiling in a friendly way, "though *she* always calls me Patricia. Come on, I'll show you where to go. What's your name?"

"Annie. Annie Gibson."

"Here, give me one of those bags. You look tired."

"I am," Annie admitted. "Those coaches make your head ache after a bit. And Mrs Lewis never stopped shopping in London. My feet are still aching from it."

"They're all as bad. I went up to London with *her* once. I hated it! And dirty! I never saw anywhere as dirty. Glad to come back to Brighton, I was, I can tell you!"

They went up the stairs to the first floor. "She's put your Mrs Lewis in the spare front bedroom. See, this door here."

"Oh, what a lovely room!" exclaimed Annie involuntarily. She went across to the window and stared out. "This is the first time I've seen the sea," she confided. "I didn't think it'd look like that!"

"Like what?"

"So big – and – and stretching so far away."

"You should see it in the winter. Waves as high as houses."

"No!"

Patsy smiled at Annie in a friendly way, feeling superior, for once. "I'll see if we can some time get off together an' I'll take you paddling on the beach," she offered.

"Will we be allowed to do that?"

"Who's to stop us? Besides, it's fun."

"Is it safe?"

"Of course it is! The gentlemen go out in a bathing machine and they dip their whole body in the water, but not many ladies do it."

"But they'll get wet through. They'll spoil their clothes and catch their death of cold!"

Patsy giggled. "No, they don't! They wear special clothes, just for bathing, an' take them off afterwards. They reckon the sea-water does them good. My brothers go swimming sometimes. Not in a bathing machine, though. And not in special clothes." She giggled again. "They just wear their under-drawers – or nothing, if it's after dark! It's all right for men. They can do what they want."

The boy and the cab driver panted into the room with the rest of the luggage.

"We'd better start unpacking," said Patsy. "I'll help you, if you like. They'll have their tea and a natter, then they'll both be up to change. If she's anything like Mrs Dwight, your Mrs Lewis will expect her things to be ready for her, then. They never think whether you're tired or not, do they?"

With Patsy's help, Annie unpacked the gown that Mrs Lewis had told her she wanted to wear the first night. A flat-iron, brought up from the kitchen by the obliging Patsy, soon got the creases out of it. There was even time for Annie to be shown her own room. It wasn't at the front of the house, to her disappointment, so she hadn't got a sea view. It seemed strange to be given a room all to herself, though it was just a tiny cupboard of a place. The only time she'd slept alone before had been when Bet was dismissed. She wasn't sure she liked it. If only Ellie were here, it'd be such fun. Still, Patsy was nice. How funny that she'd had

time to spare to help get Mrs Lewis's things ready! Annie's limited experience of domestic service did not include mistresses who staffed a house lavishly and left their servants to get on with things unsupervised.

After she'd got Mrs Lewis ready for dinner and cleared up the bedroom, Annie went down to the kitchen, tiptoeing past the dining-room, because there were no back stairs for the servants to use. She was ravenously hungry by now. Patsy introduced her to the cook, Mrs Fitton, and told her that the boy's name was Billy. Patsy couldn't spare much time to talk to the visitor, because she was helping the parlourmaid, whose name was Maud, to get the next course ready and carried up. Maud was now wearing a very pretty lace cap and apron, and was just as condescending as before to Annie.

"Can I do anything to help?" Annie asked the cook, who looked a bit flustered. "I help our cook sometimes at home."

"Thought you was a lady's maid?"

"Not really. Mabel broke her arm, so I had to come with Mrs Lewis instead."

"Well, it's nice of you to offer, I must say," said Mrs Fitton. "You didn't need to. Could you just keep an eye on that pan of sauce? Give it a stir and don't let it stick. Billy! Where are you, you lazy young devil?"

Billy's head appeared round a door at the other side of the kitchen.

"You get these dirty things into that scullery and give 'em a wash."

The head disappeared and Billy came out with a wooden tray and took the dirty dishes away.

"Can't take your eyes off him for a minute, that boy. Bone idle, he is!" grumbled Mrs Fitton. "Thank you, dear. Just don't let it get lumpy."

When the meal had been served upstairs, the servants ate theirs, consuming the left-overs with careless abandon. It would have made Mrs Lewis go mad to see such extravagance, thought Annie, enjoying the food. Mrs Fitton was a good cook and even Maud unbent a little and confessed that she was dead tired and her feet were killing her.

After the meal, Annie helped to clear away, then she and Patsy got the water jugs ready to fill and take up later for their mistresses to have a wash. She popped in to lay out Mrs Lewis's night attire and to put a towel to warm by the low fire that was burning in the grate, in spite of it being a warm June night. She yawned as she did this and wished Mrs Lewis would hurry up. Annie was exhausted, even if her mistress wasn't.

Two weeks went past in Brighton in the most delightful way, with never a word of visiting Mrs Parton. Mrs Lewis remained in a good mood nearly all the time and Annie managed not to make too many mistakes. Mrs Lewis rapped her knuckles once or twice for brushing her hair carelessly and once she smacked Annie's face for dropping a bowl of pins. Annie accepted these chastisements philosophically. She was getting used to Mrs Lewis and her little ways, and had lost a lot of her awe of her mistress, though not of her mistress's temper. You didn't rub Mrs Lewis the wrong way if you could help it, however human you now knew her to be.

Once or twice, Mrs Lewis asked her to mend something and seemed pleased by the results. Annie loved handling the fine materials and beautiful clothes. She also proved adept at pinning up the shining mass of blond hair, which was washed twice a week and polished with a piece of silk, to keep it looking perfect. Annie had never heard of anyone washing their hair so often, but had to admit that it was worth it. She began to take more care with her own and to try out a few new ways of pinning it up. Annabelle noticed, but said nothing, because the girl was not aping the fashions of her betters, just keeping herself smart. Annie also altered one of the dresses she had been given, changing the trimmings, which had seemed wrong to her, though she could not have said why. That, too, was noticed and commented on, but favourably, thank goodness.

Mrs Lewis and Mrs Dwight went out a lot and sometimes, while they were away, Patsy was allowed to take Annie for a walk down to the beach or round the town. Mrs Fitton was a kindly taskmistress, as long as you did your work properly. Annie had never known such freedom and comfort since she went into service. She loved watching the sea, though she didn't like walking on the beach. All those pebbles hurt your feet! She was fascinated by Brighton and told Patsy that she'd never seen a place like it. As for that Pavilion, well, it was the strangest looking building she'd ever seen and why old King George had wanted it built like that she'd never know. That roof was just plain silly!

She'd never seen so many grand people walking or driving about, either. "Are there no slums in Brighton?" she asked Patsy one day.

"Oh, yes, but *we* don't need to go near such parts of the town. Most of the people you see here are visitors, even though the season really hasn't started yet."

"How wonderful to be able just to go away on visits whenever you like!" sighed Annie. "I never realised before what interesting lives some people have." She was even beginning to feel a sneaking sympathy for Mrs Lewis's complaints about Bilsden.

One day Annie was taken to tea at Patsy's home. Patsy's father had lost one leg in an accident and now made a living by making things to sell to the visitors. He was good with his fingers. He gave Annie a little box, all covered in tiny pearly shells, and she spent a precious penny or two on one of his shell ladies to take back to Ellie. If she had bought her dad anything, it would only have wound up in the pawn shop.

Annabelle Lewis was having as wonderful a time in Brighton as her maid. Barbara Dwight was a dear creature; they'd always got on well. Women were so much more comfortable to live with than men. And then there were all Annabelle's old friends, giving dinner parties for her and inviting her round to tea or taking her out for drives. It was quite fashionable now to take 'carriage airings' and to drive up and down the front from Kemp Town to Brunswick Terrace. She read the 'Fashionable Chronicle' in the local newspaper every day to see which notabilities were in town, and then she and Barbara would try to spot them among the visitors.

There were endless things to do in a town like Brighton. Even if one only walked into the centre to do a little shopping, one was sure to see a face one knew or to have a celebrity pointed out. Annabelle listened eagerly to the talk of building a railway to connect Brighton and London. She was not yet sure whether she approved of the railways or not. Frederick Hallam admitted that they were smelly and noisy, but assured her that their convenience and speed would ensure that they spread across the face of England. Coaches, he insisted, had seen their day. Dear Frederick had several times ridden from Manchester to Liverpool on the train and was talking about raising the money to build a spur line to Bilsden now.

Even Mabel's accident had been providential, Annabelle decided, for Annie Gibson was not doing at all badly as a lady's maid. She was quick-witted and nimble-fingered, and possessed of a surprising degree of natural good taste. Jeremy had been right about the girl, though he was right about very little else. Whenever she thought about the way Jeremy had thrown away their chance to live here and remembered that she must eventually return to him and to Bilsden, she grew furious and at those times she would speak sharply to Annie, criticising whatever the girl did. Mostly, however, Annabelle managed to forget her husband and to enjoy herself.

Her plans for the future were rather vague as yet, but it was time to start taking a few preparatory steps. "Can you recommend a good lawyer, one who specialises in buying and selling properties?" she asked Barbara casually one day early in her stay.

"A lawyer! Is something wrong?"

"Of course not! Quite the contrary! I've had a small legacy from an aunt, only a hundred or two, but I thought I might like to invest it in a small piece of property here in Brighton." She smiled wrily. "It won't buy much, I know, but I'd like to think that I owned a bit of my beloved Brighton."

"I didn't realise that you were such a businesswoman. What does Jeremy say about it?"

"Oh, you know Jeremy. He's *so* impractical! Well, you've seen for yourself. Utterly immersed in his work. No, he'd be of no help. He just said I must spend it as I pleased."

Her hostess smiled. Poor Annabelle! It must worry her to have such an unworldly husband. And to have to live in a place like Bilsden. Barbara had been horrified by the place on her one and only visit. She was glad that her own husband had been more sensible and worked hard for the future. He had left her very comfortably provided for, even if not as rich as she would have liked. It was much more pleasant to be a widow with independent means than to have to humour a man's whims or (far worse!) share his bed. She cooed her sympathy and offered to introduce Annabelle to her own man of business who was not a lawyer, exactly, but such a sensible person and *so* understanding of one's needs.

Annabelle took to Mr Minton straight away, because the two of them were birds of a feather. During a surprisingly frank exchange, he was shrewd enough to see the frustrated businesswoman behind Annabelle's fragile exterior, and to sense her lack of scruples and her greed where money was concerned.

"Should you object to purchasing a row of four slum cottages?" he asked.

"Not if they gave a good return on my money."

"Oh, they'll do that, all right. The best, for the amount you've got. They'll pay back your capital in a few years, then you can knock them down and sell the land. They're in a good position if you look at how the town's expanding – which most people don't bother to do. It'll be prime land within ten or fifteen years, that will. You'll sell it easily and for a good deal more than you'll pay now."

"If that's so good, why haven't you bought the cottages yourself?"

He grinned. "I've bought one or two places in the same area. I'm not stupid. But I'm not made of money, either. It takes time to build up one's capital."

"Unfortunately, yes."

He pressed her hand sympathetically. "I do understand, dear lady. I've got a good rent-collector in my employ, as well. We only charge five per cent and we're *very* reliable when it comes to collecting the money. My man won't stand any nonsense from tenants. If they can't pay, they're straight out."

They went to see the cottages the next day.

"They look ready to fall down," Annabelle commented, holding her skirts carefully out of the dirt. "Are you sure they'll last ten years?"

"Oh, yes," he reassured her. "No need to spend much on maintenance, either. The sort of tenants who live in such places wouldn't appreciate good clean housing if you gave it to them. And there *is* a water tap. They're very lucky there. Not that such people are concerned about cleanliness."

Annabelle inspected the four dwellings very carefully, ignoring the tenants and their sullen glances. After that, she asked Mr Minton to drive her round the area. Only when she was satisfied that he'd been telling her the truth on all points did she agree to buy the cottages.

By the end of their fourth week away from Bilsden, the contract was signed and sealed. Mr Minton undertook to manage her properties and to deposit her rent money in a bank. He advised her to introduce herself to the bank manager as a widow. "Less fuss about getting your husband's permission, that way."

"Excellent idea! And if I should acquire any more small sums?" She raised one eyebrow.

"I'll be happy to invest them for you, Mrs Lewis. And you won't lose by it."

"You're *so* kind, Mr Minton!"

"It'll be a pleasure to earn my commission from *you*, Mrs Lewis." He bowed in a very gallant manner.

"As long as you earn it, I'll be happy to pay it." Sweet words were all very well, but money was what counted.

After that was settled, Annabelle reluctantly prepared to visit her mother, before returning to the north. She'd already stayed away for longer than planned, but she didn't suppose that Jeremy would be missing her. He'd be only

155

too happy to have the chance to spoil Marianne. He was a ridiculously doting father.

Annie was just as reluctant to leave Brighton. In spite of missing Ellie and Matt, she had enjoyed her stay there enormously. She felt quite a woman of the world now, after all her travel. The trip had opened her eyes to another world, one neither dominated by mill chimneys nor populated by pale, stunted people, who rarely saw the daylight.

She carried the wonder of it all in her heart for a long time afterwards – until other troubles intervened.

10

September 1837 to January 1838

It was strange to be back in Bilsden again. Annie found it very hard to settle down to the routine and restrictions imposed by Mrs Lewis.

"That Mrs Dwight," she told Ellie, "lets her servants eat what they like. You wouldn't credit the meals we had."

"Really?"

"And," Annie paused for effect, "we could go out sometimes for an hour in the afternoon. If the ladies were out, that was."

Ellie sighed. "Eh, that'd really be something. I'd love to go out for a little walk sometimes." They both sighed. "Tell us about the sea again," Ellie begged. She was never tired of hearing about it. She fondled her shell lady, which stood in a place of honour next to Annie's shell box on top of the rickety old chest of drawers in which they kept their clothes.

Annie described again the wonders of the sea and went on to catalogue the marvels of London and Brighton.

"I'd give anything to see it!" Ellie said longingly.

"Maybe she'll take you with her next time."

"Why should she?"

"If she took Miss Marianne, she might. She wouldn't want to look after a child all the time. She knows hundreds

157

of people down there. She's always out visiting and if she isn't, they come to see her. I've never seen her in a good temper so often."

Ellie sighed again. "Just think of it!" Annie's words had given her a plausible-enough basis for dreaming of such a wonderful trip.

On her first Sunday off, Annie had the full attention of even her stepmother and her sister Lizzie, as she retold the tale of her trip. Men sometimes left Bilsden on the tramp for work, and sent for their families if they found it, but the idea of travelling for pleasure was strange indeed for people from the Rows. Several other people from the street found an excuse to pop in and listen to Annie's tales. It was all very flattering, but it meant that she had less time to spend with Matt.

"You want to think about what you're doing, Annie," Emily told her before she left.

"What do you mean?"

"Me an' your dad've been talkin' about it." Emily looked at John for corroboration and he nodded at them both.

"About what?" Annie was bewildered.

"About your future."

"I don't know what you mean!"

"About you gettin' wed."

"But I'm not getting wed yet!" Annie was impatient at being delayed when Matt was waiting at the end of the street for her. He usually walked her back to Park House on her days off.

"You might do better for yourself stayin' in service, makin' a life there. No, you listen to me, girl! I'd tell t'same to me own daughter an' I'll do no less by John's."

John nodded. "You give it some thought, our Annie. There's a lot of sense in what our Em'ly's tellin' you."

Annie repressed a sigh and resigned herself to listening.

Her dad didn't like being interrupted by his children.

"Your Matt's a good lad," began Emily. "I'm not sayin' anythin' against him. But sometimes a girl can do better for herself in service. You could even get to be a housekeeper or – or a cook. You could have yer own money an' you could get to travel. An' you'd not have to worry about whether t'mill were on short time or not. Nor you wouldn't have to risk having childer." She looked down at her own swelling belly and smothered a sigh. She'd never thought John Gibson would give her so many babies. It fair wore you out. "Think about it, eh? We're only sayin' that it's worth thinkin' over, that's all we're sayin'."

"Aye," echoed John. "You think it over, lass, that's all we ask." He looked at her proudly. He had never thought to see his daughter dressed so fine and looking like a real lady.

Annie nodded her head. It was no use arguing with them. Best to let them think they had put an idea in her head and that she was thinking about it as they asked. Emily would never understand how she felt about Matt, though her father ought to, for he'd loved her mother in a way he clearly didn't love Emily. "It's kind of you to think about me," she said carefully. "I won't do anything hasty."

"That's right," said Emily. "An' don't you do nothin' wrong, neither, you an' Matt. You don't want to hafta get wed."

Annie blushed. "I wouldn't! He wouldn't! You should know me an' Matt better than that."

"That's as may be, but we're all human, aren't we? We've all got our needs." The look she cast at John as she said that was distinctly unfriendly, and his face flushed.

It was a relief to get out of the stuffy little house and to run down the street towards Matt. Annie didn't know how she stood her family sometimes. Every month she realised

159

afresh how glad she was that she had got out of Salem Street. The visits home never failed to make her appreciate Park House and her comfortable position there.

She didn't tell Matt what her stepmother had said; she told him instead how much she had missed him and how glad she was to be back. She also shyly produced a small framed aquatint of the sea which she had bought for him in Brighton, her first present to him. She hadn't liked to give it to him with everyone watching. Then she listened to his news of the mill and let him tell her about the books he had been reading. At the edge of the park he kissed her hungrily, then put her resolutely from him.

"You'd tempt an angel, Annie Gibson!" he said huskily. "I missed you."

She swayed towards him. "And I missed you."

He kissed her again, then stood back. "Nay, lass. We mustn't! We want better than this for ourselves."

They remained there for a moment, motionless, only a foot apart and aching to touch one another, then Annie moved away, jerkily. "I'll – I'll go in, then."

"Aye. Goodbye, love." Matt stood and watched her until she disappeared beyond the high walls of Park House, then swung round, half-whistling under his breath. It was hard, sometimes, to control your feelings, especially with a lass like Annie. Who'd have thought that the scrawny little girl with the long red braids whom he'd met all those years ago at the water pump, would have turned into such a pretty woman? No, pretty wasn't the word. She was – she was elegant. She had style. And she'd make him exactly the right sort of wife. He knew that he couldn't have married a woman, however pretty, who wouldn't be able to rise in the world with him.

It frightened Matt sometimes that he should have this burning urge to get on, to make money, to live somewhere nice, somewhere as unlike Salem Street as possible. He'd talked about it to Mr Hinchcliffe, but the minister had not thought it so wrong. If he got on in life through honest toil and he lived as a Christian should, where was the harm in that? No, Mr Hinchcliffe did not think Matt had anything to be ashamed of in his feelings. Matt had slept easier at nights since then, but he still had a niggling little worry at the back of his mind. He knew how strong his ambitions were, how ruthless he would be if he had to.

The next day Mrs Lewis stopped Annie as she was coming down the stairs. It had taken a week or two to convince Jeremy that she needed a personal maid. In the end he had given in, mainly because his wife was making life so unpleasant for them all. He had become a lot keener on the idea when he had heard that it was Annie Gibson whom she had in mind for the position. Annabelle took note of that. He showed far too much interest in the girl. He'd even encouraged the governess to lend books to Annie and Ellie to develop their minds. As though servants needed their minds developing! Strong bodies were of more use to them! Still, letting him help them was a way of letting him indulge his philanthropic urges without taking money away from his family, since the books had already been bought. Stupid man! What a fool he was!

Annabelle had always known a lot more than Jeremy realised about his comings and goings. She'd known about the girl in Brighton almost from the start, not only known, but been relieved. He had to have his little amours. All men were made like that. Even Frederick Hallam had hinted at his desire for her, though he was better than most men and had accepted no for an answer, without arguing. Perhaps it was because he was so much more sophisticated than Jeremy and could recognise a lady when he met one. Jeremy had been just – just absolutely disgusting at times.

161

Not that Jeremy seemed interested in her present maids in that way, thank goodness! She always kept a sharp eye open for that and had never seen any signs of it. She knew some wives turned a blind eye to it, but *she* wasn't having such filthy business going on under her own roof!

She blinked and realised that Annie was still standing there waiting for orders. "Come into my room. Now, how would you like to become my personal maid, Annie?"

The girl's eyes widened in surprise. "I never thought about it, Mrs Lewis. I thought Mabel would be . . ."

"Mabel! That clumsy creature!"

"I don't mean to be impertinent, Mrs Lewis, but Mabel was hoping that you would – would ask her. She's very eager to become a lady's maid."

"And you are *not?*" Surprise as well as annoyance edged Annabelle's voice with vinegar.

"I just – I never thought about it. I've been learning to cook and to run a house. It – I thought it was just a temporary thing when you took me to Brighton, because Mabel had broken her arm. I never . . ." Her voice faltered to a halt.

"Whether you accept the position or not, I shall not offer it to Mabel. She is too clumsy and she lacks imagination. You are inexperienced, of course, but you have possibilities. You have a way with hair, you can sew neatly and you are not clumsy. Oh, no! I should never take Mabel." She looked at Annie from the corner of her eye. "It would mean a rise in wages to ten pounds a year," she said casually.

Annie took a deep breath. Ten pounds. She would be able to save more money.

Annabelle looked at her, half-amused, half-indignant that she should have to tempt the girl. But a week or two of Mabel's ministrations since their return to Bilsden had made her appreciate Annie's deft touch. "Well?" she asked, tapping her fingers impatiently on the arm of her chair.

"In that case, ma'am, I'll be very happy to become your personal maid. And – and thank you."

There was a stormy scene in the attic that night, no less stormy because the protagonists did not dare raise their voices, for fear of the mistress hearing them.

"You sneaky worm!" hissed Mabel. "Stealing my job as soon as my back was turned!"

"I didn't!" protested Annie, who had been aware of Mabel's glowering looks ever since she came back from her interview with the mistress and told Mrs Cosden the news. "I didn't do anything!"

"Expect me to believe that! You done it on purpose! I always knew you was a sly one." She gave Annie a push.

Annie's temper flared up. "And you're a stupid one!" she said scornfully. "You'll never make a lady's maid in a thousand years! You're too stupid and clumsy!"

Mrs Cosden erupted out of her room, massive symbol of authority in a voluminous pink flannel dressing-gown. "Do you two want the mistress to hear?" she demanded in a fierce whisper. She stretched out a ham-like fist and pushed Mabel away from Annie. "Get off to your beds, the pair of you! And as for you, Mabel Clegg, you're wasting your time *and* your spite! If Mrs Lewis wants Annie, then there's nothing *you* can do about it! I'm not so happy to lose Annie myself. I've been training her for years and she's just getting into a real help in the decorating and serving. But I know better than to make a fuss about something that can't be mended."

Ellie pulled Annie back towards their room, but Mabel hadn't finished. "I'll pay you back one day, Annie Gibson!" she said viciously, arms akimbo. "I'll not forget an' I'll pay you back good and proper. You see if I don't!"

The next few months were to be a golden period in Annie's life. Never again, however happy she felt, would she be so carefree and so sure of life and the future which lay in store for her. She found that she really enjoyed being Mrs Lewis's personal maid, in spite of her mistress's uncertain temper. It was a challenge to try to prevent that temper being worked off on herself, which she could usually do, if she kept all her wits about her.

Inevitably, in the closeness of the association, both women came to know each other better. If you took a genuine, creative interest in her appearance, Mrs Lewis could thaw out amazingly. With practice, Annie became expert not only at dressing her mistress's silky blond hair, but also at creating new styles like the ones in the ladies' magazines. Annabelle would happily sit for hours almost purring with pleasure while her maid experimented. And Annie found it a delight to care for such beautiful clothes. Her sewing improved even further, for when she bothered, Annabelle was an accomplished needlewoman, and was able to pass on a few skills. At present, she considered it well worth her while to train her new maid properly; indeed, she was enjoying doing so.

In return for the devoted service and what Annie mentally referred to as 'the buttering-up', Annabelle went through her wardrobes and bestowed upon her maid several more dresses, petticoats, shifts, pairs of darned stockings and shoes. She even took an interest in how these were altered and allowed Annie an occasional hour off in the afternoon for her own sewing. Anything to do with clothes fascinated her, whoever they were for.

The rest of the household marvelled at Mrs Lewis's improved humour and said Annie was a witch. Mabel glowered, muttered beneath her breath and played one or two nasty tricks upon her rival until Mrs Cosden told her to stop that or she'd inform the mistress. After that, Mabel just bided her time. She would get even with that sneaky bitch one day.

The advantages of serving Mrs Lewis were not restricted to cast-off clothes and an easier life at Park House. Annie found herself making regular trips into Manchester as her mistress's companion on shopping expeditions. She came to know the shops and warehouses there quite well, especially those dealing in female apparel. There were not the luxurious dress salons there had been in London, but one or two of the dressmakers could meet Annabelle's exacting requirements in dress – though Annie was often called upon to make minor adjustments, even to these. There were also the warehouses, where one could, if one was careful, purchase accessories and lengths of material at ridiculously low prices.

Annabelle had nothing but scorn for Miss Pinkley, Bilsden's only ladies' dressmaker. She had used Miss Pinkley to make clothes for Marianne, *faute de mieux*, but bemoaned the lack of a real dressmaker in the town. Now she found that, with some help from a sewing woman for the straight seams and basic work, she and Annie between them could do a reasonable job of making everyday garments for Annabelle at a fraction of the price one would pay in a London dress salon, and that Annie had an eye for a good fit that was quite amazing. Annie joked to Ellie that her title should now be lady's maid and sewing-woman. But who cared? Life had suddenly become very interesting indeed.

Throughout those months, Mabel kept a watchful eye on her enemy. She still considered that Annie had stolen her job from her, and she refused to admit Annie's undoubtedly superior talents as a lady's maid. If she had to wait for twenty years, Mabel would get even with that sly sneak. Annie Gibson would be sorry for what she'd done!

The rest of the year flew by. It seemed incredible to Annie that it could be Christmas already. Mrs Lewis kept Park House in a whirl of activity, with parties, soirées and festive preparations. The servants grumbled, but not too loudly. Never had their mistress been so easy to work for. Jeremy, too, noticed how having a personal maid had sweetened Annabelle's temper and reminded himself to give Annie a bonus at Christmas. She had more than earned it.

January the tenth was cold and it had snowed heavily. Annie, suffering from a severe head cold, felt it to have been a poor start to the year she turned eighteen. She struggled to get on with her normal duties, but received several sharp reprimands from Mrs Lewis, who was feeling let-down and bored after the festivities. Annabelle was not sympathetic to other people's troubles and she particularly disliked servants being ill. There was too much to be done and would Annie *please* stop sniffling!

Annie felt her eyes sting with tears and blinked them hastily away. It wasn't fair! Her head was throbbing and she kept having to turn away to sneeze. How could she help sniffling?

On her first Sunday off in the New Year, she went home, because there was nothing else she could do in this weather. She still felt less than her normal self and, to make matters worse, Matt was away. Mr Hallam had sent him over to Liverpool for a few weeks to learn about the maintenance and proper use of some new machinery that had been ordered. Annie was not looking forward to a day with her family.

"Oh, it's you," said Emily ungraciously as she entered

Number Three. "I'd forgotten it was your Sunday off. Surprised y'even bothered to come, with Matt away!"

Annie leaned over to cuddle her little half-sister, Rebecca, who had looked just like a skinned rabbit when she was born, but who was now a pretty child. "How are you all, then?" she asked, as cheerfully as she could.

"'Ow d'yer think?" replied Emily. "You try losin' a baby an' see 'ow well you feel!" She had just had a still-born baby and was looking tired and unhappy.

"I'm goin' into t'mill," announced Lizzie, self-importantly. "Our dad's got me set on. I'm startin' on Monday." She seemed quite pleased at the prospect.

Annie looked at her father in surprise. He had always said that he'd keep his girls out of the mill at all costs.

"There wasn't anythin' else," he said apologetically. "There's seven of us to feed an' our Tom's not bringin' in so much just now." He couldn't meet his eldest daughter's eyes.

"Oh, Dad," she said softly. "Mam would've hated that!"

"Your mam's long dead!" Emily's voice seemed even shriller than usual. "Time to complain when *you* c'n find your sister summat better! I didn't see *you* helpin' our Lizzie to find a place in service, like you did for Ellie Peters, Miss High an' Mighty! An' the reason we're short is because that brother of yours don't hand all his wages over, like he should. That's what! Ungrateful, you are, the pair of you! Give nothin' to y'family, *you* two don't!"

"I didn't know of any places going." Annie felt uncomfortable, but knew that Lizzie could never have got taken on as a maid. Her very appearance militated against her. Employers wanted pleasant, cheerful faces around them. Lizzie was an ugly, unappealing child with a surly nature, and it showed in her face.

"Right, then! Don't complain when someone *does* find

her a job. It might not suit *you*, but it'll bring in half a crown a week an' more later, an' that suits us!"

"But will Lizzie be able to manage it?" asked Annie. "She's not quick with her hands, never was." She ignored Lizzie's scowl. "You have to be quick in the mill, or you can get injured. Ellie told me about it."

"She'll learn," replied Emily sourly. She never looked happy nowadays. "A person does what they have to. The Lord doesn't give you a burden too heavy to bear."

Rebecca fell over and started to wail and Emily turned to pick her up. Annie went over to the fire and began to stir the stew. It looked greasy and unappetising. Emily was as bad a cook as she was a housekeeper. The place smelled very sour nowadays and all the extra bits and pieces of furniture, like the brass fender, had long disappeared into the pawn shop.

The day dragged on. The whole family went to chapel, even little Rebecca, though the child shivered all the time in her inadequate clothes.

"She ain't got no fine clothes like her big sister!" snapped Emily, seeing Annie's look.

"I'll see if I can make her something." But she had made other things for her brothers and sisters, and they had unaccountably vanished.

Later, Emily shrilled, "We ain't got no fancy food, so you can like it or lump it!" as Annie picked at the gristly meat in the watery stew.

John sighed, but didn't intervene. Emily hadn't been well since she lost the baby.

Shut up in the tiny house, which had once been her home, Annie tried not to let the barbed remarks provoke her into answering back, for her father's sake. He was looking worn and unhappy, and she felt sorry for him. When she put sixpence on the table in front of Emily and said it was a present for the children, he gave her a little nod and a half-ashamed smile. The children would never see the money, of course, but Emily picked it up quickly and was thereafter a little less sharp with her elder stepdaughter.

At least they were not cold here, thought Annie, trying to look on the bright side. The tiny room was full of people and that generated warmth. The two little boys rolled around the floor, playing like puppy dogs on the dirty flagstones. Why had they not been swept? But she did not dare offer to do it. Once, Emily would have rebuked the children for playing on the Lord's day, but now she only smacked them for getting in her way. May and Lizzie sat in a corner on some old sacks, whispering and giggling together. They completely ignored everyone else. Why had her father not made them some more stools? He was handy with bits of wood. He used to make all sorts of things when her mam was alive. It was awful seeing how they lived.

At two o'clock Annie could stand it no longer. "I think I'll pop along to see Mr and Mrs Peters," she said.

"Not good enough for you, aren't we?" asked Emily. "You'd think a person'd be glad to spend a day with their family once in a while."

"Em'ly!" When John spoke in that tone of voice, even Emily fell silent.

"Come again, lass. It's allus nice to see you," he told Annie as he stood in the doorway. "She's not feelin' so well just now," he added in a whisper.

Annie kissed her father goodbye and left the house. Poor Dad! He wasn't getting a lot of joy from his second marriage. Emily was becoming a shrew and was increasingly slatternly in her ways. How could her dad stand it?

Annie had intended to go along to Number Seven, where

she knew Sam would have made her welcome, though
Elizabeth had not been very friendly since she and Matt
had started walking out together, but on an impulse she
called in at Number Six instead. She had not seen Sally for
ages.

Matt didn't really like her associating with a woman like
Sally. He fussed a lot about respectability and Annie
blamed that on his mother. Elizabeth Peters thought
herself a cut above everyone else in the street and had
talked frequently lately about finding a better place to live.
Annie didn't blame her for that; she couldn't understand
why the Peters hadn't left already. After all, Sam thought
the world of Dr Lewis and his employer felt the same about
him, so Sam's job was safe.

Annie smiled to herself at the thought of Matt. Dear
Matt! Where was he now? What was he doing? She wished
he were here. No, she didn't! She was glad he was in
Liverpool, glad he was getting some good experience, glad
that Mr Hallam and his overseer, Benson, were singling
him out for attention.

Sally opened the door, her face wreathed in smiles.
"Annie, love! Well, I never! Come in, come in! I've just got
t'kettle on." Her house was a haven of warmth and
comfort, its floor cleaner than Emily's tabletop.

Sally was getting plumper and had begun to dye her hair
yellow to hide the grey. She had lost some of the colour in
her cheeks, as women did when they grew older and now
used rouge when 'my Harry' was expected. He still came to
see her as regularly as ever and she seemed to live very
comfortably.

"You've got new curtains, I see, Sally."

"Yes. The others was gettin' worn, so my Harry brought
me some material. He knows I like to keep the place
nice."

170

"Yes, you always did keep it nice. I love coming here."

Sally beamed with pleasure. She bustled round, brewing a pot of tea and setting out a plate of drop scones. Annie sat back and relaxed. What a difference to Number Three! Respectability didn't give you peace of mind! Or even a clean house.

"Missin' your Matt, are you?"

"Yes. Yes, I am."

"Well, he'll not be away much longer. And one man's loss is another man's gain, as they say. You wouldn't've had time to visit me if he'd been around. Oh, don't look so bedithered! I know how it is! You can't blame him for wantin' his girl to keep respectable company."

"You're respectable enough for me, Sally. And I shan't stop being friends with you, whatever happens. Not for Matt, not for anyone. Besides, you've been with your Harry for – how long is it, now? – ten years? That's near enough respectable for me."

"It must be ten years." Sally laughed comfortably. "He's a nice man. I've been very lucky."

"He's lucky, too."

Sally blinked away a tear. "Get on with you, Annie Gibson! Now, tell me what you've been doin'. I'm real glad that you've got to be a lady's maid. If anyone deserves to get on, it's you. Your mam would be that proud of you. An' just look at that dress! You look a proper picture in it. A bit peaky, though. You feelin' all right?"

No one in Number Three had noticed how she was looking. "Oh, it's just a cold. I'm over the worst now."

They chatted comfortably until it was time for Annie to return to Park House. She decided that she would come and visit Sally more often, no matter what Matt said. Why were people so against Sally? She was clean and kind, worth more than a slattern like Emily any day of the week!

171

It was dark outside. She had stayed longer than she meant to at Sally's. It had snowed again during the afternoon, covering the frozen slush and making walking a hazardous business, and the wind had risen. She shivered and pulled her cloak more tightly around her, wishing she had Matt to walk her back. She'd have felt warm and safe with his arm around her shoulders. Carefully she picked her way along Salem Street and down Boston Street. There were few people around.

As she was passing the end of Florida Terrace, her head down against the driving snow, she bumped into someone. She started to apologise and tried to step aside.

"Well, if it ain't Miss Annie Gibson!" a voice exclaimed and a hand shot out to grab her arm.

She cried out in fright. She'd know that voice anywhere, even though she'd never expected to hear it again. As usual, Fred Coxton reeked of gin.

"Let go of me!" she said, pulling in vain. "My Matt told you to leave me alone!"

"But your Matt isn't here, is he? Your Matt's in Liverpool an' they tell me he won't be back for weeks." He leaned over her, pawing at her with his free hand.

She was terrified now. "But he will be back!" she cried. "He'll be back soon." She struggled to get away. Snow whirled into her face and the wind shrieked derisively.

Fred took a quick glance up and down the street. There was no one in sight. He stood for a moment, swaying slightly, his desire roused by the soft warm curves he'd felt under the cloak. Suddenly, decision taken, he clapped a hand over her mouth and began to drag her along Florida Terrace towards the warrens of Claters End. Half-suffocating under the hand, Annie fought desperately to free herself. Why did no one come to her help? She tried to bite his hand, but he didn't even seem to notice. She kicked out and felt him stumble as she caught him on the shin. The hand slipped from her mouth for a moment and she screamed as loudly as she could, but the wind was howling more loudly than she ever could and there was no one around to see her plight.

Angrily Fred hit her on the head and clapped his hand over her mouth again. For a minute or two she lay limply against him, partly stunned by the blow, then she started struggling again. She might as well have saved her efforts. The few blows that landed seemed to make no impression on him, and he laughed hoarsely in her ear. "I'm goin' to enjoy takin' Matt Peters' woman," he said and chuckled as this remark panicked her into a frenzy of useless struggling.

He kicked open the door of a house and dragged her in with him. He seemed to know the way without a light, because he pulled her across the room and dropped her on to a bed. Nearly demented with terror, she redoubled her efforts to escape and screamed as loudly as she could. He hit her on the head again. She bit him and scratched him, but he pulled off his neckerchief and tied it round her mouth to gag her cries. Still holding her hands, he felt about on the floor and swore as he didn't find what he sought. For a moment his grip slackened and she tore herself away from him, but he caught her skirt and pulled her back. She tore the gag down and screamed again. A voice in the next room shouted out to keep that whore quiet and this time Fred did.

Methodically he tied her arms and gagged her again. He then tore the front of her dress open and slobbered over her breasts. She could do no more than whine in her throat and he paid no attention to that. She prayed to faint, but she didn't. Vomit rose in her throat and she nearly choked on it, but she stayed conscious. He rolled off her for a moment and came back minus his trousers. Quickly and happily he lifted her skirts and raped her. Even the pain of that didn't make her faint. Why didn't she faint? Why didn't she die? How could this be happening to her?

Then Fred started again, for he was a man noted for his sexual prowess. This time he worked more slowly and his proddings and gropings seemed to go on and on and on. He hurt her and used her as she had never imagined possible. When she tried to sob she could only make stifled, whining noises in her throat, and he just laughed at that. When tears of pain and terror poured down her face, that too seemed to amuse him.

After he had finished for a second time, he put his mouth close to her ear and said slowly and distinctly, "Don't forget to tell your Matt everything what I done to you. He won't like that, won't Mr Spick an' Span. Bleedin' cissie, he is, allus washin' his hands! When he lost me my job, I said I'd get even. I reckon I'm ahead with this. Nice little bit of stuff, you are!" And he started to handle her body, hurting her purely for the pleasure of seeing her wince and writhe about. It took him a while to get roused again, then he held her legs apart and the painful thrusting started again. This time, the grunting, jerking animal on top of her didn't stop for an eternity.

Then, quite suddenly, he rolled off her and to her amazement, he began almost immediately to snore. She lay there for a moment, still weeping, then, as she realised that this might be her only chance to escape, she tried to pull herself together. She pulled cautiously at her bonds, but she couldn't loosen them. Her arms were numb, so tightly was she bound. The movement roused him and he muttered something. She froze and, after what seemed like hours, he started snoring again.

She lay there in despair worse than anything she had felt in her whole life, then stiffened as she heard steps outside the door. The wind must have dropped. Perhaps if she could get this gag out, she could shout for help. She rolled her head from side to side, but in vain. The filthy material was tied so tightly it was cutting into her and all that came out was a gurgle of sound. Voices muttered and a woman laughed, then someone fumbled with the latch and the door opened. They couldn't see her because it was pitch dark and she had to lie there, helpless and ashamed, as they fumbled to light a candle. They didn't notice her at first, then the man gave a muffled exclamation.

"What the bloody hell's that?"

The woman brought the candle over to the bed and they both peered down at Annie.

"Wouldn't mind a bit of that meself," said the man. "All laid out nice and ready, it is."

Annie could only look at them and plead mutely with her eyes. The man stretched out his hand and the woman slapped it away.

"Oh, no, you don't! You come here with me an' I need the money. You're not gettin' it free. Besides, the poor bitch's had enough. You can see that. Fred's a devil when he's on the jump." She laughed and strutted up and down. "Now me, I'm ready to go! I'll give you far more fun than she ever could."

The man was distracted. He echoed her laugh and turned back to paw at her, but she held him off for a moment.

"What's the matter now?"

"I'm just goin' t'let that poor bitch go."

"He'll kill you, if he finds out."

"He won't find out if you don't tell him. He's out cold. I know him. He don't wake for hours after he's been on the booze. I'll just tell him she'd gone when we got back."

"Why bother lettin' her go? She won't get in our way an' he might want her again."

175

Annie could feel tears running out of her eyes and she tried her hardest to will them to let her go.

The woman sighed. "I don't know, dearie. I must be gettin' soft in me head. But it just don't seem right to leave her lyin' there like that while we 'ave our little bit of fun. Besides, she's still cryin'. She didn't come willing, you can see that. He's give her a right old thump or two."

After a while the woman managed to persuade the man, so she came over quickly to Annie and untied the ropes. Trembling uncontrollably and unable to stand at first for the pins and needles in her arms and legs, Annie covered herself as best she could with her torn clothes. When she could manage to walk, she stumbled towards the door. She tried to thank her rescuer, but couldn't speak for her chattering teeth.

The woman gave her a shove. "Go on!" she said, with rough friendliness. "Get out of the town, if you can. If Fred fancies you an' you don't fancy him, you'd be best gettin' right away from Bilsden. Nasty bastard, he can be! Find yourself another pitch and a strong chap to protect you this time."

Annie stood outside in the darkness, oblivious to the icy wind and the snow, and tried to stop herself from having hysterics. More by instinct than by reasoning, she got her bearings and made her way back to Park House through the deserted streets. If she could only get in without being seen, Ellie would help her. Mrs Lewis must never know! No one must ever know, except for Ellie. She could trust Ellie.

It was just after midnight when she got there. She stood and sobbed, because the house was dark and locked up for the night. She didn't dare knock on the door and show herself in this condition. Like an injured animal, her one instinct was to hide and tend her wounds. She caught sight

176

of a light in the doctor's surgery and stumbled towards it. He often worked late. Perhaps she could slip in that way without his hearing her.

Slowly, carefully, she turned the knob and pushed open the outer door, breathing a sigh of relief when she found it unlocked. It opened silently and she held her breath as she listened. Smothering the sobs that still threatened to burst from her throat, she closed the door slowly, terrified of betraying her presence. She tiptoed across the room, her one thought to get upstairs to Ellie.

And then, just as she thought she was safe, the door to the doctor's room opened unexpectedly and Jeremy Lewis came out, murmuring something to himself and holding a lamp in his hand. They both stopped dead at the sight of each other.

"My God! Annie! What's happened?"

Her hand flew to her mouth in a child's gesture of pain and hurt and she began to cry quietly and hopelessly. The cloak dropped to one side and he took in her torn clothing and bruised face.

He put the candle down and moved towards her, speaking gently, realising that she was near hysterics. "What happened, Annie? Who did this to you? Oh, Annie, Annie!" The trim, pretty girl of the morning was barely recognisable in this white-faced, trembling creature. He ached at her pain and, without thinking, he made as if to take her in his arms. She flinched from his touch, flinched as if he were going to hit her, and he promised himself that whoever had done this should be found and punished.

"Come into my surgery," he urged, still gently. "I won't touch you if you don't want me to, but you need help. You've a cut on your head and who knows what else."

She followed him in and sat huddled on a chair in front of the fire, still shivering and whimpering to herself. He poured out a glass of brandy, but when he offered it to her, she made no attempt to take it from him, just sat there, gazing numbly at him. She hadn't spoken a word yet.

"You must take some," he said, with all the authority he could muster. "You're suffering from shock. Take it and drink some. It'll help."

She stared at him, as if he had spoken in a foreign language and she hadn't understood a word, but when he held the glass out again, she took it from him and, after a further pause, took a gulp. She coughed and choked and was suddenly sick, retching and retching, though there was little in her stomach but bile.

As if it were the most natural thing in the world, he wiped up the mess and got her another glass of brandy and water. And then she started crying again, sobbing in that quiet, hopeless way that distressed him unbearably.

"Tell me about it, Annie. Tell me what happened. Perhaps I can help."

Between gulping sobs, she told him how Fred Coxton had dragged her back to his room and raped her. Her voice faltered as she tried to put into words the terror of that night, the degradation of his touch and her present feelings that she would be dirty for ever more. By the time she had finished, she was sobbing despairingly.

He took her limp hand and said, "Oh, Annie!" very softly and she saw that he too had tears in his eyes. This time she did not flinch from his touch.

"We must get you cleaned up," he said at last. "And in the morning we'll inform a magistrate . . ."

"No! No!" she cried, pulling away, panic in her eyes.

"Why ever not? That brute can't be allowed to get away with such an assault. I'll go and fetch Mrs Lewis now and we'll . . ."

"No!" This time her voice was even sharper.

He looked at her in puzzlement.

"I don't want anyone to know," she managed at last, "no one except Ellie, and most of all, not Mrs Lewis! Oh, please, please, don't tell them, doctor! I'll die if anyone finds out. And I'll be turned off, I know I will!"

"But it wasn't your fault!"

"That wouldn't matter," she said dully. "If anyone knew, they'd say – they'd say I wasn't respectable any more. No one would take me on as a servant, least of all as a lady's maid."

"I'm sure you're wrong!"

"I'm not! And if you think about it, you'll realise I'm not! You know what Mrs Lewis is like. *Please*, doctor! This is my only chance of keeping my job!"

He was silent for a moment, unwilling to believe that she could be right, unwilling to admit to himself that her words carried a conviction that was frightening. Would people really penalise the victim of this crime? Would Annabelle . . . Yes, she would! Of course she would. And so would other people.

She could see him wavering and pressed her advantage. "And if you take it to a magistrate, sir, you'll not get a conviction. There are no witnesses, you see. And I'm only a servant. They'll say I encouraged him."

He shook his head.

"Yes, they *will*, sir! You know they will!"

His shoulders slumped. "It's wicked to let him get away with it."

"He won't get away with it!"

"Oh?"

"No, sir. I've got a young man, Ellie's brother. He's away just now, or I'd not have had to walk back alone. But when he comes back, he'll . . ." Her voice broke at the thought of Matt.

"I didn't know that you had a young man. I'm glad for you, though I suppose it means you'll be leaving us soon to get married."

"Oh, no, sir. He can't get married for years. We need to save our money. Matt wants to make something of himself." Talking of Matt helped more than anything, though she didn't know how she was going to tell him about this. It made the world seem more normal again, made her feel that everything was not spoiled, that there was some hope after all.

She started to stand up. "Thank you for your help, sir." She winced and swayed dizzily.

He pushed her down again. "Give yourself a few minutes more, Annie. You've had a nasty shock. Besides, I want to examine you."

She shrank away from him. "What?"

"You've got a cut on your head that needs dressing. You may have – other injuries. I'm a doctor. I won't agree to help you unless you let me check first that you're all right. Besides, we still have to think of a tale for Mrs Lewis and the others. She was angry when you didn't get back on time. And if I'm not mistaken, your face is going to be badly bruised. You'll be in no condition to work for the next few days."

He busied himself getting some water, then asked her quietly to lie down on his couch. His touch was light and impersonal and, after the first minute or two, she lost a lot of her embarrassment. This was not a man; it was a doctor. She was not to know how hard it was for him to maintain that impersonal calmness at the sight of the bruises on her body, especially her breasts, and the dried blood between her legs. She had obviously been a virgin and had been taken very brutally.

"Now," he said, when he had finished and had helped her

180

to wash in water that smelt of clean herbs, "we must think what to tell them."

He helped her up to the servants' stairs and left her in a shocked Ellie's hands. Next morning he told Mrs Cosden that Annie had had a bad fall in the snow and had been knocked unconscious. She had lain in the snow for hours. It would be a miracle if she did not develop a congestion of the lungs. She was to stay in bed for a few days.

He himself took in his wife's morning tea tray and gave her an account of how Annie, half-frozen from lying unconscious in the snow, had knocked on his surgery door late last night and then fainted clean away again. From the way he told it, Ellie had come down to help him treat Annie.

Annabelle offered up some token words of sympathy and then started worrying about how long Annie would need to stay in bed and how she would manage with only Mabel to help her.

"As you managed before!" Jeremy said impatiently. "Now mind, I'm not having Annie disturbed or I won't answer for the consequences! You don't want her dying on us, do you?"

She pulled a moue of annoyance and told him pettishly to send Mabel to her, then.

Upstairs Annie spent a long weary day tossing around in bed, muffling her bouts of weeping in the lumpy pillow. Ellie popped in to see her a couple of times and Susan brought up her lunch on a tray, but she could eat nothing. The horrors of the previous night kept replaying in her mind. Worst of all was the thought of what she was going to say to Matt.

11

March 1838

Six weeks later Annie was forced to admit to herself that she must be pregnant. She'd missed twice, she who was normally as regular as clockwork, and what's more, she was feeling queasy in the mornings and her breasts were tender.

Ellie had been appalled when Annie told her about that night's horror, saying men like Fred Coxton should be taken out and shot. Afterwards, she had been kind, hugging her friend frequently, as if to show that it made no difference to her feelings for Annie. But the rape had made a difference to Annie. It still kept her awake at nights and it made her jump in terror if anyone came up behind her unexpectedly. The idea of a pregnancy from that man was too horrible to contemplate and for a long time she hoped she was mistaken.

Annie didn't know what she'd have done without Ellie during those weeks. Many a night she'd woken up sobbing, to find Ellie's arms ready to comfort her. But there was no comfort that Ellie or anyone else could offer that would help with an unwanted baby. Annie was filled with icy horror at the prospect, a horror that stayed with her night and day, and never left her for a moment. Mrs Lewis couldn't fault her on efficiency – Annie did her job as well as always – but she noticed that the girl had not been the same since her fall.

Mabel noticed, too. She wasn't sure what it added up to but she was pleased to see her enemy looking pale and strained. She kept her eyes open. You never knew what you could pick up.

In the end, Annie slipped in to see Dr Lewis while the mistress was out and told him what she suspected. He examined her and confirmed that she could indeed be pregnant, though it was a bit early to tell for sure.

"Sit down, Annie." She sat in front of him, saying nothing. Her pallor worried him. "Have you thought what you'll do?"

"Pray to lose it!" she said savagely. "Oh, doctor, isn't there anything I can do, anything I can take that will . . ."

"No!" How he hated to hear women say this! He had to admit, though, that Annie had more justification than most. "Look, it's not the baby's fault. It's done nothing to deserve to be murdered."

She looked at him, startled by his vehemence.

"It *is* murder, Annie," he insisted, "to kill an unborn child. And what's more, women who try to get rid of unwanted babies often damage themselves permanently, so that they can bear no more children. It's dangerous and it's wrong. I would definitely call it murder."

"What they'll do to me will be worse than murder," she said bitterly.

"What do you mean?"

"I've lost my respectability. It doesn't matter how it happened. People won't care about that. As far as they're concerned, I'll be a loose woman from now on."

"Have you told your young man yet?"

"No, sir. He's still away, in Liverpool. I haven't seen him

since it happened. But he's due back this week. On my next Sunday off I'll have to tell him – somehow."

"Surely, if he loves you, he'll stand by you?"

"Perhaps." Her voice was calm but hopeless. "But why should he father a bastard, sir? And a bastard with a real father like Fred Coxton!" She shuddered. "I know I'll hate the baby for being his. I hate it already."

He looked down at his hands. What could he say? She knew her world and her young man better than he did.

"Would you mind not telling the mistress yet, sir? It won't show for a while and I might as well earn as much money as I can before I lose my place."

"There's no reason for you to lose your place, Annie! Even if Annabelle doesn't want you as her personal maid, we can keep you on in some other capacity."

She looked at him indulgently. He was a kind man, Dr Lewis, kind and gentle, but he didn't understand what the world was really like. He only knew about people's bodies.

"The mistress won't want me in the house when she finds out," she told him patiently, as if she were talking to a child.

He drew in a deep breath and sat there for a minute, reluctant to face the thought of Annabelle's reactions. Finally he sighed and said slowly, "I hate to admit it, but I suspect that you're right. What shall you do, then?"

"I don't know yet. That rather depends on Matt, doesn't it?" She stood up, shoulders drooping. "And now, sir, if you can't help me, I'll have to get back to my work."

Two Sundays later, Annie went out to meet Matt, feeling like a prisoner waiting to be hanged. She tried to tell herself that he'd help her, stand by her, want to marry her, in spite of the baby, but she couldn't seem to believe it. Why couldn't she believe it? Even Ellie hadn't been able to make her believe that there was any hope, though Ellie herself was certain sure that Matt would not desert her.

Ellie had taken a message to Matt for Annie the previous week, asking him to meet her in the park before chapel, and he was there waiting for her, his face happy with anticipation. She walked slowly towards him and he began to look puzzled, for she usually rushed to throw herself into his arms.

"Annie, love!" He pulled her towards him and she stood there stiffly, willing herself not to burst into tears. "What's the matter? Aren't you well?" He held her at arm's length and scanned her face anxiously.

"I've been ill. And – and there's a problem. I have to talk to you. Can we walk round the park? I don't want to go back to Salem Street yet."

He fell into step beside her. It was a cold early March day and the park was bleak and grey, the trees still leafless and the few daffodils that had come out early looking as if they realised they had made a mistake.

"I – I don't know an easy way to tell you this," she began. "Two months ago I was – I was attacked on my way back to Park House."

"Attacked? What do you mean, attacked?"

"Attacked and raped."

"*What!*" He stopped, seized her arm and swung her round to face him. "Annie – no!"

She just stood and looked up at him mutely.

"Who?" He could hardly get the word out. He felt as if he were choking.

"Fred Coxton. I bumped into him going home and he dragged me to his room and tied me up." She spoke tonelessly, factually. She knew of no words adequate to describe the horror of that night.

"Couldn't you have screamed for help? Was there no one around?"

"I did scream. And I fought. There was no one to hear me. There was a howling snowstorm that day. Fred's very big and strong. It was dark and s-snowing . . ." Tears were streaming down her face, and down Matt's face, too. They stood in the chill wind like two frozen creatures, only the tears alive.

He didn't move towards her, didn't touch her, and somehow she knew then what his answer would be. She took a deep breath and forced herself to speak again. "There's worse, Matt."

"Worse?" His voice was a cry of anguish. "In God's name, how can it be worse?"

She couldn't look him in the face. She couldn't put it into words with his eyes staring at her.

He took her arm and shook her roughly. "What can be worse? Tell me, Annie!"

"It looks like I'm having a child from it."

Horror crawled over his face and he let go of her arm, taking an involuntary step backwards.

She saw the revulsion in his eyes and moaned. "Oh, Matt! Don't look at me like that! Matt, I couldn't help it. I fought . . ." She broke down completely, covering her face with her hands and sobbing broken-heartedly, but still he didn't touch her.

Matt stood and looked at her, unable to think clearly. His Annie! Carrying Fred Coxton's child! It wasn't possible. It was disgusting . . . filthy . . . obscene! "Fred Coxton – threatened to get his own back – when I got him dismissed."

After a long pause he added bitterly, "I'll kill him. I'll kill that bastard!" But she knew he wouldn't. Matt Peters would never kill anyone.

When Annie half-fell into his arms, Matt forced himself not to push her away. He knew he should be comforting her. He wanted to comfort her, but he couldn't. She was – he gulped back a wave of nausea – spoiled. Spoiled, rotten, like tainted meat. Filthy.

"What are you going to do now?" he asked woodenly. It was a huge effort to force any words through his stiff lips.

She pulled away from him, rocking to and fro with the pain of his rejection. "I wanted to see you first, Matt. I wanted to see how you felt before I – before I made any plans. Ellie said you'd still want me – but you don't, do you?"

He didn't answer. He stood there with a red face and tears in his eyes, looking down at her hopelessly.

"I knew it. I knew it inside all the time." Her voice was steady now and she had stopped those anguished move-ments. "I've loved you since I was ten, Matt Peters. I thought you loved me. But you don't, do you? If you did, you wouldn't let this come between us. I was just suitable, I reckon, the sort of wife you would need one day. You don't love the real me at all."

"I'll help," he said desperately. "I've got some money saved. I'll give it to you. You could go away somewhere. Start again."

"I wouldn't take your money! And I'm *not* going away!" She spat the words at him, then turned suddenly and ran from him, not caring who saw her crying, making towards Salem Street, because it was the only place left, because her father was the only one she could turn to now. If he didn't help her, she'd kill herself.

Matt stood there and watched her go, fists knotted by his side, tears blurring his eyes. He despised himself, but he couldn't take her, not with another man's child in her belly. He couldn't even touch her any more. She was tainted. "Tainted. Filthy." He realised that he'd said the words aloud, cursed and turned grimly towards Claters End. The only relief he could think of was the relief of beating Fred Coxton to a pulp.

It was easy to find Fred's old room, but Fred had left Bilsden over a month ago and no one knew where he'd gone. The woman Matt spoke to seemed to think that was a good thing.

Matt walked aimlessly along the street and stopped in front of an open door, from which sounds of a fiddle scraping out tunes tempted passers-by to enter. It was the first time he had ever been into a gin house and the first time in his life he had ever got drunk. Two hours later, he was so drunk that he had to be carried home by some men who knew that he was Sam Peters' lad.

When Matt woke in the morning, with a thumping head and a dry sour taste in his mouth, he refused to tell his horrified parents why he had got himself into such a condition.

"I'll not do it again. I was troubled about something. But drinking doesn't help. Nothing helps. I won't – I can't talk about it – not yet. Just leave me be." And he set off for work without waiting for his breakfast, leaving his mother in tears. He would tell them about it later, he decided; at the moment, he couldn't bear the thought of their sympathy, or his mother's joy at his release from his engagement.

When she left Matt, Annie ran all the way home to Number Three. She burst in and leaned against the front door, gasping for breath, her face so white that they thought at first she was ill.

"Nay, lass!" exclaimed John. "What's wrong?" He came over to her and she fell into his arms sobbing wildly. He sat her down and looked at Emily, who had come in from the back room.

"What's wrong with her?" Emily asked in amazement.

189

She'd never seen Annie cry, even as a child, let alone falling about and sobbing aloud like this.

"Send – send the kids out." Annie managed at last. "Send them out! I can't tell you with them listening."

Lizzie and May were bundled out into the cold with orders to take young Mark and Luke for a walk. John himself cut short their protestations.

"Get out, an' don't come back till it's time for chapel! Em'ly, get the lass a cup of tea."

Annie sat cradling the warm cup in her hands and in a tense, clipped voice she told them what had happened and what Matt had said to her. They listened in stunned silence, then John put his hand on her shoulder. "You'll have to come home then, love. If Matt Peters isn't man enough to marry you, then you'll have to come here."

"How can she? Where can we put 'er?" asked Emily shrilly. The last thing she wanted was for her stepdaughter to come back. With Annie around, it'd be a lot harder to manage John. "We've no room. Tom's already sleepin' down here. She *can't* come back!"

John turned on her. "We've allus got room for my children! I'm still master here an' she's still my daughter! If she's in trouble an' she needs somewhere to go, then we shall *make* room."

In open-mouthed astonishment, Emily fell silent and offered no more protests. She'd never seen John quite like this before, because she hadn't known him when Lucy was alive.

Annie held her father's hand and managed a watery smile. "Thanks, Dad. I don't know what I'd have done if you'd let me down, too. Thrown myself in the river, I think." She turned to Emily. "I'm sorry, Emily, really I am!"

Emily sniffed, but dared make no comment.

"I don't need to come here yet," Annie went on. "It won't show for another month or two. I'll go on working, get a bit of money saved."

"Aye, that'd be best," said John. "We've not got a lot to spare. The more brass you can save, the better, lass."

"We must tell Mr Hinchcliffe," said Emily abruptly. "He'll be able to advise us."

"No!" Annie's voice was sharp and they both looked at her in surprise. "We won't tell him yet," she amended. "If it gets out, if *she* finds out, I'll lose my place. Let's just wait, eh? Go on working and wait."

12

April 1838

But the news soon got out, in the Rows, at least. Matt, under the influence of the gin, had confided his woes to a sympathetic listener. The listener, more accustomed to his drink, had not forgotten the tale and the whisper was soon round the Rows that Annie Gibson was expecting a child.

Serve the stuck-up bitch right, said some of her contemporaries, who had not been fortunate enough to get a place in service and who had been swallowed up by the drudgery of the mill. Serve you right, too, Matt Peters, said some of the lads still working at lowly jobs in the mill where he had been given such preferential treatment. If you will go off to Liverpool and leave a pretty lass like that on her own, what can you expect? No one seemed quite sure of the exact details or who the father was, however.

Matt was aghast when one of his drinking companions made a few sly digs about 'unwanted babbies' and he realised what he must have done. He didn't remember much about that day. Surely he hadn't told a complete stranger about Annie? While he was still trying to think what to do, the rumour came to Mabel's ears. She knew at once that this was her chance to get even and she seized it with both hands.

"Excuse me, ma'am," she said to Mrs Lewis after breakfast. "May I have a private word with you?"

Annabelle's assent was cool and uninterested. She was wondering how soon Jeremy would let her make another visit to Brighton.

"It's about Annie Gibson, ma'am."

"About Annie? What on earth do you mean? If Annie wants something, she can surely ask me herself!"

"It's not like that, ma'am. It's – well – some information has come my way that I thought you ought to know."

"I hope you're not going to be wasting my time with spitefulness, Mabel."

"Oh, no, ma'am. This is something important. I'm sure you'll want to hear about it." Mabel felt a thrill of intense pleasure at the thought of how angry Mrs Lewis would be with Annie.

"Then come to the point and tell me, Mabel! I have a lot to do today."

"I believe Annie Gibson is going to have a baby, ma'am." There, it was out! And just look at her highness's red face! She'll be spitting fury in a minute, thought Mabel gleefully, remembering how angry Mrs Lewis had been with Bet all those years ago.

"*What did you say?*"

"They – er – they don't say who the father is, but it's not her young man, that's for sure."

"Her young man?"

"Oh, didn't you know she was walking out, ma'am?"

"You must be mistaken! I don't believe you!" Annabelle didn't want to believe Mabel. For once, she was more than satisfied with a maid. If this news were true, she'd have to dismiss Annie and find someone else. It *couldn't* be true!

Mabel smirked. "I think you'll find that it is true, ma'am. I've had my suspicions about her for a while." The words poured out. It was balm to Mabel's jealous soul to be able to blacken Annie's reputation. "She's been walking out with Matt Peters, Ellie's brother. And he's got a way with the girls, they say. He won't go out with a girl for nothing, won't take no for an answer." Might as well lay it on thickly! "But the baby's not his."

Annabelle sat staring at the unopened letter in her hand. Could this tale really be true? She drew in a sudden sharp breath. Annie had been very quiet lately, and pale.

"And ma'am, she's been seen going into Dr Lewis's rooms. Late at night. On her own." The voice continued to drip its insidious poison.

The letter was suddenly screwed up in Annabelle's clenched fist. If Jeremy had been doing that – with her own maids – under her own roof . . . "That's enough, Mabel! You did right to tell me what you'd heard, but I'll attend to the matter myself from now on. Send Annie to me!"

Mabel curtsied and left the room. She found Annie in the kitchen. "You're wanted upstairs. She's found out about you know what." She looked suggestively at the girl's stomach.

Annie's face went chalk-white. Without a word she went upstairs, leaving a clamour of voices behind her.

Mrs Lewis looked at the best maid she had ever had and knew from her face that Mabel had been right. "So it *is* true. You *are* having a baby! You filthy little slut! After all I've done for you!"

Annie flinched. "It's not like that!" she said desperately. "It wasn't my fault! Please, ma'am . . ."

"I don't want to hear the sordid details. You may pack your things and leave. I do not tolerate immorality in my household!" The thought that Jeremy and this slut had actually dared to gratify their lusts under *her* roof made her feel physically sick.

"But, ma'am . . ."

"*Did you hear me?*"

Annie shrank back as Annabelle's fury boiled over.

"How dared you behave like that in a respectable household! How dared you! After all my kindness to you! Get out! Get out! *Get out!*" She was shrieking at the top of her voice. Making love to the master, then laying those same hands on the mistress! Revulsion coursed through her. "One hour! Make sure you're out within one hour!"

"What about my money, ma'am?" Face pale, but determined, Annie remained where she was. Now that the initial shock of being treated like that was over, she was determined to stand up for her rights.

"Money! You dare to ask for money!" Annabelle's voice rose to a piercing scream that could be heard all over the house. "*Just get out!* And be thankful I don't have you up before the magistrate for immorality."

Ellie, in Miss Marianne's rooms, pressed her hand to her mouth. Mabel, in the kitchen, smiled at Susan. Mrs Cosden rattled her pans and muttered under her breath.

Annie stood her ground.

Annabelle continued shrieking at the top of her voice, wanting only to get the girl out of her sight. "It's not money you need; it's a sound whipping!"

The door opened and Jeremy came in. "Please keep your voice down, Annabelle. You can be heard all over the house. What on earth is the matter?" He caught sight of Annie. "Oh!"

"You might well say 'Oh!'" said his wife viciously, her suspicions confirmed, she felt, by his reaction. "How dared you bring a slut like her into a respectable household? Into *my* house! How dared you?" Her voice was rising again.

"Annie's not a slut."

"Well, if you don't like the word, there are plenty of

others to choose from – whore, strumpet, fancy piece. Just take your pick!"

"Annie's none of those things."

"It's all right, sir. It doesn't matter what she calls me. They'll call me worse in the Rows. Only I've got to have my money, sir. I've earned it and – and I need it!" Her voice broke.

He turned to his wife. "How much is owing to Annie?"

"Nothing! One does not pay wages to a servant dismissed for improper conduct."

"How much is owing, Annie?"

"Two pounds, sir."

He felt in his pocket. "Here." He pressed a handful of change on Annie, much more than two pounds and folded her fingers round it when she opened her mouth to protest. Then he turned to his wife. "I'll deduct that from your next quarter's housekeeping allowance, Annabelle. We don't cheat those who work for us."

Two red spots were burning brightly in Annabelle's cheeks, but she said nothing. She would not so demean herself as to argue with him in front of the girl.

Annie turned to leave.

"Don't go yet, Annie," said Jeremy quietly. "My wife may not wish to know the truth, may not even believe us, but I intend to tell her exactly what happened in January. Sit down in this chair, please." For once, he was brooking no opposition; for once, Annabelle was not going to ride rough-shod over him.

"It doesn't matter, sir," Annie whispered, "really it doesn't!"

"Oh, yes, it does. My wife obviously believes that you are my mistress."

Annie gasped aloud at this and sat down. How could people think such things?

197

"In January," began Jeremy, "Annie was brutally raped on her way back here."

Annabelle sniffed disbelievingly. "So she says!"

"I found her in great distress, creeping in through my surgery. As a doctor, and *only* as a doctor, I examined her! She had been beaten and tied up – oh, yes, the marks of the cords were still on her wrists! – and she had obviously been a virgin when attacked."

He looked at his wife, willing her to show some sign of relenting from her self-righteous stance, but she just tossed her head. He sighed and continued. "I can't force you to believe this, Annabelle, but it is none the less the truth and I owe it to Annie to tell you – as I shall tell the other servants. A few days ago Annie came to me because she feared she was pregnant. Unfortunately she is. It seems grossly unfair."

Annabelle glared at him. "You're taking her side against me!"

"If you think that I would either bring a mistress into your house or molest one of your servants, then I can only say that it is *you* who have a filthy mind!"

He stopped and waited for her to say something, but she didn't speak, merely glared from him to Annie and back. He sighed. Annie had been right. Annabelle would not listen. And the other women with whom she associated would probably be the same. He felt sickened, as he always was by cruelty and injustice.

"Go and pack now, Annie," he said sadly. "I'm sorry you've been treated like this. If you ever need a reference, you may give my name. If you're ever in need, come to me."

When the girl had gone, Annabelle, bosom swelling with rage, stood up to leave, too.

"One moment, please," Jeremy said, his voice cold.

She stood there looking at him resentfully.

"Do you really believe that I took Annie as my mistress?" he asked. "My own wife's servant! And that I am lying to you now?"

"You took Mary. The fact that she was my servant didn't stop you then!"

"But you know that Mary didn't become my mistress until *after* you had dismissed her."

"She was a slut as well."

"Not until you ruined her life for some trivial offence – if there was an offence. I found her starving on the streets."

"It's a servant's place *not* to give offence," she stated, and her calm superiority sickened him. "It's a mistress's right to dismiss anyone who doesn't give satisfaction. *And*, Jeremy Lewis, if you ever speak to me again like that in front of a servant, I will make you rue the day!"

"I already rue the day I met you and I wish that I need never speak to you again as long as I live," he said wearily and turned to leave her. "What else you do is a matter of indifference to me. But, madam, if you take out your spite on anyone else, Ellie for instance, I shall halve your housekeeping and refuse to pay any more dress bills."

She watched him leave with murder in her heart, but did nothing to provoke further wrath. It was the servants who felt her anger and who had an extremely uncomfortable week or two, especially Ellie.

Annie packed her things quickly, managed to snatch a hurried word with Ellie, who was distraught and vowing that she would leave, too. Having made her friend promise to do nothing rash, Annie then walked slowly down the stairs. Taking a deep breath she entered the kitchen. She was not going to slink out as if she were ashamed of herself.

Mabel was standing there with a triumphant sneer on her

face. "Not so high and mighty now, are you?" she jeered.

Annie ignored her totally. "Goodbye, Mrs Cosden," she said quietly, "and thank you for all you've taught me."

Mrs Cosden looked at her reproachfully.

"Dr Lewis will confirm," said Annie, still in a tight, controlled voice, "that I was raped. I wouldn't like *you* to think badly of me, Mrs Cosden, though I don't care what others say."

The cook muttered something, then turned away.

Mabel stood holding the door open and grinning.

Annie took a deep breath. "I'll send someone for my box this evening, Mrs Cosden."

"The sooner the better!" said Mabel.

Annie didn't go straight back to Salem Street. She couldn't face it yet. She had thought she would never again have to live in such a place and now she was going back there in disgrace. It would be very hard to bear. It was all very hard to bear. She wished she were dead. She went and sat on one of the new wooden benches in the park, oblivious to the cold wind and equally oblivious to the beauty of the daffodils swaying under the trees.

How had word got round so quickly? That was what she didn't understand. It wasn't Dr Lewis, she was sure of that. He wouldn't tell anyone once he'd given his word. That left Ellie, her dad and Emily, and Matt. It hadn't been Ellie, and she didn't think Dad or Emily would have told anyone, either. They knew how much she needed the extra money she could earn. No, she reasoned, working her way through the people who knew, her father would not have told anyone and Emily was as close and secretive as her tightly-pursed mouth. How could her father have married someone like her after Lucy? At the thought of her dead mother, a tear trickled down Annie's face. Lucy would have stood by her if she'd been alive, stood by her and comforted her. Not offered the grudging help Emily had been forced into. Not turned away from her, like Matt!

Annie tried to tell herself that it was reasonable for Matt not to want another man's bastard, but the revulsion in his face had hurt her deeply. She'd seen that he couldn't even bear to touch her, and she, God help her, had longed even then, and still longed now, to feel his arms around her. She should hate him, she told herself fiercely. He was a coward and perhaps worse, for who else could have given her secret away? But she'd loved him for so long that she couldn't just turn that love off. Her greatest ambition had been to become Matt's wife. She'd have cooked good meals for him, kept his house clean – for she knew he was almost as fussy as his mother about cleanliness . . .

She dashed her hand angrily across her eyes. What use was it thinking of such things? That was all over. She must decide what to do now. She didn't have much choice for the moment. All she could do was pick up her bag and return home to Salem Street. But she wasn't going to stay there. She wasn't! She looked up at the grey sky and said it aloud for emphasis. "I won't stay there!"

Emily's reception of her was chill and unfriendly. "What are *you* doin' here? I thought you were goin' t'work till it showed?"

"I couldn't. Someone told Mrs Lewis about it and she turned me off. Did you or Dad tell anyone?"

"What d'ye take us for? Let alone we need the money you could've earned, it's not somethin' we'd go boastin' about, is it?"

"What's our Annie talkin' about, Mam?" asked May, who'd been sitting quietly in a corner, listening.

"Never you mind!" her mother told her sharply.

"She's bound to find out," said Annie. "She might as well hear the truth."

"Aye, I suppose so." Emily turned to her daughter and spoke curtly. "Annie got attacked by a man one night an' she's goin' to have a baby from it. She's just lost her place with Dr Lewis because of it as well, so she's comin' back here to live."

May's pale, protuberant eyes nearly started out of her head. She opened her mouth to make a comment and her mother told her savagely that she wasn't to talk about it to anyone, *not anyone*, or she'd take a belt to her.

"I thought your May went to Granny Marker's school," said Annie. "What's she doing at home? Is she ill?"

Emily flushed. "We – we've had a bad patch. We didn't have the pennies to send her to school."

"Oh."

"An' I don't know how we're goin' t'manage with *you* here t'feed either, let alone findin' t'beddin' for you. We've no spare blankets, none at all."

"I'm sorry, Emily. I really am. I did try to go on working. If it wasn't you or Dad who let my news out, it must have been Matt Peters. He's the only other person who knew."

"What would he want to do that for? He might not want to marry you himself now, but he wouldn't go an' do somethin' like that, surely! I mean – it's not your fault, is it? It's not as if you done it on purpose." Emily shook her head and looked at her stepdaughter with something approaching sympathy.

"No, it's not my fault, but who's going to believe that? The doctor spoke up for me to Mrs Lewis, but it made no difference. She still turned me off."

For the rest of the day Annie helped Emily in the house and Emily had to admit grudgingly that the girl wasn't afraid of hard work. In fact she threw herself into the cleaning like one possessed. "You sit back and have a rest, Emily. I'll do this."

Emily sat back, but she felt resentful. John would be bound to notice the difference.

Later Annie produced a shilling. "I don't eat much," she told Emily, "so I reckon three shillings a week should be enough to pay for my food. I'll give it you every day or two." If it had been her mother, she'd have tipped all her money out on the table and together they'd have schemed to make it last as long as possible. But you might as well throw money away as give it to Emily. She spent foolishly, even on food, and it was always either feast or famine at Number Three. No wonder Tom refused to hand over all his wages!

Annie had no intention of telling Emily that she had several guineas saved. Her money was sewn up in her best petticoat, a trick the nursemaid, Katy, had taught her, and after they'd all gone to bed tonight, she would sew up the money Dr Lewis had given her. Seeing the sudden greed in Emily's eyes, Annie resolved to wear that money petticoat all the time until she was able to make some proper plans and arrangements.

When John came home, he was deeply upset that Annie had been turned off and said at once that she must now consider this her home. When she told him her suspicions about how the news had got out, he was for going straight along to Number Seven and confronting Matt Peters. With difficulty Annie dissuaded him from doing this and made him promise to leave that to her. After he'd eaten she asked him to go round to Park House for her box. He'd have to borrow Barmy Charlie's handcart, for it was heavy. "You'll need sixpence for that," she said, trying to press it into his hands.

"No, I don't think so. I've done old Charlie a favour or two. If I tell him why we need the cart, he won't charge me now. You keep your sixpence, love. You're goin' to need it. He's all right, Charlie Ashworth is. An' he'd not be so barmy if folks left him in peace."

Only when her father had left did Annie steel herself to go along to Number Seven. "I want to see what he has to say for himself," she told Emily. There was no need to explain who the 'he' was. "I also want to make sure Mr and Mrs Peters know the truth. They've been good to me, especially Mr Peters, and Ellie's still my friend."

Tom, who'd come in late and who was wolfing down his meal, told her that she was wasting her time. "It's all round t'Rows that you're no better than you ought to be," he told her. "You might as well face up to that an' find yourself a cosy little nest, like Sally Smith. She's done all right for herself, an' you've got twice her style."

His words were cut short by Emily clouting him on the side of the head. "I've told you afore that I'll 'ave no such talk in here!" she shouted. "You godless young devil! As long as you live under my roof, you'll watch your tongue. We might be poor, but we're decent folk an' we don't talk like that."

"Aye, well, I won't be here for much longer!" he shouted back at her. "An' if you ever try clouting me again, I'll clout you back, an' a damn sight harder than you c'n manage, too! Have you told Annie about your little gin bottle yet?"

Emily flinched away from him, her face going red.

Tom swung round to his sister. "She hides it under the stairs, Annie. Takes a nip now an' then to keep the cold out. Thinks I don't know about it. Dad doesn't, but he will if she causes any more trouble for me!" He pushed his plate away, grinned at the shock on Annie's face and swaggered out of the house. "Don't bother to wait up for me!" he called back over his shoulder. "I'll be late. An' you think over what I said, our Annie! You could earn yourself a mint of money once you've had the little bugger. But don't think for too long. There might even be time still to get rid of it, if you want. I've got friends who'd help."

"Good riddance!" said Lizzie as the door slammed behind him. "He's in with a rough crowd, our Tom is. He'll get hisself into trouble one of these days." She looked at Emily. "Where's our Annie goin' t'sleep, Mam? Me an' May think she should sleep in t'kitchen. We don't want her in our room. We've got Becky already an' we're not havin' *her* in our bed as well! An' there's only room for the boys' bed as well as ours."

Her fat white face became faintly pink from the vehemence of her feelings, then resumed its customary pallor. She'd been unlovely as a child, but she was positively ugly now she was twelve, her features heavy, her gingerish hair unflattering and her eyes filled with slyness and malice. Contrary to Annie's fears, Lizzie had coped well with working in the mill. She wasn't sluggish where her own safety and welfare were concerned, just about doing things for other people. She and May were as close as real sisters and presented a solid front of hostility to Annie every time she came round.

It was only a few hours since Annie had returned to Number Three, but she was already wondering how she would stand the crowded conditions and lack of privacy in the tiny house. It was a relief to close the door behind her and walk along to the Peters' house, even though she wasn't looking forward to the interview.

Sam Peters opened the door. "Annie! I didn't expect to see you, lass!" He seemed embarrassed. "I was sorry to hear about your trouble with Mrs Lewis."

"Yes. Thank you. Is Matt in?"

"Er, yes, but . . ."

"I know he won't want to see me, but I have to speak to him."

"Are you sure that's wise, love?"

"I *have* to speak to him," she repeated.

"Aye, well, you'd better come in, then." He held the door open and she stepped past him, head held high.

"Good evening, Mrs Peters, Matt," she said quietly.

"Annie!" Elizabeth flushed and looked at her son, who, after a first horrified glance at Annie, stared pointedly into the fire.

"I want a word with Matt. No, don't go away! I'd like you and Mr Peters to hear what I have to say. But I think it'd be better if the children went into the back room, perhaps. That's up to you, though."

"Go into the kitchen, you kids," Sam said quietly. "An' no listenin' at the door, or I'll tan your backsides."

"It's no use, Annie," Matt blurted out, "I haven't changed my mind."

She ignored him completely until the children had filed into the kitchen and Sam had shut the door between the two rooms. Three-year-old Jonas was asleep in front of the fire and they left him there, his thumb in his mouth, his rosy, peaceful face bearing a strong resemblance to his elder brother. The thought that this was what Matt's sons would look like brought a lump to Annie's throat, but she swallowed it resolutely. She'd get nowhere if she weakened. Life had been hard on her and she was just about to give her first demonstration of the lessons she'd learned in the past few weeks.

"The word seems to have got round that I'm expecting a baby," she began, "so I thought you'd better hear the truth about how I got it."

"There's no need," said Elizabeth, seeing that Matt didn't intend to speak. "That's your business."

"Oh, no! I insist!" said Annie, in the clear unaccented

English she had learned at Park House. She might have to live in Salem Street, but she had no intention of sliding back into slack speech and dirty ways. Her whole bearing and voice had a dignity of which she was unaware, but which made a strong impression on the others, as she recounted the sordid events of that night in January.

"If you don't believe me," she finished, "you can ask Dr Lewis, who will be glad to bear out what I have said."

"Nay, we believe you, lass," said Sam, when neither of the other two spoke. "We've known you since you were a child. We know you don't flirt and lead men on. And I'd've been glad to have had you as a daughter, Annie. Still would be."

Matt avoided looking at Annie, staring into the fire as if his life depended on it. He knew that his father thought less of him for abandoning Annie. He knew it was cowardly and he thought less of himself, but he couldn't ruin his life by marrying her now. Mr Hallam was speaking of a course of training, trips to other mills, a bright future. All right for a single man, but not for one with a wife and child to support. And besides, he couldn't – no, he just could *not* touch Annie now. There she stood, as lovely as ever, the baby not even showing in her body, but to him she was dirtied, defiled. He was sorry that he'd betrayed her, though. They were right when they told you not to drink; he'd never touch the stuff again as long as he lived. He regretted most bitterly what he'd done and wished there were some way to atone – but even that regret was not enough to make him marry her.

"Thank you, Mr Peters," Annie was saying to his father.

What did she want, Matt wondered? Why had she come? He looked at his mother for support and she nodded encouragingly at him.

"It was you who told people about me, wasn't it, Matt?"

Annie said suddenly, moving round so that he had to face her.

He raised his head and looked her in the eyes for the first time. "Yes. I was drunk. I don't really remember what I said. It's no excuse, but I'm sorry."

"I'm sorry too, because I lost my job this morning as a result of your loose tongue."

The scorn in her voice! He winced and dropped his eyes again.

"I'll try to get another job," she said, "but times aren't easy and all I know is being in service. I'd have been able to work for another three months but for you, Matt, so I think you owe me some compensation for what you did. I still have to live, you see. Three months is two pounds ten shillings in wages. I know you don't want to marry me now, but I do think that morally you owe me that money."

Three people were staring at her in shock. This was the last thing any of them had expected.

"Nay, lass, that's a bit thick!" exclaimed Sam.

"You cheap hussy!" cried Elizabeth.

Matt realised with a lift of his heart that here lay his way of atonement. "All right," he said.

"You'll not do it, Matthew Peters!" shouted his mother. "Annie Gibson, I never thought I'd see the day . . ."

Annie cut her short. "I never thought I'd see the day either, Mrs Peters," she said, with her new-found hardness. "I didn't think I'd get raped – did Matt tell you that it was partly in revenge for something he'd done? No, I thought not! – and I didn't think Matt would let me down. Do you know, my own brother suggested today that I become a whore? I didn't expect that, either. And I'm not going on the streets!"

They gasped in unison at this blunt speech, but she continued to speak calmly and slowly, as she had planned.

"I don't intend to become a whore, but I don't intend to starve, either. And there'll be the baby to think about, too. So I'm going to need as much money as I can get, aren't I? It's letting you off cheaply, really, Matt, isn't it? I can see the relief in your face. Your conscience will be clear now, because you'll have paid your debt to me. You can wash your hands of me, just like Pontius Pilate."

He ignored that gibe and stood up, anxious not to prolong the interview. "Give her two pounds ten out of the savings, Mam."

"I'll not!"

"It's *my* money. If you don't get it, I will." Their eyes locked for a long minute, two pairs of bright blue eyes in two pink, well-scrubbed faces. After a moment, Elizabeth's eyes dropped and she went into the back room.

"Here!" she said, and flung the money at Annie's feet. Annie sighed and stooped to pick it up. Sam moved across to help her and pressed her hand as he put some coins into it. "Thank you," she said, near to breaking down. "I shan't bother you again."

Once outside she leaned against the wall, because she suddenly felt too weak to stand up without support. She was shaking uncontrollably. "Oh, Matt!" she whispered. "Matt, Matt, Matt!"

After a few moments, she moved slowly back along the dark street. She'd not let herself care, she told herself, that she'd blackmailed the money out of Matt. She wouldn't let herself care, either, what the Peters family thought of her. All she would let herself care about from now on was money. If she managed to scrape enough of it together to see her through till the baby was born, she'd not have to sell her body to live. She didn't think she could bear to do that under any circumstances. And afterwards, after the child was born, she'd find something to do, something away from

209

Salem Street, away from Bilsden, too, if she could manage it.

She would make that her future goal and would concern herself now only with earning money. She wouldn't ever be able to marry anyone decent, after what had happened, and anyway, she didn't want a man to touch her body again, not as long as she lived. Fred Coxton had spoiled her for that. Perhaps she could move away and pretend she was a widow. Dr Lewis had said he would give her a reference. And whatever she did, she'd stay respectable. She would, if it killed her! Other people could think what they liked about her, but she could live with herself despite all that had happened if only she stayed respectable.

13

April to May 1838

The next day, after an almost sleepless night on the kitchen floor, lying on a makeshift bed of old sacks and covered with her cloak, Annie let her stepmother persuade her into going to see the minister, Mr Hinchcliffe. Emily was most insistent that they do this. She seemed to have complete faith in his ability to solve the problem. Annie could not see what good it would do, but she was willing to try anything.

Mr Hinchcliffe lived in the end house of a new terrace belonging to Mr Hallam. The houses in Durham Road were bigger than average, designed for the new generation of skilled workers and supervisors. It was just outside the Rows, near the chapel.

Emily and Annie found Saul Hinchcliffe at home and were at once invited in and offered a seat in his front room. Annie, who had never been inside his house before, looked around curiously. It was amazing what a difference a bit of good furniture and a carpet made. Even living in Salem Street would not be too bad if you could surround yourself with a few comforts like these.

Sighing, Annie leaned back against the leather upholstery of the armchair, enjoying the comfort and listening to Emily mouthing a few polite phrases about the Sunday service. What Annie most envied the minister, after his

211

furniture, was his books. He had several shelves full of them. She'd have given a lot to be able to read all those books sitting here in this cheerful room. How lucky some people were! No one would ever tip Mr Hinchcliffe out of his cosy little nest. She sighed again and tried to keep her attention on what Emily was saying.

"It's Annie we've come about, Mr Hinchcliffe. She's in a bit of trouble, lost her place, you see. An' it's not her fault. She's done nothin' wrong. So I – we – we wondered if you could 'elp us. She needs to find work for a few months. There's not room for her in our house an' we haven't the money to keep her, anyway, let alone the child."

Emily was most worried of all about the money side of things. She could never seem to make ends meet. Annie obviously had a bit saved, but how much? And how could she be made to give it to them? She had refused point-blank to do so, or even to tell Emily how much she had, and that wasn't right. Children should give all their earnings straight to their parents. It was only fair, a return for bringing them up. Besides, it was needed. Few men earned enough to feed and clothe a growing family and every extra penny helped. But Annie had said no, and John had backed her up, as long as she paid for her keep. She was to give them three shillings a week and help Emily in the house, and the rest was her own business.

A hasty search through Annie's bundle when she was out at Sally's had revealed nothing and the big tin box was locked. Somehow Emily had not dared to break the flimsy lock, for fear of what John would say. But it was a crying shame if Annie, who had so much, didn't even share the clothes she'd brought with her from Park House with her sisters and her stepmother, who had so little.

Emily prayed with all her heart that the minister would be able to help them. She didn't want Annie living with them, cleaning things up and cooking fancy meals, till you hardly knew your own house. And the girl took all John's attention, as well as spoiling Becky, making a pet of her!

Annie sat in stony-faced silence while Emily told Mr Hinchcliffe the story of Fred Coxton's brutal attack and its consequences. She was tired of going over it again and again. She just wanted to forget it as best she could.

Saul Hinchcliffe looked at the young woman sitting in front of him. So far she'd hardly said a word. She was very pretty, and neatly dressed, but she looked pale and tired. He remembered having her in one of his Sunday School classes when he'd first come to Bilsden. She'd been a bright little thing, eager to learn. A pity she'd not been a boy, with a brain like hers. Her brother was a surly lad, sharp enough when he bothered, but only willing to exert himself in his own interests. What a shame that this terrible thing had happened to her! He would check it all out with Dr Lewis, of course, but he was inclined to believe the tale. The Lord's will was very hard to fathom sometimes and even harder to accept.

"I thought – aren't you going to marry young Matt Peters?" he asked in puzzlement when Emily had finished. "Surely . . ."

"I was going to marry him. Not any longer," said Annie. "He doesn't want me now."

She spoke calmly, but he could see the pain in her eyes. "I'm sorry," he said gently. "Shall I have a word with him?" A true Christian would not have abandoned the girl like that. The lad put too much emphasis on material advancement. He'd admitted as much a while ago. Of course, you couldn't blame him in one sense. Taking on someone else's bastard would be a hard thing. Still, it was a shame. It would have been the easiest way of solving Annie's problems.

213

"No, thank you," she replied quietly. "It'd do no good."
"Do you know of anyone as wants some extra help in their house, Mr Hinchcliffe?" pressed Emily. "It's not goin' to be easy for us if Annie can't put away a bit now to tide 'erself over. And we haven't room for 'er. She has to sleep on t'kitchen floor an' Tom sleeps in the front room. What we'll do when t'babby comes, I don't know, I just don't know!" She mopped her eyes with a corner of her shawl.

"I can't promise anything, Mrs Gibson, but I may be able to help you. Leave the problem with me and I'll ask – er – someone I know who may be able to help. Could you come round at, say, three o'clock tomorrow afternoon, Annie? Alone might be best, I think. I may have some news for you by then, and if not, we could pray together."

"Yes, sir," said Annie, but without much real hope. She might as well give him a chance. And if it cost her a few hours of praying to a God she no longer believed in, well, this was a nice warm house and it would be a relief to be out of Number Three.

When Annie went back to Durham Road the next afternoon, she found Mr Hinchcliffe entertaining a pale, thin-faced lady, who had called at the Lewis's once or twice. He was behaving with a degree of deference amazing in one who preached that all people were brothers and sisters in Christ. Annie couldn't remember the lady's name, because she wasn't one of Mrs Lewis's close friends or even, she thought, searching her memory, one of her former mistress's regular acquaintances. The lady was quite old, thirty at least, and plainly, but expensively dressed, with her sandy hair pulled back into an unflattering knot, rather like Emily's. Someone should teach her how to make the most of herself, thought Annie, remembering the care and effort that had gone into the adornment of Mrs Lewis's person. But it probably wouldn't have done much good, because this lady had a certain look on her face which said she wasn't particularly interested in attracting the attention of the opposite sex, a sort of no-nonsense, I'm-doing-very-well-thank-you, look.

"Come in, Annie," said Mr Hinchcliffe encouragingly, mistaking her hesitation for nervousness. "This is Miss Collett, who may be able to help you."

That's it, thought Annie, Collett! How could I have forgotten? The richest family in the district, old money, Mrs Lewis had said once, landowners, but with business interests, too. Mrs Lewis had been piqued when Miss Collett refused her overtures of closer friendship.

Mr Hinchcliffe was speaking again. "Miss Collett lives outside town, Annie, at Netherden. She has a large house there. She has recently become a member of our congregation."

Annie knew what was expected of her and dropped a curtsey. "Good afternoon, miss."

"Good afternoon, Annie." The woman's voice was cold and devoid of any warmth or real interest in Annie and her problems.

She didn't seem the type who would go in for charity work, thought Annie cynically. You could usually spot them a mile off. And what was she doing joining the Methodists? She didn't seem the type for that, either. Landed gentry usually attended St Mark's.

This time no one asked Annie to sit down. It would never have occurred to Pauline Collett to allow a servant to sit in her presence, unless it was necessary for some task or other. And at her request, Saul Hinchcliffe was leaving this interview entirely to his visitor, of whom he was slightly in awe.

Pauline Collett was a wealthy woman in her own right and had been since the age of twenty-two, when her father died and left her, for lack of a male heir, the family fortune and estate. She had, even by that age, resigned herself to spinsterdom. There were few eligible gentlemen in Bilsden and those few had shown little sign of being interested in anything but pale, colourless Pauline Collett's prospects of inheriting money. When she was in full possession of her father's fortune the same gentlemen had intensified their pursuit, but Pauline had found she enjoyed the power of her money, and was not going to be fooled into making any gentleman a present of it and then retiring to breed his children while he continued to enjoy himself.

However, eight years later, she had begun to tire of her single state and to feel lonely and unfulfilled. And what would happen to Collett Hall when she died? She had decided that she must marry and have children. But she would not marry a man who would take the management of her fortune out of her own very capable hands! The law was cruel to women, handing all their money over to their husbands. So Pauline had set out to survey the neighbourhood and find someone who would not try to take over.

She had noticed Saul Hinchcliffe one day in Bilsden's High Street, and had thought him a fine figure of a man. It hadn't taken her very long to find out who he was and she had started going to Todmorden Road Chapel in order to get to know him better. Netherden, where she lived, was too small a hamlet to have its own church and she was not a regular attender at any other church or chapel, preferring to stay home during the worst of the winter and to choose her church in summer according to which route she felt like driving along. You could afford to be eccentric when you were rich.

Liking what she saw of Mr Hinchcliffe, Pauline began to give lavishly to the chapel furnishing fund and to look around for other ways of involving herself with him.

Heavens, what a primitive, uncomfortable place the chapel was! She allowed Saul to lead her to salvation, and she then took over the Ladies' Charity Committee. Her pursuit of the young minister was very circumspect. She had no intention of providing a raree-show for her fellow Methodists, let alone for the other people in the town.

Unaware of her designs on him, Saul was delighted with his helpful new chapel member and was fooled by her many charitable acts into believing that she was behaving simply as a caring Christian. Gradually, he learned to enjoy her company and to admire her fine brain, as well as to turn to her for help and advice about any female member of the congregation who had problems.

He sat there now, nodding approvingly as Miss Collett conducted the interview in her own way. He looked plump and smug and pink, no longer the zealous young minister with a poor congregation, but the established incumbent of an expanding and thriving chapel.

"I believe you are expecting a child, Annie?"

"Yes, miss."

"Mr Hinchcliffe has told me your story and I have verified it with Dr Lewis."

Annie lowered her eyes to conceal the anger that this statement aroused in her. She couldn't afford to be angry.

"Dr Lewis also explained his wife's misinterpretation of the situation as the reason why she would not give you a reference. It was a most unchristian act to turn you out like that!" Pauline Collett did not like Annabelle Lewis, which had also influenced her in Annie's favour. She noted the approving nod from Saul Hinchcliffe and reflected cynically that this might be just the thing to provide her with an excuse for seeing more of him. "What exactly were your duties at Park House?"

"I went there as a general maid when I was twelve, miss.

217

Later I became a parlourmaid, then personal maid to Mrs Lewis. I did a lot of sewing. Before this – thing – happened, I believe that Mrs Lewis was very satisfied with my work."

Presumably the girl had also learnt to speak properly in the Lewis household. She seemed to be a sharp little piece and would bear careful watching. Pauline was, however, inclined to believe her story. It had a ring of truth to it, and she liked and trusted Jeremy Lewis as much as she disliked his wife. He had spoken very highly of Annie, said he had known her from a child. It would seem strange to have a pregnant maid around, but it would be worth it. She would need, Pauline thought, smiling to herself, to consult Saul very regularly about Annie's welfare.

"Very well, then. I am prepared to offer you a position as a general maid. You may also help with the household sewing. When is your baby due?"

"In late September or early October, miss." Annie kept all expression out of her voice and face.

"In that case, you will leave my service at the beginning of September and return to your family until after the child is born. If you're able to make arrangements to have it cared for, and if your work has been satisfactory, you may later return to my employment.

"Thank you, miss. I'm very grateful. And – and what about wages?"

Miss Collett frowned. It was, she considered, impertinent to ask this when the girl should just have been thanking providence for a roof over her head. On the other hand, it argued a realistic approach to her situation. "Five pounds a year and all found."

The old skinflint! thought Annie. Even Mrs Lewis paid more than that. "Thank you, miss," she said aloud. "When shall I start and how do I get to Netherden?"

"I presume you can start immediately?"

"Oh, yes, miss. I'd prefer to, miss."

"You may go home now to fetch your box. Meet me here in an hour – if Mr Hinchcliffe will allow me to wait here for you?" She raised an eyebrow enquiringly at her host and he hastened to assure her that he and his home were both entirely at her service. His daily housekeeper was still in the kitchen and would, he was sure, make them both some tea.

Annie curtsied herself out, then walked quickly back to Salem Street. She told Emily what had happened. She would have to borrow Barmy Charlie's handcart for her box. May agreed sulkily to come with her to the minister's house and trundle the empty cart back for a halfpenny.

Barmy Charlie opened the door of Number Eight and stood there peering at her. It was funny, but before he'd always seemed very old to her and now she realised that he wasn't any older than her father. He didn't seem all that barmy, either, today, just a bit slow.

He smiled at her. "I was sorry to hear about your trouble, lass."

"Thank you, Mr Ashworth. Can I borrow your hand-cart? I've got myself a job with Miss Collett, and I have to take my things along to Mr Hinchcliffe's house, so that I can go back with her."

"Of course you can borrow it! An' I'll come with you myself to push the cart and bring it back. That's what I'll do. Yes, I will. We should all help one another. We should."

"That's very kind of you, Mr Ashworth. Er – it's sixpence, isn't it, for borrowing the cart?"

"Nay, I don't want nothin' from you, lass. If we can't help one another when we're in trouble, it's a poor look-out, it is that. An' you'll have enough other things to pay for. No, I'll lend you the cart an' come with you to push it. I will. That's what I'll do."

219

Tears came to her eyes at this kindness from an unexpected source. "Thank you, Mr Ashworth."

"An' if there's owt else I c'n do, lass, you just let me know. Yes. Let me know. I'll start looking out for a cradle for the baby. I get 'em sometimes. You'll need a cradle. An' I'll find you one. I will."

She tried to smile at him, but it was a poor effort, she was so touched by this unexpected kindness from a near stranger. "Thank you, Mr Ashworth," she whispered, close to weeping, then turned to her stepsister. "I shan't need you after all, May."

"You promised me a ha'penny. I come out of the warm house for you."

"So you did. And I've said thank you." She stared at the pale eyes. She liked May less the more she got to know her. Besides, she was glad to save her sixpence ha'penny. She resented spending even a farthing at the moment. Fancy Barmy Charlie being so kind to her! "I'll be ready in a few minutes, Mr Ashworth," she said. "I'm really grateful for your help."

"It's a pleasure, lass, a great pleasure. I'd like to help you. I would that." He stood in the doorway and watched her walk briskly back down the street, sighing. He wished he could help her more. What a pretty lass she was, and kind. She'd never thrown things at him like the other kids had.

It didn't take Annie long to get her things ready. She could tell that Emily was pleased to see her go. Well, she was pleased to be going. She hated Salem Street.

"Will you tell Dad for me?" she asked.

"Oh, aye," said Emily. "I'll tell him. You've been lucky, Annie, an' I hope you show your appreciation to Miss Collett."

"She'll have no cause to complain about my work."

"No. You're a good worker. I'll say that for you."

"And – I'll be back at the beginning of September."

"Mmm." There was no enthusiasm in Emily's voice.

Annie put two shillings down on the table. "That's to help out a bit," she said, knowing that she had to buy Emily's goodwill from now on. If her stepmother thought that there was money to be had from helping her, she'd not cause any trouble about letting her come back to have the baby.

Emily's face brightened a little. "Oh, thanks. That'll be a big help."

"Well, you *are* my family, aren't you?"

Emily nodded and picked up the money, eyes gleaming.

"Is it all right if I come here on my days off?"

"Yes. Yes, that'll be all right."

And no doubt she'll expect a contribution every time, too, thought Annie. "Well, I'll be going, then."

"Yes. You look after yourself. I'll tell your dad what's happened. He'll be right glad for you."

May scowled behind her and stuck out her tongue at Annie. It was a relief to turn round and see Charlie's smiling face.

Collett Hall was a big grey-stone house on the edge of the moors. It stood squarely on top of a slight rise, as if defying the elements to do their worst. Rain lashed against it, the wind screamed against the window-panes and all around were stunted, wind-bent trees. Annie, perched on the outside of Miss Collett's carriage, was soaked to the skin and shivering by the time they got there. Even Mrs Lewis had let her ride inside. This didn't bode well.

The coachman beside her was a dour old man and not inclined to gossip, so she'd found out very little, either about her new employer or about the household. She didn't fancy the job. She was sure that Miss Collett would be a hard taskmistress. Well, beggars can't be choosers, she told herself, gritting her chattering teeth. At least it'd get her out of Salem Street and keep her fed until the baby was nearly due. And she'd be able to add a bit to her savings, too. She was lucky, really. But she didn't feel lucky at the moment, just cold and alone.

She followed Miss Collett into the house and was kept waiting in the entrance hall in her wet things until her mistress had changed and had a cup of tea. She tried not to shiver, but she was so very cold.

At last a plump maid came up to her. "You're wanted in the parlour," she said. She showed Annie where to go, then left.

There was another woman with Miss Collett, who turned out to be the housekeeper.

"I've told Mrs Marsh your story," Miss Collett said. "I shall expect you to work hard and to give satisfaction, Annie. You're not to gossip about your condition. Mrs Marsh will tell the other servants all they need to know and then it need not be mentioned again. Is that clear?"

"Yes, miss."

"That's all."

Still shivering, Annie followed Mrs Marsh to the housekeeper's sitting-room. Here she was at last allowed to warm herself by a fire and was given a cup of tea. Mrs Marsh questioned her carefully about what she had done at Park House and seemed pleased by her answers.

"I'll put you to work with Rose," she said at last. "She'll show you what to do. Miss Collett wants the whole house spring-cleaned, so we'll be glad of another pair of hands. Later on, when you're getting a bit big for heavy work, we'll give you some sewing to do. There's plenty of that, too. Now, if you'll take my advice, Annie, you'll remember exactly what the mistress said and not gossip about your condition. She doesn't like to be disobeyed in any way. She's very strict about that."

"Yes, Mrs Marsh."

Annie hated life at Collett Hall from the start. The house itself made her uneasy. It was dark, even on a sunny day, and she wouldn't have been surprised if it'd been haunted, except that no ghost would have dared to intrude uninvited on Pauline Collett. The wind was for ever sighing and moaning round the house, too, which unsettled town-bred Annie. She wasn't used to such bleak, open spaces. She decided that she preferred even the Rows to this – though not Emily's house, of course.

The other staff treated her like an animal which might bite. They were not actively hostile or unfriendly, but they kept their distance. There were ten indoor servants, all female, ruled fairly, but with a rod of iron, by Mrs Marsh, who was in turn ruled by Miss Collett. They worked from five in the morning until eight or nine at night, with an hour's break during the afternoon, and were then allowed to sit around the fire in the servants' hall until ten o'clock, when they must go to bed. These were better conditions than many employers offered, but Annie found herself so tired at nights that more often than not she went straight to bed after her work was finished.

From Rose, who was nearly forty and who had worked for the Colletts all her life, Annie learned a little about The Family, of whom Rose spoke in tones of awe. Old Mrs Collett had died when the mistress was fifteen and Miss Pauline had taken over the housekeeping straight away. She was clever, was Miss Pauline. You should see the books she read and the newspapers that came for her from London.

Rose never mentioned Annie's condition, nor did the

other servants. Miss Collett had forbidden it, so they didn't even whisper about it when they were on their own. They were like a bunch of silly sheep, thought Annie, and Miss Collett the shepherd.

On the second Sunday after her arrival there, Annie was told to get ready for chapel. Miss Collett would take her into Bilsden to the service and then she could have two hours with her family. Annie guessed that she was to be shown off to Mr Hinchcliffe and the Ladies' Charity Committee, who met each week. She didn't mind too much. It'd give her a bit of a rest and she'd like to see her dad. She hoped it wouldn't rain, though. Her only worry was that she'd have to see Matt at chapel, and she wished, she wished very desperately, that she need never see him again.

Matt had been relieved when Annie got a job and left the street. Her pale unhappy face was a reminder of things he would rather forget and it seemed to loom at him accusingly wherever he went. His mother had said he should ask for his money back now Annie had a job, but he wouldn't. Giving it had eased his conscience a little. He'd told his mother to mind her own business and had refused to talk about it any more. These days he didn't discuss many things with his parents.

Sam grieved over this distance between them and prayed hard for guidance from the Lord, but he could make no headway with his stubborn son, who remained polite, but uncommunicative.

Mr Hinchcliffe had had a word with Matt, and with him Matt was a bit more open. He was not proud of himself, he agreed, but he couldn't marry Annie now. He just couldn't have brought himself to touch her. No, he knew it was not her fault, but that didn't make any difference to how he felt. There were things you could do and things you

224

couldn't do. Marrying Annie was something he couldn't do any more. He was going to concentrate on his work from now on; he would study a lot and leave women alone until he was much older.

It came as an unpleasant surprise to Matt, therefore, that Sunday, when Annie walked into chapel behind Miss Collett and quietly joined her parents at the rear. He couldn't help gasping aloud when he saw her and then he could feel himself going red. He had felt guilty every time he had seen her in the street, but he felt worse here in the Lord's house.

Annie's eyes swept coolly across his face, but she gave no sign of even recognising him. She did, however, smile in genuine pleasure when she saw that Ellie was there. She'd forgotten that it was Ellie's Sunday off. Ellie beamed back at her.

After the service, Annie waited until Miss Collett nodded dismissal, then went off with her parents. She had two whole hours free. As they passed the Peters family, she smiled at Ellie, who called out that she'd meet her in an hour's time, ignoring the nudge her mother gave her.

In Number Three, John treated Annie like an honoured guest, to Emily's disgust. He sat her down with him in front of the fire and wanted to know all about her new place. "I was fair set up when our Em'ly told me you'd got a place," he said. "It was a good idea of Em'ly's, goin' to see Mr Hinchcliffe, wasn't it? She's a good woman, she is." It wasn't clear whether he meant Emily or Miss Collett, but Emily was smirking by this time.

"Yes. I'm very grateful to you, Emily." Annie picked up her basket. "Mrs Marsh, the housekeeper, gave me some food to bring home. She's all right, is Mrs Marsh, as long as you do your job."

"There now. Fancy that!" said John. "You just be sure to

thank her kindly from us." Once he would have scorned to take charity, she thought sadly.

Emily unpacked the basket, eyes glistening. She added the loaf from it to the stuff on the table. The packet of tea she put carefully to one side, together with the generous wedge of cheese and the bag of somewhat withered apples.

"You've fallen on your feet there," she said to Annie. "Don't you do anythin' to upset that Miss Collett – or the 'ousekeeper. You don't want to lose this place!"

"No, I'll be careful," said Annie wearily, not bothering to point out that it hadn't been her fault that she had lost her other place.

"Are you sure you'll be all right out there, love?" asked John. "You seem – well – a bit quiet-like."

"I'm just tired. I get tired more easily now."

"Oh, aye, I was forgettin'. It don't even show yet, does it? Eh, it's a rare pity the first grandchild 'ad ter come this way! I'd been lookin' forward to havin' grandchilder." He had always loved children.

"It's a pity that that Matt Peters didn't stand by you," said Lizzie, jealous of the attention her sister was getting. "Addy says their Ellie'll not speak to their Matt no more. Are *you* goin' t'speak to 'im, our Annie?"

"Not unless I have to."

"I don't blame him," said Lizzie, with a toss of her head. "No man'd want you like that!"

"Lizzie!" thundered John.

"Well, how could he take another man's leavin's?"

John's hand shot out and cracked her across the face, he who rarely laid a finger on his children. Lizzie's heavy lids flickered over her dull-pebble eyes, but she said nothing. You couldn't control Lizzie with thumps; you couldn't seem to get at her with anything. John never admitted, even to himself, how much he disliked her. She'd been an unattractive child and she was growing into a strange sort of woman, nasty and unwholesome, somehow. He couldn't see any man ever wanting to marry *her*, more's the pity. Only May seemed to like her; the two of them were devoted to each other. And May was nearly as bad as Lizzie. But the other little 'uns were as nice as their two sisters were nasty. His eyes softened as they lingered for a moment on little Becky.

Annie ignored Lizzie. As soon as the meal was over she said her goodbyes and went out to join Ellie. With Mrs Marsh giving her the food, at least she did not feel the need to slip Emily any money.

The two young women threw themselves into each other's arms, then started off for a walk around town. It was cold but fine, and how lovely it was, Annie thought, to see so many people after the bleak loneliness of the moors around Collett Hall. She walked down the High Street, trying to ignore the speculative glances she got from people who knew her and concentrated on exchanging as much news as she could with Ellie.

"Mrs Lewis has a new maid called Cora. Got her from an agency in Manchester. She's an experienced lady's maid." Ellie pulled a face. "I can't stand her and she has to share my room. It's awful!"

"Never you mind. You keep her in her place. You're the nursery maid, not a skivvy. She's no call to look down on you." Annie sighed. "I'm in a bedroom of my own and that's worse, I can tell you. The other servants are all about a hundred and they keep their distance. There's no one young there and I've got no one to talk to. And I absolutely hate that house! The wind never stops blowing up there. It drives you mad. If I had *her* money, I'd not live in a place like Netherden." They walked on for a few moments, then Annie said with relish, "I'm glad Mabel didn't get the job, though. Serves her right, spiteful old cat!"

Ellie giggled. "Well, she's wild with jealousy and she hates Cora even worse than she hated you. If looks could kill . . ." She then remembered her own big piece of news. "Guess what! Mrs Lewis is going to Brighton again this summer. And – guess what else!"

"I don't know. What?"

"I'm to go too, because she's taking Miss Marianne, and Cora refuses to look after a child. Says she was hired for a lady's maid, not a nursemaid, and she can always find herself another place. I wouldn't have dared say that to Mrs Lewis, but she did. Isn't it wonderful?"

"What, Cora speaking back to Mrs Lewis?"

"No, stop teasing! You know what I mean – me going to Brighton. You said I might go one day and you were right."

"I'm really glad for you, love." Annie squeezed her friend's hand, though the comparison between them made her feel very bitter about her changed circumstances. Brighton! How lovely it had been there!

"And as well as Brighton – I can't *wait* to see the sea! – we're to go on to stay with Mrs Lewis's mother afterwards. She's not been very well. We're to be away for several weeks. Just fancy!"

A little later in their walk Ellie broached the subject of Matt. "He's gone very quiet and he's always got his head in a book. Mam says he'll ruin his eyes. I hope he does!"

Annie made a non-committal sort of noise in her throat. It hurt to talk of Matt, yet though she wouldn't have admitted it for the world, she wanted to hear how he was.

"I don't speak to him any more. I told him he's no brother of mine, deserting you like that. He just looked at me in a funny sort of way and shrugged. Dad's not happy about how he behaved, either, and *he* told Matt so, too. Said he should have stood by you. But Mam – well, she seems to have taken against you. Told me to keep away from you. I told her I'd not and we had a row. I don't care. She gets funnier every year. If she had her way, I'd come home an' spend all day cleaning the house. You daren't touch anything, these days."

The hour with Ellie passed more quickly than any other hour had since that terrible night. Annie was hard put to hold back her tears as they parted, but she wasn't going back to Collett Hall with red eyes. Her pride would not let her. No one there had ever seen her cry, had ever seen anything but a calm expression on her face. And they were not going to.

14

May 1838

After the visit to Bilsden, Collett Hall seemed bleaker than ever. Annie often wept into her pillow at nights and several times she dreamed of Matt, dreamed that he had married her after all. She was angry at herself for this, but the dreams still came back unbidden, however much she tired herself out before going to bed. By the time April was drawing to an end, a cold, wet, windy April, with storms that rattled every window in the Hall and a pale, fitful sun that didn't warm you, even Miss Collett had noticed Annie's pallor.

"Is your work too arduous, Annie?"

"No, miss. No, of course not!"

"You're not looking at all well. Mr Hinchcliffe will be upset about that. He thinks a lot about you and prays every day for your welfare."

"Thank you, miss. It's – er – most kind of him."

"What is the matter, then?"

"Nothing, miss. Really! I just – just feel a bit down, that's all. I expect it's my condition."

A look of distaste flitted across Miss Collett's face and her cheekbones took on a momentary tinge of colour, but she didn't pursue the matter further, just dismissed Annie.

On the next Saturday, however, Mrs Marsh told Annie to pack her things for the night.

"What?"

"Are you deaf, girl? I said pack your things."

"But – but, please, Mrs Marsh – where am I going? I haven't done anything wrong, have I?"

"Dear me, no! Miss Collett thought you might like to spend a night with your family, that's all, to cheer you up a bit. As she's going out to dine with the Hallams, she can drop you off on her way tonight and then pick you up again after chapel tomorrow."

"But I don't want to go!" said Annie, rendered bold enough by her desperation to protest. It was one thing to visit her family on Sundays, quite another to sleep on a hard stone floor in her condition. "Please, can't you ask Miss Collett if . . ."

Mrs Marsh sighed. "Haven't you learned yet, girl, that if Miss Collett wants something, it's best to fall in with her wishes?"

"But there's nowhere for me to sleep!" Annie blurted out. "I'll have to sleep on the kitchen floor – and they've only got sacks to lie on, and no blankets! It's cold there, Mrs Marsh, and damp as well. I'll catch my death!"

Mrs Marsh frowned at her for a moment, then nodded. "I shall inform Miss Collett of your problem. In the meantime, pack your things as instructed."

Miss Collett provided an old straw-filled mattress and some even older blankets, and took along a stable boy as well as her coachman, to help Annie carry the things.

Annie, shivering on the outside of the carriage between the driver and the stable boy, thought despondently that she would go mad if Miss Collett kept doing things like this to her. She was just being used in order to impress Mr

Hinchcliffe. No one cared what *she* wanted – or even whether their charity was of any practical use! It was bad enough having to go to Bilsden on Sundays and face Matt in chapel. She always dreamed of him afterwards; she couldn't help it. Spending the night with her family was the very last thing she wanted.

She hated Salem Street! Why did fate keep pushing her back there? Now she'd have to slip Emily a shilling for food, and when you only got five pounds a year, shillings weren't so plentiful. It was awful to be the object of someone's charity. The thought of several more months of it, followed by a return to Number Three to have the child, made Annie feel very bitter indeed, bitter and desperate. If only there were some alternative!

Emily's face, when her stepdaughter turned up at seven o'clock on a Saturday evening, escorted by the stable boy carrying a big bundle, was a study in fear and dismay. If she hadn't been feeling so miserable, Annie would have burst out laughing.

"You've never been turned off again!" gasped Emily.

"No, of course not!" said Annie sharply, mindful of the listening lad. "Put that down there, Pete, and thank you very much." When he'd gone, she explained to Emily and her father what had happened, ignoring the sour expression on May's face and the downright hostility on Lizzie's.

"Well, that's all right then," said John, relieved. "It's nice to see you, lass. Get our Annie a cup o' tea, will you, Em'ly, love."

Annie sat in the dark stuffy little room for an hour, talking mainly to her dad about Collett Hall and the ways of the gentry. Even May and Lizzie stopped whispering at times to listen. They were all of them fascinated by the lives of the rich. After a while, she couldn't stand the close atmosphere any longer and stood up.

"I think I'll pop in on Sally for half an hour. I haven't seen her for ages."

"You should keep away from her sort!" snapped Emily. "Your name's black enough without you gettin' seen with such as her."

"Em'ly!" said John warningly and Emily fell silent. She was a little wary of John when he spoke in that tone of voice. He looked as if he might thump her as her first husband had. The fact that he'd never laid a finger on her made no difference to this fear.

Once outside Annie strolled to the end of the street and back to get a little fresh air. A figure came shambling along and bumped into her. "Sorry," it mumbled, cringing back, "sorry." It was Barmy Charlie.

"That's all right, Mr Ashworth," she said soothingly.

"Who's that?"

"It's me, Annie Gibson," she replied. She hadn't forgotten how kind he'd been to her, taking her box round to Durham Road and refusing any payment.

"Oh, Annie Gibson," he repeated, sounding relieved. "How are you, lass?" He seemed as if he wanted to linger and talk, so she humoured him.

"I'm all right, thank you, Mr Ashworth. Just come to see my family."

"That's good. Are you lookin' after yersen'? You're a good lass. I like you. I've allus liked you. I don't believe what they say. You're a good girl. You are."

"Thank you, Mr Ashworth." She spoke gently. Poor old man! He sounded as lonely as she felt.

"Would you – would you like a cup o' tea?" he asked hesitantly. "I've got some o' the good sort an' I've got a pretty cup and saucer you'd like."

Why not? It'd please him and it wouldn't hurt her. Anything to stay away from Number Three! "That'd be nice, Mr Ashworth. If it's no trouble."

"No trouble! No trouble at all! An' call me Charlie, will you, lass? I'd like it if you did that. Yes, call me Charlie." He almost pulled her along the street in his eagerness, fumbling at the lock for ages till he got the key in. Once inside he told her to stand still until he got a light, then led her through the mounds of junk in the front room to the back kitchen.

She didn't remember ever having been inside Charlie's house before. Few people got further than the yard. Would-be intruders were driven away by the barking of his dog. He had a new one now, a big black dog, lean and vicious-looking. It was throwing itself against the back door in a frenzy of yelps and snarls. She drew back nervously.

Charlie grinned. "Don't mind Sammy! He won't hurt you if I tell him you're a friend. I'll bring him in an' I'll introduce you an' then he'll shut up. Don't worry, lass. He won't hurt you. No, he won't never hurt a friend of mine. Not Sammy."

She stood there tensely whilst the dog sniffed at her skirts and then she relaxed as he wagged his tail.

"There!" said Charlie in delight. "He's took to you! I knew he would. You're a nice lass. Allus were. Sit down, sit down!"

She sat down and looked around curiously. Unlike the front room, this one was bare and neat, with a few cups and plates set primly in a row on a shelf and tea in a pretty tin box next to the kettle. Charlie seemed different here inside the house, more relaxed, less awkward. The dog sighed and lay down in front of the fire, its head on its crossed paws.

"You've got it nice in here, Charlie," she said, to make conversation.

He nodded. "Yes. I like things nice." He took down a delicate blue and white china cup, set it on a white saucer

and filled it with strong brown tea, not the cheap sort that
Emily used and re-used. Annie could smell the difference
at once.

"You're right. It's a lovely cup. And good tea, too."

He nodded again, complacently, accepting her compliment as his due. "I knew you'd like it, knew you would. I
did."

They sat together for a few minutes in a companionable
way, without the need to speak for speaking's sake. She
began to relax a little, really relax. It was cosy in here. And
Charlie was a nice old man. What did it matter if he was a
bit simple? He was kinder than most of the people she
knew.

"How's y'new place?" he asked after a while, not just to
make conversation, but as if he really wanted to know.

"Oh, it's a place," she said. "I don't like it much out on
those moors, to tell you the truth, but it's better than
nothing. I can stand it till the baby's born." It was funny to
talk about a baby, when the thing in her belly was hardly
showing yet. She'd been feeling sick in the mornings, but
that was beginning to pass now. Her waist was a bit bigger
and her breasts swollen and tender, but she'd not even had
to let out her dresses yet.

"Yes, yes. The baby. I like babies, I do. Wish I'd had one
of my own. I'd've looked after it, yes, an' been kind to it,
too. I would've."

"I'm sure you would, Charlie. You should have got wed,
found yourself a nice girl years ago."

For some reason, this seemed to upset him. Tears came
into his eyes and he shook his head from side to side,
blinking rapidly.

She leaned forward to pat his hand. "I'm sorry. What
have I said?"

He breathed deeply a few times, then said gruffly, "It

wouldn't 'ave been no use. I had an accident in t'mill. I wouldn't have been much use as a husband after that – no, nor got me any childer, neither."

"Oh! I – I didn't realise! I was only a child myself when it all happened. I'm so sorry!" She should have remembered that. It was common knowledge in the Rows. Poor Charlie! He was holding her hand now and patting it gently and she didn't like to pull it away, so she let it lie there. For some reason she felt no fear of this gentle creature.

"What'll you do, Annie, lass? Afterwards, I mean. What'll you do?"

"I don't know, Charlie. I can't bear to think about it. I thought I'd hate the baby, but already I don't want to give it up."

"Why d'you hafta give it up?" he asked, frowning in an effort to understand.

"So that I can earn the money to feed it."

"Ah." He was silent for a minute, then burst out, "That Matt's no good. No good, I tell yer! Thinks too much of himself, he does, an' allus has done. If it'd been me, I wouldn't've let yer down, whatever happened, Annie, lass. No, I wouldn't! I'd've stood by you! I would! Yes, I would." He bobbed his head up and down, like a little toy man Miss Marianne had, then he started to gabble something. She couldn't follow what he was saying and he realised it, stopped, shook his head, as if to clear it, then started again, slowly.

"I get like that sometimes," he said. "When I try to speak fast. What I wanted to say . . ." He stopped and swallowed painfully.

"Go on. What is it?"

"I said – I'd marry you, if it'd help."

"What? But . . ."

"Let me finish, lass. I've been thinkin' about it, ever

237

since I pushed your things round to Durham Street. After I've finished tellin' you, you can say no if you like, an' I'll not bother you no more." He took a deep breath. "I'm not as daft as people think, but I get the words mixed up sometimes an' I don't think so fast. I got hit on the head as well as down there, you see. Bad thing, that accident were. Bad. It were t'master's fault for not lookin' after t'machinery. Not *this* Mr Hallam – but his father, Mr Tom. He didn't think I'd live for long, so he agreed to give me some money every week. He knew me dad as a lad. They used to go fishing together. He were all right, were Mr Tom, if he liked you, kinder than this one under it all. In his way. So when I were hurt, he got this lawyer chap to draw up the papers. Mmm. I had to sign me cross on 'em. An' then he give me this house to live in. I don't pay no rent. An' his son has to do the same. It said so in the will."

He laughed softly at her surprise. "That rent man don't come to *take* money every week, but to give me some. Five shillin' a week, for life. Yes, for life. Folks don't know about that. I mustn't tell and I haven't told no one, 'cept for you. But *you* won't tell. I know that. You're a nice lass. You are, that." He paused for a moment to collect his thoughts, then went on slowly.

"An' I make some money, too! I do, Annie. I've got a tidy bit tucked away in my box, I have. There's good money in rubbish, if you know what to look for. An' I know. I didn't at first, but I do now. I haven't told no one else about my money. Why should I? They think I'm barmy and they laugh at me, but they give me their old bits an' pieces. An' then I laugh at them back, inside me head, like. Only – only sometimes I get a pain in me head and then I have to have a drink till it stops." He paused, then added softly, "I get lonely, too. I'd *like* to marry you, Annie. I would. I'd really like it. I'd be kind to you. I wouldn't hurt you. Nor I wouldn't touch you in that way. I couldn't. But you'd have a name for your baby and a house to live in. I'd like to have a baby around, I would. I'd look after him, an' work hard for you both."

He faltered to a stop, for she had bowed her head and was weeping quietly. He leaned over her, patting her back in his agitation. "Don't cry! Please don't cry! I'm sorry. I only wanted to help. What is it? Just say no. I'll not bother you no more, lass."

She raised her head and looked at him, her cheeks all wet and tears quivering on her lashes. "Oh, Charlie, Charlie, you're the kindest man I've ever met. You haven't upset me with your offer. It's not that. I was crying – oh, because you're so kind. And most people aren't. My dad's been kind too, but he can't do much to help me, because he's got Emily and the rest of them to look after. That Miss Collett isn't really kind. She's just using me and I hate taking her charity!"

He sat there with his head on one side and listened carefully. He couldn't understand all she was saying, because she was speaking too quickly, but she didn't seem to be angry at him and she hadn't laughed at his proposal. He sat and watched her with utter patience as she thought over what he'd said. She was thinking hard, he could see that. It'd taken him a long time to think out how he could help her, so he could understand that now she needed time to think out her answer. He waited silently, humbly, not daring to move in case he disturbed her. He knew that he was a poor old wreck of a man, but she was in trouble and she had no one else to turn to.

Annie rested her head on her hands and shut her eyes. Her first impulse had been to dismiss his offer out of hand. Marry Barmy Charlie! Impossible! But then, as he spoke, she'd begun to think. Fancy not paying any rent! Not to mention getting five shillings a week for doing nothing. It wasn't enough to live on, but it'd be a nice help. And he'd said he made money from his junk as well. She could help him with that. Or take in sewing. Make more money. But to marry Barmy Charlie! No, she couldn't! No man was going to touch her again! But – he wouldn't touch her. He couldn't. She'd be safe with him. She'd be respectable again. She wouldn't have to accept anyone's charity.

She lifted her head and looked at him thoughtfully. "How much money do you make every week from your junk, Charlie? I have to ask, because we'd have to have enough to live on after the child was born."

He gazed at her incredulously, opened his mouth and shut it several times, then managed to stammer, "Some weeks a lot – fifteen shillings, more even, others less, but never less nor five. An' sometimes I find nice things, things folk have thrown out and I repair them. And that's extra money. I like mendin' things, I do." An idea came to him and he jumped up. "Wait! Wait there, Annie lass!" He stumbled up the stairs, his clogs making a great clattering noise. He'd taken the candle and she was left in the firelight, but she didn't mind. The dog lifted its head and blew a sigh through its nostrils at her, then settled down to sleep again, only to start up as Charlie came clattering back.

He had a box in his hands, a dusty, battered tin box. When he dropped it into her lap Annie was surprised at how heavy it was. As it fell open, it showered her with coins which glittered and winked on the dark woollen material of her skirt. She touched them with trembling fingers while he held the candle up for her to see better and the shadows danced around them on the walls. They were guineas, mainly, and there must have been well over a hundred of them.

She took a long slow breath. "That's a lot of money, Charlie. You want to be careful with it."

He nodded. "Yes. Very careful. I hide it away. I do. An' no one knows about it. They think I'm barmy. But I'm not barmy, just slow. Not too slow to earn good money, though. No. An' not too barmy to save my pennies, eh?"

"Are you sure that you want to marry me? Don't you mind about the baby? Someone else's baby?" she questioned. He had to know what he was doing.

"Sure?" His voice squeaked and he had to stop and swallow again. "Oh, yes, I'm sure, Annie, lass. Very sure. I do want to marry you. Yes, I do. And I'm glad about the baby. I *want* the baby! I do, that."

A great weight slid off her shoulders and she held out her hand to him. "Well, then, we'll do it. I'll marry you. And Charlie – I'll make you a good wife, I promise. I'll look after you and your house and – and you won't be sorry." It meant going back to Salem Street but that was a small price to pay for her freedom and a home for her child.

His face was a blaze of joy and for a moment she caught a glimpse of the good-looking lad he must once have been. "You – you do mean it, Annie, lass? You wouldn't tease me about that? No, not you. You're a nice lass. The best. You won't be sorry, neither. No! You won't! You won't be sorry at all! I'll look after you proper, I will. And the baby." He pressed her hand, then sat back and stared at her wonderingly. "Eh, what a day! What a lovely, lovely day!"

They both sat there very quietly for a few minutes, and it would have been hard to say which of them was the happier.

15

May to June 1838

Annie went back to Number Three alone to tell her father the news. As she had said to Charlie, why wait? She hated it at Collett Hall. They might as well get married straight away. She nearly said 'get it over with', but she changed the words just in time. She didn't mean the marriage, so much as the fuss she knew people would make about her and Charlie. They'd laugh at her for marrying him, but let them! She'd know about the money and they wouldn't. She could still feel the coins in her fingers. How round and shiny! They had made all the difference when it came to marrying Charlie, for they represented the thing she craved most, security.

She had already begun to feel protective towards Charlie. He was a nice man, kind and generous. She wouldn't do anything to hurt him and she wouldn't let other people hurt him, either. She'd look after him well, better than he'd ever been looked after before.

She went in through the front door of Number Three and leaned against it. They were all there round the fire, even Tom, and they turned to stare at her, their interest caught by the aura of excitement that hung around her.

"You all right, our Annie?" asked John.

"Yes. Yes, I'm fine." She drew a deep breath. "I've a bit of good news to tell you."

"Oh, aye?"

"I'm going to get married."

"What?" That was Emily. "Matt's never changed 'is mind!"

"Matt? Oh no! It's not Matt."

"Who is it, then? Who else is there?"

"It's – Charlie."

"Charlie who?"

"Charlie Ashworth."

They still didn't understand. This was the bit she'd dreaded. She hated to say it. She'd never say the word again after today. Never. "Barmy Charlie."

She shut her eyes tight as they all hooted with laughter. They fell about the room, wiping the tears from their eyes, then breaking into fresh paroxysms of mirth. From time to time, one of them would say, "Barmy Charlie," and this would set them all off again. Even John joined in the general mirth. Annie stood rigid, waiting for them to finish.

But after the first burst of laughter Tom didn't join in. He sat and gazed at Annie speculatively and waited for the rest of them to stop laughing, waited for her to explain her action. She wasn't daft, their Annie wasn't; she'd not marry anyone without a good reason. What did a man like Barmy Charlie have to offer a girl like her?

"You're goin' as soft as he is!" said Emily at last, scornfully, when they realised that Annie meant it.

"You're not serious, are you, lass?" asked John sadly. "I mean – you *can't* be serious!"

"I'm serious," Annie said. "I'm very serious. I want you to come with me to see Mr Hinchcliffe tomorrow and get him to call the banns."

"I'll not!"

"Why not?"

"Why not? You know why not, Annie, lass! It's disgusting even to think of it! Why, he's old enough to be your father and he's not right in the head!"

"I don't find him disgusting. I think he's a nice man. Kind. And he's not barmy, he's just a bit slow, that's all!"

John suddenly smacked his hand on his knee. "But he can't get wed! I mean, not properly he can't! Not after that accident!"

"I know." Annie's voice was quiet, but sharp. "That's why I feel I can marry him. I don't want any fellow touching me again. Fred Coxton's done me for that."

"Nay, lass!" There was a world of sadness in the way he said it.

Emily spoke now. She'd been following what they said almost as closely as Tom. "But how will y'live? You'll need a husband as can keep you, with the baby coming."

Annie had her tale ready. "Charlie earns more than you'd think with his junk. Not a fortune, but a steady income. And," she paused for dramatic effect, "he's got some savings. Not much, but enough to tide us through till I've had the baby. After that, I'll probably take in sewing to help out. I'm a good dressmaker."

"I knew you'd not marry him for nothin', our Annie," said Tom, nodding in satisfaction.

"Oh, there's more reasons that that, even," she said off-handedly. "I can help him with his business. He's a good hand at mending things and I'll have the sense to see what's worth doing, yes, and to help him to get properly paid for his work, too. I've learned a lot since I've been in service. With that an' the sewing, I reckon I can double what he earns now."

If they estimated him to earn a few shillings a week, then doubled it, they'd think she was doing all right for herself. The money was the only reason people would accept for her marrying him. She'd got to make them believe Charlie would be able to provide enough for her and the baby, without giving them the idea that there'd be any to spare for them. She nodded at her brother. "If I see any extras for you, our Tom, I'll tell you. Charlie's not as strong as he was. He might need help lifting things or fetching them – or dealing with people. Some of them have treated him a bit roughly, taken advantage of him. That's goin' to stop from now on. I'll see you don't lose by helpin' us, I promise. We'll keep the money in the family, eh?"

Tom nodded. "Aye. Keep it in the family. An' look after your own." He grinned at her knowingly. "You an' me's not allus got on so well with each other, our Annie, but I reckon we want the same things out of life now." He rubbed his fingers together as if they held imaginary coins and she nodded. "I reckon we can pull together all right if there's money to be made."

He was only sixteen, but he had a muscular man's body and a hard expression on his face. He was already known in the Rows as a lad not to be crossed. He hadn't done well with his learning, and could still only read and write with difficulty, but he was shrewd enough when it came to looking after himself. She remembered how he'd threatened Emily when she'd slapped him. He'd frightened Emily, too, and she'd done as he wanted. Annie wanted him on her side from now on.

Lizzie and May were tittering away together in the corner and she caught the word 'barmy'. She turned on them in a sudden fury. "If I ever hear you calling my Charlie barmy again, I'll lay into you!" She shouted so loudly and looked so fierce that they cowered back before her, mouths gaping in shock. "He's slow, that's all he is, slow! He can't think quickly, but he's not barmy! And you'd better all remember that!"

"Nay, lass, calm down!" begged John, shaken by this sudden resurgence of Lucy in his daughter. Just so would Lucy have protected one of her own, eyes blazing and hands on hips. "None of us'll call your Charlie barmy any more. You hear that, our Lizzie an' our May?"

"Yes, Dad."

"It's Mr Ashworth from now on, an' see you remember that."

"Yes, Dad."

"But what about the baby?" asked Emily. "Does he understand about the baby?"

"Yes. Of course he understands. He *wants* the baby. He must be the only person in this town who does. He can't have one of his own, so he wants this one." The fury was subsiding and she felt her knees start to tremble. "I – I'd like to sit down a minute. It's been a long day."

"Get our Annie a cup of tea, May," said Emily, seeing how pale Annie's face was and beaded with sweat.

"She can get her own!"

Emily raised her hand. "You heard me! Do as you're told or you'll get a clout. Cheeky young devil! Here, John, let your Annie have that chair, so she can lean her head back." With rough sympathy, she pushed Annie down and saw that she drank the tea. Who knew better than she how weak a pregnant woman could feel? She'd been pregnant just about ever since she married John Gibson, pregnant and tired.

Annie understood the sympathy and fussing for what it was – insurance for the future – but she accepted it gratefully. She'd need help with the baby and if she could spare the odd sixpence, it'd keep Emily willing. After a while she asked John to go along the street and speak to Charlie, to reassure him. He was to arrange to go and see Mr Hinchcliffe in the morning before chapel. They'd all three go. And they'd ask Mr Hinchcliffe to intercede with Miss Collett. Annie didn't

247

want to upset anybody. She just wanted to save what she could from the ruin of her life.

Saul Hinchcliffe was as surprised as the Gibsons had been by Annie's news. He insisted on taking her into the back room and talking to her alone. With him she was a little more honest about the weekly money. At last, when he was satisfied that she knew what she was doing, he agreed to call the banns, but he expressed his deep sadness that she should feel obliged to take such a step.

"You're only seventeen, Annie."

"Nearly eighteen. Eighteen next week." The thought surprised her. She had completely forgotten about her birthday until now.

"That makes very little difference. Charlie is – what – about forty?"

"About that." She didn't even know, but was not going to admit it.

"That's a big difference. And then – you're a very intelligent girl, and pretty, too. How shall you feel living with someone who's so – er – slow?"

She looked at him and all at once she looked old and what she had to say remained impressed on his memory. "Yes, I'm young and pretty, Mr Hinchcliffe, and look where it got me! Now I'm poor and in trouble and there's nothing, nothing respectable that is, that I wouldn't do to save myself and the child. You're rich, to a person like me, rich beyond my dreams, and you'll never have to worry about getting enough food, but if I don't take this chance, the best chance I'm likely to get, and marry Charlie Ashworth, I'll likely wind up on the streets, because no one will believe I'm respectable."

"But Miss Collett gave you a place!"

"Miss Collett's been kind to me, sir, and I'm very grateful to her, but what'll I do after the baby's born? Who'll look after it well enough for what I can spare from my five pounds a year? And I couldn't leave it with my stepmother." She did not need to enlarge upon that statement.

He bowed his head. Her reasoning was only too sound. "Very well, Annie. I'll call the banns. Go and bring your Charlie in to see me."

She hesitated. "Sir, will you speak to Miss Collett for me, as well? I'm a bit afraid to tell her. Will you speak to her *before* the service? Please? I'd be very grateful."

"Yes. Yes, I'll do that for you, Annie. But I think you should wait here in case she wants to see you."

"Very well, sir. I'll send Charlie back with my father after you've spoken to him."

Miss Collett was a much easier hurdle than either of them had expected. She listened gravely to all that Saul had to tell her while Annie stood and waited in front of them, and then she said quietly, "I think it's probably the best way out for Annie."

Annie nodded. "Yes, miss."

"Do you really think so, Miss Collett?" Saul looked relieved.

"Yes. Yes, I do. Go back to your family now, Annie. Mr Hinchcliffe will call the first banns today."

When Annie had left, Saul turned to his guest. "So you really think that Annie's doing the right thing?"

"I do. Besides, we can keep an eye on her, can't we, and help her if she needs it?" She lowered her eyes. "If I may be allowed to link myself with you in this?"

"My dear Miss Collett, I am overwhelmed, absolutely overwhelmed, by your continuing Christian generosity. You are a shining example to the ladies of my congregation, a shining example."

"It's a pleasure to help you in any way, my dear Mr Hinchcliffe. You must so often feel the lack of a wife to help

249

you in your duties. If I can be of assistance in any way, it would give me great pleasure. I am a lonely woman, a very lonely woman, I'm afraid."

His eyes flew to hers in a startled reflex and she smiled tenderly at him. There was no mistaking her meaning. "My dear Miss Collett, I don't – I . . ."

"Could you not call me Pauline?"

"Pauline." He said the word reverently, his fists knotting as he nerved himself to speak. "I had not dared to aspire to . . . not thought that . . . What could I offer a woman like you?" He gestured round the little room. "Annie just told me that I was rich, but I'm not."

"Ah, Saul, what is the use of wealth such as mine if one is lonely? Even helping you in your parish has given such meaning to my life, wonderful meaning. I had long since given up hope of," she hesitated delicately, "of marriage. Surely an honest man would not let my wealth stand in the way?" She stretched out a hand to him and he took it in a bemused way.

"Pauline . . . my dear Pauline . . . could I . . . would you do me the honour, the inestimable honour, of becoming my wife?"

She allowed him to enfold her in a reverent embrace.

"Yes, Saul, oh, yes!" Behind his back her eyes were triumphant, but when she faced him again, they held only encouragement and quiet warmth.

After achieving her goal, Pauline made her way to the chapel, face inscrutable, but mind working furiously to plan her future. She was most affable to Annie, whom she met outside, suggesting that she should work on at Collett Hall for another two weeks, then come home to prepare for the wedding.

"I'd rather work for the three weeks, if you don't mind, miss."

"Have you no preparations to make?"

"Not many, miss. And my father's house is very crowded. I have to sleep on the kitchen floor."

"Will your husband's house be any better?"

"It will when I've finished with it, miss, but it wouldn't be proper for me to live there yet, would it?"

Pauline looked at her. She felt a sympathy for the girl, perhaps because she herself was also soon to be married. "What made you decide to marry this man, Annie? From what Mr Hinchcliffe says, he is not – er – not very bright."

Annie sighed, tired of this question already. She decided on the brutal truth. "He has money saved, miss. And he earns a decent living, too. And he might be slow, I'm not denying he's slow, but he's kind as well. But it's the money that outweighs the other things."

"Very sensible. I wish you luck. What shall you do with the money?"

"Put it to work, maybe start a business. I haven't decided yet."

Pauline nodded her dismissal. How intriguing! She had realised from the start that Annie was a sharp little piece, but not just how sharp. Pauline only respected people intelligent enough to direct the path of their own lives. Most people just drifted along and she had absolutely no respect for them. And as for social butterflies like Annabelle Lewis, she despised them utterly. It would, she thought, looking at Annie, be interesting to see what this one made of her life after such an inauspicious start. She would keep an eye on things. It might be quite entertaining.

The only major hurdle remaining, as far as Annie was concerned, was for the banns to be read and for Matt – and the rest of the congregation, of course – to be faced. She was standing behind the Peters family, next to Charlie and

251

flanked by her father, stepmother, brothers and sisters, when Mr Hinchcliffe started speaking. She felt somewhat protected by their presence, but she was dreading people's reactions.

As the fatal words were pronounced by Mr Hinchcliffe, she saw Matt Peters jerk and heard him gasp out loud. Most of the rest of the congregation made similar sounds of surprise, but Matt's gasp rang out clearly above the others. He listened in stunned silence until Mr Hinchcliffe finished speaking, then he threw his father's restraining hand off his shoulder and turned to face her.

"You can't do it!" he shouted hoarsely.

"Oh, yes, I can!" She reached out blindly and Charlie took hold of her hand. She forced herself to smile at his anxious face. "It's all right, Charlie. Pay no attention to Matt Peters. It's nothing to do with anyone else what we do."

"Nothin' to do with you, Matt," Charlie echoed, keeping a tight hold on Annie's hand. It was a long time since he'd been in a church, or, indeed, anywhere with so many people. He was bewildered and frightened, but Annie's dad had said that they couldn't get wed unless he went to church, so he had come. And now, there was Matt Peters telling Annie that she couldn't marry him. Still holding her hand, he repeated loudly, "Nothin' to do with you, lad! You mind your own business."

A murmur of laughter ran round the chapel. Matt went bright red, pushed past his family and ran out. Saul, annoyed and distressed by this scene, exchanged glances with his own fiancée and dismissed the congregation.

Annie walked out of the chapel on Charlie's arm, head held high, ignoring the glances and the buzz of conversation that followed her. In response to a signal from Miss Collett, she made her way over to rejoin her employer, telling Charlie to start back for home with her family. Tom, she was pleased to see, stepped forward and began talking to him.

"Ah, Annie. Congratulations on your engagement, my dear," Miss Collett said loudly. "I'm very pleased for you."

"Thank you, miss." Annie saw heads turning and was grateful for this public support.

"I find that I must delay my own departure. Will you please come round to Mr Hinchcliffe's house in, say, two hours' time?" She did not wait for an answer, but nodded kindly to them and left.

Annie strolled after her family, in no hurry to be surrounded by them again. What had happened to put her mistress in such a good mood? Whatever it was, she'd gained two more hours of freedom because of it.

As she was passing the end of Florida Terrace a hand shot out and dragged her into the ginnel between the backs of the houses. At first she cried out in terror, but then stopped as she saw that it was Matt Peters.

"Let go of me!" She tried to shake off his hand.

"You can't do it, Annie! You can't!" He almost choked on the words. "Not Barmy Charlie! Not that old loony! It's *worse* than Fred Coxton attacking you, far worse! Because if you do this, you'll be doing it willingly, you'll be selling yourself!"

She stood there, looking at him coldly and waiting until he'd finished. "Charlie's a kind man," she said flatly when he was through. "I need a kind man, Matt Peters, because I've been hurt badly by two unkind men this year."

He flushed scarlet and let go of her.

"I don't see you offering to marry me," she added contemptuously. "If it was up to you, I could go and rot in the union workhouse, couldn't I? Me and the baby both."

He closed his eyes, as if in great pain. "I – I can't marry you now," he whispered.

"No, because I'm spoiled, aren't I?" she said viciously.

"Well, I wouldn't marry you now, Matt Peters, either, because you're a sham and a coward. I'd rather, I'd *much* rather snuggle up in bed to Charlie than I would to a cold, calculating fish like you!"

He turned away, feeling nauseated as she painted this picture of conjugal bliss for him.

"You're disgusting," he whispered.

She stared at him, hard-eyed. "And you're sick, Matt Peters!" she said. "It doesn't show, but it's you that's barmy inside, not my Charlie." She turned away and left him.

Annie Gibson was married to Charlie Ashworth on the final Saturday in May at four o'clock in the afternoon. To her relief, she did not have to go through the strain of a ceremony in the parish church before the one in her own chapel, as Emily and her father had had to do, for Dissenters could now be legally married in their own places of worship. She wished her family did not have to be present, but her dad was on short time and she had not the heart to tell him to stay away. All she wanted was to get the whole business over as quickly and quietly as possible, and then to pick up the pieces of her life again.

She wore her best dress of blue wool, with a straw bonnet, trimmed in dark blue ribbons and white lace, and she was pale but composed during the brief ceremony. She made her responses in a clear voice and she signed the register with a firm hand, in her round careful writing.

The bridegroom was very neatly dressed, too, in a brown jacket and a grey waistcoat, chosen for him from his stock and carefully sponged and mended by his bride. As Lizzie said spitefully, he looked almost normal.

The whole family walked with them to the chapel, seen off by Bridie and Sally, for once united in something. Charlie's arm trembled slightly in Annie's all the way there and she forgot some of her own nervousness as she tried to reassure him. He trembled even more during the ceremony and his replies were mumbled in a low voice. He signed the register with a shaky cross, then turned a supplicatory gaze on his new wife. She squeezed his hand in a way more maternal than wifely, thanked Mr Hinchcliffe and led the way out of the chapel.

Back at Number Three, where they all gathered for a celebration meal afterwards, at John's insistence, Annie sat Charlie in a corner, kept Lizzie and May away from him and gave him a plate of food and a cup of Emily's weak tea. Tom came over to chat to him and did it sensibly, keeping to simple everyday topics. Charlie began to relax and Tom winked at his sister.

As soon as she politely could, Annie said her farewells and took her husband back to Number Eight. There she made him another cup of strong tea in one of the pretty cups he was so proud of, praised the way he had behaved and took possession of her new home. Her main regret about the day was that Ellie couldn't be there.

Only when she got to bed did Annie's self-control slip and the tears begin to fall. She thought she had muffled her sobs in her pillow, but a gentle hand on her shoulder announced Charlie's presence.

"Nay, lass, he's not worth it."

"I know. But I – Oh, Charlie!" And she threw herself against the comfort of another warm human body and burst into fresh sobs.

He let her cry herself out, patting her shoulder from time to time and making inarticulate noises that seemed to comfort her. He stayed till she was asleep and then wandered sadly back to his own bedroom, murmuring, "Poor lass, eh, the poor lass!"

That was the only weakness Annie allowed herself. The

next day she initiated a frenzy of spring-cleaning that left every inch of Number Eight sparkling clean. She went through all the piles of rubbish with Charlie and made him explain just what resale value each item had.

"Some of these clothes have a lot of wear still left in them," she said thoughtfully, after a while. "Can you get more like them?"

"Oh, yes," he nodded happily. "Get 'em at the big houses an' farms. They know me an' they keep things for me. Don't make much money from 'em, though. Sell 'em to Mr Thomas for a few shillin' a load."

"I think we could get more money for them if I washed them and remade some of them."

"Mr Thomas won't pay more."

"I won't be selling them to Mr Thomas," she explained patiently. "I shall mend and remake them for people to wear, and then sell them – Oh, I don't know, maybe at the markets. I'm a good sewer, Charlie."

"You're a nice lass," he said. "Kind. I like you. I do."

"I like you, too."

He blinked and tears came into his eyes. He was always pathetically grateful for a kind word. "Do you?" he asked wistfully.

"Of course I do! I wouldn't have married you if I didn't like you." She patted his hand. "Now, let's get on with things. If I can help you to make more money, maybe one day we'll be able to move out of Salem Street. We'll get ourselves a house with a garden." She had already noticed how much he liked flowers, bringing back bunches of bluebells and other wild flowers from his travels. "You'd like a garden, wouldn't you? But don't tell anyone else about it. Not anyone. It's a secret between you and me. If we tell people, they might try to stop us."

"I won't tell," he said obediently. "I do like gardens. I like flowers. I like hens, too. Sammy'd like a garden to dig in. He's a good dog, is my Sammy. He is that."

Annie was amazed at some of the things she found in the house. There were dresses in funny styles, which she'd never seen women wearing. There were bits and pieces from a score of attics, the debris of many lifetimes. A pleasant find for her was a bundle of old books, dog-eared and with the binding half eaten away by mice, but still readable. She asked Charlie if she could keep them and he pushed them into her hands, trembling with delight at being able to give her a present. After that, he would sometimes bring home books or old newspapers, and she would read them aloud to him at nights.

Another good find in the early days was a set of torn curtains in a faded brocade. She washed them carefully, cut out the worn bits and had enough left over to cover their small front window. She was determined to make her home more comfortable, remembering the difference between Mr Hinchcliffe's house and those of his parishioners. She would not be like the other women in the Rows! She would not!

She was so busy that she had no time to waste gossiping, as the other women did, though she always had a pleasant word for anyone she knew. People like Polly Dykes said she was a snob and always had been, and it took Emily quite a while to accustom herself to the idea that she could not just pop along the street and borrow things from Annie, as she had expected to be able to do. Annie's door sported a brand new lock, so you had to knock and wait for it to be opened. And Annie would say quite bluntly that she was too busy to stop and chat, and no, she had no bread to spare.

One Saturday after work, Tom came round and helped Charlie to load a borrowed cart with the old clothes Annie had rejected as too far gone to salvage. They took this round to Mr Thomas's yard, leaving a lot more space in the small house. Annie paid Tom sixpence for his trouble and invited him back for a meal afterwards. She wanted to get to know him better, for she thought he would make a useful ally.

"We made old man Thomas up his price, didn't we, Charlie?" he boasted when they returned. "I reckon that bastard's been diddling Charlie for years, our Annie. He won't find me so easy to cheat, though."

"Don't push him too far!" Her voice was sharp. "I don't want him to stop buying from us."

"I'm not stupid." His voice was relaxed, as he was himself once away from Emily. "I still let him beat me down a bit. It's money for old rope, that, after t'mill. I like buyin' and sellin'. I want to get out of Hallam's one day. There's no future working there."

"You get out," agreed Charlie. "It's dangerous. All mills is bad. Bad in the old days, when they were smaller, and still bad now! Oh, yes! I know."

Tom cleared his plate of stew. "That was good!" he said, smacking his lips. "Got any more?"

Annie gave him another helping and another piece of bread and he began to shovel it down noisily. "You're a good cook, our Annie," he said when he'd finished. "Better'n Emily. Only things she's any good at are prayin' an' havin' babies."

"Too many babies. They can't afford them."

"Well, you know our dad. He does like a bit of a tumble. Not doing badly for an old 'un, either. Though Emily's not a patch on our mam."

There was silence for a moment as they both remembered their mother. It was Tom who broke it. "You've changed a lot since you left home, Annie. You learned a lot in that doctor's house. You allus were smart. Too smart, I used to think, but I were wrong."

"You can't know too much in this world. *You*'d have done

better for yourself if you'd learned more at school and kept out of that mill."

"Aye, well, I didn't, did I? I didn't know then what it'd be like in t'mill. Mind, I've learned a few useful things there. I can fight an' take care of meself, an' that's never wasted round here, is it? You might be glad you've got me to look after you one of these days."

"I'll just be glad if you stay out of trouble," she retorted. "And I'll look after myself, thank you."

"Oh, I stay out of trouble most of the time, don't you worry I'm not stupid! Er – Annie."

"Yes."

"I – I wouldn't mind gettin' a bit better at figuring. I don't bother much with readin', but figuring and ciphering can be very useful."

"Oh, yes?" She wasn't exactly encouraging. She remembered all too clearly those years when Tom had been sent to school and had wasted his chances, while she had had to stay at home.

"Will you help us? Give us a bit of practice, like?"

"I might. When I've time. If you really mean it."

He relaxed, then sat upright again. "You won't tell anyone, though, will you?"

"Why should I? It doesn't pay to blab your business to other folk."

In the middle of June, Annie made a big effort and invited her family round for a meal, the excuse being a belated celebration of her eighteenth birthday. She did this mainly for her father's sake, but, to her surprise, Charlie enjoyed the party as much as anyone. He sat in a corner and took little active part in the conversation, but Tom and her father both made an effort to talk to him, little Becky made him laugh and he beamed all evening long. He must have been starved of company for years, she realised. Poor man!

"You're a good cook, lass," John told her after the meal, "like your mam was."

She could see Emily's scowl. "I'm glad you enjoyed it, Dad. I used to enjoy cooking. I wish I had a proper oven here."

"You'll have to forget your fancy ways now!" said Emily sharply. "This is Salem Street, not Nobs Alley."

Annie took a deep breath. She had taken just about as much as she could stand from Emily and her sister, Lizzie. It was Charlie who saved the day. "Annie *is* a right good cook," he said, nodding emphatically. "She's a good lass, too. I've never been so well looked after in me life." He blushed at his own temerity in volunteering a remark.

Even Emily hadn't the heart to contradict him, not while the poor old fellow looked so happy and while she was eating Annie's food. It were wonderful, Emily thought, sighing, to have a meal bought and cooked for you. This were what it must be like to be rich.

Tom trod on Lizzie's toes as she opened her mouth and said loudly, "You're a lucky man, Charlie, a very lucky man." He looked so menacingly at Lizzie that even she didn't dare to spoil the mood of the moment. The kids were all a bit frightened of Tom when he got that sort of look on his face.

It was funny, Annie thought afterwards, that she should get on so well with Tom nowadays. Lizzie she still detested and she had never taken to Emily, but she found she could really talk to Tom. Her dad came into Number Eight to see her sometimes, and that was lovely, too. He was a nice man, though a bit weak, she now realised. He didn't come to see her too often, because of Emily's jealousy. He would always avoid trouble, rather than put his foot down about something. The younger children were also discouraged from having much to do with their half-sister, but Tom popped in several times a week and she began to look forward to his visits and his cheery voice telling her all the news from the Rows.

In fact, she admitted to herself it was Tom's visits that kept her sane, because Charlie had his limitations as a companion, kind and well-meaning though he was. She could not help wondering sometimes what life would have been like with a normal husband, with someone like Matt, for instance.

16

June to July 1838

One Sunday after chapel Miss Collett beckoned Annie over
and began to catechise her about her married life.

"And how are you managing, Annie? I've been worried
about you since I gather that your husband is a little – er . . ."

"Slow," Annie finished for her. "My husband is a little
slow, Miss Collett – but that doesn't prevent him from being
a good man and a hard worker."

Pauline Collett was impervious both to sarcasm and
offended pride. "Good. And your home? I hope you're
keeping it clean. So many of the women from the Rows are,
unfortunately, very slovenly in their habits."

"Well, I'm not slovenly!" Annie didn't know what had got
into her lately. She only knew that she had had enough of
charity and condescension. And her condition was definitely
affecting her temper. Some days she was even sharp with
Charlie, who never contradicted her in any way and always
tried to please her. "You may call any time and check, Miss
Collett. You won't find *my* house dirty."

Pauline drew herself up and stared at Annie. Few people
ever dared to argue with her, and certainly she had never
been spoken to like that before by an ex-maidservant.
"That's a rash invitation," she said dryly. "What if I took you
up on it?"

263

"Come any time," repeated Annie recklessly. "Come to tea!"

Pauline's eyes began to gleam wickedly. "Very well. Tea it is. Will Tuesday suit you?"

"Perfectly."

Miss Collett inclined her head. "Until Tuesday, then." She didn't know whether to be amused or offended at such impudence, but she intended to keep that appointment and set the girl in her place. Come to tea, indeed!

When Annie got home, she sat there aghast at what she had done. What had got into her? Fancy daring to invite Miss Collett to tea! Tom was of the opinion that she should send a note of apology, but this only made Annie more stubborn. "I won't!" she declared. "She had no right to talk to me like that!"

"But what are you going to do about her?"

"What I said. Give her tea. If she comes."

By Tuesday, the house was scrubbed and polished, scones were made and fine white bread purchased, as well as good tea from the grocer who served the gentry. He seemed to have no objection to Annie's custom and money, and she gained a little confidence about going into his shop. Maybe she would come and buy a few things here again. Just every now and then. For a treat.

By the afternoon, Annie was so apprehensive that she could not sit still, but had to keep going over to peer out of the window. One moment she was sure Miss Collett would not come and the next that she would, if only out of spite.

In fact the visit hung in the balance in Pauline's mind until noon that day and only a chance remark by Mrs Marsh to the effect that her mistress could not possibly go and take tea in the Rows tipped the balance.

"Nonsense! Of course I'm going. As a minister's wife, I

shall have to learn to move among people of humble birth. Order the carriage for half past two."

When she saw Miss Collett coming along the street, Annie's knees turned to water and she rushed to stand in the back room, hands clasped at her breast. When there was a knock on the door, she moved to open it like an automaton. However, the challenging expression on her visitor's face and the greeting, "Well, here I am!" stiffened her resolve and gave her the courage to say quietly, "Won't you come in, Miss Collett?"

Pauline was, if truth be told, feeling rather ill-at-ease herself. What if the house were dirty? What if she were offered some unpalatable mess to eat and drink?

She looked round in relief. Small, but immaculately clean.

"Please take a seat," said her hostess graciously. "The rocking-chair is the most comfortable." There were, in fact, only three proper chairs, but each shone with polish.

"Thank you."

Annie sat down, and began to make conversation, as she had seen Mrs Lewis do. "A lovely day, is it not?"

"Beautiful."

Annie had thought out in advance what she could talk about safely without giving offence. They started with the weather and then went on to the coronation of the new girl queen, which was to take place on the twenty-eighth of the month.

Pauline began, albeit reluctantly, to admire the girl. She had certainly learnt a few tricks while she was in service. She told Annie how two hundred thousand pounds had been voted by Parliament to cover the expenses of the coronation, and how bands were to play festive music in the parks of London.

"I wish I could see it," said Annie wistfully. "I loved my

stay in London. One feels so cut off here, sometimes – especially in the Rows." The last admission escaped before she had realised it.

"Well, even in Bilsden, the mill-owners are to let their employees off work an hour or two earlier on that day," said Pauline.

Penny-pinchers! thought Annie. They might have given people a whole day off, or at least a half-day. "I wonder if you'll just excuse me for a minute or two while I brew the tea?"

"Certainly." Pauline waved a hand in gracious dismissal.

In the kitchen Annie leaned for a moment against the table and closed her eyes. How long could she keep this up? She gritted her teeth. As long as necessary. She moved towards the fire and seized the kettle.

She carried the tray into the front room and set it down upon a stool. "Please excuse the china. My husband delights in pretty cups and saucers, but people rarely throw out ones that match." She gave her visitor a defiant toss of the head as she said this, daring her to take umbrage.

Pauline looked at the tray, made by Charlie, who had a small gift for wood-carving. An immaculate little cloth covered it, sewn by Annie, presumably. The unmatched crockery was indeed pretty and the scones looked appetising. "It looks delicious," she said generously. "Did you embroider that cloth yourself?"

Annie had made it for herself and Matt. It was exquisite. Tears came to her eyes, for all that she bit her lip and dug her fingernails into the palm of her hand. "Yes." She saw that Miss Collett was frowning at her and added harshly, "It was part of my bottom drawer."

"For the other man?"

Annie nodded, still trying to control the tears.

"He must be a fool!" said Pauline. "And you're very

brave, Annie. I was wrong to patronise you like that. Will you forgive me?"

"I should be asking you that, Miss Collett. I was in a bad mood the other day. I shouldn't have spoken to you like that. I get – well, funny sometimes. Sharp. Too ready to take offence. I'm sorry."

"I'm not. I'm glad I came today. Now, may I have one of those delicious-looking scones? And you must tell me about your husband's business . . ."

The rest of the visit was a great success. When Pauline relaxed she could be a very entertaining companion. And once she grew to like someone, she was doggedly loyal. For all the differences between them, she had begun to like Annie Ashworth.

The best times for Annie during that first year were when Ellie had her Sundays off and appeared at chapel. The two young women would then spend the whole afternoon chatting and drinking cups of the good tea, which Annie now thought of as Miss Collett's tea.

The first time Ellie visited her after her marriage seemed a special enough occasion to warrant its use and afterwards it became a symbol of celebration.

Charlie stayed with the two young women for a few minutes, then said he had things to do in the yard.

"Oh, Annie, how are things really going?" asked Ellie at once. "It's so awful to think of you married to . . ."

"To a very kind man," said Annie firmly. She gave Ellie another hug. "I'm happier than I'd ever expected to be, really I am! Charlie's a nice man, easy to live with. And so kind! You couldn't ask for a kinder husband. And it's good to have my own home. I didn't realise how much I'd enjoy that."

After that, Ellie spent most of her free Sundays round at

Annie's house, to her mother's fury.

"You know, you've certainly got this place nice," Ellie said, looking round on her next visit. "There's something new every time I come. I like the curtains and these are good solid chairs."

"They weren't when Charlie found them. But he's good with his hands."

"He seems – er – very pleasant." Ellie had still not come to terms with the marriage, and she was still not speaking to her brother Matt.

Annie looked round and smiled proudly. "It's a start. You wait a year or two. I'm going into business on my own account. See!" Annie held up the brown material she was sewing. "This'll make a good skirt. When I've got more things made up, I'll start selling them at the market."

"Doesn't Charlie make enough money for you to live on, then?"

"He's made enough to live on every single week." Annie's voice was proud. "And we've saved something every week, too – even if it's only a few pence."

"You're very brave about everything, Annie."

"No, I'm not brave; I'm a coward. I'm afraid of a lot of things, Ellie, but most of all, I'm afraid of having no money behind me. I'm never going to be charity-poor again! Never!" She laughed shakily. "Listen to me going on after the way folk have been kind to me! Let's not talk about me any more. Tell me what's been happening at Park House instead."

Even Ellie was not told about the box of money, which had proved to hold over two hundred guineas. Annie worried about keeping it in the house, though, at the same time, she loved to count the shining coins and think how long she could live on that money if she had to.

Ellie didn't need much prompting to launch into a flood of

news. "Well, Cora and Mabel are still not speaking to each other, except in the course of duty. It's a bit of a laugh, really. Mabel's grown as sour as vinegar lately."

"She always has been. Go on!"

"Cora's not a bad sort. She just laughs at Mabel and calls her Old Speckle, because she says Mabel looks just like a cow her uncle used to have called that. Mind, it's not as nice as sharing a room with you, love, but Cora's all right. She's teaching me some new ways of doing my hair and trimming up a bonnet."

"And the doctor? How's he going on?"

"We hardly see anything of him in the house these days, except when we have visitors. He spends most of his time shut up in the surgery, even in the evenings. He's had a big box of books delivered and when he isn't seeing patients, he's reading or writing. And every now and then he goes away for a night or two to meet other doctors in Manchester or even London. Mrs Cosden says he'll wear his brain out and ruin his eyes with all that reading, but Dad says the doctor's interested in the problems of women having children and he wants to make things easier for them. Just fancy a man being interested in something like that! It doesn't seem decent somehow. Oh, sorry, Annie, love, I forgot you were – well, you're not very big yet, are you?"

Annie managed to smile, though Ellie had touched on one of her fears. What if she were like her mother? "That's all right. I'm used to the idea of the baby now. Go on! You were telling me about Dr Lewis."

"Well, the doctor doesn't even eat with Mrs Lewis most of the time. Funny way of being married, if you ask me! They hardly ever see each other at all. And she doesn't seem to mind at all. It's only when she has her parties that they really spend time together. What do you think of that, then?"

Annie made a non-committal sort of noise, which Ellie

269

took as a sign to continue. "This will be my last visit for a while, love, because we're going down to Brighton in September. I'm that excited about it, I could burst! I've made myself a new dress, not as nice as you would have made, but Cora helped me to fit the sleeves. Look, I've brought a snip of the material to show you."

Annie felt the material and nodded approval. "I expect Miss Marianne is excited about the trip, too?"

Ellie rolled her eyes. "Excited! She jumps up and down every time she talks about it. Mrs Lewis said she'd have to learn to behave better than that. I think the mistress has changed her mind about taking Miss Marianne with her – she doesn't spend much time with her, you know – but the poor little love's been ill so the doctor just put his foot down, for once. I heard him say that the child needed some good sea air and either she went with her mother, or her mother could stay in Bilsden to look after her. Mrs Lewis was spitting fury for days about it."

"Yes, she's got a mean temper."

"Anyway, Miss Marianne's dying to see the sea and so am I. Tell me again what the beach is like."

Ellie's visits did Annie a world of good. For a few hours she relaxed, and felt young and carefree again. It was a bitter-sweet pleasure, however, because it showed her how much she had changed. She felt years older than Ellie nowadays.

The next day Charlie came down with a cold. It didn't seem much at first, but then he started groaning and holding his head. By Tuesday he was rocking about in pain and had produced a bottle of gin. She tried to stop him drinking it, but he clung to it obstinately. "It's the only thing that stops the pain. Only thing, Annie, love. Jus' – leave me alone. I'll go to my bedroom an' drink it there."

Annie remembered the times he'd had his funny turns

when she was a child and the way he'd talked and sung and shouted for hours on end. She didn't want to face that, and wondered if something could not be done about it. After all, doctors knew a lot more nowadays.

When the mill came out, she slipped along to ask Tom to fetch the doctor. While she was waiting for him, she tidied up her kitchen and picked up a piece of sewing, but she couldn't seem to settle to it. She could hear Charlie upstairs, moaning and shouting incoherently. It was a relief when someone knocked on the door. She opened it to find Tom standing at one side and Dr Lewis at the other.

"Here he is!" said Tom, with his usual impudent grin. "I'll be round at our house if you want me, Annie."

"Thanks, Tom. Er – won't you come in, doctor?"

Jeremy Lewis brought with him the smell of soap and the cologne he always used. She'd forgotten how clean and fresh he always smelled. Whatever you did to keep clean here, you couldn't prevent the other people in the Rows from smelling sour.

"How are you, Annie?" he asked gently, seeing that she was tongue-tied.

"Oh, I'm fine, thank you."

"You look well. How's the morning sickness?"

"Gone, just like you said it would." She felt strange to be entertaining her ex-employer after all that had happened. She was having difficulty in thinking what to say and do, and that was unlike Annie.

If she'd only known it, he was feeling awkward too. He'd meant to have kept his eye on her when Annabelle dismissed her, but she'd found others to help and he'd not been needed. He'd asked Ellie a couple of times how Annie was getting on and it had seemed that she was managing all right. He was glad of that. Annie was as nice as she was pretty. Unlike his own wife, who grew more elegant by the year, but who had the soul of an iceberg and a tongue dipped in acid.

He'd hardly spoken to Annabelle since the day she'd dismissed Annie, and wondered sometimes if he were being a coward, avoiding her like that. He was glad that she was going down to Brighton again, though he suspected that she had only suggested taking Marianne with her out of spite. But the child was happy and excited about the proposed visit, so he'd said nothing. And now that Marianne was run down after her illness, she really needed the change and the bracing sea air. He wasn't going to let Annabelle make a habit of taking Marianne away on these trips, though. She wasn't a good influence on the child.

"What can I do for you, Annie?"

"It's my husband, doctor. He has these funny turns – I don't know what to call them. His head hurts and he goes – well – funny. He was badly injured years ago. I think it's a result of that." They heard a moaning sound above them and Annie winced. "He's been drinking gin. He says it's the only thing that helps. Normally he doesn't drink at all."

Upstairs, Charlie started to shout incoherently.

"May I go up and see him?" Jeremy was as polite to the poorest of his patients as to the richest.

"Yes. Mind how you go. The stairs are rather steep." She led the way up the dark narrow stairs and knocked on Charlie's door.

"Go 'way!"

"It's the doctor, Charlie. Dr Lewis." She pushed the door open. "He's come to help you."

Charlie was sitting on the bed, rocking to and fro, and clutching the gin bottle. Annie would have gone across to him, but Jeremy held her back.

"Wait for me downstairs," he whispered, and after a doubtful glance she left him.

Jeremy was shocked when he recognised the man on the

bed. Barmy Charlie was a well-known figure in the town. He hadn't associated the old man with the name Charlie Ashworth. How had Annie come to marry such a person? He'd assumed that she was marrying someone of her own age. This man was old enough to be her father!

As he sat on the bed and talked to Charlie, Jeremy realised that the poor chap had suffered some brain damage, and he was filled with horror and pity for Annie. That lovely young girl married to a wreck like this! What had made her do it? Surely there were others willing to marry her? Any man would be proud of a wife like her. Or a mistress. The thought rose unbidden and he banished it immediately. Annie was not that sort of girl.

All the time he was thinking about Annie, he was talking to the man on the bed and noting his responses. There wasn't really much he could do. Brain damage was one of the most difficult things to treat. Doctors knew so little, really, and tampering with the human brain had such serious effects that most doctors left it strictly alone, even after accidents. Jeremy did, however, manage to take the gin bottle away from Charlie and persuade him to take a sleeping draught instead. He waited until his patient was snoring gently, then he went downstairs.

"You can get rid of this." He handed Annie the half-empty gin bottle with a grimace. "I've given him a sleeping draught and I'll send Sam round with some more."

"Thank you, Dr Lewis, but don't trouble Mr Peters. My brother can come and collect it."

"There's no need. And, anyway, Sam lives right next door. Why shouldn't he bring it?"

"I – I'd much rather he didn't," she insisted, embarrassed.

"Why not, Annie?"

She closed her eyes for a minute. What could she say? "We – we're not on good terms, sir. It was – it was Matt Peters that

I was going to marry and – and I'd rather not . . ." Her voice broke and with it, her iron self-control.

He came across the room and gently sat her down in the rocking-chair, then felt her pulse.

"You're feeling the strain. Sit down for a minute and close your eyes. No! I insist!"

She did as she was told and gradually the colour came back into her cheeks. He sat there quietly in the other chair and watched her. She was even more beautiful than he had remembered. The last few months had set character into what had been merely girlish prettiness. How long her lashes were and how creamy her skin! He realised that he'd like to touch that skin, not as a doctor, but as a man. It was a long time since he's wanted a woman as a person. His body had its needs, but since he'd been in Bilsden his worsening relationship with Annabelle had soured him for other women's company. He remembered suddenly the comfort he'd found in Mary, his mistress in Brighton. Her kindness had been a balm to his spirit. There'd been no one permanent since. He wondered for the first time in years how she was getting on.

Annie opened her eyes, gave him a half-smile and let out a deep sigh. "I feel better now. I was upset, and I didn't get much sleep last night."

He smiled back at her. "You must look after yourself too, you know. Annie – forgive me, but I didn't realise that you'd had to make such – such an unequal marriage."

She looked at him warily.

"He's quite an old man. And you must realise that he can never be a husband in more than name. You're young and healthy. You should be thinking of a family and a life together – not of tending an old man."

"Everyone says that to me," she told him in a flat, emotionless voice, "but young men weren't queuing up to wed me. You told me that it'd be murder to get rid of the baby – and I came to see that you were right – but you didn't tell me what I was to live on, or how I was to keep my child afterwards!" Her voice rose a little.

"I should have come to check that you were all right. I was going to give you some money, help you myself. Then I heard – my wife told me – that Pauline Collett had found you a place. I assumed that you'd be all right. Miss Collett has a reputation for charitable acts."

Annie gave a short, mirthless laugh. "Oh, yes! She's very charitable. Five pounds a year and all found. You can't keep a baby on that!"

"No, I suppose not. I'm sorry. I shouldn't have spoken about it. It's not my business any more."

"No, it's not! But I'll tell you something anyway, doctor. Charlie's a good man. He's kind and he works hard and he *wants* the baby. And I couldn't have married him if he'd wanted my body, too. I don't want any man to touch me again!" She shuddered at the memories this raised.

Like her father, Jeremy shook his head sadly. "That's a great pity, Annie, because the love between a man and a woman can be very beautiful. You've only seen the worst of it so far."

"Yes, well, I'll manage without the rest, thank you. Now, how much do we owe you?"

"It doesn't matter."

"Yes, it does! We can pay our way. Charlie's not as daft as folk think. He's a good provider."

"Very well. That'll be two shillings, please. And a shilling for the sleeping draught."

He took his leave of her, but was back the next day in person with a large bottle of milky liquid. He went to examine Charlie, who was lying half-dozing in bed, then came down and gave Annie the bottle. "It has to be

275

measured carefully. It's very strong. Show me your spoons? Right. That one. Two spoonfuls when an attack starts, one twenty-four hours later and if that doesn't do it, call me in. That'll be another five shillings for the medicine. It's expensive, but it's worth it. I've left your name and the details with Mr Tyndell, the new apothecary in the High Street, so that you can buy more bottles when that one runs out."

"Thank you." She handed him the money, then said impulsively, "Won't you sit down and have a cup of tea, doctor? I'm sorry if I was a bit sharp yesterday. I was tired."

He smiled warmly at her.

He had a lovely smile, she thought. It made him look rather boyish.

"If that's a peace offer, Annie, I'll be happy to take you up on it. I'm always ready for a cup of tea. And I'll even admit that I shouldn't have spoken as I did."

She bustled round, brewing some of the good tea and getting two cups from the shelf. They didn't match, but they were clean and they were real china, not the heavy pots or tin mugs that most people in the Rows used. She also produced some little cakes, which he ate with relish, biting into them just as her brother Tom did. Fancy comparing a gentleman like Dr Lewis with her brother!

Before he left, he made her promise to let him give her a check-up once or twice before the baby was due. "There won't be any charge for that," he said firmly, "because you'll be helping me to learn more about women and childbirth. We have to study normal pregnancies, as well as problems." She didn't like to refuse, because he seemed so set on it, but the idea of seeing a doctor when you weren't ill seemed strange to her.

The only real problem during the first month or two in Number Eight was Matt Peters. Annie did her best to avoid him, keeping to the house at those times when he was likely to be going to work or coming from it, but it was inevitable that they should meet occasionally. The first time that he turned his head away and muttered the word 'whore', she couldn't believe her own ears and stopped dead in her tracks, cheeks flaming. By the time she'd pulled herself together, he was out of sight.

The second time she met him, she was better prepared, and when he treated her in a like way, she barred his path. "You've done enough harm to my life, Matt Peters," she said. "If I hear you saying such things about me again, I'll take legal action against you!" She hadn't the slightest idea what legal action was or how to take it, beyond going to see a lawyer, which no one she knew had ever done. It was just a phrase she'd heard Mrs Lewis use, but it seemed to serve her purpose now. She had the satisfaction of seeing his mouth drop open as she said it. She followed it up with, "And Dr Lewis has already spoken up for me about the attack, so I don't suppose I'll have much trouble in defending my good name. I'm a respectable married woman now, and don't you forget it!"

"Married! To that!" He jerked his head scornfully towards Number Eight. "It's disgusting!"

"Don't you talk about my Charlie like that! He's more of a man than you are!"

His face was as white as hers was red. "Well, I wish you luck of your bargain!"

"Oh, Matt," she said softly and sadly. "What's done is done. Can't we forget the past and be – polite, at least?"

For a moment it seemed as if her plea had touched him, then his mother came out of Number Seven and he swung away down the street.

Mrs Peters stood on her doorstep and looked down her nose at Annie. "You're wasting your time with my Matt! He knows better than to get mixed up with your sort again."

Annie looked her straight in the eyes. "I was just telling Matt," she said slowly and distinctly, "and I'll tell you, too. If I hear that anyone's been blackening my good name, I'll see a lawyer about having them stopped. Dr Lewis has been very kind to me. I'm sure he wouldn't like to think that Mr Peters' family were going round spreading lies about me."

Elizabeth Peters fell back before that threat. Even after years of Sam being in continuous employment, she still had nightmares about him losing his place.

Annie turned and walked slowly up the street with her bucket, feeling weary and old. All she wanted was to live in peace and make enough money to feel secure! She'd accepted her new life and the fact that it didn't include Matt. She might not be able to banish him from her dreams, but that didn't hurt anyone except her, did it? Why did he hate her so? Why did he keep trying to hurt her?

Matt couldn't have said why he was behaving like that. He had tried to accept the Lord's will and to bury himself in his work, encouraged by his mother, who hovered over him and fussed till he could have screamed at her to leave him alone. His father was deeply disappointed in him, he knew, though Sam said little. It was just that every time Matt saw Annie in the street, looking as fresh and lovely as ever, something boiled up inside him and he wanted to hurt her, because losing her had hurt him so much, because in spite of everything she was managing without him and because he, too, was tormented by dreams of what might have been.

17

July to August 1838

Pauline Collett and Saul Hinchcliffe did not announce their engagement until July, because she knew what a nine-day wonder it would be. Annie had heard of it from Miss Collett herself beforehand, but kept her own counsel. She had received several more calls, and had grown used to the visitations now. Pauline, who said quite frankly that she admired what Annie was doing, would leaven a round of tedious calls upon humble, grateful women from Saul's flock with a visit to Number Eight. Annie was not humble or grateful, and her sharp perceptive comments on the poorer members of the congregation made Pauline laugh.

She would sail along the street, nose in the air, ignoring the smells and debris, followed by the stable boy with some offering for Annie, tactfully chosen not to give offence – a newspaper or a book or a bag of precious oranges.

The second time she came to visit, Pauline insisted on being shown all over the house. She rapped on the thin walls, poked into corners and demanded to be told exactly how one made a living from such rubbish. Sammy, banished at first to the yard, whined and growled at her through the door, but when Miss Collett grew tired of this and herself let him in, he instantly recognised her as a superior being and abased himself before her, tail wagging tentatively. To Annie's astonishment, Miss Collett gave him a pat or two, before telling him firmly to go and sit in the corner now whilst she talked to his mistress

After a while Annie began to enjoy the visits. Pauline was as different from Mrs Lewis and her friends as chalk from cheese. One day, when her visitor was in a particularly good mood, she plucked up the courage to ask her what was the best thing to do with a sum of money one had saved. Should one put it in a bank or one of the new friendly societies, or should one do something else with it, like perhaps buy a house? That was what Sally had done with her savings, for 'my Harry' continued to be more than generous with her.

Annie didn't really like the idea of banks. She hadn't quite worked out what they did with their clients' money, but Darton and Forraby's new bank on High Street looked so imposing that she couldn't dismiss it out of hand and had several times made an excuse to walk past in order to peer into its mahogany and marble interior. As for friendly societies, she wasn't a member of any group which ran one, and again, was rather suspicious of someone else handling her money.

"I suppose by that question you mean that your husband has some money put by?" asked Miss Collett, never one to beat about the bush. "How much?"

Annie hesitated.

"Come, come, Annie! If you don't trust me, why mention the matter in the first place? Besides, I'm hardly likely to try to steal your money, am I, and I give you my word that I won't mention it to anyone else. But if you don't tell me how much, I can't advise you."

"Well – there are over two hundred guineas." Even to say the sum aloud made Annie look round nervously.

Pauline blinked in surprise. "That much!"

Annie could only nod.

"Lying idly in some box, I suppose?"

Annie's flush betrayed the accuracy of this guess.

"Then it's a good thing that you mentioned it to me. You must definitely invest it in property. Buy a house!" She looked round disparagingly. "Not like this place! The rents wouldn't be secure enough." She saw Annie's puzzled expression and tried to explain. "Nearly all the people in this street and in most of the Rows are very poor. They depend on the mills, so if the cotton trade is slack, they'll find it hard to pay their rent. With the amount of money you have, you'll be able to buy a nice pair of cottages, with gardens, the sort that overseers or clerks live in. People like that don't have as much trouble with paying rent as the people in this street, for example. I presume you weren't thinking of moving elsewhere yourself?"

"Not at the moment, not while this one is rent-free." An image flashed into Annie's mind of the sort of house she and Matt had planned for and she closed her eyes for a moment to shut out the pain.

"Are you all right?"

"Oh – yes, miss. Just – just the baby moving."

"Are you sure you're all right? You look quite pale."

Annie pulled herself together. "Oh, yes. I'm fine now, thank you. Please go on."

"Well, as I was saying, property is the thing for you, I'm sure. You must buy a house, maybe two." She took Annie's consent for granted. "I'll introduce you to my own lawyer. You should always deal through a lawyer, Annie. They make sure that everything is in order. You can't be too careful."

"Yes, miss."

Miss Collett consulted a little gold fob watch. "No time

like the present. I have an hour to spare. Change your dress
and we'll go to see my lawyer now. Put on that blue dress
you wear to chapel. And bring the money with you. How
can you bear to leave it lying around? Someone might steal
it and then you'd have lost your big chance in life."

Bewildered, feeling as if she were being dragged along by
a runaway horse, Annie went upstairs and changed her
dress. Then she got the box out of its hiding place, but
before she went downstairs she took ten guineas out and
hid it among her clothes. She wanted to be prepared for any
emergency. You never knew what could happen. She
didn't ever again intend to be left without a good sum in
cash to fall back on. When she returned to the kitchen, she
found Miss Collett reading a book.

"Yours, I presume?"

"Yes, miss."

"Are you enjoying *Ivanhoe*?"

"Not really. I don't understand enough of the words – or
the background. But I don't get much choice. Charlie
brings home books people have thrown away and I try to
read them. Lamb's *Tales From Shakespeare* was the best,
though it had some pages missing." She flushed. "I know it
was written for children – but I'm like a child when it comes
to book learning. One day, perhaps I'll know enough to
read Shakespeare himself."

"You're a strange girl, Annie Ashworth. Have you
always lived in Salem Street?"

"Yes, miss. Except when I was in service."

"And where did you learn to read?"

"At the chapel." She wasn't going to mention Matt and
those early lessons. She mustn't think of that any more.

"It's amazing!"

"What is?"

"Your intelligence – and the way you use it. Most girls in

your condition would have given up. Instead you marry a man old enough to be your father, a man everyone calls 'Barmy Charlie', and it turns out that he has money saved. Did you know that when you married him?"

"Oh, yes! It was one of the main reasons. That and the way he wanted the child."

"Admirable!"

Annie followed Miss Collett along the street and into her carriage, which was waiting in Boston Street. She enjoyed the luxury of the short drive to the better part of the town and was quite sorry when they stopped in front of one of the large houses on Market Street, one with a shiny brass plaque on the wall beside the door.

Miss Collett led the way inside and upstairs to the offices of Bromford and Pennybody. A clerk received her with flattering deference, but stared curiously at Annie, in her simple gown and with an unmistakably pregnant body. He offered them chairs and went into another room, reappearing almost immediately. A rotund gentleman with a rosy face was following him and beaming at Pauline. It must be wonderful, Annie thought, to be so important that people made a fuss of you. She watched with great interest as the gentleman clasped Miss Collett's hand with all the familiarity of an old acquaintance.

"My dear Pauline! This is an unexpected pleasure. Do come into my office! May I offer you a cup of tea?"

Miss Collett interrupted the flow of words. "Thank you, no. I haven't time today. Jonas, may I introduce Mrs Ashworth, one of my fiancé's congregation. It's she who has need of your services, not I. Annie, this is Mr Jonas Pennybody, my lawyer."

Like his clerk, Jonas was a little surprised by Annie, but he gravely shook hands with her before shepherding them both into his office, where he settled them in two comfortable upright armchairs which smelled of polish and old leather, before taking his place behind a big, untidy desk.

"Well, now, Mrs Ashworth, how can I help you?"

Annie waited for Miss Collett to speak for her, but she didn't "Oh, I – I . . ." She paused for a moment to gather her wits. They would think her a real simpleton if she stuttered like this. "My husband and I have some money saved. Miss Collett suggested that we invest it in some property and kindly brought me along to see you about it." She sat back, trying to look relaxed and confident.

"Well, yes, we do occasionally help clients in that way," he admitted. "Er – how much money is involved?"

"Over two hundred pounds." She gestured towards the tin box on her lap. "I brought it with me. Miss Collett said – she suggested that it might be safer to leave it with you rather than keep it in this box."

Miss Collett smiled at the way he shuddered and said emphatically, "Indeed, yes!"

"Give it to one of your clerks to count, Jonas, then look after the money till we need it."

Mr Pennybody looked at Pauline, whom he'd known all her life. She had one of the sharpest business brains in Bilsden, in spite of being a woman. What on earth was she doing bringing this girl and her paltry life savings to him? One of the clerks could have seen to such a minor piece of business. Oh, well, he had some time to spare and Pauline never did anything without a good reason.

"Had you anything special in mind, Mrs Ashworth?"

Pauline judged it time to join in. "No, we're relying on you for that, Jonas. Do you know of anything suitable for sale, a nice pair of cottages, perhaps?"

"Well, as it happens, there are one or two places on the market that might be worth consideration. Perhaps Mr

Ashworth would like to come and look at them?" He glanced enquiringly at Annie.

"My husband is – is too busy at the moment. He said he would rely on me," faltered Annie, inwardly quaking at the thought of how Mr Pennybody would react to Charlie, or vice versa.

Again, Pauline saved her. "I have agreed to help Annie instead. I can take her round in my carriage if you will send your clerk to show us what's available." Pauline was deriving a great deal of entertainment from her altruism. Really, life had become so much more interesting since she had got engaged!

A dazed Annie was presently dismissed to walk home clutching the receipt for the two hundred and forty-seven pounds ten shillings and sixpence that the box had contained. She had arranged to meet Miss Collett the next day to look at some properties. She was also clutching the empty box, wrapped up in paper. It felt awful not to hear it chink. She must start filling it up again as soon as possible.

When she had gone, Jonas Pennybody cocked an eye at Pauline. "Now, what about that tea? You're not leaving here till you've told me a bit more about your protégée!"

"I'd love some tea."

He rang for his clerk, ordered a pot of tea, then asked her bluntly, "What's all this about, then? You know I don't usually concern myself with small fry."

She leaned back in the comfortable armchair and smiled provocatively at him. "What do you think Annie's background is?"

"What?"

"Go on, guess! What do you think her background is?"

"How should I know? Shopkeepers, clerks, something like that."

Pauline smiled again, like a pale cat contemplating a

juicy fish "Do you know Salem Street?"

"Yes. It's in the Rows . . ." He broke off. "Do you mean to tell me she comes from Salem Street? I can't believe it!" He broke off again. "Ashworth. Charlie Ashworth lives in Salem Street. Not *that* Charlie Ashworth? That lovely young girl and that old wreck?"

"Mmm. Annie married him a while ago."

"But – he's not right in the head! He had an accident, a bad one. I remember the case clearly." He looked at her sideways and said, "In strictest confidence . . ."

"You know I never break confidences, Jonas."

"Well, we handled the matter for old Tom Hallam. Gross negligence by the overseer. Shocking injuries Ashworth had. They didn't think he would recover. Tom was furious, because the negligence cost him a lot of money, but also because he knew Ashworth and had a soft spot for the family. I think he knew this man's father, or something of the sort. So Tom arranged for the free house and for weekly payments for as long as Ashworth lived. He chose to be amused when Charlie got better – as better as he'll ever be. He even put a clause in his will that the house and payments were to continue for as long as Ashworth lived. Laughed himself silly about it, actually. Said his son would be furious. And he was. Still, Frederick Hallam won't miss a few shillings a week. He's twice the businessman his father ever was."

"And twice the womaniser, from all I hear."

"Yes, well, that's not our concern, is it? So your protégée married old Charlie Ashworth, eh? Goodness me! You'd think she could have done better than that for herself."

"Not in the circumstances. She was raped and left pregnant. She had a young man, but he wasn't prepared to marry her afterwards."

"Another of your charity cases?"

"No!"

"What then?"

Pauline shrugged her shoulders. "I don't know exactly. She was a charity case until she arranged to get married. I knew then that she had more to her than most of the people I help. I'm just – taking an interest."

He cocked an eyebrow at her. "Amusing yourself, Pauline?"

"If you like. It's nice to see another woman with the sense to make something of her life. I think Annie will go far. She's turning into quite a shrewd businesswoman. You men have things too much your own way, you know."

The following day a nervous Annie joined Miss Collett and one of Mr Pennybody's clerks in a tour of inspection of some properties that were for sale. She had told Charlie what she had done and asked whether he wanted to come too, knowing he'd shrink from the idea, but feeling that he ought to have a say in how his money was spent.

"You're sure it's what you want, Charlie? It *is* your money, after all. If you'd rather I didn't . . ."

"No! No! You take it! You look after it!" he insisted. "Buy a house. A nice house, with a garden. I like gardens."

"I will, then. But don't tell Tom about this."

He frowned at that. "I like Tom. He's my friend."

"Yes, I know. Tom's all right. But this is *our* secret. Just you and me. Don't tell anyone till I say it's all right, and then you can tell Tom."

She didn't really suppose it'd hurt if Tom knew, but better safe than sorry. What people didn't know about, they couldn't spoil.

Annie sat quietly in the carriage and let Miss Collett do the talking. She went round three pairs of cottages in the older part of town, taking everything in, missing nothing, but saying little. She listened when the clerk pointed out their advantages and disadvantages, and mentally added a few items of her own to the list.

"Well?" asked Miss Collett, after they'd left the last house. "What do you think, Annie?"

"I'm not sure, but . . ." Annie hesitated.

"Go on."

She took a deep breath. "The second pair," she ventured.

"Why?"

"They were – better."

"In what way?" Miss Collett was giving her no help.

The clerk looked supercilious. Annie scowled at him. How dared he look down his nose at her! "They looked better from the outside, for one thing. They were prettier than the others. People who have the money would prefer to live in pretty houses, I think. And – they were in a better position, higher up the hill."

Pauline raised her eyebrows. "Is that all?"

"Well, they were nicer inside, too. The kitchens were good. You could work properly in them. And three bedrooms are better than two." She stopped, wondering if she'd made a fool of herself. Miss Collett's expression had not changed while she was speaking. Then, slowly, the thin lips relaxed and a smile appeared.

"Not bad, Annie. I would also have told you to look at the other houses in the street. You don't want to be near something that would reduce the value of your property." She turned to the clerk. "I'm surprised we had a choice. Why are there so many places for sale?"

The clerk did not dare look superciliously at her, but he felt resentful that he had had to spend the whole morning at the beck and call of two females. In his opinion, females should leave business matters to their husbands or fathers, and tend to their houses and families. "There used to be a shortage, miss, so all the mill-owners built houses for their workers. Now there are plenty of places, so there are always one or two of the older properties on the market, especially the larger ones."

When they had returned to Mr Pennybody's rooms and were getting out of the carriage, Annie turned to Miss Collett in a panic. "I don't know anything about prices," she whispered.

Pauline patted her arm reassuringly. "Enough new experiences for the time being, eh? Shall I do the bargaining for you?"

"Please."

Annie listened in amazement as Miss Collett and Mr Pennybody bargained briskly over the price of the cottages. This was like no haggling she'd ever heard. The two protagonists didn't raise their voices, but somehow the price was reduced and she got the cottages, on her husband's behalf, for two hundred and twenty pounds the pair. Mr Pennybody congratulated her on her bargain and offered her the services of his firm to manage them and collect the rents. He assured her, with a twinkle in his eye, that Miss Collett would be able to vouch for his firm's efficiency and honesty, and all for a mere five per cent of the rentals.

Annie was tempted to accept his offer. Firstly, she did not want it known that she and Charlie were property owners. Secondly, the thought of collecting the rents terrified her. How would she ever dare to go and check up on people who would be likely to consider themselves her social superiors? Then she thought of Tom. He'd jump at the chance of earning some extra money, she knew. She could pay him sixpence a week. He'd not be afraid to collect the rent money.

"No," she said slowly. "No, I don't think so." She smiled

at Mr Pennybody and told him with disarming frankness, "You see, that five per cent is important to me at the moment. I – we – my husband and I want to make money. We need every penny at this stage.

Miss Collett smiled in approval. "Very sensible, Annie."

"Right then," said Mr Pennybody, "all that remains is for you to bring your husband here to sign the necessary documents. That's one thing you can't do for him!"

When Annie had left, Mr Pennybody looked at Pauline. "How old did you say she was?"

"Just eighteen."

"Incredible! And born and bred in the Rows, too! I wonder what she'll be like when she's thirty. I hope I'll be around to see it."

"You will be, Jonas. You're indestructible. Oh, and when they come in to sign the papers, you'd better get him to sign a will. Get your clerk to draw it up. Tell Annie I said she should do it, just to be on the safe side. It need only be very simple: he leaves everything to her. She's to lodge it with you."

He shook with silent laughter and then changed the subject. "Are you going to devote yourself to good works from now on, Pauline, or are you interested in another little business deal I have in mind?"

"I'm interested, of course," she said instantly.

More laughter. He was the only person she knew who dared laugh at her to her face.

"What about your fiancé? How will he feel about your doing business on your own behalf?"

"He'll leave it to me. He has his ministry to worry about."

"I'd have thought you were the last person to be marrying a minister – and a Methodist at that! Are you going to abandon business and take up philanthropy?"

"You know me better than that, Jonas. I'm marrying Saul because I want a family before it's too late. He's a nice man, healthy in body and intelligent enough to be a good companion. I think we shall deal very well together. He's also got no interest in my money, which is equally important to me. I couldn't bear to hand over the reins to a husband now. I like running my estate and making a little extra money here and there."

"Not to mention collecting a few lame ducks."

"Annie's no lame duck, and I shall enjoy helping her. I'm beginning to suspect that I shall enjoy her company, too, when she loses her fear of me and learns a bit more about the world."

That same evening, Annie offered Tom the job of rent-collecting. "You mean old Charlie had that much money saved!" he gasped. "And you knew it all along?"

"Of course."

Annie noticed that Charlie was beginning to look a little anxious and nudged Tom.

"My, you did well there, Charlie!" he said at once, patting his brother-in-law on the shoulder.

Charlie's face cleared. "Saved it up in my box. Not so daft, eh?"

"Not daft at all, Charlie, not daft at all." Tom looked at Annie with new respect and then looked back at Charlie thoughtfully. Who'd have thought that there'd be so much money in rubbish! He'd have to learn a bit more about all Charlie's stuff.

"It's to go no further, Tom!" said Annie sharply. "No one, no one at all, is to know! Especially the family. They'd never leave us alone if they thought we'd got money to spare. You know what Emily's like."

"Aye, you're right there. Silly bitch, she is! Dad were a fool to wed her."

291

"I don't want to collect the rents myself, so will you do it for me? I'll pay you for it."

"Of course I will!"

"It'll only be sixpence a week, mind."

"An' all I 'ave to do is walk over to Cloughside and hold me hand out for it! When do I start?"

"As soon as the houses have been handed over. I'll let you know. Tom – what'll you tell the family about it? They're bound to hear that you're doing the collecting."

"I'll tell 'em nothin'. It's none of their business. I do as I please nowadays, our Annie. I don't hand me wages over any more an' I come an' go as I want."

"And Dad lets you?"

"He's got no choice. They know I'd leave home if they didn't let me be."

"Do you manage to save any of your wages?" she asked curiously.

"I've started," he admitted. "But it's a bit difficult. She goes through me things. She had five bob away last week, the bitch! She couldn't deny it, but she couldn't pay me back, either. Money just burns a hole in her pocket. Can I leave my money here from now on?" For some reason, he trusted Annie absolutely.

"Of course you can. Emily went through my things too when I was back at Number Three. If I hadn't had a good lock on my box, she'd have been into that, too. Do you – do you remember Mam, Tom?"

"Aye. A bit. She had red hair, too. You take after her."

"I don't know how Dad can stand Emily after Mam!"

"She has her uses. You know what he's like. Can't do without it."

"I don't like such talk," she said primly.

"Then you shouldn't live in the Rows."

"I won't have it in my house, Tom!"

He looked at her in surprise.

"I mean it! I may have to live here, but I'll set my own standards, thank you."

He shrugged. "All right, then. It's your house." He didn't want to do anything that would upset her. She could be a stepping stone to a better future for him. Something told him that the sixpence a week was just a start. It had taken him a while to realise that nowadays Annie was just as eager to make money as he was. He was sure that they would do well together. He knew he would be able to trust her.

18

August to September 1838

The wedding of Saul Hinchcliffe and Pauline Collett took place on the second Saturday in August at eleven o'clock in the morning. The little chapel was full to overflowing with the bride's friends and relatives. Saul's family had managed to arrange for the farm to be looked after and were also there in full strength to lend their support to the only son. Although Pauline had been very gracious to them, they could not feel at ease in her company and would be glad to return to their quiet acres in Cheshire when all the fuss was over.

Todmorden Road was lined with waiting carriages, and groups of humbler spectators were standing between them, watching the goings-on of the gentry. Annie was among the crowd of onlookers, for she was curious to see how Miss Collett would look, and besides, she'd not been feeling too well lately and she thought that a walk in the fresh air might do her headache good.

Pauline had insisted on decking the chapel with flowers, even though this caused mutterings among some members of the congregation. It smacked too much of high-church idolatry for plain people like Sam Peters. Miss Collett silenced her critics in no uncertain manner.

"Rubbish! The flowers will be picked from my own

gardens. The Lord did not despise flowers, so why should you or I? 'Consider the lilies of the field, how they grow; they toil not, neither do they spin: And yet I say unto you, That even Solomon in all his glory was not arrayed like one of these.' Matthew 6, verse 28. I think I have my quotation and references correct." No one was brave enough to voice any more objections to her face.

Standing just outside the little chapel yard, Annie watched Mr Hinchcliffe alight from a carriage belonging to his bride. As if you needed a carriage to cover the short distance from Durham Road to the chapel! The visiting minister, who was to conduct the ceremony and take over for two weeks while the bride and groom were away visiting London, had declined the offer of a carriage and had walked across earlier.

Annie had to bite her lip not to laugh aloud at how harassed the bridegroom was looking. Just wait until he was married and living at Collett Hall! He wouldn't be able to call his soul his own then. Only too well did she remember what a tight rein Miss Collett kept on every member of her household, right down to the gardener's boy. She smiled and slipped into the chapel to watch. Only regular chapel attenders were being allowed inside, so she was alone in the back pew.

During the ceremony, Saul Hinchcliffe looked as nervous as his bride was composed. His colour was high, clashing unbecomingly with the maroon of his new frock-coat. From time to time he eased his high, starched stock away from his neck, as if it were too tight, or he cleared his throat with a dry little cough.

Annie could tell at a glance that most of the guests were friends of the bride, local gentry, conservative in their tastes and members of the Established Church. They were sitting bolt upright in their hard wooden pews, disapproval writ large upon their faces. She repressed a chuckle. She supposed that they had felt it to be their duty to attend the wedding, the Colletts being so important locally, but they were not at ease in the bare little chapel. She could tell that from the way that they fidgeted and turned to whisper to each other. She looked at the flower decorations and remembered what the flowers had been like at St Mark's, and the stained glass, and the carved wooden panels. If she had her way, that would be the church she attended, but it would upset her father too much if she left the Methodist fold, and she would not do that to him.

Although Saul, standing rigidly at the altar, believed that all men were equal in the Lord's sight, he was also fully aware of how low a farmer's son turned Methodist minister ranked in their guests' eyes. He was somewhat overawed by the guest list and only hoped he would not let dear Pauline down in front of such august members of county circles. He glanced anxiously towards her as she walked up the aisle and took her place by his side. She gave him a reassuring nod and smile, before bending her eyes modestly to the posy she carried.

Pauline was wearing a cream silk gown and matching bonnet, with a light lace shawl around her shoulders. She had declared herself too old for virginal white and veils, and was only carrying a posy because her sole surviving aunt had made such a fuss about it.

Annie frowned when she saw what Miss Collett was wearing. Although the gown was of heavy expensive silk, it was not the colour best calculated to enhance a pale complexion and mousy hair. Miss Collett should have chosen a soft blue or green, or certain shades of apricot pink. Funny that with all her money she couldn't manage to dress in a more flattering way!

Mrs Lewis would have stood out among the wedding

guests for elegance, Annie decided, looking round at the guests, her eyes lingering for a moment on Christine Hallam's unflatteringly fussy gown. But Mrs Lewis was still away in Brighton and consequently Annie was missing Ellie's companionship. Ah, there was Dr Lewis now! He was not handsome, but he looked quietly distinguished, a true gentleman.

At last the ceremony was over. Annie moved outside through the little side door and lingered to watch the bridal party leave.

Pauline Hinchcliffe walked down the short aisle on her husband's arm, savouring the fact that she was now a married lady, no longer to be pitied and excluded from intimate little conversations. She allowed Saul to hand her into the carriage and smiled triumphantly at the world.

For a moment, Annie thought, Mrs Hinchcliffe had looked almost pretty. She must be feeling happy. As the carriages started to drive away, Annie turned and walked slowly back to Salem Street. She was glad to have seen the wedding, but the day was chillier than she had expected and her headache was as bad as ever. She tried not to let her condition prevent her from doing anything, but inevitably it slowed her down. And she was feeling a bit depressed too. Ellie was away and Miss Collett – no, Mrs Hinchcliffe now – would not be coming to see her for a while, either. And kind though he was, you had to admit that Charlie was not the most interesting of companions. Thank goodness for Tom and her books!

The rest of the month seemed to pass very slowly. By the beginning of September Annie was very big and had lost all her energy. Even Charlie noticed how pale she was looking and began to worry about her. He brought home little presents, delicacies to eat or books for her to read. He tried to do things for her in the house, but she would rarely let him help and snapped at him sharply once or twice. He was so worried that he took his problem to Tom.

"Annie's not well." He looked hopefully at his brother-in-law, seeking help and reassurance.

"Well, she'll soon be better," said Tom, trying to jolly him out of his miseries. "It won't be long before she has the baby an' then she'll be better again."

Charlie wrinkled his brow in laborious thought. "Annie's very tired," he started again. "She's not well." His face lit up suddenly. "Get the doctor!" he said. "Dr Lewis. He's a nice man. I like Dr Lewis. When my head hurt, he made it better." He took hold of Tom's arm and shook it to make his point. "Get the doctor for Annie!" he repeated. "He'll make her better. You go an' get the doctor. Go on! Get him!"

"I don't know," said Tom. "She's only havin' a baby. Women have babies all the time." And die of it, said a voice inside him. Annie might die, like their mam had died, and where would you be then? He stood there indecisively for a moment or two, then he slapped his hand on his thigh. "Why not, eh? You can afford it, after all. Right, then, Charlie, I'll go and fetch the doctor. You go home to your wife and wait there."

Annie was sitting by the kitchen fire, sewing. Grimly she stabbed her needle in and out of the material, ignoring the pain in her head and the puffiness in her fingers. Charlie stood over her, fidgeting and watching until she could bear it no longer.

"For goodness' sake, go and find yourself something useful to do, Charlie Ashworth!" she exclaimed at last. "You're driving me mad, standing there twitching!"

He moved slowly towards the front room and stood looking back at her from the foot of the stairs with mournful, worried eyes. Then someone knocked on the front door and he hurried to answer it. Annie sighed and leaned her aching head tiredly on her hand. The next thing she knew, someone was taking the sewing away from her. She blinked up and saw Dr Lewis.

"Why didn't you call me, Annie? You're not well."

"I'm not ill!" she replied crossly.

"You're not well, either. You should be in bed, and that's where you're going."

"I'm all right!" she repeated, but her tone was unconvincing. "I'm just a bit tired, that's all."

Ignoring her protests, he pulled her to her feet and turned to Charlie. "You stay here, Charlie. I'll have a look at Annie, then I'll come back and tell you what to do."

He looked at Tom, who had followed him into the house. "Will you stay, too?"

"Aye, I'll stay. Me an' Charlie'll make a pot of tea, eh, Charlie? Make some tea for Annie and the doctor."

Charlie, who was jigging about in nervous misery, snatched gratefully at this idea. "Aye, we'll make some tea for Annie an' the doctor," he repeated, and began to bustle about. "We will. We'll make some tea."

How did Annie stand it? Tom wondered. The way Charlie repeated everything fair got on your nerves at times.

Jeremy Lewis carried Annie upstairs, in spite of her protests that she was quite capable of walking, thank you. "Be quiet!" he told her. "Which bedroom?"

"The front one, doctor."

He pushed open the door with his elbow and walked in. It was still light enough for him to see the neatness of everything. The room had a curiously virginal feel to it, with its narrow bed and rickety chest of drawers, upon which a shell-covered box sat primly. One wall was half-covered with bundles of what looked like rags or old clothes, but even they were neat and orderly.

He deposited Annie on the bed, told her to be quiet and checked her pulse. Then he held her swollen hand in his and examined it. "Why didn't you send for me before?" he demanded angrily. "I told you to send for me if you weren't well, didn't I? You said nothing about this when I saw you last month! You must have been feeling poorly then!"

"It didn't seem serious enough."

"Heaven preserve me from foolish women!" he exclaimed. "Not serious enough, when your hands and feet are swelling? And I'd guess that you have a bad headache, too. I'm right, aren't I?"

"Yes." Her voice was low and tears were not far away.

"Get your clothes off! I want to examine you properly."

She opened her mouth to refuse, then changed her mind and did as he had ordered, while he looked out of the window, tapping his fingers impatiently on the sill.

"I – I'm ready, doctor."

In silence he examined her carefully, noting that the baby was a large one, but that at least it was lying in a normal position, and seemed to have a strong heartbeat. When he had finished, he looked down at her.

"Annie, you must surely realise that things aren't going as well as they should?"

"I thought it was just – just the last bit. Emily says you always get t-tired then."

"Well, you and Emily were wrong. Annie, you've got to rest, or you'll lose the baby – and maybe your life, too."

She swallowed convulsively and looked up at him. "Like Mam?"

"Yes, just like your mother. Some women are like that. But if you do as I tell you, you'll stand a much better chance. Will you promise to follow my instructions?"

Without realising it, he had taken hold of her hand and just as instinctively she was clinging to his.

She sighed. "Yes. Yes, I promise."

"Very well, then. Firstly, you must stay in bed."

"But . . ."

"You must stay in bed all the time until the baby is born. You *must* do this! Is there anyone who could come in and look after you?"

"I don't know. There's my stepmother – but she has a family of her own to look after, and she's not very – er – energetic. Perhaps – I don't know – perhaps Sally Smith might help. She lives at Number Six. Yes – I think she'd help. And there's Charlie, of course. He's very handy. He's looked after things for years on his own."

"Right, then. Bed it is. Now, secondly, I'll come and see you every day or two. The minute your pains start, you must send for me and wherever I am, whatever I'm doing, I'll come to you. You've asked Widow Clegg to come in and help you, haven't you?"

"Yes."

"Good. She's the best. I'll tell her to send for me when your pains start. Now, you will rest, won't you? Promise me!"

Annie lay back on the pillows, her face white and her eyes dull. "Yes, doctor." Now that she had given in to her illness, she was glad to be in bed, glad to lie back and rest. She gave a long, soft sigh and he smiled down at her.

"You're relaxing already," he said, with his warm, boyish smile.

"Yes. Yes, I am." She sounded surprised.

"That's good. I'll go and talk to your husband now. I'll call in and see you tomorrow."

Downstairs Charlie and Tom were sitting in front of the little kitchen fire with cups of tea in their hands.

"Is there a cup for me?" Jeremy asked.

"Yes. Cup for you." Charlie bustled around and handed the doctor some tea in a pretty pink cup. He then stood and looked at him hopefully.

"Sit down, Charlie," said Tom. "The doctor can't talk to you when you're hoppin' around like a flea at the market. Sit down in your chair. You, too, doctor. Take this chair. That's right. Now, how's our Annie?"

"She's not well, obviously. She needs to rest until the baby is born. There's no medicine I can give her, but if she can just rest, really rest, no housework, no cooking, no sewing, just complete rest in bed, then she'll stand a better chance. It's very important indeed."

Charlie didn't answer, just sat looking trustingly at the doctor.

"Will that do it? Make her better, I mean?" asked Tom.

"It'll help."

"An' that's all you can do for her? We wouldn't care what the medicine cost." For this crisis had made Tom realise suddenly how much he had grown to care for his sister and how much she needed him. Poor old Charlie wasn't up to much, though he did his best.

"There is no medicine for women like her. One day, when doctors know more about childbirth, perhaps . . . But at the moment, there's nothing but rest. And that's a thing most women can't manage. Look, Annie said she thought someone called Sally might come in to help in the house. Do you know her? Could you ask her?"

"Aye, I'll see her. She an' Annie are good friends. An' I can come in an' help a bit too."

Dr Lewis nodded. "Good! Well, I'll call back tomorrow evening." He drained the cup and set it carefully on the table. "Thank you for the tea, Charlie. It was good. Now, you look after your wife. Annie's to stay in bed. You understand? No getting up. No housework. Just bed."

Charlie nodded obediently. "Stay in bed. I'll look after
'er. She's a good lass, is my Annie. She is."

At the door, Jeremy turned round and looked at the ill-
assorted pair. Would they really look after Annie properly?
A sixteen-year-old lad and a slow-witted old man! Should
he stay to check that this woman she'd mentioned could
help her? No, better not. He was late already. Mrs Cosden
would have his meal ready. At least Annabelle would not
be waiting for him tonight. He was looking forward to the
time when Marianne would be old enough to dine with
them. Her chatter might help fill the awkward silences. He
contented himself with repeating his warning that he was to
be called the minute Annie started having the baby and
then he left.

Two weeks later Annie's pains began, a couple of weeks
earlier than expected. Emily, who was with her at the time,
sent out for Widow Clegg.

"Has tha sent for t'doctor?" asked the widow, as she
stumped up the stairs.

"Nay," protested Emily. "She's only havin' a baby, an'
she's hardly got started yet. What d'you want t'send for *'im*
for?"

"He said to send for 'im straight away," insisted Widow
Clegg. "And he allus means what he says. Tha'd best
send."

"But it'll cost money!"

"They've got the money. Send for 'im!"

Dr Lewis arrived half an hour later, nodded to the
women and went upstairs. He smiled down at Annie, lying
uncomfortably in the bed. "Last bit. Nearly over now," he
said encouragingly.

She managed a smile. "Yes. I'll be glad to have it over
with." Now that he was here, she felt much more confident.

The widow had followed him up. "She'll not be havin' it yet a bit. I s'all have t'go an' get tea for me lodgers."

"That's all right. I'm here to stay now till it's over." Jeremy smiled down at Annie. "You go and do what you have to, Mrs Clegg. I want to see my experiment through."

Widow Clegg clattered off down the stairs.

"Her clogs always make more noise than anyone else's," Annie whispered.

Jeremy grinned. "Much more noise."

The widow stopped to peer into the back room and say, "Your Annie'll be a long while yet," to Emily and Sally, who were sitting waiting. "The doctor's stoppin' with 'er."

"Is she that bad?" gasped Emily, who equated doctors' visits with death or serious injury.

"No, not bad. But not well, neither. She takes after 'er mother that way." The widow folded her shawl carefully around her head to give her some protection from the rain that had been falling all day. "He's a good doctor," she admitted grudgingly. "He's saved some as I'd given up for dead."

Emily shrugged her shoulders. She had no faith in doctors and thought Annie was making a fuss about nothing. She'd never had the doctor to any of *her* birthings, no, nor ever would want a man to see her like that. "Can you stay for a bit?" she asked Sally, whose company she was now tolerating because she didn't want to be left with the job of looking after two households. "I have t'get tea for my John, an' if I leave them kids for long, they'll get at the bread. Little devils, they are! You no sooner fill their bellies than they're hungry again!"

"Yes, I can stay for a bit," said Sally easily, and watched Emily scurry off. The second Mrs Gibson would be late for her own funeral, she thought with a grin. She didn't like to interrupt while the doctor was with Annie, so she did a bit of cleaning up downstairs. When she could find nothing else to do, she went and listened at the foot of the stairs, but could hear nothing.

Upstairs Annie had lost a lot of her shyness and was chatting to Dr Lewis about her plans for the future with more animation than he'd seen in her face in weeks. The pains weren't bad yet and she was hoping for a good birth, with Dr Lewis to help her.

Jeremy encouraged her to chat and they went on to exchange opinions of the servants at Park House. He made her laugh out loud several times.

He noticed more than you thought, she realised. The only person he didn't mention was his wife.

Sally, downstairs, marvelled that they could find something to laugh about at a time like this. She'd had a baby once and it'd been born dead after several hours of agony. She hadn't fallen for one since and was glad of it, too. They hurt to bear and they were a burden on you for years. She'd never have got where she was now if she'd had a bunch of kids to look after. And as for being the comfort of your old age, your children were as likely as not to put you in the union poorhouse because they hadn't the space to lodge you or the food to keep you alive. Give her the comfort of owning a few cottages any day!

Charlie came home from his rounds just as Sally was getting restless. Her gentleman friend was due that evening.

"The baby's started," she told him. "The doctor's with her now." His face paled. He gave her a strange look and went to sit by the fire, all hunched up in his chair and rocking slightly. You couldn't help feeling sorry for the poor old sod. "Annie's all right, you know," she said gently. "An' he's a good doctor."

"Mmm."

"Look, why don't you pop up an' see her for a minute?"
He shook his head and rocked harder, so she shrugged
and left him to it.

About midnight the pains started to get really bad and
began to come more often. Annie couldn't help crying out
sometimes. Three hours later she was only half-conscious
and the baby had still not been born.

"She's not goin' t'get it out without a bit of 'elp," said
Widow Clegg.

"No. I'll have to cut her. The baby's too big." Jeremy
opened his bag and took out some instruments.

"I'll go an' wash 'em for thee." The widow picked them
up and disappeared downstairs before he had a chance to
say anything. He smiled wryly. She was a terror, the
widow. A lot of the women in the Rows didn't like having
her to help with a birth. She insisted on washing their
bodies and she hectored them about their dirty houses.
They only called her in if they knew they were in for a bad
time. Jeremy had thought himself clean until he'd seen the
way Mrs Clegg scrubbed and rinsed his instruments. And it
seemed that her extra fussiness paid off. Few of her patients
dared to fall ill once they had been safely delivered.

Charlie looked up as Widow Clegg came down into the
back room. "Annie?" he asked, his face full of mute
misery.

"Not finished yet. Here, tha can help us, Charlie
Ashworth. Go an' get some more water. Every time I
empty that bucket, tha mun go an' fill it up. All right?" She
spoke impatiently, but she had struck the right note. He
needed something to do.

Tom, who was waiting with him, patted his hand. "I'll
leave that job to you, Charlie lad."

Charlie nodded and seized the empty bucket. Whilst he
was out of the house, Jeremy made a quick, but careful

incision, ignoring Annie's screams. Tom, downstairs, turned pale. He didn't give a toss what happened to Emily in her birthings, but Annie was different.

Matt, lying sleepless next door, heard the sounds through the thin walls and buried his face in the pillow. That settled it! He couldn't stand any more. Tomorrow, he'd start to look for lodgings. You needed peace to study. Who could get any peace with that noise going on? Oh, God! Was Annie all right?

Within minutes the baby had been born – a boy, a big healthy child. His head looked a bit bruised, but otherwise he seemed normal enough. Jeremy handed him over to Widow Clegg and waited for the afterbirth. As soon as that was out, he began to stitch Annie up. She moaned a little, but didn't seem really aware of what was going on until the baby started to cry angrily, protesting at being left on its own.

Annie's eyelids fluttered open. "Is it over?" she whispered. "Is it really over?"

"Yes, and you have a fine son."

She blinked as he picked the baby up and held it out to her, but she didn't make any attempt to take it from him.

Widow Clegg stepped forward. "Here – take him!" she said and pushed the baby into Annie's arms. "It's best to give 'em t'babbies straight off," she explained unnecessarily in an aside to Jeremy, who had seen her do it many times. "They need summat to love after their trouble."

Jeremy had never seen the bonding happen so visibly. Oblivious to her aching, exhausted body, Annie gazed in wonder at the little red face peeping out of the shawl. She'd seen dozens of babies before and not thought much of them, but this one, *her* baby . . . A tender smile crept across her face and she leaned forward to kiss the soft downy skull. Then she lay back on the pillow and her eyes flickered shut as she fell into a light doze, still with that tender expression on her face.

The widow started to clear up the mess and Jeremy gathered his things together. He'd never seen anything remotely like that loving expression on his own wife's face. She regarded Marianne as a possession, a toy to be shown off to visitors and then put firmly away in the nursery. Jeremy was suddenly furiously jealous of Charlie. What wouldn't he give for a loving wife and some more children! And how stupid Sam's son must be to reject a girl like Annie!

He forced himself to stop thinking such unproductive thoughts and concentrated instead upon the clinical aspects of the case. He would write a treatise about it and see if he couldn't contact other doctors with similar interests. If they could share their observations . . .

In the kitchen, Jeremy found Tom and Charlie waiting anxiously.

"Couldn't sleep," Tom said shamefacedly. "You'd think I was the bloody father, wouldn't you? How is she?"

"She's fine," said Jeremy, "though very tired, of course. And it's a boy. He's large and healthy."

Charlie beamed at him. "A boy! Large an' healthy," he repeated. His eyes filled with tears. "Eh, to think of it! A little lad."

"An' you're sure our Annie's all right?" persisted Tom, not much interested in the baby.

"Like I said, she's tired, but she should be all right in a day or two." Jeremy looked around. "I'd have thought your stepmother would want to be here."

Tom scowled. "That Emily's not our mother, not in *any* way. She's only me father's wife. She says she'll come along if she's needed, but she might as well get some sleep in the meantime."

"Oh. And Mrs Smith?"

"Sally?" Tom grinned. "She's busy tonight. Her gentleman friend calls round on Tuesdays and Thursdays.
Regular. Very regular." He winked expressively.

"I don't want Annie left on her own," said Jeremy,
frowning. "She's too exhausted to see to the baby without
help."

"I'll stay for a while," said Widow Clegg, who had just
clattered down the stairs. She pushed Tom aside with an
ungentle hand. "It's nearly mornin', not worth me goin'
t'bed. When it's light, tha can get thy stepmother along,
Tom Gibson. Let that Lizzie do summat for a change,
or that May. They're old enough to get breakfast for
t'rest."

Charlie went over to the doctor and timidly pulled at his
sleeve. "The baby. Can I see it? An' Annie, too? I won't
touch 'em. I just want to see 'em. I do."

"I'll show him," said the widow, who had now taken
complete charge again. "I've washed thy instruments,
doctor. Tha'd best be off home. There'll be other folk
needin' thee today."

"Yes. I suppose so." Jeremy didn't want to leave, to
return to an empty house. He'd write to Annabelle the very
next day. It was time she brought Marianne back.

"Come on, then, Charlie Ashworth," said the widow.
"Tha can see thy wife – an' tha can carry this bowl of water
up for me while th'art goin' up."

Eager anticipation shining on his big round face, Charlie
took the bowl and followed her upstairs.

"He's a nice old chap, really," said Tom. "Pity he's a bit
slow, but he's not so daft as folk think. Our Annie did all
right for herself weddin' him, didn't she, doctor? She's not
daft, neither!"

Upstairs, Annie was still holding the baby and Charlie

was standing next to the bed, looking down at them. Even Widow Clegg did not dare to interrupt that moment, for Charlie's face was lit by sheer rapture.

19

Ellie: July 1838 to January 1839

While Annie was enduring the last months of her pregnancy, Ellie Peters was adjusting to a life without her. She missed Annie dreadfully at first, but gradually got on better terms with Cora, the new lady's maid. Later there was all the excitement of getting ready for the trip to Brighton. Annie had said that Ellie might get a chance to go one day and now, here it was, rushing fast towards her.

The weeks before they left were very busy, what with the packing for Miss Marianne and the sorting out of Ellie's own modest wardrobe. Mrs Lewis was in a bad temper most of the time, because she didn't want the bother of taking her daughter. Ellie reckoned she'd only suggested it in the first place out of spite. Ellie could not help overhearing several sharp exchanges on the subject between her master and mistress.

"Jeremy, I really think a long journey will be too much for Marianne! She's not fully recovered yet."

"Then don't go!"

"I need a holiday! I'm worn out."

"So is Marianne."

Jeremy was growing very hard to manage lately, Annabelle thought resentfully. He could be quite stubborn at times. "And what about Miss Richards?" she demanded.

"Surely you'll be taking her with you?"

Annabelle sighed in exasperation. Miss Richards was far too sharp-eyed. She wasn't having the governess with her in Brighton, noting all her comings and goings. There was no harm in the occasional little dinner or drive with Henry Minton, her man of business, but it was still better to keep such things quiet. She could trust Barbara's discretion, because dear Barbara also had her gentlemen friends, but she was not having the governess privy to her little diversions. "It would be too much of an imposition on Barbara's goodwill. Her house is not a large one, and a governess cannot be expected to eat with the servants."

"Then Miss Richards can take a well-earned holiday," said Jeremy impatiently.

"I'm not paying her good money to do nothing! I can't afford such extravagance!" Annabelle'hated to spend money on anyone but herself.

The new, tougher Jeremy merely looked at her cynically, so she flounced out of the room to give herself time to think. Miss Richards and Ellie, who had heard every word from the nursery, exchanged expressive glances, but said nothing in front of the child.

Marianne, who had been listening too, tugged at her governess's sleeve. "I don't think I want to go with Mama, after all," she whispered. "She's always so cross with me."

"That's for your parents to decide, I'm afraid, my dear."

In the end, it was Miss Richards herself who solved the problem by accepting a post as teacher in a school a friend of hers had just opened in Bilsden. Annabelle was delighted. Marianne could go to the school in the autumn, which would save the expense of housing and feeding a governess. With a bit of luck Jeremy would pay the school fees and not think to reduce her housekeeping allowance. Really, things were beginning to look quite promising! And

Ellie should go with them to Brighton, to look after the child. She would be adequate for this unimportant task.

"I thought Barbara's house was too small for you to take anyone with you," commented Jeremy, when informed of the new arrangements.

"Oh, too small to take a governess, who must have a room of her own, but quite large enough for Cora and Ellie, who can sleep together and eat with the other servants," replied Annabelle airily. "I still think it's foolish to drag Marianne all over the country, when she's been so ill, but if *you* insist, what can I do?"

They left Bilsden in the middle of July, travelling by mail-coach. Frederick Hallam, a progressive spirit, had urged them to use the new railways, which would make their journey much faster, but Annabelle refused even to consider it. They would have to go into Manchester first by coach, then change trains several times between Manchester and London, if they did that. Without a gentleman to supervise all these changes and see to their luggage, she would not feel safe. No, better to use the mail, which was slower but safer. You knew where you were with the mail.

Annabelle, who had remarkable stamina when it came to doing things for herself, showed no signs of fatigue on the journey and became quite affable once they had left Bilsden. Cora, who was a seasoned traveller, endured the journey philosophically, but to Ellie and Marianne it was a new and exciting experience. They goggled out of the windows, whispered together and enjoyed every minute. Far from being annoyed, Annabelle laughed at them indulgently and turned back to converse with a fellow traveller, who was very gentlemanly and who was looking at her with admiration. She always enjoyed a mild flirtation when it could have no serious consequences.

In London, Mrs Lewis gave gracious permission for Ellie to take Miss Marianne out sightseeing. She also gave them a guidebook to the metropolis and a small amount of money to cover expenses. However, Dr Lewis had secretly given Ellie a generous sum to buy treats for the child, so there were no restrictions on their enjoyment. If they got lost or grew tired of walking, they simply took a cab.

"Mama seems different here," said Marianne. "She keeps smiling all the time. I'm glad now that we came, aren't you, Ellie?"

"I am, miss," said Ellie, clutching her purse tightly and watching the fascinating goings-on around her. "Just look at that lady over there! Did you ever see such full skirts? It's a wonder she can walk in them! They must be heavy!"

Within two days Annabelle, too, was wearing extra petticoats stuffed with horsehair. She set Cora to adjust her skirts to the new fashionable instep length and ordered some new bonnets from a clever little milliner in a back street, for bonnets were being worn smaller nowadays. She also began to lace herself more tightly, which would have brought Jeremy's wrath down on her head, but which showed off her tiny waist to perfection.

Cora was not quite as good with her needle as Annie had been, Annabelle thought, trying on the results of her maid's labours, nor quite as inventive, but then, Annie had been exceptional, with a real feel for clothes and their trimming. Then Annabelle grew angry with herself for remembering that slut and turned her mind firmly back to getting herself in fashion again.

They moved on to Brighton and Ellie fell in love with it on sight, as Annie had done. For the first time she began to feel some sympathy for her mistress. No wonder Mrs Lewis hated Bilsden so much when she had been used to living in such a heavenly place! Ellie took Miss Marianne down to the beach or out for long walks on every fine day, earning Mrs Lewis's approval by keeping the child out of her way.

Ellie and Marianne were equally fascinated by the sea and would spend hours gazing at it or walking along the edge of the water. The few times Cora was able to go with them, she complained that the pebbles on the beach hurt her feet and retreated to the promenade, so they went mostly on their own.

The little girl rapidly regained her health and grew quite brown. Mrs Lewis said that the sun and wind were bad for the complexion, but then thought of the penalties of keeping her daughter indoors with her and said that as Marianne was only ten, they need not bother about such things just yet. More likely, thought Ellie, you don't really care! She was beginning to wonder what Mrs Lewis was up to. She had seen her mistress in the company of the same gentleman several times, and had thought it wiser to whisk Miss Marianne round corners and change their itinerary, just in case the child commented on it later to her father.

Then a message came from Mrs Parton's doctor to say that the old lady was very ill and would Mrs Lewis please come quickly. Ellie had her first experience of life in the depths of the country and found it very flat after Brighton. There was nothing to see but cows and trees, the people spoke so strangely that she couldn't understand them and Mrs Parton's house was small and dark, smelling of illness. Miss Marianne hated it there, too, and was fractious and hard to manage the whole time, which was not like her.

Old Mrs Parton got worse and worse. Congestion of the lungs, the doctor said. You could hear her from all over the house, gasping and wheezing with each painful breath. It upset Miss Marianne and she couldn't sleep, so Ellie had to go in with her. And the mistress had no sympathy, but just told Ellie to keep that stupid child quiet.

On the third day, Marianne burst into tears when spoken to sharply at the breakfast table and her mother slapped her face, a thing Jeremy would not have allowed. A great red mark it left, too, which made Ellie very angry, though she was powerless to do anything about it. She decided to take Miss Marianne for a walk to get her out of the house for a bit, but just as they were leaving, Cora came down to summon the child to her grandmother's deathbed.

"No! I won't go!" screamed Marianne, thoroughly frightened. She hardly knew her grandmother and was terrified of the skeletal, yellow-faced creature lying gasping in the big bed. She clung to Ellie and kept on screaming and refusing to move until her mother came downstairs and commanded her to behave herself. Then Annabelle dragged the white-faced, sobbing child up to witness the death of her grandmother.

Ellie waited for her with lips tightly compressed. What a way to treat a child! She was not in the least surprised when Miss Marianne had nightmares about it for years and she heard Dr Lewis have another big row with his wife when he found out what had caused the nightmares. Ellie had rarely seen him so furious.

When the funeral was over, Mrs Lewis stayed on for several more dreary days, going through the contents of the house with a fine tooth-comb and arranging its sale to the local squire, who was very gallant to the pretty Mrs Lewis, and very indignant that her husband had not even bothered to come and support her in her time of trouble.

In fact, Jeremy had not been asked to come to his wife's aid. Annabelle had merely informed him of her mother's death and asked his permission to invest her small inheritance in a house in Brighton, which would bring in a better rent than a property in Bilsden.

He sat and stared at her letter for a while, then gave a

wolfish smile. "Why not?" he said aloud.

Armed with his written permission and with Mr Minton's assistance, Annabelle bought a pair of small houses on the sea front, one for her own use and one to rent out. Really, Henry Minton was a most stimulating companion, sharing to the full her own fascination with making money! She wished Jeremy had half his initiative and business acumen. With Henry's help, the money and properties were beginning to mount up nicely. In a few years' time, she would be able to leave the filth and squalor of Bilsden and come to live in Brighton permanently. And she would make very sure that Jeremy did not prevent her.

Jeremy, who had more idea of what his wife was planning than she realised, would have been glad to see her go immediately, but for Marianne. He did not wish his daughter to grow up with the stigma of separated parents. He therefore confronted Annabelle when she returned.

"So you now own a house in Brighton?"

She eyed him sideways. "Yes. I did write and explain about the investment value."

He gave a short, bitter laugh. "Oh, don't worry! I have no intention of interfering with your investments – or with your escapes to Brighton."

"I go there for my health," she insisted. "The air there agrees with me, after the damp of Bilsden."

He sat and looked across the breakfast table at her, studying her as he had not for years. She was carrying her years lightly. She was not beautiful, but she was elegant, witty and attractive – unless you knew the cold and selfish soul under that well-cared-for exterior. He could see that his scrutiny was making her nervous and waited a moment or two longer to speak. "I do have certain conditions, my dear Annabelle. Unless you meet them, I shall be obliged to take a closer interest in your investments."

Fear held her rigid for a moment. "You have *no* interest in business matters! You'd not know what to do with my little legacy."

"No, indeed. Absolutely no interest. Why, I might even lose all your money for you with my ineptitude." He allowed a few minutes for that to sink in.

"What conditions?" she asked at last, when she could control her voice.

"I shall require you to spend enough time in Bilsden to allay gossip and to provide Marianne with a secure background. If you do this, we can maintain the fiction that your delicate health necessitates regular stays in the bracing air of Brighton. If not, well . . ." he shrugged and let the threat remain unvoiced.

Annabelle's soft white fingers curled into claws as he said this, but she kept a calm expression on her face. "Very well. For Marianne's sake." Time enough to worry about getting his permission to leave permanently when she had enough money to live on comfortably.

Ten days after the birth of Annie's son, there was a knock on the door of Number Eight and Ellie came bouncing into the kitchen. She flung her arms round Annie and then hung over the cradle that Charlie had made from scraps of wood. He had carved and polished it with loving care, and it was a beautiful piece.

"Oh, Annie, I'm so glad you're all right! I was that worried, not knowing how you were getting on. The doctor told me you'd had the baby when we got back last week, but I couldn't come to see you till now. How are you?"

Annie smiled at her. Ellie was wearing a bonnet with far too many bright artificial flowers on it. But that was Ellie. "I'm fine now, though I still get a bit tired. How do you like my son?"

"He's bonny!" said Ellie. "I didn't think he'd be so bonny."

"What did you expect? Horns and a tail?"

Ellie laughed shamefacedly. "Sort of."

"He's only a baby. It's not his fault what happened." Annie picked the infant up and cradled him in her arms.

"What've you called him, then?"

"William." Annie dropped a kiss on his button of a nose and stroked the soft auburn fuzz on his skull.

"Who's that after? There's no one in your family called William, is there?"

"No. He's called for himself – and for the old king. That's where I got the name from."

"You should have called him Victor, then, for the new queen."

"Oh, no! I don't like that! Victoria's bad enough for a girl's name, but Victor – ugh!" She put the baby back into the cradle and picked up her sewing. "Now, you tell me all about your stay in Brighton. How did you like it? Did you get on well with Patsy? And how did you like London? Aren't the shops marvellous? What are the latest fashions?"

Nothing loath, Ellie launched into a full description of her trip and of Mrs Lewis's new clothes. "Flounces are in again, you will be pleased to hear, and dresses *en tablier*, which look as if you're wearing a fancy pinafore. Though why ladies want to look as if they're wearing pinnies, like we have to, is more than I can fathom!"

"Go on."

"Well, there's a new sort of sleeve called a bishop's sleeve, tight at the top and full at the bottom." She giggled suddenly. "*She's* got some, of course, but they're set in so low she can't lift her arms properly. I think she loses all her sense when it comes to fashion. If they said wear a feather up your nose, she'd do that, too!"

They both chuckled.

"Oh, an' she's got a new cloak, a sort of two-layer thing with a cape down to her wrists. It makes her look as wide as a house, but it'll be warm come the winter, I expect. An' – let me think – oh, she has a thing called a burnous for evening wear. It's like a shawl with a hood, only she never puts the hood up in case it disturbs her hair. She'd freeze to death, that one would, if it were the fashion!"

Annie sighed. "I really miss her and her clothes," she admitted. "She's got better taste than any of the other ladies, even Mrs Hinchcliffe. I'll have to see if I can catch a glimpse of her in the street. What's her hair like now?"

"She's got it in a low knot at the back, but she ties ribbons an' flowers an' things round it. Cora tried putting it in ringlets for the evening, but you know how soft her hair is and they just didn't hold, so," Ellie leaned forward and grinned, "guess what?"

Annie shrugged.

"She bought herself some false ringlets!"

They both rocked with laughter.

"Do they look false?"

"No. They're a real good match. I don't think the doctor even realises. She keeps 'em hidden in her cupboards, Cora says. Eh, me an' Cora do have a few laughs at the things she gets up to!"

Annie couldn't help feeling a pang of jealousy at Ellie's growing friendship with Cora, but forced herself to ignore that. No good ever came of wishing for the moon.

Although Annie was now pottering round the house, she wasn't well enough to attend chapel, so Ellie decided not to go either, that day. Since the Park House servants had to attend St Mark's, the parish church, Ellie had lost a lot of her old loyalty towards the Todmorden Road Chapel.

Mrs Peters, who felt that Ellie had spent enough time

with *that woman* and her bastard brat, sent one of the younger children round to summon Ellie to go to chapel with them. When a refusal was sent back, she came and banged on the door of Number Eight herself, for Matthew and Sam had both flatly refused to interfere. Mother and daughter had a short, sharp argument on the doorstep, but there was no way that Elizabeth could force her recalcitrant daughter to go with them. Ellie was bigger and stronger than her now, and cared nothing for her threats.

Ellie came back into the house tossing her head angrily. She'd been on cool terms with her mother ever since Annie's troubles had started. "I don't care if she won't have me round there on my days off. It's no pleasure visiting *them*! She's getting funnier all the time. Takes your cup and washes it before you've even finished your tea, and she's for ever sweeping the floor. I don't know how Dad stands it!"

Elizabeth Peters had changed greatly in the past year or two. She was at that awkward time of life for a woman and although she was glad to be done with childbearing, she was not in very good health. She often took offence at Ellie's independent ways and this wasn't the first row she had had with her eldest daughter. She had no desire to see Matt get married, especially after what she thought of as his lucky escape, but she was longing for grandchildren.

She had tried to get Ellie interested in some of the lads at chapel, those with good prospects, sons of farmers or shopkeepers, and the lads had not been at all averse, for Ellie was a plump and pretty girl. But Ellie tossed her head at the mere idea of marrying and discouraged the lads from hanging around her. She was happy in her job, she told her mother firmly, and had no intention of leaving it, no intention at all.

Elizabeth was also worried about Matt. He had grown quieter and quieter since Annie's return, living only for his job. He had little time now for cosy chats with his mother, for he always had his head in a book. And besides, the things he talked about were incomprehensible to a woman who never read a newspaper or opened a book. Mr Hallam had sent Matt away two or three times on business, and although Elizabeth was very proud of that, it had changed her son and made him less hers. Now Matt was talking of leaving Salem Street, though she'd begged him not to. He needed his own room for doing his studies, he said, but she knew it was because of that woman.

Since Annie's baby had been born, Matt had grown very tense, because you could hear its crying through the thin walls. She could see that the noise set his teeth on edge. Indeed, it set her teeth on edge, too. Not just the noise, but knowing who was there on the other side of the wall.

Soon after Ellie's return from Brighton, Matt made the break and found himself lodgings with a widow from chapel. Elizabeth tried by every means she knew to stop him from leaving, but she failed for he was as stubborn as she was, once he had set his mind to something. When he'd gone, she cried for days on end and nothing Sam said or did seemed to comfort her. He worried about her health generally, for she had put on weight and looked puffy and tired most of the time. But when Sam tried to persuade her to go and see the doctor, she turned on him like a wildcat.

"I wouldn't go an' see your precious Dr Lewis if he were the last doctor on earth!" she spat at him. "The way he hangs around that slut next door is disgustin'. He's not comin' near me, not after he's been pawin' at her! Besides, there's nothin' wrong with me! *Nothing!* I'm just a bit tired, that's all. You'd be tired if you had this house to keep clean."

Annie was relieved when Matt Peters moved out. Her heart still lurched in a most disobedient way every time she saw him. She tried not to let her hurt at his scornful attitude show, but the pain of losing him was slow to fade and even now she would sometimes lie awake and weep for what might have been. She had her son and a busy life with Charlie, but there was still something missing, though she would not have admitted that to anyone.

20

Annie: November to December 1838

At the end of November Annie sat feeding her son and talking to her husband, who still fussed over her a lot. "I'm better now, you know, Charlie."

"Yes. A lot better." He was only half-listening, his eyes glued to the child he considered to be his son.

"Dr Lewis won't stop coming round, though."

"He says he's keepin' an eye on you," Charlie pointed out.

"Yes."

"He likes coming. Likes your scones."

"So do you. I don't know who's greedier, you or him."

He just grinned. He was looking a lot better, now that she had the feeding of him. Mind, they'd had to spend some money on cooking equipment, but she hadn't grudged that. She enjoyed cooking and was quite skilled, thanks to Mrs Cosden. For Number Eight, she had bought herself a new spring jack to turn a roast, so that she wasn't for ever tending it, and a lovely dutch oven, so that she could bake properly. And only last week, Tom had found her a proper chimney crane to hold her new cooking pots, and her dad had fixed it up for her. That beat trying to raise and lower the chains holding the hot cookware. How Charlie had managed with only an old black frying-pan and a pan for boil-ups, she didn't know. But then, Emily had much the same equipment.

Even with her improved utensils, Annie still found cooking at Number Eight very limited and the constant need to boil hot water was very wearing. Oh, for a decent closed stove! Mrs Cosden had had one of the first in town, thanks to the doctor's fascination with what he called 'progress'.

"I think the doctor's lonely," she said thoughtfully. She patted William and when he had burped, passed him over to Charlie to cuddle, enjoying the beaming smile on her husband's face. As she cleared up and put William's dirty clouts to soak, her thoughts dwelled on Jeremy Lewis. "He's not a happy man, the doctor isn't, Charlie. Ellie says he and Mrs Lewis don't even eat their meals together unless they have guests. She says he only smiles when he's with Miss Marianne."

"Well, he likes coming here," Charlie repeated, cradling his son in his arms. "He comes a lot."

"Yes." She frowned. "But I'm not sure I like him coming so often. People will talk." But Charlie wasn't even pretending to listen, and anyway, she thought sadly, the subtleties of the situation were really beyond his understanding.

By mid-December, business matters had reached crisis point in Number Eight. Annie had more folk knocking at the door, wanting to buy her second-hand clothes than she could produce clothes, and she had started doing alterations for people as well. It gave her great pleasure each week to drop the shillings she earned into the black tin box, for they could live adequately on what Charlie made. In with her earnings went the rent from the cottages, which seemed a marvel every time Tom brought it back, money that had earned itself, money that just kept coming in, without you having to lift a finger.

The crisis was caused by other factors, as well as Annie's skill with a needle. Helped by Tom and spurred on by his desire to do his best for William, Charlie had extended his rounds over the past few months and was now bringing home more and more stuff. Some of it was so good that Annie couldn't bear to send it away for rags. It was a marvel to her how careless and wasteful some people were. They threw away things with years of wear still in them, just because of a few little holes or a worn hem. But she hadn't the time to mend and alter them all herself, so the bundles began to mount up along her bedroom wall.

"I don't know where I'm going to put this lot!" she exclaimed one day, as Tom helped Charlie carry in some more stuff. "I haven't started on the last lot yet. I can't keep up with you two lately!"

"Why don't you set someone on to help you, then?" suggested Tom. "You could get a young girl to sew the easy bits. You'd not have to pay 'er much."

There was a pause. "Hire somebody? Me!" said Annie faintly. "Don't talk daft! I couldn't! Do I look like an employer?"

Tom grinned. "No, but if you've got the money to pay 'em, people won't care what you look like. What matters to us is, would you make more money out of it?"

Annie sat there, her brain working furiously as she got over her first shock at the idea. Would she make more money? Yes, of course she would! The clothes she made from the stuff Charlie brought in were becoming popular for 'best' among the more affluent inhabitants of the Rows, and returned a good profit on Charlie's original outlay of paying a few pence by weight for people's clean rags. The women who bought Annie's things were those with a bit of money to spare, even in these hard times, the young unmarried girls and the older women with several children working. And she knew her clothes were more than just body coverings to them. She had an eye for colour and could 'do up' an old dress till you'd think it was new-bought that year. A couple of young women had already got wed in her simple creations. Oh, yes, she thought, she could definitely make more money if she had some extra help.

She looked at Tom. "Do you really think I could do it?" she asked hesitantly. It seemed such a big step to take. "Dare I?"

Tom had no doubts. Even at seventeen, he had an entrepreneur's soul and could spot talent in others a mile off. "Why not, our Annie! Any road, it wouldn't cost much to try, just a few shillin' a week till you see how it goes. You could always get rid of her if it didn't pay."

"Ooh, I don't know. We'll leave it be for the moment. I'll have to think about it." She refused to discuss the subject any further. She could not just dive into something. She had to be sure that it would work, that she wouldn't lose from it. Security was just as important as making a profit.

She was still thinking about the matter when Mrs Hinchcliffe dropped in to see her. Annie screwed up her courage and asked if Pauline thought it would be a good idea to expand her business and take on another woman to help her with the sewing.

"Why not?" Pauline echoed Tom's words. "It'll only cost you a few weeks' wages and you're not telling me you can't afford that! You have to spend money sometimes to make it."

"Yes, I suppose so. It's just – everything's happened so quickly."

"It's happened quickly, Annie, because you've filled a

need, and because your clothes are nice to look at as well as practical."

"So you think I could cope?"

"Of course you could!"

"The thing is, if I do get someone, I'd not want an untrained girl." She looked at Mrs Hinchcliffe apprehensively, fearing her scorn. "I've been thinking about it. I don't need someone who just knows how to do straight seams. It's alterations and awkward bits I mainly have to do with my re-makes. Oh, I don't know. I just don't know."

"Think it over. You don't have to do things immediately, do you? It's nearly Christmas. You *are* allowed to relax and enjoy yourself occasionally."

Annie, who even worked on Sundays, shuddered at the thought. She looked round at the bundles. "I'll have to do something, that's for sure. There won't be any room in the house for people, at this rate."

In the event she found someone sooner than she had expected. She mentioned her plans casually to Sally the next day and Sally began to look thoughtful.

"I know a woman who'd like a place," she told Annie after a few moments' hesitation, "only – well – you might not want to set her on."

"Oh? Who is she and why not?"

"She's a friend of mine. I've known her for years. She trained as a seamstress in Manchester, but then she – well, no use tryin' to dress it up – she went on the streets. That's how I met her. But she's had enough of that now, love. She wants a change. If she could get a respectable place again, she'd leave that other business tomorrow. But it's hard to get a respectable place without references, specially for someone like her. She's not been as lucky as I have."

Annie was dubious. "I don't know. Folks talk. I wouldn't want customers put off coming to me."

"How would they find out?"

"You'd be surprised how things get round," said Annie darkly.

"Oh, well, it was just an idea."

"No, wait! I wouldn't mind seeing her. At least she wouldn't turn her nose up at working in Salem Street. Could you ask her to come and see me? But tell her to dress quietly. And I'm not promising anything, mind. What's she called?"

"Alice is her real name, Alice Turner. She's been callin' herself Marie, because it's better for business, an' she's been dyein' her hair blond. I don't think folk would recognise her so easy if she changed it back to brown, though, an' stopped curling it."

When Sally brought her friend round the next day, Annie recognised her at once. It was the woman who had set her free from Fred Coxton. She saw by the woman's face that she, too, had been recognised.

When Annie shook hands, she kept hold of Alice's for a moment or two longer. "I never thanked you properly for helping me last January. If you can sew, the job's yours." Sally looked puzzled, but Annie didn't explain just then.

Alice shrugged. "I was glad to help. That Fred Coxton was a pig. I heard tell that he died in a fight, over Liverpool way. I hope he did!"

Annie shuddered. She still had nightmares about that evening. Or about Fred returning to Bilsden. "What about your sewing?"

"Well, I made this dress I'm wearing," Alice pirouetted in front of them. "It's not bad, is it? I call it my go-to-church dress, because it's dark and respectable." She grinned at them. "I made it from some flawed pieces I got at the market."

Annie examined the stitching, then looked at the fit and

style. The stitches were neat and even, and the only fault she could find was that there was too much trimming.

"If I take you on, you must give up the other," she warned. "I run a respectable business."

"Just give me the chance! I hate it! Most men are bastards!"

"Why did you start, then?"

"I was workin' for an old bitch in Manchester. She treated us like slaves. Didn't even feed us properly. Then I met this fellow. He said he'd marry me. I wouldn't have gone off with him else. Only he didn't marry me. Turned out he was already wed. We made me work for him instead. What could I do? *She* wouldn't have taken me back, an' I've no family left that I know of! An' anyway, George treated me all right at first. We had a bit of fun together." She looked at them defiantly. "I'd never had much fun. My parents were old and strict with me."

"So what went wrong?" asked Annie.

"I fell for a kid. He didn't like it when I wouldn't get rid of it an' he turned me out of my room when I got too big to work. Things was never so good after that. I went from one place to another. In the end I wound up with Fred Coxton. Dunno how. A right bastard, he turned out to be! I were glad when he left, but I had to go on workin' or I'd have starved."

Sally nodded. "That's how a lot of the girls get started, Annie, love. They'll believe anything a man tells 'em, young girls will. You're just lucky you haven't got no kids, Alice."

"I had two," Alice blinked her eyes rapidly, "but they died. Fever, it was, with Billy, an' Jane just never thrived. Only two months old, she was, when she went. Fred said good riddance, but I were upset. They were nice babies. I tried to look after 'em, but you know what it's like. You have to give 'em Godfrey's Cordial to keep 'em quiet. An'

333

then they're not so hungry. An' so things go from bad to worse."

Annie's eyes turned to her own baby, who lay in his cradle waving his chubby arms about. How lucky she was that Charlie had married her! Who knows what she might have been driven to do otherwise? She'd heard Jeremy Lewis's views on Godfrey's Cordial, which he called 'an iniquitous brew', for it contained laudanum and babies given a lot of it were often slow to learn and mature.

She patted Alice's arm. "All right. I'll take you on. I'll pay you eight shillings a week, your clothes found and two meals a day. That's to start. If business goes all right and you work well, I'll pay you more later, but I can't afford it yet. You'll start here at seven in the morning till seven at night. Saturdays we'll finish a bit earlier. You'll sew mostly, but you'll have to help with the baby or do the cooking or whatever else needs doing." She cut short Alice's stammered thanks, embarrassed by the tears in the older woman's eyes and the warm expression on Sally's face. "Where do you live? Still down in Claters End?"

"Yes."

"Well, you can't stay there. It's not respectable. An' it's dirty. You'll have to find a lodging nearer. And Sally said you could maybe change your hair, stop dyeing it, wear it differently. We don't want anyone recognising you."

"Yes, I'll do that. Be a relief not to have to keep bleachin' an' curlin' it, to tell you the truth."

"You could stay with me most of the time, Alice," Sally volunteered. "Except on the nights when my Harry comes." She winked. "He likes us to be private then."

"You could sleep here in the kitchen on those nights, if you don't mind a mattress on the floor," offered Annie. In for a penny, in for a pound, she thought to herself. Besides, she owed this woman a lot.

Tears were running down Alice's face. "You won't be sorry," she promised huskily.

When she'd gone to get her things, Sally looked at Annie. "I must be goin' soft in me old age. I don't know what my Harry will say."

"If you're getting soft, so am I," answered Annie.

"You'd no need to do all that. Why did you, love?"

"She's the one who helped me to get away from Fred Coxton that time. I owe her the same chance."

"Eh, she's never said anythin' about it, an' I've known her for years. She's a nice lass. Reminds me of meself a few years ago. But I were lucky. I met my Harry."

Years later, when Annie looked back on those early days, she felt that she must have had a guardian angel watching over her, because she had a few pieces of luck. Alice Turner was the first. Alice worked enthusiastically right from the start, taking as much interest and trouble as if the business were her own. Her face soon lost its pallor, her body filled out and she became a plump vivacious woman with a bounce to her step. The blond hair was dyed a dirty brown before she ever joined Annie, and gradually grew into her own soft brown, which suited her complexion, to Annie's mind, much more than blond.

It was Alice who took charge of selling the clothes at the market. The first time they tried it, Annie was almost too nervous to think straight. She paid the market fees and then she and Alice stood behind Charlie's handcart, loaded with remade or mended second-hand clothes. It was Alice who called out their wares, and Alice who bantered with the customers and passers-by. By the end of the day, they'd sold nearly half of the things they took along, especially the dark, serviceable garments. They couldn't make enough clothes to fill the cart every week, but from then onwards they went to market about once a month. Or at least, Alice did. Annie soon left the selling to her.

On the second visit to the market, they had a bit of trouble from some bullies, who tried to make Annie pay protection money. When she mentioned their threats indignantly to Tom, he grinned. "Leave it to me, Sis."

She was troubled no more.

"How did you do it?" Annie was worried at his familiarity with the rougher element in the town. "Won't they come back next time, if they see Alice there on her own?"

"No. I know their boss. He won't trouble my sister, or anyone doin' business for her. He owes me a favour."

"You know some funny people, Tom. I don't like it."

"It's useful. Why do you think no one's bothered your Charlie lately? Did you know he used to have to pay the bullies twopence every time he came back home?"

"No! But still, Tom . . ."

He shook her arm. "Leave it be, our Annie. That's how things are done in the Rows, whether you like it or not."

"I don't like it. In fact, I hate it!"

"Well, you've got no choice, have you? You're stuck here now yourself. Like the rest of us."

She watched him go. Yes, she was stuck here – but not for ever!

Annie's first Christmas back in the street passed almost unnoticed so busy were they. The mills had been on full time for the past few weeks and people had a little money to spare, so she'd sold a lot of her clothes. She did make the effort to put on a specially nice meal after chapel on Christmas Day, to which her family, Sally and Alice were invited. John had squashed Emily's protests about Sally's presence and made sure she was not left out of things on the day.

Annie gave everyone a present, little things she had sewed herself. She watched her little stepsister, Becky, playing with a rag doll, loving it in her arms and staring around her wide-eyed and protective. Poor child! She looked half-starved and that dress was a disgrace. Emily was a rotten mother.

Her eyes caught her father's and he shrugged, taking Becky and her dolly on his knee. Annie smiled as she watched them. Just so had John bounced her when she was little. He was as good a father as life allowed. And he was looking pretty tired himself lately. Seeing how poorly dressed her stepbrothers and sisters were made her resolve even more fiercely that William should do better than that, that she would get the two of them out of Salem Street one day, if she had to work her fingers to the bone to do it.

Charlie, sitting in state at the head of the table, never stopped beaming all day and the good food and small presents kept even Lizzie and May on their best behaviour. William gurgled his way through the day with his usual sunny nature. A better baby, Annie thought that evening, looking at him lying kicking in the cradle, was never born. Almost worth the trouble he'd caused her, she realised with a shock. He beamed up at her and caught her finger in his little pink hand and she amended that. "You're well worth the trouble, my lad," she said aloud. It was strange how her feelings had changed towards him.

One day in February Annie was walking back from the shops when a small body catapulted into her just before the turn into Salem Street. The child cried out and went sprawling in the half-frozen mud. Annie bent to pull her up, recognising that it was one of the Dykes children. She exclaimed in horror at a fresh burn mark on the bony arm.

Just at that moment, Polly Dykes came puffing round the corner, a smoking poker in her hand.

"There y'are, y'little bastard!" she screeched, brandishing the poker. "I'll give it you! Run away from me, will you!"

Annie put the trembling child behind her and confronted Polly, now a draggled, blowsy woman, ageing rapidly. Polly spent as much of her time as she could afford drunk, and the rest beating her children and quarrelling with her husband. It was a minor miracle that George Dykes was still in employment, because he was as fond of the drink as his wife. It was a wonder, too, that any of the Dykes children had survived infancy, so irregularly were they fed. Neighbours slipped them a crust, when they had a bit to spare, but they were a sickly, undersized bunch and two of the younger ones had died in the last outbreak of fever.

"What's the matter, Polly?" Annie asked quietly.

"What's the matter?" Polly mimicked Annie's accent and flounced her hips. "What the 'ell's it got to do with you? Ain't you got enough on yore plate with yore barmy 'usband?"

"You watch what you say about my Charlie, or I'll make you sorry."

Polly shrieked with laughter and brandished the poker, but Annie easily avoided her wild swings and pushed her over, wrenching the poker contemptuously out of her hand as she fell.

She thumped the poker on the ground, making Polly whimper and jerk backwards. "If I *ever* hear you calling my Charlie barmy again, I'll pay someone to fix you, Polly Dykes." She tossed the poker aside and bent to pick up the basket she had dropped, becoming aware that the little girl was still clinging to her skirt and shivering uncontrollably, though whether from cold or fear it was hard to tell.

"What's the matter, love – Kathy, isn't it?" she asked gently.

The child shuddered and said nothing, but her eyes flickered towards her mother in a tell-tale way.

Annie sighed. She shouldn't really get involved. What a parent did to a child was nobody else's business. But since she'd had William, she was looking at the children around her differently.

"What's your Kathy done wrong?" she asked Polly, who was struggling to her feet.

"Her! Lazy bleedin' sod, she is! They won't set her on at t'mill, because she looks too weak. She will be weak, I told 'em, if she don't get a job soon! Albert Thomas tried her on rag-pickin' an' she couldn't keep up with the others. It's more than time she were bringin' summat in, more'n time! I'll learn her to do as she's told! Couldn't keep up, indeed! We'll see 'oo can't keep up!" She waved a threatening fist at the child, who shivered and pressed closer to Annie.

"I didn't know you were wanting her set on," Annie said casually. "Why didn't you come to me, instead of insulting my Charlie?"

"Huh?" Polly stood there, swaying a little, already reeking of gin, though it wasn't yet noon.

"I've been thinking of taking a girl on," went on Annie, "an apprentice, to learn the trade."

Polly hooted with laughter. "Well, we've got sod all to pay for her to go as a bleedin' apprentice, so y'wastin' y'time talkin' to me."

"I know you couldn't pay, but I could give you special terms for old times' sake, because you knew my mother."

"Ah, Lucy was a fine woman," said Polly, with a sudden switch of mood. A maudlin tear wound its way down her grey, dirt-encrusted cheek. "Many's the cup of tea we supped together, y'poor mother an' me." She seemed to have completely forgotten her animosity. "I often think of Lucy, that I do."

Liar! thought Annie, but she didn't say so aloud. "Well," she said, in the tones of one making a huge concession, "just for you, just because you knew my mother, Polly, I'll set Kathy on without charging you the usual apprenticeship fees. Just for old times' sake. And – because I know you've a hard time feeding them all – I'll give Kathy all her meals. Now, how about that?"

Polly's brow creased in laborious thought. "That won't help us," she said at last. "She won't be bringin' no money in."

"She's not bringing anything in now, and you still have to feed her. I can't do any better than that, Polly. I'm only just starting up in business. I haven't got any money to spare. I'm only doing this as a favour to you."

The older woman wavered.

"She'll be able to make you a new dress when she's been with me for a few months," added Annie persuasively, wondering why she was even bothering. "Just think of it, a nice new dress."

There was a moment's pause, then, "A new one?" Polly fingered the filthy grey skirt she was wearing and her eyes were briefly young again. "I haven't had a new dress for years."

"Well?"

"All right, then."

Annie became her usual brisk business self. "I'll bring round the papers for you to sign tomorrow."

"Papers! Sign!"

Annie feigned surprise. "Well, of course! You've got to do these things legally. One day your Kathy will be earning a good wage, if she sticks with me for the five years. But you and George have to sign. You're the parents."

"George'll not sign no papers. How will we know what's writ in 'em?"

"I'll tell you what's in them."

"Yes, but we won't know if it's true or not."

"Well, if you don't trust me, that's that, then." Annie shrugged her shoulders and turned away. The child gasped in dismay.

Polly grabbed Annie's sleeve. "No, wait... What do these soddin' papers say?"

"They say that you agree to leave Kathy with me for five years." Inspiration struck. "And that you agree to pay me twenty pounds if you try to take Kathy away from me."

"Twenty pound! Twenty pound! We've not got no twenty pound! Never will 'ave, neither!"

"That's only if you try to take her away." Annie's patience was wearing thin. "Make up your mind! I can't stand around here talking all day. I have a baby to feed and a business to run."

"Well, I dunno. I'll 'ave to ask my George."

Annie smiled. George Dykes was an amiable bear of a man, who would do anything to keep the peace. "Your George won't say no to me. He's known me since I was a child. Look, I'll take your Kathy with me now and start her off, eh?"

"Well – Oh, all right."

Annie strode away, followed by a patter of footsteps. She stopped and the child was so close behind, she trod on Annie's skirt, then flinched back, as if expecting a slap.

When they went into Number Eight, Kathy remained gaping by the door. Neighbours were not encouraged to run in and out of Number Eight, and most of the people in the street had not been inside the house. To Kathy, the place seemed a palace. There were coloured rag rugs on the floor, soft to the feet, and beautiful curtains at the windows, none of whose panes were broken, and as for the furniture, well, she'd never seen anything like it in her life, with its polished wood and bright-coloured cushions. The Dykes children sat and slept on sacks on the floor, and their parents had rickety stools. Kathy had heard people say that the Ashworths were rich and now she knew that all the stories were true.

Annie explained to Alice in an undertone how she'd acquired Kathy's services and they both looked at the child, who was still standing patiently by the door, waiting to be disposed of.

"Poor little devil!" said Alice softly. "How old did you say she was?"

"Twelve, I think."

"Some people shouldn't have kids," said Alice scornfully. "Why, she's nothin' but skin and bone! And she'll be lousy, you know. She'll have to be washed and combed clean. An' what about her goin' back at nights? She'll pick things up again if she does."

"Ugh! I never thought of that," said Annie. "I just felt sorry for her. You know what that Polly's like."

They both looked at Kathy again. She was standing as patiently as ever by the front door, waiting for her rescuer to tell her what to do.

Annie sighed. "I can't send her back, Alice, I just can't! Look at the burn on her arm. Polly had just hit her with a red-hot poker. On purpose! She'll have to live in, that's all. She can sleep down here. I'm not sharing my bedroom with anyone. You won't mind having her around on Mondays and Thursdays, will you?"

"Not if she's clean!"

They burst out laughing. "Come on, then," said Annie. "Let's get it over with!"

Kathy made no protest at the stripping and cleansing of

her person. Indeed, she almost fell asleep in the tin bath. Never in all her short life had anything felt so warm and soothing! The two women were appalled at the bruises and scars on her emaciated body, but they kept their thoughts to themselves, merely exchanging expressive glances from time to time.

Once the bathing was over, they wrapped the child in a blanket and settled her in a chair by the fire. When they gave her some bread and ham, and a cup of tea, she wolfed it down as if she expected someone to snatch it away again. Then her eyes closed and her head rolled backwards against the chair. Annie left her to sleep. There was no question of work just yet.

"I never thought I'd say this," muttered Alice, "but she'd have done better in the union workhouse."

"I don't know about that." Annie shivered. "My mam was put on the parish and she wouldn't ever talk about what had happened to her."

"But look at what's happened to Kathy!"

"Yes." They both fell silent again.

Charlie, when he came in, just smiled at the idea of having Kathy live with them. "It'll be nice, havin' you here, lass." He loved children, as long as they weren't rough and noisy. He always shrank away from May and Lizzie, but this thin little creature instantly aroused his compassion.

Kathy stared at him as if he were the man in the moon.

"I'll make you a bed chair," he promised her. "Saw one once. Not hard. Get some wood tomorrow. The bottom pulls out to sleep on. It does. Neat as anythin'."

Annie intervened. "Let her get used to you." She kissed her husband's cheek. "You're a kind man, Charlie Ashworth. And don't worry. She'll earn her keep. She can learn to sew and help me with William when she's stronger. She'll need feeding up first, though, poor thing. You wouldn't think she was nearly twelve, would you? She's only a year younger than Lizzie."

He scowled at the name. "I don't like Lizzie. No, I don't like her."

"I don't either, but she's my sister, so we'll have to put up with her. The only one who does like her is May. The two of them are as thick as thieves, and welcome to each other, as far as I'm concerned."

When Tom came round, as he did most nights, he was less pleased. "You're gettin' soft, our Annie," he said scornfully. "There's plenty of kids as'd come an' work for their food. Smart kids. Why did you have to pick this one? Everyone knows that Kathy Dykes is slow. That's why no one'll take her on. She'll be no use at all." He took a very proprietorial interest in Annie's business and often turned up at the market once the mill had closed on Saturdays, to try his hand at selling.

In spite of his disapproval of the transaction, however, he agreed to go round to Number Two with his sister, "if only to stop them tryin' to get any money out of you."

"I'm not that daft, our Tom!" retorted Annie. "If they thought there was money to be got from me, they'd never be off my doorstep."

They took a big piece of paper with them, to impress Kathy's parents. Annie giggled as she wrote it out, using all the long words she could think of and her very best handwriting. She even drew flourishes on the top.

"That looks good," said Tom. "I didn't know you could draw so well."

"Oh, I used to have a go sometimes at Park House. Miss Richards taught me and Ellie a few things. I like drawing. I only wish I had time to do it properly."

As Tom had predicted, George tried to get Annie to pay him a shilling or two a week for Kathy's services. Tom took over the bargaining at that point. When George started threatening Annie, Tom marched over to him and grabbed him by the shirt. George made a feeble attempt to fight him off, but then subsided on to a stool. Like Polly, he was drunk most evenings. Several filthy, half-clothed children watched wide-eyed from the back of the room till George shook his fist and roared at them to get into the back kitchen.

"Now, George Dykes," said Tom, "either you sign an' let Annie take your Kathy an' train her to sew, or I'll go an' bring her back right now, this very minute. I don't mind. I think Annie's soft to take her on at all. I wouldn't! She don't know how to sew or do anything else much. She's not worth a farthing scrape of dripping, that one!"

Grandpa Jack spoke up then. "You do as he says, our George. Tom's right. The little lass is good for naught else. She's not strong enough. You said so yourself only yesterday. Let 'em take her off your hands." Jack Dykes was beginning to show his age and now that he could no longer beat his son in a fight, tended to sit quietly in his corner after work. He was terrified they'd put him in the union workhouse once he grew too old to work. But he had a soft spot for little Kathy and enough wit to see that here was her big chance in life.

Reluctantly George Dykes agreed to sign his cross.

"Go an' fetch our dad, Annie," said Tom, who'd now taken complete charge. "We need a witness to this. That lawyer chap said it was to be done proper." They had consulted no lawyer, but the word impressed Polly and George into complete silence.

John Gibson came round and solemnly signed his name after George and Polly's crosses, then they all left. Before he went back into Number Three, John patted Annie's shoulder. "You're a nice lass doin' this. Your mam would've been proud of you." Then he whisked inside, his eyes suspiciously bright.

At the door to Number Eight, Annie stopped and looked at Tom. "You handled that well."

He grinned. "Told you I could take care of meself. Wait till your business is goin' proper! I'll come in full-time, then. We'll make money, you an' me, one way or another. Lots of money. You'll see."

"Yes. I hope so. But not till times get better. Charlie can cope with things himself for now. I want to make money as much as you do, Tom, but I'm going to be very careful how I do it."

Part Two

21

1839 to 1844

Engrossed in her business and her son, Annie hardly noticed how the years were passing. The Chartist movement went by almost unobserved by her, although Sam Peters talked about it to her father, and her father mentioned it to her once or twice. Annie still did not get on with her stepmother, but Emily had changed over the years. She seemed to have withdrawn into herself, to find everything just too much to cope with. She had absolutely no comprehension of what Chartism meant and took no interest in the wider world. She only cared that John brought home enough money to feed them all. Some of the mills in Bilsden had a struggle to survive, though Hallam's always did better than the rest. Emily was quite bewildered by all the changes going on around her, as were many of the older people.

In almost no time, it seemed to Annie, William was turning six, a sturdy little boy, too much of a mammy's boy, some would have said, for he spent a lot of his time with her, doing his lessons and helping her in his childish way. He hardly played out at all because she didn't want him associating with riff-raff. The rest of his spare time was spent with the man he called Dad, for Charlie adored him and always had time to talk to the child or play with him or teach him new skills. Sheltered and cared for by Annie and Tom, Charlie grew gradually to near normality, slow still, but achieving a kind of gentle dignity and acquiring an aura of cheerful kindliness that made people stop calling him 'barmy', even out of Annie's hearing.

Every now and then, as the years passed, Annie would pause to marvel at the changes in herself, but mostly she was too busy making a living and putting a bit by to waste time in introspection. Until William was five, times were hard in Bilsden. A general recession, trade fluctuations in the cotton industry, the death of a leading mill-owner, a fire in one of the big mills, all these hit the small town hard and, of course, inevitably reflected on the junk trade. No question yet of bringing Tom into the business full-time; there was sometimes barely enough work for Charlie. They would just have to bide their time.

Fortunately they were not only dependent on what Charlie could bring in. There was the five shillings a week from Hallam's still, the rent money on the cottages and what Annie could earn with her sewing. There was no week in which she did not put at least a few pennies away in the tin box, and more often it was a few shillings.

Annie grew into a lovely woman, but it was a cool, reserved loveliness that offered no promises and held out no lures to the men with whom she came into contact. Indeed, she kept everyone except William and, to a lesser degree, Charlie and Tom, at arm's length. So engrossed was she in her work that she paid little attention to her own appearance, as long as she was clean and neatly turned out. But when the sun shone on her auburn hair or when she smiled at her son, men sometimes turned to look at her admiringly. Most of the time she didn't even notice them.

She had no time to waste on chit-chat and rarely paused to gossip with the other women in the street, except Sally and Bridie O'Connor. And even with them, she spoke decisively and crisply, and did not linger for long. Time was money.

Little by little she grew used to giving orders to her employees. The orders were usually couched as polite requests, but Alice, Kathy and the other women who intermittently sewed for her obeyed them without question, for Annie would stand no nonsense. Only Tom sometimes questioned what she said and did; only Tom could provoke her into a quarrel, for they were too alike to co-exist in complete harmony.

During those years Tom had no choice but to stay on in the mill. Although this fretted him greatly, he generally managed to hide his feelings and he gained a reputation as a good, steady worker, one of the most skilful, for all he was so young. He could turn his hand to anything and was always one of the last to be put on to short time. He eked out his earnings when Hallam's was on short time with odd jobs, or made extra money from the bits and pieces, as he called them, in the good times. So, like his sister, he began to accumulate money, make contacts and hone his skills.

However, Tom also acquired a reputation as a mean man to cross. Neither Benworth, the overseer, nor Matt, now assistant to Benworth, found occasion to criticise Tom's work or dock his money for minor infringements of the rules – he had too much native cunning to be caught out doing anything against the mill rules – but neither of them marked him out for further advancement. Tom Gibson had a way of looking you straight in the eyes, as if he were daring you to find fault with what he was doing and there was not a subservient bone in his body. Even Frederick Hallam frowned at his attitude, but there was nothing that he could put a finger on to complain about and the man was such a good worker that it'd be a pity to lose his services, just because he had the wrong expression on his face at times. Frederick had developed an obsession about building up a more skilled workforce and had no intention of training men to serve other masters.

After work Tom associated with a dubious crowd whom Annie didn't like and about whom she and Tom had words regularly. He was also fond of women, though he was careful to confine his attentions to married women or women of loose morals, because he had no desire to let himself get trapped into marriage. He'd seen enough of what a bad marriage did to a man, with Emily and his father.

In appearance Tom was not prepossessing, for he was one who would come late to full physical maturity, and his face still reflected the youthful uncertainties that raged within him. He had grown little since he was fifteen and was of barely medium height, only an inch or two taller than Annie and about an inch taller than his father. He was, however, as strong as an ox and seemed to take a perverse delight, every now and then, in testing out his strength and fighting prowess in what he called 'a bit of a rough-house'. Annie called it brawling, and she called most of his friends 'scum'.

When he was eighteen Tom left home and went to lodge with Widow Clegg, because he could no longer stand the crowded conditions at Number Three, even for the sake of living cheaply. John Gibson's second marriage continued to be disastrously fertile and Emily was still presenting him with a new child almost every year. By the time William was six, Mark, Luke and Rebecca had Peggy, Joan and baby Edward to keep them company. Another baby, a boy, had died at birth and Emily had also had two miscarriages. A bewildered Emily found it hard to cope with the demands of such a large brood of children. She changed gradually from a shrew into an apathetic, overworked drudge, who turned more and more often to gin as her only means of solace.

But in spite of her backsliding, Emily still clung to her religion and regularly staged scenes of fervent repentance about her drinking and general inadequacies. The help of her brothers and sisters in Christ was one of the main things that prevented her from going completely downhill, like Polly Dykes. Cast-off clothes, gifts of food, a helping hand when she was ill or confined to childbed, all these were forthcoming when things grew too much for her or when the mill was on half-time.

Within the Gibson family, Lizzie and May always kept themselves very much to themselves. Both now worked in the mill, but in a community where early marriage was the rule, neither had ever shown the slightest interest in boys. By 1844, Lizzie was nineteen, pale, plump, with lank gingery hair. May, at seventeen, was a younger version of her mother, scrawny and with sharp features and mousy hair. When May was fifteen, she and Lizzie had issued an ultimatum to their parents. Either they got the small back bedroom to themselves or they would leave home. John blustered and protested, but he had lost a lot of his old forcefulness and in the end he and Emily had to give way to their daughters' demands and move themselves down to the front room, putting the rest of their brood in their old front bedroom. A year after that, Lizzie and May moved right out, giving no warning, just packing their things one day and moving to a room in Florida Terrace. The loss of their earnings was a big blow to the family.

Pauline Hinchcliffe, usually the organiser of help for Emily Gibson, shook her head over the woman's improvidence and said that she was one of life's incompetents, but Saul would not countenance any diminution in help to one of his congregation and reminded Pauline sternly of the parable of the lost sheep.

Annie helped, too. Emily had completely forgotten her old animosity towards her stepdaughter and was humbly grateful nowadays for the help she regularly gave.

"The woman's a fool!" Pauline would exclaim to Annie. "You're just wasting your time with her."

"I know," Annie would sigh, "but if I don't help out a bit, it's my dad and the children who'll suffer."

"And so he should! If he were more continent, they would not have such difficulties!"

"I know, but . . ." And Annie would dip into Charlie's junk to provide clothes for the new baby or a dress for little Rebecca. But she never gave them money, for she knew Emily would only spend it on gin. She also discouraged her father's family from popping in and out of Number Eight, because she didn't want interruptions to her business.

Except when she was pregnant, Pauline kept up her practice of dropping unexpectedly in at Number Eight and demanding a cup of tea. She said she needed someone intelligent to talk to once in a while. She was a stimulating conversationalist and not one to bow to the prevailing mores. She had found and wooed a husband when she felt the need for one and she would bestow her friendship where she chose, too. She was not a regular member of the local social circles. Chapel did not usually associate with church and she owed her husband some loyalty. However, her family had been landowners in the district for a long time, and she would occasionally condescend to exchange hospitality with her peers and even with those higher up on the county's social scale.

During those years Pauline bore two sons. Her narrow body was not well suited to childbearing and it was over two years before she first conceived, years in which she came near to despairing over her inability to have a child. She was in poor health all the time she was carrying a child and her first labour was long and arduous. It was only thanks to Jeremy Lewis's skill that young Stephen Collett Hinchcliffe emerged unharmed into the world.

It took three more years for Pauline to conceive again, and this time, the birth was so difficult that Jeremy forbade her to have any more children if she valued her life. This child she allowed her husband to name Wesley Emmett, and for a few years Saul nourished hopes that his son would follow him into the ministry. But in spite of his name, the boy was as like his mother as his elder brother was, and neither of them ever paid more than lip service to their father's religion.

One day, when Pauline had fully recovered from the birth of her second child and was looking round for more challenges, she announced to Annie, "It won't do, you know."

"What won't do?" Annie was puzzled.

"That dress."

"What's wrong with it?" Annie looked down in surprise. "It's clean and I mended it carefully. I don't know what you mean."

"Heaven grant me patience!" Pauline shook her head, and then cast patience aside in favour of brutal honesty. "How a person dresses is most important. What must people think of you when they see you in a dress like that? It's faded and patched and the hem's been turned."

Annie shrugged.

"Put down that sewing and listen to me! In that dress you look just like any other woman from the Rows – a bit cleaner, maybe, and certainly prettier than most, but a woman of the poorer classes."

355

"I don't see what's wrong with that," said Annie defensively. "I live in the Rows. I can't change that. What need is there to dress more smartly?"

"Because better times are coming and because you want to improve yourself, to make money, to *leave* the Rows – or so you've always said. Have you changed your mind about that?"

"You know I haven't! That's why I'm so careful with my money. But there'll be time enough for fancy clothes when I have some real money behind me."

"Raise your eyes from the ground, girl! You don't make real money by grubbing in the mud for farthings! Why aren't you making new dresses for people, instead of patching up those pitiful rags? Why aren't you dreaming of becoming a proper dressmaker? This town abounds with silly women, who have nothing better to do than fritter away their husbands' money on fancy clothes and falderals in Manchester. Why don't *you* take their money away from them, since they're so eager to spend it?"

Annie's full attention was caught now. "Do you really think I could do that?"

"I don't know, but I think you should try." Pauline was not one to boost morale without foundation. "Anything would be an improvement on those rags you're for ever patching together. I'll think less of you if you don't have a try."

"We make good money from what you call rags!"

"Good money!" snorted Pauline. "You mean you make a living and a bit to spare. I don't call that good money."

"It's good money in the Rows."

"The Rows! The Rows! There's more to the world than these filthy terraces, Annie, my girl! It's a pity you ever had to come back to Salem Street!"

"I didn't have much choice about that, did I?"

Pauline sighed and spoke more gently. "I know. You've done well, all things considered. But now it's time to make some changes, to take a step forward. And the first thing to do is to change the way you dress, so that people can *see* that you're different."

"I suppose you have a point there."

"You know I do. If you dress more fashionably yourself, other women will want to look like you and they'll come to you for clothes. Not ladies, not yet. One step at a time. But there are plenty of farmers' wives, and clerks' or shopkeepers' wives around nowadays, not to mention their daughters, some of them in our congregation. *They* have money to spend, too." Satisfied that she'd made her point, she left things at that and changed the subject by asking for another cup of tea.

When Pauline had left, Annie sat and stared at the pile of fashion magazines Pauline had given her. A few days later, for the first time in years, she bought some lengths of material and made herself some brand new dresses. She also experimented with her hair and started wearing it in a more fashionable style, though she grudged the extra time she had to spend on putting it up every morning. Here Kathy proved unexpectedly helpful, for she turned out to have a way with hair and loved to experiment with new styles. They joked about Annie having her own lady's maid now.

The first time Annie went out in her new clothes, she felt very self-conscious. She'd tried them out the evening before on Tom and he'd been loudly appreciative.

"Turn round. Walk across the room." He whistled softly. "I didn't know you could look so – so . . ."

"So what?"

"So fashionable and – and pretty. You're a proper

357

stunner, our Annie, and I never realised it!" He grinned at her. "What brought this on?"

"Pauline Hinchcliffe. She said I should dress better, start making new clothes for people."

"Well, if those are anything to go by, she's right. You look downright elegant." He seemed surprised by that.

"I'd forgotten what it was like." Annie stroked the material of her skirt.

"Forgotten what *what* was like?"

"Oh, forgotten what it's like to wear pretty clothes and fuss about my hair. All that sort of thing. Kathy did my hair tonight. Do you like it like this?"

"Aye. You look – well, you look like a proper lady. You really do."

Charlie just sat and smiled at them. "Annie allus looks pretty," he said complacently. "I've got the prettiest wife in town, I have."

"Thanks, both of you. She knew Tom wouldn't have said that if he hadn't meant it, not to her. She looked down at her hands thoughtfully. "I'll have to do something about these, though. They're too rough to sew delicate fabrics. I think you'll have to take over more of the housework, Kathy. Would you mind?"

"'Course not! You know I'd rather cook an' clean than sew," said Kathy in her gentle voice. "I'm not a good sewer like you, though I can run a neat seam as quick as anyone. But I am a good cook."

Annie nodded. "You certainly are. All right, then. You can be my new housekeeper, as well as lady's maid." They laughed at each other.

The next day Annie went out into town in her new clothes. Before she got to the end of Salem Street, she met Bridie O'Connor, whose mouth dropped open at the sight of her.

"Annie, me darlin', have ye come into a fortune, then?"

Annie flushed. "No, I decided to – to make myself a new dress or two, that's all."

"Well, don't ye look a proper lady! Sure, your mother would be proud of ye the day!"

"I hope so."

Bridie had some good news to share. "I've had word from Danny again."

Annie forgot her new clothes. Danny O'Connor had been away for several years and she knew how much Bridie had missed him and fretted about his safety. "Oh, Bridie, I'm so glad for you! How is he? When is he coming to see you? It must be – what – ten years since you've seen him?"

"Aye. It'll be a good ten now. Ah, but he was a bad boy to go away like that! But maybe it's all been for the good. An' he *has* written from time to time, at least he's written. There's some poor women as never hear from their sons again. Danny sent us a letter through that new penny post this time. I had nothin' to pay for it at all; they just brought it to the house and give it to me. Isn't that a miracle, now?"

She shook her head at the wonder of it all and continued eagerly with her news. "He writes a good hand, Father Shaughnessy says, a good clear educated hand. Just fancy that! Our Danny! The father read the letter to us. Danny says he's doin' well for himself an' he sent us some money too, a banknote for five pounds. The father's going to change it into real money for us. Paper never looks worth anythin' to me. Not that we need it, mind – we're managing fine – but it's a lovely thought for him to send it. And Annie, oh, Annie, best of all, Danny says he'll be comin' home to visit us in a few weeks, takin' a little holiday, like." She wiped her eyes at the thought.

"He must be doing well for himself, then."

359

"Aye, he must. But he was always the clever one. An' to think how I cried when he went for a navigator to build them railways!" She dabbed at her eyes again. "Me and my Michael, we went and lit a big sixpenny candle to the blessed Virgin yesterday, to thank her for bringin' him back to us."

Ignoring possible damage to her new clothes, Annie hugged Bridie and kissed her cheek. "I'm so glad for you!"

That good news made her forget her own appearance and helped carry her through the morning's shopping. She put a little card into the window of Hardy's, the draper's, to say that Mrs Ashworth would be pleased to do dressmaking or alterations for ladies, and would attend them in their own homes. Mr Hardy agreed to send her word by one of the street urchins if anyone was interested. She also bought trimmings for her other new dresses, and was waited on with flattering attention by the proprietor, because, if Mrs Ashworth was setting up as a dressmaker, she could bring him more custom. Annie was not sure that she liked his fulsome manner or the way his hand lingered on hers as he handed over her parcel, but she knew she could not afford to alienate him, so she gritted her teeth and said nothing. She noticed that Mrs Hardy was watching them and scowling from the back of the shop.

As she was coming out of Hardy's, Annie bumped into Jeremy Lewis and the latter's patent astonishment and approval set the seal on her day.

"My dear Mrs Ashworth! How – er – well you look!" He always addressed her formally in public, though it was 'Annie' in private.

Several heads turned in their direction.

Flushing slightly, she shook hands with him. "Mrs Hinchcliffe said I should dress better," she confided with unaccustomed shyness.

"Then we must all be grateful to her, because you look lovely."

She went even redder. "It's for business purposes," she said, trying for a less personal tone. "I'm hoping to start doing some proper dressmaking and – and so I need to show what I can do by what I wear. But I mustn't keep you. I have a lot of things to do." She hurried off down the street, both pleased with and embarrassed about the success of her new outfit. She didn't notice Matt Peters come out of a side street and stop dead at the sight of her. Nor did she know that both he and Jeremy Lewis carried the image of the new Annie around with them for days.

Jeremy went on his way, worrying about Annabelle. She now spent the whole of each summer in Brighton, and since the most popular tourist season had unaccountably shifted to the winter months, she often went down for a few weeks then as well. She had not attempted to take Marianne with her again, and Jeremy would not have let her do so, but he was growing increasingly concerned that the amount of time she spent away from her family would give rise to talk.

Thank goodness his daughter had Ellie Peters to look after her when she was not at school! The relationship between Ellie and her charge was a strange mixture of mother, maid and friend, and no one realised better than Jeremy how important Ellie was to Marianne, who, at fifteen, spent little time with her mother.

Jeremy Lewis actively encouraged this close relationship with Ellie, who was warm, loving and not above having a bit of fun, for there were times, when an epidemic raged in the town, or when he went to attend a series of lectures in London, that he had to be away from home for longer than he liked. Annabelle didn't interfere with Ellie, either. Apart from the fact that she was not greatly interested in her daughter, she knew that Jeremy would not have let her go away from home so often if Ellie had not been there.

Annabelle, who had continued to skimp on the house-keeping, now owned several properties in Brighton, one of which she kept permanently available for herself. That was the only one Jeremy knew about, believing it to have been purchased from the money her mother had left her. He had never visited it, nor did he question how she afforded its upkeep. He continued to live with Annabelle and to be seen with her socially solely for Marianne's sake. Apart from that, as far as he was concerned, the less he had to do with his wife, the better.

Like many another person frustrated in his family life, he submerged himself in his work. He was becoming quite well known in the medical profession as a practical authority on the problems of pregnancy and childbirth, and had written a treatise on it that was standard reading for the new breed of doctors being trained in Edinburgh and London. He had followed with interest the work of a Viennese surgeon called Semmelweis, who was using antiseptics in his maternity wards, and who was finding a remarkable reduction in the number of mothers dying of childbed fever. Widow Clegg was the one who embraced his new methods most readily, for many of the women he treated regarded his antiseptic procedures with deep suspicion. He began to think longingly of founding a hospital where he could put more of his ideas into practice, but that was far beyond his purse. Somehow, his expenses always seemed to keep up with his income.

While Annabelle was indulging in her taste for reading melodramatic novels, Jeremy subscribed to *The Lancet*, which had first been published twenty years previously and which, as far as he was concerned, was crucial for country doctors like himself who wished to keep abreast of the times. He read its articles and papers with intense interest and occasionally wrote to their authors. He also, in 1842, began to develop a deep concern about sanitary conditions in the poorer parts of Bilsden, after he had read Edwin Chadwick's report on *The Sanitary Condition of the Labouring Population*. Strangely, Frederick Hallam was the main person in Bilsden to share this interest, for he was attracted to the new ideas on urban cleanliness as he was attracted to every modern development in the cotton trade, especially its machinery.

Jeremy had been offered a number of teaching positions in universities, several of which had now established schools of medicine, but he had turned them down, for he preferred to do the work he loved rather than just talk about it. He knew of no greater thrill than to bring a child safely into the world or to win against one of the myriad illnesses that flared up in his town. From time to time, however, he did go away to attend a conference or agree to give a course of lectures, engaging a locum to cover the needs of his patients if he were to be away for more than a day or two. He needed, he told Sam, often his only confidant, to meet new minds and ideas.

Ellie rarely saw her family nowadays, except for her father. Elizabeth Peters had never really forgiven her for taking Annie's side against Matt. The Peters family moved out of Salem Street within a few months of Matt leaving home. Dr Lewis found them a nice cottage with its own garden closer to Park House and Elizabeth persuaded Matt to come home again, since he could now have his own bedroom. But he felt suffocated by his mother's fussing and attention, and not all her tears and hysterics had persuaded him to stay. Like the doctor, he lived mainly for his work, but he was also a member of the newly-founded Bilsden Mechanics' Institute, a grand name for a group of men who met in the Church Hall. He occasionally attended a lantern show with these new acquaintances, or a lecture. None of them were close friends, however, and he avoided eligible women like the plague.

As time passed, Matt saw Annie and the little boy around the town and that made him wonder yet again if he had made the right decision in rejecting her so arbitrarily, but by that time it was too late. She was married to that loathsome old man and she always looked happy and well-fed. Even her son, the fruit of sin and violence, was a pleasant-looking lad, with an intelligent face, the sort of boy any man would be proud to father. So, when he saw Annie that day in town, resplendent in her new clothes, it was like a blow to his heart and she once more began to invade his dreams.

Annie had long since stopped dreaming about Matt, and her dreams were filled with clothes nowadays, beautiful clothes in the latest styles, like those in Pauline's magazines. As Pauline had prophesied, when women saw the new Annie in chapel or shopping in town, they began to wonder where she got her clothes. Since it was known that she did some sewing, albeit of second-hand garments, one or two women from the chapel ventured to ask her if she were now making new clothes for people. There were also one or two replies to her little card in Hardy's window. Slowly she began to acquire a regular clientele. Miss Pinkley, for long Bilsden's only real ladies' dressmaker, joined the ranks of Annie's critics and began to glare at her when they passed in the street or met in Hardy's.

When Danny O'Connor did come home for the long-promised visit, a flushed and tremulously happy Bridie brought him along to meet Annie again, though as he was nearly ten years older than her, all she had known of him was an occasional kind word from a man to a child.

Danny had changed beyond recognition. Gone was the thin, gangling young man Annie vaguely remembered. He was now nearly six feet tall and broad-shouldered. The biggest surprise to Annie was that he looked and acted almost the gentleman, though his voice still had a touch of an Irish lilt in it, and his face and hands were more weather-beaten than a gentleman's would be.

She felt a little shy as she shook hands with him. "Won't you come in, and take a cup of tea with us, Mr O'Connor," she said formally.

"Mr O'Connor, indeed!" said Bridie, giving him no chance to answer, but leading the way in. "And what's wrong with callin' him Danny, then? Isn't that his name, and didn't the two of you grow up together?"

"Hush now, Mam! If Mrs Ashworth wishes to call me Mr O'Connor, then sure, she has every right to do so in her own home." A pair of astonishingly blue eyes twinkled down at Annie. "Unless you'd prefer to be calling me The Gentleman, for everyone has a nickname on the diggings and that's mine."

She couldn't help smiling back at him. "Why do they call you that?"

"Oh, now you've really hurt me!" he exclaimed in mock anguish. "Can't you see why? Aren't I the best-dressed sub-contractor on the railways?" He bowed to the two ladies with a flourish and Bridie's eyes overflowed with tears of maternal pride. He hugged her and grinned at Annie. "Will you look at me mam, now! She says she's glad to see me, but she's done nothing but weep all over me since I got back!"

Bridie gave him a watery smile. "Behave yourself now, Danny."

But he continued to tease her. His high spirits were so infectious and there was so much laughing and bantering over the teacups that it was a while before the visitors were able to explain the reason for their call. Kathy and Alice, working in the kitchen, stared at each other in amazement as Annie's clear laugh rang out time after time. Usually she was so calm and cool, rarely doing more than smile. They kept William with them lest he spoil the mood of the little party, for it was good to hear Annie laugh. They both worried about how unremittingly she always worked.

At last Bridie got round to the reason for their call. "Annie, love, Danny wants to buy me a dress – a *new* dress. He's wastin' his money on an old woman like me, but he'll not take no for an answer."

"I want to buy Mam two or three new dresses," he said firmly, serious now. "She'll need them for her new life."

"New life?" Annie questioned.

"It's – nothin's settled yet, but he – our Danny..." Bridie couldn't finish the sentence, for the tears were flowing again.

"Will you stop that, Mam!" He looked at Annie and shook his head ruefully. "It's just that I want to buy a small farm. I don't intend to stay on the railways all me days. A man gets tired of travelling. And who better to manage it for me in the meantime than me mam and dad?"

Annie looked at him, a little puzzled, for there was an air of power and authority about him, for all his joking, that didn't seem to fit with an ambition to settle down as a small farmer. As if he sensed her doubts, he rushed into speech, explaining volubly that a navvy's life was no good for an older man and he had a bit of money put by already, so what safer place to keep it than in land? Banks could fail, houses could burn down, but the land was always there, waiting. Bridie nodded as he spoke.

Annie guessed suddenly that he had no intention of settling down on a farm; he was just doing this for his mother and father. And she remembered how Michael O'Connor would sometimes spend all Sunday tramping over the moors and how Bridie had told her of his early hatred of working indoors.

Warm admiration in her eyes, she seconded his words. "What a good idea! Make your money work for you, don't leave it lying idle in a bank."

He looked at her gratefully.

Bridie seized on her words. "Do ye think it's a good idea then, Annie, love? I'd like your opinion, for we all know what a good businesswoman you are. She has dozens of women working for her, you know," she said in an aside to her son.

He looked at Annie with surprise in his eyes. "Is that so?"

"Bridie's exaggerating. It's only two people full-time and casual outwork to about ten others."

"That's not bad, though." She flushed under the admiration in his eyes.

"It's all right, I suppose, but we were talking about you, Mr – er – Danny. Where do you plan to buy a farm?"

"Oh, I'll have to have a little look round and see what's going. Something over beyond Cloughside, maybe, or in Netherden way. But we're wasting our time talking of that now. Let's get back to the dresses, Annie." He lingered over her name, as if savouring the sound of it.

"One dress!" protested Bridie.

"Dresses," he said again. "You need two or three and a good one for best. And I've had enough arguin' from you, Mam? Behave yourself, now, woman!"

"But . . ."

"Not another word! Can you fix her up, Annie?"

"It'll be a pleasure. And I'll do you a special price, so that Bridie can stop worrying about the cost. We'll go over to Hardy's this very afternoon and choose the materials, Bridie."

But Bridie would not agree to go to the draper's, knowing how they'd look down on her in her old faded clothes. "You go for me, Annie, love, you an' our Danny. I'll tell ye the colours I like an' then leave it to you. Sure, I know I can trust your taste, for you always look a picture yourself."

Strangely, Danny didn't try to persuade his mother to go with them, but arranged to call for Annie that afternoon and escort her to the draper's to look at materials. That settled, he excused himself, saying he had a bit of business to conduct and leaving the two women to finish their cups of tea at leisure. Bridie could talk of nothing but her son and his amazing success.

That afternoon, when Danny called for her as arranged, Annie felt a little strange at being out in the company of such a striking-looking man. But he was a pleasant and polite companion, and she gradually relaxed with him. They chose material for three dresses for Bridie and she dissuaded him from buying anything too grand.

"You might be able to afford it, but when would your mother wear it?"

"When she's in her farm and able to take things a bit easier."

Annie laughed. "Bridie take things easy! You must be joking. You'll never stop her from working! It's in her very bones. And what's more, she'd pine away if you tried to make her sit around like a lady, with nothing to do."

"I suppose you're right there."

"But – if you still have money to spend – she *will* need some better underclothes, some petticoats and things, not to mention some bedlinen and furniture for the new house."

"What a good idea!" Unlike any other man she knew, he insisted on staying with her to choose the materials for the underclothing and seemed to know exactly what was needed.

"Are you sure you've never been married, Mr O'Connor?" Annie teased as they came out of the shop. "You seem to know so much about ladies' needs."

He grinned down at her. "I'm a man of wide experience, Annie, that's all, wide enough to appreciate being seen with a lovely woman like you on my arm."

She stiffened at once, pulling away from him. "I don't care for such talk, thank you."

But he wouldn't let go of her arm and she didn't like to struggle with him there in the main street, so she was obliged to carry on walking next to him.

He looked down at her, frowning slightly. "You talk as if I'm insulting you!"

"I'm a respectable married woman, and . . ."

He stopped, still keeping a firm hold of her arm. "We both know how 'married' you are, Annie Ashworth, and I for one am sorry for the waste of it, for you're a woman after my own heart, one who's not only pretty, but who's got a bit of sense in her head. And its no use you pullin' away from me, because I'm far stronger than you, an' I'd suggest you smile and point to something in that shop window – unless you want those two old biddies gaping at us from across the road to think the worst."

Seething, she did as he suggested. "How dare you?" she hissed at him, trying to smile.

"Oh, I'd dare a lot more, given a bit of encouragement, believe me!"

"Well, you won't *get* any encouragement from me!"

"I know. You're afraid of men now, more's the pity!"

"I am not! But I'm a married woman and I've better things to do than waste my time flirting."

"How you keep harping on that word married! Does it

make you feel safe?" He smiled down at her, and he was so big and so exuberantly male that she caught her breath and her hand quivered in his. "It's not flirting I'm after," he went on. "Have you ever thought, Annie, lass, what it'd be like to be loved by a real man, one who cared for you body and soul?"

"No!" She was shaken to the core. It was something she deliberately didn't think about. "Please, D-Danny, please don't!"

He sighed. He could hear the real distress in her voice. "Oh, Annie, my love, I'm not such a brute that I'd force me attentions on a woman. I've never needed to do that. But I'd like to murder the bastard who hurt you so." He patted her hand. "Come on. I'll walk you home now. But you'll have to learn to accept a compliment once in a while, if you will look so lovely. Where's the harm in telling a woman she looks pretty? Tell me that, now."

She looked up at him, thankful that the conversation had taken on a lighter note. "I – I – there's no harm, I suppose. I just – I'm just not used to it, that's all."

When they reached Number Eight, he again kept hold of her arm. "Just one thing more, Annie, me love."

"Yes?" She tried to keep her voice and her expression cool, but didn't succeed.

"If you were a free woman, I'd not give up so easily. One day you'll have to come to life again, and I'd like to be the one to help you do that."

She stiffened. "I don't know what you mean."

He threw back his head and laughed. "Oh, you do, Annie, you do! You understand *exactly* what I mean. And one day, God willing, I'll show you." Only then did he release her arm. He stood there chuckling as she whisked inside the house and slammed the door.

Annie made the dresses for Bridie as quickly as she

could, anxious to take away any excuse for Danny to call in at Number Eight. But while she was working on them, he very basely took advantage of every opportunity to visit her, appearing on her doorstep several times to inspect progress, mostly with Bridie in tow, so that she couldn't refuse to see him. Each time she was aware of the way he looked at her and of the smile lurking in his eyes. She was furious with herself for stammering and blushing when she spoke to him.

She was glad, she told herself, when he found a farm, completed the purchase in record time and went back to his railways. Then, after he'd gone, she was furious with herself for thinking about him and wondering what he was doing. She only hoped that Bridie hadn't noticed anything.

The sad sequel to Danny's visit was that within a few weeks Bridie, Michael and their remaining children left Salem Street. It seemed to Annie as if she'd lost an integral part of her life, for Bridie had always been there at Number Five, to greet her with a smile and a cheery word. She could hardly bring herself to be civil to the new tenants.

It now began to seem a good idea to Annie to think of moving out of Salem Street as well. She didn't rush into things, because they had Charlie's business to consider as well as hers, and, after all, their present house was rent-free. Still, it didn't hurt to look around and to make a few tentative plans. Charlie had slowed up a lot lately. A change would be good for him. She let him buy himself a shiny new spade and chatter on happily about how good it would be for Sammy, now a very old dog, to have a nice garden to dig in.

He and William were making lots of plans for the garden their new house would have.

"Eh, lass," he said to Annie one day, "you've made me that happy, you and our William."

22

August 1844

One morning in August, Annie woke up very early, feeling restless. Outside, it was fine and sunny, with a blue sky still unmarked by the smoke from Hallam's tall mill chimney. She had not yet come to any firm decision about the move – and she should do. Things could not hang on like this.

Charlie was late in coming down to breakfast, so she sent William up to wake him. Self-importantly the little boy ran up the narrow stairs. She watched him go, smiling tenderly. With his mop of deep auburn curls, he seemed to her all Gibson. Many a time she'd studied his childish features, fearing to see a resemblance to his real father, and had been relieved when she could trace none, either in face or character. William was slim, freckled and alert, not an overly aggressive boy and with no sign of slyness or any other bad trait he might have inherited from his father. She loved him dearly and could not now imagine life without him.

Kathy smiled at Annie across the table. "He gets more like you every day," she said comfortably. The responsibility of handling the housekeeping had made Kathy grow in confidence, but she was still thin and undersized, in spite of all the good food she'd had since coming to live at Number Eight. She was totally devoted to Annie, for she knew how much she owed to her, and she was like a second mother to William.

Kathy's parents, George and Polly Dykes, no longer lived in Salem Street. When Grandpa Jack had died, George had gone to pieces and had lost his job at Hallam's. He was now making a precarious living in a string of casual labouring jobs, in between bouts of drunkenness. The Dykes family – mother, father and four surviving children – were living in filth and squalor in one room down at Claters End. When things got desperate, Polly would come and beg a few shillings from Annie, who gave them to her for old times' sake. Kathy never went to see her family and would hide upstairs when Polly came round. Funnily enough, they had never tried to take their daughter away from her 'apprenticeship' and Polly would beam with pride when told how well Kathy was doing.

After a while William came back downstairs. "Dad won't answer me," he said, "but his eyes are open. He looks funny."

Annie's startled eyes met those of Kathy. Oh, no, she prayed, not that! "I'll go up," she said aloud. "You stay here, William, and get on with your breakfast."

She found her husband lying in his bed, looking peaceful and happy, but most clearly dead. There was no sign of why he'd died or of any pain or struggle. No wonder William hadn't realised what had happened.

"Oh, Charlie," she said softly, tears trickling down her cheeks, "you never got your garden after all!" She closed his eyes and stood looking down at the man who'd given her so much. She was reluctant to call anyone or to disturb him. She would miss him greatly and what would William do without his dad?

It was only when Kathy came tiptoeing upstairs to see what was wrong that Annie came out of her reverie.

"Is everything all... Oh, no!" Kathy burst into noisy tears.

Annie put her arm round the girl and led her away from the bed. "Don't cry like that. Charlie wouldn't have wanted you to."

"But we was just goin' to move! He was makin' plans for a garden. He polished up that spade of his every night!" Kathy's sobs redoubled.

William showed unexpected maturity when Annie told him what had happened. After all, death was a normal part of life in the Rows, and Charlie, it seemed, had already prepared his little son for the possibility.

"Dad said if anything ever happened to him, I was to look after you," William said, lips quivering, but head held high. "He said he was getting old an' tired, an' if he died, I was to be brave an' to look after you."

"I don't know what I'd do without you," she told him, holding his tense little body close for a moment.

When Kathy had calmed down somewhat, Annie sent her to fetch Dr Lewis. There was nothing he could do, but it seemed right to call him in. She also sent word to her family, but would not let them go upstairs to stare at the body. She had always thought that a ghoulish custom. William stayed by her side for most of the day, earnestly carrying out the little tasks she set him, fetching things for her or sometimes just sitting quietly next to her. She didn't send him away, even when Jeremy Lewis arrived. She needed her son as much as he needed her.

The doctor came downstairs and accepted a cup of tea from Annie. "He just died in his sleep, as older people do sometimes," he told her gently. "I don't think it was anything to do with his injuries. If it's any consolation to you, it must have happened very quickly and he would have felt no pain."

"No. He looked very peaceful, didn't he?"

"What shall you do now, Annie?"

"I don't know yet. I haven't had time to think about it. We – we were just going to move to somewhere better."

"Annie – don't do anything rash or irrevocable this time." He tried to choose his words carefully, knowing that he had no right to say anything to her. "I'd be happy to help you, if you were ever in need. Think of yourself this time. You have a right to a normal happy life now."

The little boy watched him in puzzlement, not understanding what the doctor was talking about and bewildered by the emotions he could sense behind the words.

"I've been happy," Annie said firmly. "Charlie was a nice man. He was always so – so kind to me." Her voice broke for a moment. "And I've got William. I've still got William, you know."

Her arm tightened involuntarily around her son's shoulders and he looked up at her, puzzled by this whole conversation.

"I wish," said Jeremy, almost savage in his self-restraint, "I wish I were free to offer you my legal protection!" He clamped his mouth tightly shut on these words, afraid of offending her so soon after her husband's death. He'd always been so careful not to cross the line of friendship that he wasn't even sure if she knew how he felt about her.

Annie's eyes flew open in surprise. There was no mistaking what he meant by those words. She half-opened her mouth to speak, then closed it again, giving her head a little shake, though whether to clear it or to dismiss an unpalatable thought, he couldn't tell.

In fact, Annie was confused about her own reactions to what Jeremy had said. She had long admired him, considered him a friend and looked forward to his visits, but even if he had been free, she would never have thought of him as a possible husband, somehow. An image of Danny O'Connor was swiftly banished and she shook her head again.

Her sad expression was too much for his self-restraint. "Would you just wait in the kitchen for a moment, William?" he asked and when the little boy had left them, he turned to Annie a face ravaged with sorrow. "I know I had no right to say that," his voice was harsh and his expression grim, "but I meant every word. If I were free, I would ask you to marry me tomorrow, Annie – but I'm not free and I probably never will be!" People like Annabelle lived for ever. He called to William to come back and look after his mother and left abruptly, not giving her the chance to answer him.

The day seemed to Annie to drag on interminably. Widow Clegg came to lay Charlie out and together they washed him and dressed him in his best clothes. Two men brought round a coffin and had trouble getting it up the stairs. They grumbled and cursed as they edged it into the back room and gloomily predicted that it'd be nigh on impossible to get it down again with a body in it. Annie hardly heard them; she seemed to be walking around in a daze. It was Kathy who moved William's bed into their room, Kathy who attended to the household chores; Kathy who directed the men.

Mr Hinchcliffe popped in briefly to offer his and his wife's condolences and he agreed to conduct a funeral service the next day. There were so many details to attend to and yet nothing seemed to get done. Annie felt numb and disoriented. She wished she could find release in tears, like Kathy, who had hardly stopped weeping all day, but somehow, after the first shock, Annie was unable to cry.

She was jolted out of her lethargy just before teatime. Jim Catterall, Mr Hallam's rent agent, a man universally hated in the Rows, knocked on the door, then walked straight in, without waiting for an invitation to enter. Kathy and William were out on an errand at the time and Annie was alone in the house.

"Is it true?" Catterall demanded, standing at the bottom of the stairs and eyeing the house and its contents with an almost proprietorial air. He was a burly man, always scrubbed pinkly clean and neatly dressed. His presence always made her feel uneasy and she'd made sure that she was never on her own on the day when he called to pay Charlie's money. She found the way he looked at her offensive and the man himself physically repulsive, because when he held his head in a certain way, he reminded her of Fred Coxton, about whom she still occasionally had nightmares. Jim Catterall's thick pink neck bulged over his shirt collar and his small piggy eyes were never still, flicking here and there. She felt that he was calculating the value of everything he saw down to the last farthing. In his big scarred hands he always clasped a shiny black leather bag, into which he put the rent money he collected, snapping it shut with an air of daring anyone to try to wrest it from him. And such was the fear in which he was held, that no one ever had tried to steal it, not even in the worst of bad times.

"Well, is it true?" he repeated impatiently.

"Is what true?" She spoke coldly, not helping him at all.

"That the barmy old bugger's dead at last."

"My husband's dead, if that's what you mean."

He mimicked her accent. "Yes, that's what I mean, your ladyship, an' you bloody well know it, so stop playin' games with me!" He made no pretence of civility. "How'd it happen? Mr Hallam wants to know."

"Charlie died in his sleep – though I don't know what that's got to do with you, or with Mr Hallam, for that matter."

He slapped a ham-like fist on the wall. "It's got eight shillings a week to do with my employer, that's what – the rent of this house an' the money that old sod got paid every week. Disgustin', that was! Stealin' money from my employer. Anyway, it's over now, an' from today on, this house is on my rent roll, so it *is* my business. Mr Hallam says you can stay on here if you can pay the rent."

Annie tried to pull her wits together.

"Well, are you staying or not?"

"I suppose so. For the moment, anyway."

"Then that'll be three shillings, payable in advance. Mr Hallam don't allow no credit."

"Three! But the rest of the street only pay two!"

"They did. Times is hard. Mr Hallam's just had to put up the rents. Proper shame, it is, but that's life. So it's three shillings a week an' plenty of folk ready to take the house if you don't want it." His eyes flickered over the furniture. "You've got some nice stuff here an' you've got your sewing. You should be able to afford it all right." He leered across at her. "An' a good-looking woman like you will soon find someone else, someone who can give you a bit more fun than that barmy old sod. He hadn't even got all his wits, he hadn't, let alone what it takes to pleasure a woman."

She ignored his insinuations. "All right, I'll give you the money." She took out the little purse in which she kept a bit of money for her day-to-day expenses, her reserves being carefully hidden in several places around the house.

A beefy hand shot out to grasp her wrist. "Of course, if you was a bit short, well, we could come to some little arrangement about the rent. I'm not a hard man to please."

She tried to pull away, but the hand tightened on her arm and his other hand came up to squeeze her breast. It was like the nightmare of Fred Coxton suddenly coming back to life. She went rigid with shock and horror for a moment, and, taking this for acquiescence, Jim began to paw at her body. At this she screamed loudly and started to struggle like one demented. Sammy, outside, began to bark and growl and throw himself against the back door.

All at once the grip on her slackened and she was free. She staggered backwards and saw what had saved her. "Tom!" She began to sob in relief at the sight of her brother. "Oh, Tom!"

"Don't you *ever* touch my sister again!" said Tom slowly and distinctly.

"You mind your own business, Gibson," retorted Catterall, spitting on the floor. "If you an' your dad want to stay on at the mill, it don't do to cross me. Mr Hallam has a lot of faith in my judgement. He leaves things to me."

Tom stood there, arms swinging loosely, ready to defend himself. "An' if *you* want to walk the Rows safely at night, Jim Catterall, it don't do to cross *me*," he said softly, far too softly for a man with that look on his face. "I've got a lot of good friends and they don't think much of you at all. They only need half an excuse to show you how they feel."

Jim's fist came up suddenly, but Tom was ready, ducking the blow easily and smashing the older and bigger man between the eyes. Annie winced at the dull smack of fists against flesh and moved as far out of their way as she could.

"You're gettin' soft, Jim Catterall!" taunted Tom. "Old an' fat an' soft!"

All hung in the balance for a moment, then Jim spat on the floor, wiped the blood from his face and stepped back. "I've changed my mind," he said thickly to Annie. "We don't want your sort in Mr Hallam's houses. You can clear out – by tomorrow. An' as for you," he turned back to Tom, "you'd better watch *yourself* at nights! You're not the only one with friends round here. An' you can collect what's owing you from the mill tomorrow, you an' your father both."

He trod heavily out of the house and slammed the door behind him, setting Sammy off barking again.

"The bastard!" said Tom. "The rotten bastard!"

Annie burst into tears and Tom patted her awkwardly on the shoulder. "You sit down and I'll brew you up a nice cup of tea. Widow Clegg told me about Charlie when I got home from work. Poor old bugger! An' then that bastard comin' round an' pesterin' you like that. I'll fix him up good an' proper one of these days. You see if I don't!"

Annie was glad to sit there quietly for a few moments and let him fuss over her. As she sipped the strong sweet tea, however, she began to think clearly once again.

"I'm not going!" she declared abruptly, putting the empty cup down with a clatter.

"What?"

"I'm not going! Not leaving this house."

Tom was surprised. "But I thought you *wanted* to get out. You were *plannin'* to leave. You said so the other day."

"I was, but that's all changed now that Charlie's dead. We'd be fools to try to start somewhere else, when we're all set up here. And what'd we do with all the stuff?" She gestured outside at the crowded yard and lean-to, where old Sammy was lying quietly again in his corner. "I'm not going to give it away for nothing and we couldn't move it by tomorrow. So I'm not leaving." She sat there for a few minutes, lost in thought. "What time does Mr Hallam leave the mill?"

We, thought Tom jubilantly, she said 'we'. "I dunno. Later than us lot. He always stays on to see things settled for the night. He doesn't trust anyone since that big fire."

"So he'll be there now?"

"Probably. You can't always tell."

"Well, it's worth a try." She stood up and began to tidy her hair in the little mirror. "Yes, that'll do. I won't wash my face. I want it to look as if I've been crying." She whisked a woollen shawl round her shoulders and tied a bonnet on her head. "You come with me, Tom, but keep in the background. Don't say anything unless you have to, just try to look angry and upset."

"Come where?" He was bewildered by this sudden activity.

"To see Mr Hallam, of course."

"What for?"

"To ask if I can stay on."

"It won't do any good. Hallam's a hard man. And he does what Catterall tells him to about his houses."

"We'll see. It's still worth a try."

She led the way down the street and round the corner into the mill. The watchman stopped them at the gate, but luck was on their side. Frederick Hallam had not yet left. After a short time, they saw him cross the yard to his office.

"Mr Hallam, sir!" called the watchman. "Some people to see you."

"Tell them to come back in the morning."

"Please! It's very important!" begged Annie.

Hallam squinted across at them, saw that the speaker was a pretty young woman and decided that he could spare a few minutes. "Oh? very well. Send them over to my office in five minutes' time, Bill. I've something to finish first."

"Yes, sir."

Five minutes later, they were knocking on the office door.

"Come."

"He always says that," whispered Tom. "Daft, isn't it? Why can't he say 'Come in!' like everyone else?"

"You shut up and let me do the talking." Annie led the way in.

"Gibson! What do you want at this time of day?" Hallam grunted, not offering them a seat and looking bored. He was already regretting his generous impulse.

"My brother came with me to protect me," said Annie. "It's I who wish to see you."

"Protect you? From what? Do you think I try to ravish my millhands?" asked Hallam scornfully.

"I'm not one of your millhands," said Annie, in the best imitation of Annabelle Lewis's haughty tones that she could manage. "And although *you* may not attack women, one of your employees does and I was afraid that I might meet him here."

Hallam looked first surprised, then puzzled. "I beg your pardon, ma'am. Gibson, get your sister a chair. She doesn't look well."

Annie sat down gratefully. "Thank you, Mr Hallam. I'm not usually prone to such weakness, but my husband died this morning and since then your rent agent has . . . has . . ." She managed to produce a credible sob and dabbed at her eyes.

"Catterall tried to molest her," said Tom bluntly. "And if he touches her again, I'll . . ."

"Tom, please!" Annie begged. She turned back to Mr Hallam. "When Tom stopped your Mr Catterall from – from attacking me, he told me to get out of my house by tomorrow and he told Tom that he and my father were dismissed from the mill."

What a fascinating face, Hallam was thinking. Dress her in fine clothes and she'd be a real beauty. What does Catterall think he's doing? He'd better be a bit more discreet in the future, and choose his fancy pieces more carefully. It doesn't do to mix business and pleasure, not my business and his pleasure, anyway. I'm not going to lose good workers and rent money because some woman has said no to him.

Aloud he said, "You were quite right to come to me. It's Mrs – er – Ashworth, isn't it?" I remember her now, he was thinking. Saw her once or twice at the Lewis's. Used to be Annabelle's maid. That explains her fancy accent. Though why a good-looking young woman like her should have married an old wreck like Charlie Ashworth is beyond my comprehension. For the money, presumably, though five shillings a week isn't much.

He abandoned speculation and spoke soothingly. "Catterall has obviously exceeded his authority. Of course you can stay on in Salem Street, Mrs Ashworth. Shall you be able to – er – manage?"

She gave him a smile tremulous with relief. "Oh, yes. I do some dressmaking, you know, and Tom's going to leave the mill – at once, if it's convenient to you – and he's going to run Charlie's business for me."

Tom sucked in his breath, for nothing definite had been said about that yet. But it was what he wanted more than anything else. A grin crept over his face. Oh, yes, he would certainly take over Charlie's business! It was an ill wind.

"But my father doesn't know anything about this," went on Annie. "If he loses his job, I don't know what he'll do. He has a family to support."

"Did Catterall threaten your father's job as well?"

"Yes, sir. It – it doesn't seem fair, sir."

I'm not having that! Hallam was thinking. Lose a good steady worker because he's offended Catterall! That's no way to run a business. "It most certainly isn't fair," he said in a kindly tone, "and I shall not countenance it for a moment, Mrs Ashworth. Catterall overstepped his author-ity there – he can be over-zealous sometimes. You have nothing to worry about in that respect, my dear lady. Your father's job is quite safe."

Tom had been listening in admiration, firmly resisting the temptation to smile at the sight of Annie playing the helpless female so convincingly.

"Thank you, sir," murmured Annie. "I'm very grateful."

Hallam turned to Tom. "So you want to leave the mill, eh, Gibson?"

"Yes, sir. It's my big chance, you see, to set up in a business of my own."

"I wish you luck. And you needn't come in tomorrow, except to collect your pay. Your sister will no doubt be glad of your support at this unhappy time."

"Thank you, sir." The grin escaped Tom's control and took over his face for a moment.

Annie stood up. "We won't trespass upon your time any further, Mr Hallam. I know you're a busy man, and I'm extremely grateful for your help." She held her hand out to him across the desk and he found himself shaking it and escorting her to the door as if she were a lady and not a – well, what was she? He waited till they'd gone and then let a smile creep over his face. A sharp little piece, that's what she was. Far too sharp to waste her time with an oaf like Catterall. He must keep an eye on her, see what she made of herself. He wouldn't mind getting to know her better. Fascinating eyes and that glorious hair. She'd played her cards well coming straight to the master. Yes, she was a very sharp little piece. Why had he never noticed her around before?

When they got back, Tom grinned at his sister. "You did that well. Sounded just like a lady, you did. Had that old bastard eating out of your hand."

"He knew exactly what I was doing. Did you see the way he was looking at me? It must just have amused him to play along today. He wasn't concerned with the rights and wrongs of my case." She shuddered. "I hated the way he looked at me!"

"Nay, you can't blame him for looking. You've started making something of yourself and you'll not stop fellows from admiring how you look."

"I still hate it! If I didn't need to look good for my business, I'd dress in ugly clothes and hide all my hair!"

"Now you *are* talking daft!" He ran his finger along the edge of the table with studied casualness. "Er – you did mean it, didn't you?"

"Mean what?" She was still brooding over the inequities of life.

"Mean what you said about me runnin' the business."

"I meant it about you coming in and *helping* me to run the business. I took it for granted that with Charlie dead, you'd want to do that. Was I wrong?"

He sighed happily. "No, you were bloody right!" Then he eyed her sideways. "Er – wouldn't it be better if I lived on the job, like? You'll have enough room for me here, now, an' it'll save on lodgings money. Besides, you need a man around the place to protect you."

She hesitated. She wasn't sure that she wanted to live with Tom. He might start trying to boss her around and she wasn't ever going to have anyone do that again. And she knew Tom; he'd be trying to introduce a few sharp practices – and she wasn't having *that*, either! Then her common sense reasserted itself. He could only boss her around if she let him. Unconsciously she drew herself up to her full five feet two inches. She wouldn't let him. She'd keep a tight hold on the reins.

He was frowning by this time. "What's the matter? Don't you want me to live here? It'd be a lot more convenient – an' cheaper too."

She smiled. "Yes, I do want you, Tom. I need you. But just as long as you realise that *you* won't be in charge. I will."

He relaxed again and grinned at her. "All right."

"But are you sure you want to give up your job, Tom? Times are hard. People don't know you. There won't be the easy pickings Charlie used to find. They trusted him and felt sorry for him, too. They won't feel sorry for you."

"Nothin's ever easy," he said cynically. "Try workin' in the mill. That's not easy, either. An' it fair drives you mad, all that noise an' fluff. But if you're workin' for yourself an' a good chance comes along, you're free to grab it. There isn't much chance of grabbin' anythin' when you're stuck inside a bloody spinning shed. The only one that makes money in a mill is the master."

"What do you want out of the business? We ought to settle that before you start."

"Half the profits," he said promptly. "I'll earn it, I promise you. Wait and see. But I'm comin' in as a full partner or I'm not comin' in at all. Half's fair. You can't quarrel over that."

She nodded. "All right. But I want to make one thing very clear right from the beginning. There are to be no sharp practices, no cheating, no dealing in stolen goods. Nothing like that!"

"Aw, come on, Annie. Everybody fiddles a bit. People are so stupid! You could get a lot more . . ."

"No!" Her tone was emphatic. "Cheating's a short-sighted thing. I've worked hard to build up a reputation for treating people honestly, and poor old Charlie couldn't have done anything else. People will always remember that I came from the Rows, but they'll never be able to accuse me of anything worse than that. I learned early on, Tom, that you've got to be respectable. I've fought hard to keep my good name. If you do anything to spoil that for me, anything at all, you're out – even if I have to ruin my own business to kick you out! I mean it! I've been planning things for a long time, thinking how the business will be years from now."

He blinked at the vehemence in her tone. "I never thought of plannin' for years ahead. I just thought of – well, makin' as much money as you could, havin' a better life than our dad's got."

"You don't have to cheat to make money. And surely you want to go on making it?"

"Yes. I suppose so. All right, then. No funny business. But am I in as a partner?"

She relaxed and smiled at him. "Yes, you're in. You can move in here tomorrow after the funeral, but you'll have to share William's room."

Charlie's funeral was an elaborate affair, for Salem Street. Annie did everything properly, out of gratitude for all that the kindly old man had done for her, and she hired a real hearse drawn by two black horses to carry the coffin to the chapel. She knew he would have loved that. Most people in the Rows borrowed a handcart to do this final service to their dead, but she was determined that Charlie should have a more stylish last ride.

Annie, Alice and Kathy worked late into the night to sew a black dress for her and a little black suit for William. They were sewing almost up to the minute the cursing men struggled down the stairs with the coffin. Women in the Rows couldn't usually afford the extra expense of going into mourning, but Annie was different and she intended to show it. Staring into her mirror as she adjusted her bonnet and veil, she thought how well she looked in black. It might be a good thing to continue wearing it. Good for keeping men away from her and good for the business. She caught herself up guiltily. Fancy thinking of how she looked at a time like this!

But she couldn't help looking round and thinking about things as she rode with her son and her brother in a carriage behind the hearse. Even on a rainy day like this, the park looked pretty. How nice it would be to live in the older part of Bilsden! To see the green of trees around you and live among quiet people, who didn't scream and shout and get drunk. She promised herself that one day in the not-too-distant future, one day, when she was sure that Tom could run the business successfully, they would move to a better part of the town and they would live among people who could afford to wear mourning and to rent nice houses and to send their children to good schools.

This was just a temporary set-back, she vowed. Her dressmaking business was getting nicely established, but she still made more money from her second-hand clothes and from the junk. She had to be sure that Tom could keep her supplied with cast-off clothing and could manage the rest of the business. No, she decided, she couldn't afford to take any risks until Tom was firmly established in Charlie's place and the money was flowing in steadily again.

There were quite a few people at the chapel. Emily and the children had walked there, as well as Kathy and Alice. There were a few older women too, members of the congregation who made a practice of going to funerals, goodness only knew why. And Dr Lewis also turned up, driven by Sam in the gig. This was as much a surprise to Annie as to the onlookers and she was not sure that it was a sensible thing to do. It was bound to cause gossip, for he wasn't even a member of the congregation.

"My dear Annie!" he said, coming over to take her hand.

"Dr Lewis. How kind of you to remember Charlie!" she

said, removing her hand quickly from his and taking her brother's arm. She wished Jeremy hadn't come. And calling her Annie in public, too!

She was relieved when Pauline Hinchcliffe turned up as well, and came over to join them, because that made Jeremy's presence seem less strange. Pauline behaved very affably to Tom, praised William's appearance and took Jeremy Lewis to sit in a pew with her. Afterwards she insisted on driving Annie home in her carriage, while Tom and William walked – for Annie had not seen the necessity to waste good money on keeping the carriage to take them back to Salem Street when the funeral was over.

Pauline didn't beat about the bush. "Stupid of Jeremy Lewis to come to the funeral! It's bound to cause talk. You mustn't encourage him to hang around you now that your husband's dead. Oh, it's all right. I know *you* wouldn't do anything stupid. But he might. He doesn't get on with that wife of his and he's too soft for his own good, that man. His patients trade on his kindness. It's a good thing I was here to step in this time."

"I didn't know Dr Lewis was coming," protested Annie. "And I've done nothing to encourage him or to cause talk. He's just a friend. How stupid people are sometimes!"

"Well, stupid or not, that's life. I'll have a word with him myself. He must realise that his little calls at Number Eight have to stop, now that you're a widow." She rapped on the roof. "Drive round the park!" she called to her coachman. "Miserable day," she added, turning back to Annie, "but I wanted to have a talk with you, and there's always someone around in that little house of yours. What are your plans now?"

"My brother is coming to live with me. He'll take over Charlie's rounds."

"Good. You're too young and pretty to live on your own.

But what about your move? I thought you were going to leave Salem Street."

"I've postponed that. I daren't risk anything until I see how Tom shapes up."

Pauline laughed, a dry, disbelieving spurt of sound that made Annie flush. "Some would say that this was the ideal time to leave. I'm beginning to think that you're afraid to move out – afraid to come to life again. But you'll have to leave the Rows one day, my dear Annie."

"I will leave! I'm *longing* to leave. You know how I hate Salem Street!"

"Do you?" Pauline asked coolly, taking Annie's breath away. "I'm not so sure about that. I think you're frightened to move."

"I'm not! I just – I can't take any risks at the moment – not till I've seen how Tom goes on."

"Mmm. Well, you do have a point there. Perhaps this is not the most auspicious moment. But you're not staying in Salem Street for ever. Make up your mind to that!"

23

August to October 1844

Tom moved into Number Eight as soon as he and William got back from the funeral. The moving in was well under way by the time Annie arrived home. Tom let William help him to carry his things along from Widow Clegg's and joked with his nephew as he rearranged the bedroom they were to share. Annie realised with a pang that her son was already transferring his allegiance from his dad to his uncle, and she wasn't sure that she liked that. Not so soon.

After he'd unpacked, Tom started poking into every corner of the house. He even walked into Annie's bedroom, frightening Kathy, who now shared it and who was having a wash. She let out a little scream of fright and clutched the towel in front of herself, but he just grinned and walked out, tossing a "Sorry!" over his shoulder.

He was the same downstairs, looking into drawers and cupboards, which he'd never dared do before, and moving things around till Annie got mad at him.

"You can just stop that, Tom! This is *my* house and these are *my* things, and I'll thank you to leave them alone!"

"Just lookin'." He was quite unabashed. "No harm in lookin', is there? After all, I live here too, now, and I'm the man of the house."

"You live here, yes, and I'm not denying that I'll be glad

to have a man around, but you're not taking over, Tom, not now, not ever. You'd better understand that from the start. You're not my husband; you're my partner. It's still *my* house. And what's more, it's *my* ideas and *my* hard work that have made the business so profitable, so nothing, *nothing at all* is to be changed without my say-so!"

Two pairs of eyes met challengingly across the table and William, sitting by the fire, waiting for his tea, looked anxiously from one to the other, upset by their tone and the tension he could feel in the air. Kathy kept her eyes on the pan she was stirring. She wasn't sure she liked the idea of Tom coming to live with them. She didn't like young men. They shouted and fought and pestered you. If only all men were like Charlie. He hadn't shouted. He'd been gentle and kind and she missed him greatly. A tear splashed on to her apron and a little hand stretched out to pat her arm.

"Don't cry, Kathy," said William. "I'll look after you now. Dad said I was to look after you and Mother."

The tension was dispelled as everyone smiled at the little boy's words.

Inevitably business slowed down when Tom first took over the collection and sorting of the stuff. He had thought he knew most of what was needed, but there was a surprising amount still to learn, and of course, he made one or two mistakes, though not as many as Annie had feared.

In a few weeks business began to pick up again, as Tom grew more expert at wheedling rubbish out of farmers' wives and out of the housekeepers and maidservants of the wealthier citizens, not to mention the women in the older part of the town. He gradually learned the values of each type of item and the profits began to rise again. And he went further afield than Charlie ever had, sometimes staying the night in some small inn or even a farmer's barn.

After a while he began to take on commissions for

women in the outlying districts, making a penny here and a halfpenny there. Nothing likely to show a profit was too much trouble for Tom, who was revelling in the open air and the freedom to do as he pleased after the stifling years in the mill. Not that this was not hard work! It was. He was out from dawn to dusk most days and footsore when he returned, until his body grew used to the new routines. Even his face changed. He would never be good-looking, but he began to look more attractive as his face gained colour from the sun and his expression began to reflect his growing confidence and satisfaction with life.

Tom even did errands for some people for nothing, building up goodwill, he said to Annie, who was still keeping a careful eye on everything he did. He wouldn't have admitted it, but he had a soft spot for old people. He liked to get them talking about the old days, before the mills had grown so big, when families did a bit of weaving or spinning at home and most folk had their own patch of ground to grow a few greens and keep a pig. He would flirt shamelessly with toothless old women, leaving them convulsed with laughter, and he would slip a small packet of tobacco to the old men, who were dependent upon their families' generosity. He was drunk with happiness himself those first few months and wanted to share it with the world.

Gradually Tom began to make his own niche in Number Eight. He developed a friendly, no-nonsense relationship with Alice and he teased Kathy as if she were his younger sister, seeing even more clearly now that he lived there how useful she was to them all, for she was a good housekeeper and an excellent cook. It only increased his respect for Annie when he remembered the filthy waif she'd rescued from Polly Dykes and saw what she'd made of Kathy.

William followed his uncle around whenever his mother

would let him. His mother didn't like him to play out with the dirty children from the Rows and his young uncles and aunts from Number Three rather despised him. Consequently, he was a lonely child, with no real friends. Tom's liveliness and vigour seemed to fascinate him.

Annie would have preferred not to let William go outside into the streets at all, but that wasn't possible. There were many little errands he could run for her, and it would have been stupid to leave her sewing and do them herself. But she was so terrified of him growing up as roughly as Tom had that she discouraged him from fighting or getting himself dirty or from doing most of the things the other children of the Rows did.

As a result, William Ashworth was regarded as an outsider by everyone, a stuck-up little mammy's boy, who talked differently from them and who wore fancy-nancy clothes. When he did go out and there were no adults around, they pelted him with rubbish and taunted him with being a softie and barmy like his dad. He bore this stoically, hiding most of his hurts from his mother and cleaning himself up as best he could.

One day, Tom turned the corner from Boston Street and startled a group of children yelling and struggling with someone in their midst. When they ran away, leaving a child doubled up on the ground in the back alley that ran between Salem and Boston Streets, he realised that it was William and hurried over. The boy was bruised and covered in filth, crying in a despairing way that upset his uncle.

Tom bent down and offered him a handkerchief. "What happened, then, kid?"

"They – they threw things at me." William started scrubbing at the dirt.

"They? Who're they?"

"The other children."

"Oh, fights, eh? And the other gang won."

William blinked up at his uncle. "Other gang?"

"Yes. We used to have gangs too, when we were little 'uns. Whose gang are you in?"

Tears welled up again in William's eyes. "I'm not! They won't have me!" He burst into noisy sobs and flung himself into his uncle's arms. "They shout at me – an' they throw things – an' – an' this time they hit me an' kicked me. But I'm *not* a softie and I'm *not* barmy!"

Tom patted the quivering little back. "Nay – shhh, now." After a while the sobs stopped and William mopped his eyes with his uncle's handkerchief. "I shouldn't have gone along the back," he stated bitterly, "but I wanted to see what they were doing. They were laughing." He looked up, his face streaked with tears and dirt. "Don't tell my mother. She doesn't like me talking to the other children."

"She'll not need telling, young fellow. You're going to have a nice black eye there. Besides – she'll have to know. We've got to do something about this. We can't have people calling my nephew a softie, can we? I reckon I'd better teach you how to fight."

"Mother doesn't want me to fight," said William, in the bleak tones of one unjustly denied a treat.

"Well, your mam's wrong this time. Women don't know about things like that."

Two greenish-brown eyes stared gravely up at Tom, as William struggled to digest the idea that his mother didn't know everything. "My mother knows a' awful lot," he said dubiously.

"Well, she don't know about men an' fightin'," Tom insisted. "She's a woman. They're different from us men."

"Oh?"

"I'll teach you a few tricks, show you how to fight, then

you'll have to get into a few fights for practice. You won't win 'em all – you're too little. But if you show 'em you're not a softie, they'll let you join one of the gangs. You'll see." He took hold of William's hand. "Come on! We'd better go an' face your mam before we do anything else."

Annie nearly went mad when she saw the state William was in. She went even madder when he informed her that his Uncle Tom was going to teach him how to fight.

"You'll not!" she threw at Tom. "I'm not having my William fighting. You leave him alone."

"He needs to learn," said Tom flatly. "All kids have to learn how to stick up for themselves."

"William's different."

"He's not!"

"I *want* to learn to fight," said William, walking over to stand next to his uncle.

"You be quiet! You'll do as you're told."

"I won't! I won't!" William burst into tears and clutched his uncle's arm for support.

Tom looked across at Annie. "He has to. You're wrong about this, our Annie."

Kathy, sewing by the window, nerved herself to interfere. "They'll keep on bashin' him if he don't learn to hit 'em back," she said. "I've helped him clean hisself up a few times now, Annie, but I didn't say owt about it. All kids fight. Didn't you?"

Annie's resistance crumbled suddenly as a vivid memory of beating the 'Bosties' came back to her, a battle in which she had played a leading role.

"They call him a softie, say he's barmy like his dad," Tom urged. "Do you want him to be called Barmy Willie?"

Annie opened and shut her mouth, then collapsed into a chair and covered her face with her hands. "I didn't want him to grow up like we did," she faltered. "I was trying to make sure he had a better life. He doesn't need to mix with dirty kids from the Rows."

"Doesn't need to? He *lives* in the Rows!"

"I should have moved out when Charlie died. I should have got away then."

"You know as well as I do that it wasn't the right time to move. An' it wouldn't have made any difference to William's problem," said Tom. "You *are* trying to make him into a mammy's boy and you'll succeed if you go on like this. Wherever he lives, our William has to learn to stick up for himself, yes, and to take a beating without showing he's afraid. Everybody fights. Some of 'em use fists, an' some of 'em knives, an' some use money, like Hallam, an' some use words."

Annie stared at her brother, amazed at his perceptiveness. What he'd said made sense. She thought of Mrs Lewis – just look how that woman bullied everyone, even the doctor and Miss Marianne. She used words and airs and graces as her weapons. Annie looked at her brother with new respect. "All right," she said in a tight voice. "All right, then. Teach him to fight, if you must. But don't teach him to look for fights or to bully people, just to defend himself."

During the next two weeks William spent a lot of time with his Uncle Tom. He went out with him sometimes to collect junk, a rare treat, and he practised how to hit people and how to fall over, away from kicking feet. He lost his look of dewy-eyed innocence and Annie shed secret tears over the loss of her baby. For the first time it occurred to her that it might be nice to have other children. But that'd mean – no, she couldn't! She was *never* going near a man again. She didn't want to wind up like Emily, worn out and old before her time. That's what getting married did for you.

Unbidden, the image of Danny O'Connor rose before her. What on earth had made her think of him, great braggart that he was? And there was Jeremy Lewis. He'd said he cared for her, but he was already married. And she hadn't seen much of him lately. Pauline Hinchcliffe must have had a word with him. Annie was missing him, missing not only his visits, but the books he'd lent her and the ideas he'd planted in her mind. If it hadn't been for Pauline, she sometimes thought she'd have gone mad here.

Her reverie was interrupted by a banging on the door. When she opened it, she found her half-brother, Mark, and two other filthy little boys supporting a bloody, but triumphant William.

"What have you been doing?" she demanded angrily. "Just look at the mess you're in!"

"He fought Henry Jones, our Annie," Mark volunteered. "Henry threw some muck at him an' our Willie bashed him one."

"Oh, did he?"

"'Course, he didn't win, our Willie didn't," went on Mark.

"William!" she corrected automatically.

Mark shrugged. "William, then. That Henry's eight an' he's big. But our Willie, I mean our William had a good try an' he give Henry a few good belts."

"Well, don't stand there dripping blood all over my clean doorstep, come in," snapped Annie.

Mark looked round to make sure his mother wasn't out in the street to see him, then entered Number Eight. He liked visiting their Annie, when he could. You always got something to eat and her house smelled nice, too.

The other two boys hesitated. Annie Ashworth was known to be stuck-up. They'd heard their mams talk about her and seen her in town in her fancy clothes. Still, it'd be something to boast about, going into her house would. They tramped in after Mark and William.

Kathy uttered a cry of distress when they went into the back kitchen and dropped her sewing to run to William. For once he wriggled out of her grasp.

"I'm all right!" he said crossly.

Annie swallowed a lump in her throat at the sight of her son's bruised face and told the boys briskly that if they washed their hands and faces, they could have a cup of tea and a hunk of bread and butter. The two strangers hung back, but Mark and William made straight for the bucket and poured themselves a bowl of water.

"William first," said Annie calmly. "Let's get those cuts cleaned up. Then you others can wash your hands and faces. No wash, no food. I only allow clean people in my house." The other boys lined up with alacrity. An extra buttie was not to be sneered at. They looked with new liking at young Willie Ashworth as they bit into the thick slices of bread and butter.

From then on, William never looked back. He was out playing as often as his mother would let him, and his young uncles, Mark and Luke, relieved not to have a relative who was a softie, kept a careful eye on him till he'd got himself fully accepted. He grew rapidly in confidence and developed into a sturdy, independent lad. He still behaved protectively to his mother and Kathy, however, and Tom was careful not to destroy this for him. It was William who made them cups of tea, helped set and clear the table, ran errands into town and fetched the water, half a bucket at a time, till Tom got him a little cart to carry two smaller buckets.

After Charlie's death, many things had begun to change, whether Annie wanted it or not. It took her a while to get used to having Tom around the place, and several times they had words over habits of his that she objected to. She had thought that after a time the business would settle down into the old routine, but it didn't. When Tom got into the swing of things, business began to increase. Soon they were making more money than ever before and the stuff was piling up faster than they could clear it.

Unlike Charlie, Tom had no skill in mending things, so he had to find people to do it for him. He always seemed to know a man who could do a job for him on the side, usually someone in dire need of extra money, who would work cut-price. When Annie worried about paying a fair rate for the job, Tom scoffed loudly. He drew the line at dishonesty, because he knew his sister would not stand for it, but now that he had recovered from his initial euphoria, nothing she said or did could prevent him from being a sharp businessman and paring costs to the bone.

Tom loved living at Number Eight. To him it was a big step up in the world. Among the things that surprised him during the first few weeks were their fancy table manners, their mania for washing their bodies and their clothes, and the comfortable beds with sheets which were changed every week or two. No matter that the sheets were made of coarse cotton twill, reject pieces picked up cheaply at the market; they were proper hemmed sheets, not rough blankets and sacking. Tom's own table manners and cleanliness improved rapidly, as well as the way he spoke. He still kept in touch with his old friends, however, going out for a drink with them at nights and occasionally bringing the more presentable of them home for a piece of one of Kathy's cakes and a cup of tea.

Annie didn't much like his friends, one or two of whom she remembered from her childhood, but she didn't raise any objections to the visits, sensing that Tom wanted to show off his new way of life and acknowledging his right to bring friends into his own house. Some of the men essayed a heavy gallantry with Annie, for she was a lovely woman and well-off by their standards, but she cut their compliments short and behaved with such icy disdain that they didn't pursue matters any further. Tom would watch and grin. It suited him to have his sister remain a widow and grateful for his protection. If he'd thought that any chap had a chance with her, he'd have taken steps to quash the affair himself.

Tom still collected the rents for his sister. To the pair of houses she'd bought when she first married Charlie, she'd added another, in spite of the hard times. It was a house on half an acre of land in the older part of Bilsden, quite close to the park. It'd been sheer luck that she'd heard gossip about it being offered for sale. She'd got Mr Pennybody to buy it for her without even consulting Pauline, busy at the time having her second child, snapping it up at the price asked, because she knew it must be good value in such a central position. Frederick Hallam, who had also had his eye on it, tried to buy it off her through Mr Pennybody, but was refused. He would have been astonished, she thought, to know that the mystery buyer was one of his own tenants.

It amused Annie, too, when she found out that the occupier of the cottage was none other than Michael Benworth, the overseer at Hallam's. She sent Tom round to tell him that he could stay on in the cottage, on a monthly tenancy, but that it would cost him an extra sixpence a week. He accepted, for he had an ailing wife who was much attached to the house, but he grumbled for the first few weeks.

Tom made short shrift of his complaints, enjoying the reversal of roles with his overseer. In his opinion, Benworth had a bloody good job, and if he'd spent a little less on his own pleasures and saved a bit more, like Annie, he'd have been able to buy the house for himself by this time. Tom would have done that in his place. Although Benworth was Tom's boss when Annie first bought the house, Tom was not in the least overawed by him when collecting the rent. And nowadays, he wasn't overawed by anyone, except perhaps Pauline Hinchcliffe, and he was getting used even to her.

Once in a while, on a fine Sunday, Annie would tramp out of town with William and sometimes Tom, to visit Bridie and Michael on their farm. It wasn't a big place, as farms went, but after Salem Street it seemed like paradise to the O'Connors. In spite of the hard work he was putting in, Michael was looking years younger and Bridie was the same as ever, only perhaps a little plumper. She'd welcome them with open arms, talk their ears off and send them home loaded with gifts of eggs and butter. Neither she nor Michael had forgotten the old skills of their youth, and the farm was coming on nicely.

Annie tried to avoid going out to the farm when she knew that Danny would be there, for he was working only twenty miles away at present. He always unsettled her and made her feel flustered and breathless, which annoyed her greatly. In spite of her efforts, though, she ran into him occasionally. The first time he managed to get her on her own for a few minutes.

"So you're a free woman now," he said, barring the way into the house.

"I'm a widow, if that's what you mean."

"How long is it, then?"

"What do you mean?"

"How long since your husband died?"

"Two months."

"A bit soon, eh?" He smiled down at her and she drew in a sudden sharp breath. "You're a beautiful woman," he said softly, running a fingertip down her cheek.

Annie took a quick step backwards, colour flooding her face and heart pounding. Danny opened his mouth to speak, but Bridie called out from the kitchen just then. "Where are you, Annie, darlin'? The tea's ready." He stepped away from the door and bowed to Annie, but as she passed him, he caught her arm and whispered, "I can wait," smiling as she jerked her arm away and hurried into the house.

On the way home, after one visit to the farm, they passed Pauline's carriage taking Saul back home from the Sunday evening service. "That Mrs Hinchcliffe of yours is a rare madam," Tom said, watching the carriage bowl away into the distance. "I don't envy old Saul being married to her. I bet he can't even fart in his own bedroom!"

"Tom Gibson! Don't be so crude!"

He grinned. "Sorry, Annie. It's me low background comin' out. I have these lapses from time to time."

"It's the company you keep," she said disapprovingly. "They'll lead you into trouble one day. That Billy Pardy's a bad sort. It's a wonder he's kept out of prison so long. I don't want you bringing him along to my house again. And who was that – that female I saw hanging on your arm in town last week?"

He winked. "That was Rosie. A right little armful, she is. Very good-natured girl, if you know what I mean."

"She's as common as dirt. You want to watch yourself with her. You never know what you'll pick up."

"Ah, leave us be, our Annie. She's a good sort, is Rosie an' clean, too. I'm not stupid. A man has to have a little fun once in a while."

"You'd be better finding a decent girl and getting married than mixing with people like that."

"I'm not getting wed till I'm properly set up with me own

house and a good steady business. Then I'll look around for a wife who'll be some use to me, as well as giving me a kid or two. But the sort of woman I want wouldn't look at me now. So leave be, our Annie. What I do in me spare time is me own business."

"Who's thinking ahead now?"

"Who taught me to think ahead?" He winked and led the way down the hill into town at a smart pace, whistling merrily.

After a couple of months in the junk trade, Tom began to borrow a donkey and cart from one of his friends so that he could go further afield on his foraging trips. Old Charlie must have had feet of iron, he reckoned, to do all this on foot. He taught himself to drive it the hard way, persevering with the recalcitrant animal until it'd do what he wanted. Next he started to bring home all sorts of different goods. Annie nearly went mad when he turned up one day with a couple of big round cheeses and a basket of eggs, cushioned in straw.

"What do you think you're doing, Tom Gibson?" she shouted angrily, as he and William carried the things into the house. "We don't deal in foodstuffs! What do we know about cheese?" She was angry most of all because he'd dared to change things without consulting her.

"Aw, come on, Annie," he replied, trying to placate her. "People always need to eat. We won't have any trouble sellin' these because they're nice and fresh. I think we're on to a good thing. You'll see. I got them from those small farms over Hendon Dene Edge. It's not worth it for them women so far out to bring their bits of stuff to market each week themselves, when I can do it for them. I take a small share in the profits an' I save them time an' trouble, so everyone's happy."

The eggs and cheese sold well, as he'd predicted, so Tom

continued to expand their range. They were renting a stall every week at Bilsden market now, and the profits were continuing to rise. Annie, once she'd come round to the idea, made a sign for their stall and a canvas cover for rainy days. She painted the word ASHWORTH in neat letters on a piece of wood. "Though I don't know what sort of a stall you'd call it," she grumbled, "with second-hand clothes at one end and food at the other!"

"Who cares what you'd call it as long as we make money?" Tom retorted. He'd taken over much of the selling from Alice, because he adored the chaffing and banter of an open market. Alice didn't mind. She had now taken charge of the collection and distribution of the outwork they gave to a few carefully-selected women. That had changed too, because every now and then, Tom bought pieces of substandard material cheaply from one of the small weaving mills on his rounds and then Annie would design and cut out serviceable shirts or dresses or skirts and her outworkers would run them up for sale at the market.

Annie mainly turned her own efforts on to what Tom called her fancy sewing. Her customers were so pleased with what she had made that they came back for more garments, and sent their friends, too. The front room was now dominated most of the time by a huge trestle table stationed near the window to catch the light, and piled with sewing. Kathy worked on the straight seams and Annie acquired another outworker, a Miss James, who existed in genteel poverty and took in sewing secretly to eke her money out. Annie took a pride in making dresses women could be proud of. She didn't see why everyday dresses shouldn't flatter their wearers. It was lovely to work with new materials after years of making over old clothes, lovely to see the look of pleasure on a woman's face as she tried on a finished dress.

In some ways, though, Annie felt that her nose was being pushed out of joint by Tom. She grumbled about it to Ellie one Sunday.

"I don't like what he's doing! It's too chancy. Food can go bad or – or anything. And look what Tom's gone and done now! Bought a donkey and cart, if you please! Where will it all end, that's what I want to know?"

"You can always stop him if he goes too far," said Ellie, leaning back comfortably in her chair and licking her fingers. She had grown plumper with the years, for she was a hearty eater with a very sweet tooth. "Mmm, your Kathy's cakes just get better. How does she manage it with just that fire and a Dutch oven? Do you remember, Annie, when you were working at Park House and Mrs Cosden used to give you cookery lessons? You weren't all that pleased when Mrs Lewis turned you into her personal maid instead."

"Pleased! I was terrified! And I still don't envy anyone that job!"

"No, she's not an easy person to look after, is she? But she's a lot sweeter-tempered when she's down in Brighton, and she's there half the time nowadays. But she still keeps her eye on the housekeeping when she's back in Bilsden."

"She always was a mean one."

"Not mean with herself, though. She has a wardrobe full of clothes, while poor Miss Marianne has only just enough. A girl of that age feels it, you know. And anyone can tell the difference between Mrs Lewis's clothes that she gets in London and Miss Marianne's dresses, which Miss Pinkley makes. There isn't a really good ladies' dressmaker here in Bilsden. Why, *you* get a more stylish look to your clothes than that Miss Pinkley! Everyone's admired the last dress you made for me. Even Mrs Lewis asked me where I got it."

408

"Did you tell her?"

Ellie tossed her head. "I certainly did!" She spoiled the effect by giggling. "You should have seen her face!"

"What did she do?"

"What could she do? She just pokered up an' changed the subject."

"In the old days, she would have dismissed you, or forbidden you to see me again."

Ellie smiled rather grimly. "She can't dismiss me. Dr Lewis told me – so I suppose he must have told her, too – that *he* is my employer, not Mrs Lewis. He said he would be the judge of Miss Marianne's needs."

"Goodness! Things have changed!" Annie pushed a plate of tarts across to Ellie and went to ask Kathy to make them another brew of tea. "How is the doctor?" she asked as she sat down again. "I haven't seen much of him lately."

"Oh, he's fine. He never ails." Ellie leaned forward to whisper confidentially, "But he still goes off to Manchester every now and then, and you can guess what he does there when you smell the cheap perfume on his clothes. They're all alike, are men, even nice ones like him. Can't do without it. Catch me getting married! I know when I'm well off.'

"Me, too!"

The two young women exchanged smiles, comfortable as always together. They did not need to see one another often; they would always be like sisters.

24

October to November 1844

Annie could not avoid having admirers, whether she wanted them or not. Danny O'Connor was not one to take no for an answer when he had set his heart on something. She couldn't stop going to Bridie's because she did not wish to hurt her friend and also because going to the farm was William's greatest treat. Her heart would begin to beat at a faster rate whenever Danny was there and he would always manage to make her blush, though never in such an overt way that she could take exception to what he said.

"Sure and isn't he a tease!" Bridie would exclaim complacently and Michael would smile his slow broad smile.

"What is it now, three months since your husband died?" Danny asked abruptly one day. "Time passes slowly sometimes, doesn't it?"

Colour heightened, Annie fled into the kitchen to help Bridie.

"You're looking well, Annie," Danny said over tea another day. "Widowhood must suit you."

"I miss Charlie very much," Annie said emphatically. "Very much indeed!"

"Yes," said Danny, "women need husbands, don't they?"

"Ah, wasn't he a lovely man, God rest his soul," Bridie said, automatically crossing herself.

Careful as Annie was to avoid being alone with Danny, he did occasionally manage to catch her on her own. One day, she and Bridie went out to the cowshed with William to see the new calf. On the way back they bumped into Danny, who had been helping his father. He had his sleeves rolled up and his shirt half-open, showing his muscular chest. His hair was damp where he had just been washing himself under the pump.

As they all rounded the corner by the barn, Danny took hold of Annie's arm and held her back forcibly. "I just want a word with your mam," he told William, who nodded and ran off.

"Let go of me!" she hissed, unwilling to make a scene.

"I will, if you'll promise not to run away," he said, serious for once. "I need to talk to you."

"Bridie will miss me." But when he let go of her arm, she moved back a pace and stood waiting. "Well? What's the matter?"

"My next contract is in the south," he said abruptly. "It'll be nigh on a year before I'll be able to get back again. Annie, you know how I feel about you . . ."

She turned to flee, but found herself held by a pair of strong arms. She went rigid with panic.

"Now stop that!" he commanded, giving her a shake. "I'm not about to rape you."

"Let me go! Please!" Her voice was shaking and she was trembling.

"One kiss, Annie," he pleaded. "Nothing more. I won't hurt you."

"No! *No!*"

But he pulled her slowly closer, bent his head and kissed her anyway, a long gentle kiss that terrified and yet excited

412

her. When it ended and he held her close, she did not try to break away, but just leaned against him and drew in a shaky breath.

"Now, was that so bad?" he teased, stroking her hair.

"Danny, I don't ... I can't ..."

"All I'm asking is that you'll still be here when I come back, so that I can court you properly. A year's a long time. You won't forget me, will you, Annie? You won't go off with someone else?"

She was beginning to recover her composure. "I don't want to be courted by anyone." She pulled away from him. This time he let her go.

"You will one day, Annie, my love," he said confidently. "One day you'll want to marry again. And I'll make sure that I'm around at the time." Then his mood changed and he grinned. "Only I can't miss out on this contract, for it's going to make my fortune for me."

"I wish you luck, I'm sure." She started patting her hair into place, afraid that someone would guess what had happened. She could not bear Bridie to think that she and Danny were ... She dismissed the idea firmly from her mind.

"It's not luck, but hard work that'll make my fortune," he said soberly. "I don't believe in relying on luck."

"I agree." She turned to go.

"Just one thing more, Annie, love."

"Stop calling me that!"

He reached out and grasped her wrist, swinging her round again to face him. "Make sure you *are* still free when I get back, for I'll not let anyone else have you, wedded or no!"

This time, when he released her, she fled to the safety of the farmhouse as fast as she could. Even so, his voice pursued her. "Remember, Annie!"

413

Although she told herself she was relieved when he went, she found that she missed him. Bridie and Michael were lovely people, but it was just a little bit – well, boring – at the farm with only them and the animals. Danny had been able to talk about the wider world, and talk with assurance, too. She had enjoyed listening to his tales of the railway diggings and the men who worked there, though the shanty towns they lived in sounded worse than Claters End, even. She admired the way Danny had made something of himself, in spite of his humble beginnings. She intended to do the same – she was doing the same, she corrected. But she did *not* want another husband!

Another of Annie's admirers was Michael Benworth, her tenant. He was in his mid-forties, but still a fine figure of a man, with luxuriant curly hair only lightly flecked with grey, a flourishing set of whiskers and a flamboyant way of dressing. He was a widower, now, with all his children grown up and married, except one daughter, who kept house for him. Annie had expected him to move into a smaller house when his wife died, but Tom reported that Benworth wanted to stay on at Netherleigh Cottage in Moor Close, which he was welcome to do, as long as he paid the rent on time.

Benworth turned up a few times at chapel, making it plain that it was Annie who drew him there. Once or twice he contrived to walk home with her and William, saying that he had someone to visit in the Rows. He did nothing to which she could take offence on those walks, behaving towards her in the most respectful way, but he seemed impervious to the mild snubs she gave him.

If it had not been for her father, she would have told him to stay right away from her. It made her furious to know that people were already whispering about them. But John Gibson was showing his age, and Michael Benworth was the man upon whom he depended for employment. John saw how Annie felt and begged her not to offend Benworth. He even tried to encourage her to look upon him favourably, for he had never been reconciled to seeing his bonnie daughter 'waste hersen', as he put it.

"Benworth'd make you a good husband, lass," he said wistfully one day. "A *proper* husband! It's been a good long while since all that other business. Now that your Charlie's gone, you should start thinkin' of the future, like. A woman needs a husband to look after her."

"*I* don't. I'm doing very well as I am, Dad. I don't intend to get married, not ever again." She forced the image of Danny out of her mind.

He sighed. "Eh, you're missin' a lot, love. I'm not sayin' as you should marry where there's no feelin', but it's a sad waste of a good woman if you don't get wed. Me an' your mam, well, we had some right happy times together. I still miss her. Em'ly does her best, poor old lass, but she's tallow to wax compared to your mam." He sighed again, then reverted to his original theme. "I would like to see you wed to a nice young fellow, though, one as you could love proper."

"Well, I don't love Michael Benworth, nor ever could! And he's not all that young, either. He'll be about your age, I should think."

John shrugged, tiredly. "About that. A year or two younger, maybe. But he's a well-set-up chap, he is, not like your poor old dad. I'm not the man I used to be, an' that's a fact!"

She gave him a hug. "You're still the best dad I've got." She was delighted to see how his face lit up at her words. It had been nice having a talk with him. She did not see as much of him as she would have liked, because of Emily's jealousy.

415

He looked at her fondly. "I'm proud of you, love, proud of what you're doin', but don't miss out on the other things, will you? Money isn't everything, you know. And one child doesn't make a family."

It hurt her to see him looking so old and careworn, and she blamed Emily for that. But it was his fault, too. He should never have married a younger woman. He should have found someone older, someone past childbearing. How could he ever hope to make ends meet, let alone put a bit of money by for his old age, with such a large second family and such a poor manager for a wife?

Annie's eldest half-brothers, Mark and Luke, spent a lot of time round at Number Eight, now that they had taken William under their wings and were no longer ashamed of their young nephew. William thought that Mark, who was turned eleven and almost old enough to work in the mill, was magnificent and tried to emulate him in every way possible. Annie thought that Mark was a nice lad, and kind too. If she could do anything for him, she would.

The next boy, Luke, was a bit on the slow side and very shy, hardly saying a word when he was round at her house, but he, too, had a nice nature. Both lads always looked hungry and Kathy often slipped them a bite to eat. She excused herself by saying that she knew what it was like to be hungry herself, but Annie only shrugged. She could spare the food easily enough.

The older girls, Rebecca and Peggy, were not allowed out to play very often. They had to help their mother with the younger children and with the newest baby – and there always seemed to be a new baby at Number Three! And when the girls did come round, they could hardly be persuaded to open their mouths. She knew that all her half-brothers and sisters stood a little in awe of the fancy way she spoke and lived, not to mention the sharp edge of her tongue, but she had no time to bridge the gap between them, so busy was she.

The frequency of Mark's visits declined a little when she put William into a school that had just opened in Bilsden. She had been trying to teach him at home, but as the business grew she found that she had less and less time to spend on him and that he was running wild. The headmaster of the new school was a little dubious about accepting a child from the Rows, but Annie got Pauline to put a word in for her and the man rapidly changed his tune.

William did not have an easy time of it there, because the other children made it very plain what they thought of someone from the Rows, while at home he had to prove several times that going to a fancy school had not turned him into a stuck-up sneak. Annie bit back words of rebuke and cleaned up his wounds, but she started to think seriously again of leaving the Rows. In the meantime, with calculated generosity, she volunteered to pay the school pence at a little cottage school for both Mark and Luke, so that William would not seem quite so different from the others.

John accepted her help gratefully and Mark went wild with delight at this opportunity, rapidly improving his reading and writing, in spite of his mother's gibes. Emily considered that it would have been better if Annie had found her half-brothers employment in her junk business, rather than filling their heads with nonsense. The lads could learn to read as well as they would ever need to at Sunday School, but it was more than time they brought in a shilling or two to help out. She was the one who had to manage on John's wages and growing lads never stopped eating.

For once, John put his foot down and the two older boys continued to attend the little school. He thanked Annie privately, saying sadly that he knew he couldn't give his second family the chances he'd given Tom. He seemed to have no similar concern about educating the girls. Remembering how he'd left her to find her own way to knowledge, Annie resolved to do something for them later, when she had a minute to turn round. She remembered how envious she had been of Tom when they were all children and wondered if Rebecca felt the same. How very long ago that seemed now!

Annie had thought that she was eager to make money, but Tom's hunger was even greater than hers. Their only quarrels were when he got into deals which she considered dubious or risky. Once or twice she was on the verge of telling him to get out, for she had a terror of smirching the good reputation she had worked so hard for. But the fuss all blew over and she decided that he had learnt his lesson.

Then, one night in November, just as she was about to go up to bed after working late on a special order, Tom crept into the house the back way, gasping for breath, blood pouring from a cut on his forehead.

"Tom! What's happened?"

"I . . . they nearly caught me."

Annie recoiled, sick with fear. "*What?*"

Tom closed his eyes for a moment. He knew she'd go mad at him. She might even chuck him out. Suddenly he saw his lovely new life crumbling before him and an image of the mill looming behind it. He cursed the drinks that had made Billy Pardy's proposition that they earn themselves a bit of easy money seem like a golden opportunity.

Her voice was as cold as ice. "You'd better tell me exactly what happened."

"I – Billy knew a man who wanted some stuff moving quietly. He was willing to pay well. It seemed, I don't know, it seemed an easy way to earn some good money."

"I suppose you mean stolen goods when you say 'stuff'?"

"I – yes. But I didn't steal anything. I wouldn't do that. I only agreed to move it . . ." His voice tailed away before the scorn on her face.

"I can't see much difference myself. Nor will the law. Go on."

"The town constables must have heard about it – or been told. They were waiting for us. They nearly got Billy and his friend, but they managed to get away. Only – oh, Christ, Annie, they've got our donkey and cart! They'll soon find out who that belongs to. It's got our sign on it."

She didn't say anything. She felt physically sick with anger, so sick that she couldn't speak for a moment or two. How could he jeopardise all she'd worked for? How *dared* he get involved in something illegal? If this came out, she'd not only lose her good name, but most of her dressmaking business. Women wouldn't let the sister of a convicted criminal make for them. The realisation sent a wave of fury through her and she groaned aloud. Dimly she heard his voice.

"Annie – please – you've got to help me!" Then a minute later, "Annie – for Christ's sake, say something!"

She forced herself to take a few slow, deep breaths, then she opened her eyes. "Tell me again what happened, Tom, *exactly* what happened."

He repeated his tale. "We went to pick up the stuff. They were waiting for us. They jumped on Billy. His friend hit one of the constables. I was behind them. I got away while they were fighting. I think the others got away, too. I heard shouts and a chase. They went towards the town centre and I came back here."

"Just a minute. I thought *you* must have been in a fight. You've cut your head."

He gave a mirthless laugh. "Yes. I cut me head. I was that scared once I'd got away, that I just took off and ran. There wasn't anyone chasin' me – I just ran. I fell an' banged me head. Annie, please . . ."

"Shhh! I'm thinking."

Hope flared briefly in his eyes.

"Where were you before you went off on this wonderful job?"

He winced at the biting sarcasm in her voice. "We were drinkin'. Down at Ma Corry's boozer."

"People saw you there together?"

"Must have."

"And you left together?"

"Yes. No! What am I thinkin' of? Billy went first to arrange things. I stayed on for half an hour or so. Had another drink. Then I went and joined him."

"Where?"

"Down at the shed where I keep Blackie an' the cart. It was all arranged. Poor old Blackie. I hope he's all right."

"Never mind that stupid animal! It's you I'm worried about. You said there was another man. What about him?"

"Billy brought him along. It was old Mac. He's all right. He won't give me away."

She looked at him in disgust. "All right! Nothing's all right! If I don't help you, I'll be known for ever as the sister of a thief. If I do help you and I get caught, I'll be put in prison, too!"

He winced again. "Annie, I'm sorry! I am! I promise you I won't do . . ."

"Keep your promises till you've learned not to break them. And keep your voice down! I don't want you waking Kathy and William up. The fewer people who know about this the better."

420

"But you will help me?"

"Yes!" she spat at him, "Yes, I'll help you now, but for my own sake, not for yours. And once this has all died down, that's it. You can get out. I told you before – I'm not getting involved in anything dishonest."

"Annie!"

"I mean it! You've put everything I've worked for at risk and I'll *never* forgive you for that! Now, be quiet and listen. Your story is that you left Ma Corry's tonight and you went to feed the donkey. Someone hit you over the head, which is why you're bleeding, and that's all you can remember. Right?"

"Yes," he breathed, face lighting up. "Yes, that might work."

"Go back to the stables now, as quickly as you can, and lie down somewhere as if you'd been hit. If anyone comes, moan a bit and pretend that you're only half-conscious. I don't care how cold it is, you must just lie there till they find you. It's a pity we can't knock you out properly, but we can't, so you'll just have to act the part. See that you make it convincing, that's all. I'll go back to bed, and if anyone comes round here, for whatever reason, I shall say I know nothing, except that you went out tonight for a drink. Is that clear?"

"Yes."

She had another idea. "Have you got a bottle of gin?"

"Yes."

"Then have a swig, so that you smell of it, and tip some over yourself. You were drunk when they hit you. You know nothing of what happened after that. Now, go on! You'll have to be back at the shed before anyone goes there to check. Go out the back way and don't make any noise."

At three o'clock in the morning Annie, lying tense and

sleepless in bed, heard footsteps come along the street and pause at her door. Someone beat a firm rat-a-tat on it. Deliberately she waited for whoever it was to knock again and wake Kathy before she stirred. She'd grown used to sharing a room with Kathy now, because with Tom in the house she had no choice, but she still sometimes longed for a room of her own and a little privacy.

Kathy sat up in the other narrow bed. "Annie! There's someone at the door!"

"Mmm. I heard. Who can it be at this time of night? I'd better go down and see. You stay here!"

"No. I'm coming with you."

As they stumbled down the dark stairs the knocking started again. Annie flung open the door, simulating anger. "What do you think you're doing? It's the middle of the . . ." Her voice faltered when she saw three constables in the light of a lantern that one of them was holding. The other two were carrying a limp body.

"Sorry to disturb you, ma'am. It's Mrs Ashworth, isn't it?"

"Yes."

"Your brother's had an accident, I'm afraid."

There was real fear in her voice when she answered, because she could see that Tom was genuinely unconscious and his head was covered in blood. "Bring him in! What happened?"

The two men laid him down on the rug in front of the hearth and stepped back to let her examine him. As they did, a voice quavered from the stairs, "What's wrong with my Uncle Tom? Is he dead like Dad?"

Kathy flew across to William. "No, love, he's just hurt himself. You go back to bed."

"I don't want to go to bed."

Annie spoke sternly. "Go to bed, William! You're in our

way. We have to see to your uncle. I'll come up to you later."

He knew that tone of voice, so he turned reluctantly and made his way up the stairs, but for once he disobeyed her and stayed at the top out of sight, listening.

Annie looked at the man who seemed to be in charge. "What happened?"

"Someone must have attacked him, ma'am."

She had heard how polite the new town constables were, but she had never had cause to deal with one before. "But why? He never carried much money on him."

"We found him down by the sheds at the end of Church Lane. We think someone hit him over the head and then took your donkey and cart."

"Took Blackie? What for?"

"To move some stolen goods."

"What! Did you catch the thieves?"

"Er – no. Unfortunately there were several of the villains. We were misinformed about numbers and there were only the three of us. We found the donkey and cart but the thieves got away."

She bent over Tom to hide the relief that she was sure must be showing on her face. How had Tom got knocked out? She made a pretence of examining his injuries till she had control of herself. "This cut looks bad. I can't stop it bleeding. I think I'd better send for Dr Lewis."

"I'll go an' get him," said Kathy at once.

"Ahem. I'll send one of my men, miss. Not safe for a young woman to be out on her own at this time of the night. Farnham, go and ask the doctor to come out here to Mr Gibson, then go back to the shed and see to that bloody donkey. Ahem. Pardon the language, ma'am, but it's not a very – er – easy animal tonight. Something seems to have upset it."

"Thank you. Is – is the cart all right?"

"Bit scratched. Nothing much. And – er – perhaps you could suggest to your brother that he doesn't drink so much in future, ma'am."

"Yes. Yes, I will. I most certainly will. I'll do more than suggest it. He'll get the sharp edge of my tongue when he wakes up, I can tell you."

The constables were grinning as they left.

When they had gone, Annie tried to clean Tom up a bit, while Kathy lit the fire. It was a chill night. Annie was worried about Tom. How had he got knocked out? For a moment she was taken back in time to the night soon after her mother had died, when her father had hit Tom and she'd had to run for the new doctor. Tom was breathing in the same heavy way now. She sighed. She must pull herself together. She had to keep all her wits about her.

Fifteen minutes later Jeremy Lewis arrived. He went straight across to Tom. "What happened?"

"We don't know exactly. The law officers found him like this down at the shed where we keep Blackie, our donkey. They think he was hit over the head by the person who stole the donkey and cart."

"He's certainly had a nasty crack on the back of the head. And that's a bad gash on his forehead, too. I seem to make a habit of sewing his head up, don't I?"

She smiled, as he had meant her to and their eyes met over Tom's unconscious body. As usual, she felt comforted by his mere presence.

As the doctor was finishing, Tom started to regain consciousness. "Don't . . . Annie . . . stolen!" he muttered.

"Shh! You're all right," she whispered, afraid he'd give something away.

"He'll probably be half-conscious like that for hours," warned Jeremy. "It'd be best if someone stayed with him."

"I'll sit up with him." Annie forced herself to smile at the doctor. "Thank you for coming at this hour. You look exhausted."

Kathy came in from the back room. "I've just brewed some tea. Would you like a cup, doctor?"

Annie could have screamed at her. All she wanted was to get Jeremy Lewis out of the house, in case Tom said something he shouldn't.

"I'd love a cup!"

Jeremy Lewis stayed on for a quarter of an hour, chatting comfortably until Annie thought he would never go. At last, however, he stood up. "I must go and get some sleep, or I'll be no use to my patients today." He paused for a final look at Tom. "I'll call in sometime tomorrow. Don't try to move him upstairs until he can walk himself."

When he'd gone Annie slipped upstairs to check on William, who was fast asleep on the landing, with a tear-stained face. She carried him to his bed and tucked him in, kissing his cheek. As she was walking downstairs the tiredness and reaction hit her. She turned into the front room in time to hear Tom say loudly and clearly, "They'll catch me! It's stolen stuff."

She looked at Kathy, but Kathy's expression remained calm. "It's all right, Annie, love. I heard Tom come back earlier. I knew summat were wrong. What did he steal? Is it safe hidden? Is there anythin' I can do to help?"

Only then did Annie fall into a chair and start to sob.

For the next few days Annie refused to speak to Tom. He soon began to pick up, for he had as strong a constitution as her own. She left his care mainly to Kathy and kept William away from his uncle as much as possible. She alternated between feeling furiously angry with her brother and coldly disgusted. The only time she did say anything to him voluntarily was when she asked him abruptly one day,

"How did you get knocked out? You never said how that happened."

"I did it meself."

"*You* did? I don't understand."

"You said it was a pity you couldn't knock me out properly. It seemed like a good idea, so I took a few swigs of gin and banged my head on the wall. I was a bit drunk. I banged too hard."

"Oh."

One day, two weeks later, Tom caught her on her own. "Annie, we have to talk about it."

"I don't want to talk to you. I just want you to keep out of my way." Then suddenly the anger welled up inside her and erupted into a fury. "Go on! Get out!" she screamed at him. "I told you when Charlie died that I'd have no sharp practices, no dishonest dealings. And you've let me down!" She tried to push him towards the door, beating at him with her fists till he had to hold her off him.

"Annie! Annie, listen. Don't chuck me out! I swear I've learned my lesson! I won't do anythin' like that again. I promise I won't!" He tried to dodge her flailing fists.

"I won't have to chuck you out. They'll come and *take* you away one day. It's not like the old days, with one parish constable, you know. We've got proper town constables in Bilsden now." She kicked him on the shins.

He began to get angry, too. "You bloody vixen! Ouch! Stop it, will you!" He shook her.

A small body hurtled across the room from the kitchen and attacked Tom from the rear. "You let go of my mother!"

Tom pushed William aside and gave Annie another shake. "Damn you, our Annie! You *can't* chuck me out. You need me! I've doubled the turnover and you know it. It's my business too, now!"

She sagged against him. "You rotten bastard!" For her to swear like that showed how upset she was. His grasp slackened and she pushed away from him and went to cling to the mantelpiece, for her legs were shaking. She stared unseeingly into the flames. William went and stood beside her, bewildered, but loyal.

"Annie?" said Tom tentatively, after a few minutes had crawled past without a sign from her. "Annie – I know I've been a fool, but Annie, I don't want it to end. It went to my head, I think, livin' so posh, earnin' good money, feelin' free. I got greedy. And I'd had too much to drink that night. I give you my word that I won't ever do anything like that again. Nor I won't drink so much." He shuddered.

"Your word!" she flung back at him. "We agreed to keep things honest when you came in with me. You gave me your word then. Well, I can't afford to take any more risks and I *don't trust* your word. You'd better get out." She spoke calmly now, her voice resolute and this frightened him more than her fury had.

William, at her side, gave a sudden sob. "Don't send Uncle Tom away, mother! I don't w-want him to go. Please, mother!"

She tried to gather the child in her arms, but he fought her off.

"Tom's done something wrong, William."

"But he said he was sorry. I heard him. He said he wouldn't do it again."

"He's said that before. I don't believe him."

"It's no good, William," said Tom, touched by his young defender's words. "She's right. I'd better go."

"But – who'll get the stuff for us? Who'll look after the stall? I can't do it yet. I'm too little." William burst into noisy sobs. "You can't send him away, you can't!"

427

Tom tried a desperate last appeal. "Annie, I swear I mean it this time. I've learned my lesson. I'm not cut out for crime. I was scared witless. I don't want to lose what we've got. Please, Annie, just . . ."

She was wavering, but not yet ready to give in. "I could live off the rents of my cottages, you know," she threatened. "With that and my sewing I'd manage all right. I don't need you as much as you need me."

He played his last card. "But would you feel safe at nights?"

She stared at him and let out her breath in a long shuddering sound. "I've got Sammy. He's a good watch dog."

"He's getting old. He wasn't much help to you with Jim Catterall when Charlie died, not with him shut outside in the yard. You need me, Annie, need me inside the house to protect you."

She looked at him, chewing her lip. She might have known Tom would work on her weak point. Should she trust him? Dared she trust him again? Only – how would she manage on her own? He'd struck home there. She was afraid to live alone.

"If you give up the business, Annie, what'll you do about our William? There'll be no fancy schools for him if you have to cut back." Tom let that sink in, waiting quietly, sensing that he'd hit the right note there. She'd do anything for William.

She expelled a whoosh of breath and her shoulders sagged. "All right, then." She spoke tiredly. "One last chance. But it really is the last chance. I can't go through this again, Tom. I just can't face it ever again!"

William poked his head out from behind his mother. He scowled up at his uncle. "Promise to be good now, Uncle Tom! I don't like it when you make my mother cry."

The tension relaxed and they both smiled down at the little boy.

"All right, our William." Tom ruffled his nephew's hair. "I promise to be good." He was near to tears, as he looked at Annie. "I mean it," he said softly. "I really do mean it!"

25

January to March 1845

Just after Christmas, Sally came into Number Eight, flushed and tremulous. "Annie, love! Oh, Annie!"

"Why, Sally! What's the matter?"

"Such news! I don't know whether I'm on me head or me feet!" She collapsed into a chair and sat there, shaking her head from side to side and trying to find the words to tell her news.

"Well, come on, what is it?" Annie demanded, uncertain whether the news was good or bad.

"It – it's my Harry," Sally got out at last.

"What about your Harry? Is something wrong with him? He didn't come to see you last week, did he?"

"No, he didn't come. But he came yesterday. And there's nothin' wrong – not *wrong*, no. I – it's his wife. She – she died last week. That's why he couldn't come to see me. She's been ailing for years, but no one thought she was any worse. But anyway, she just died in her sleep. Harry came to see me last night and he said – he— Oh, Annie, he asked me to marry him." She burst into tears and buried her head in her apron.

Annie went and put her arms round her friend. "But Sally, that's *marvellous* news!"

Sally looked at her through swimming eyes. "I – I can't

seem to take it in. Imagine it! Me, a respectable married woman!" The tears flowed again. "He – he says we'll have to wait six months or so, but then we can get wed and go to live in his house in Oldham. He's only got one daughter and his youngest son left at home now. He says they can like it or lump it."

Annie hugged her again. "That's the best news I've heard in a long time!"

"Yes, but – but what if someone found out about me – about what I was?"

"Why should they? You've been away from that sort of thing for how long – sixteen years? Who's to remember anything?" She sat down and sighed. "But I'll miss you, Sally. It won't be the same in the street without you. Everyone I grew up with will have left when you go."

"Then you think I should go ahead? Accept?"

"Of course I do, you daft thing! No question of it!"

Sally shook her head. "I told him to go an' think it over for a week or two, but he said he'd already thought it over and he'd marry me tomorrow if he could, only that'd put people's backs up."

"Well, he couldn't say fairer than that, could he?"

"No – I just – it's been such a shock. An' I do want to do the right thing by him. He's a lovely man an' he's been that good to me. I really love him, Annie."

"I'm sure you do."

They shared a cup of tea, then Sally remarked inconsequentially, "It'll give me time to grow me hair grey, any road."

"Your hair?"

"Aye. I've been touchin' it up a bit. But we're to say I'm a widow, so it'll look a bit more respectable, like, if me hair's grey."

Annie refrained from smiling.

"And I want you to make me some new clothes, Annie, love."

"New clothes?"

"Yes. Something a bit quieter, like, but *good*. A silk for best and some dark dresses. My stuff's too bright. I like a touch of colour, but widows don't have orange dresses, even I know that. I'll need some fancy caps and aprons, the frilly, lacy sort. *You* know."

"Don't you think you should go to a proper dressmaker in Manchester? I've never made a silk dress."

"You *are* a proper dressmaker! You always get a lovely fit, even with that second-hand stuff, an' you've a rare way of settin' in a sleeve. It takes a good dressmaker to cut a sleeve just right, 'specially with these tight sleeves. A full sleeve can hide a lot of faults, but a tight one has to fit without wrinkles."

So Annie found herself with her first silk dress to make. When she confided her fears to Pauline Hinchcliffe, she was told in no uncertain terms that it was about time she started making for ladies. After she'd finished doing Mrs Smith's dress, she could make up a new silk for Pauline. It'd be good practice for her. They'd start studying *The Ladies' Fashion Calendar* together, so that they could pick out something suitable. Not that she, Pauline, wanted one of those ridiculous creations one saw illustrated, with skirts so wide you couldn't get through a door, but she owed it to her position to dress well.

A few days later, faced with twenty yards of lustrous lavender silk, Annie felt her mouth go dry and her scissors turn to lead. "I can't!" she whispered to Alice. "I daren't! What if I ruin it?"

"Get on with you!" retorted Alice, who had no such sensitivities. "You work miracles with the old stuff an' with cheap woollens, an' them's as hard to make up as anythin'. I'm lookin' forward to seein' what you do with this."

Her mouth as dry as ashes, Annie made a hesitant first snip along the lines she'd chalked in so carefully. She'd already checked them several times, but she put her scissors down again and re-checked her measurements. Finally, unable to postpone the moment any longer, she slowly cut out a bodice front. Her movements gathered speed and in a short time, she had a pile of neatly-folded pieces on the table in front of her. She then cut out the lining, after which Alice and Kathy pulled their stools up to the table and began to help her to baste the pieces together.

"Lovely, it is!" said Kathy reverently, stroking the shiny material.

The dress was, of course, a success, not only perfect in fit and fashionable in style, but also subtly flattering to Sally's plump figure. Pauline Hinchcliffe, taking, Annie felt, an over-keen interest in the whole business, came along and demanded to be shown the results of her labours, so Sally had to be called in to parade her new dress.

"Er – this is my neighbour, Mrs Smith," said Annie, wondering what Pauline would say if she knew of Sally's past. She had to cough to hide a chuckle at the thought.

"How do you do?" Pauline shook hands graciously with Sally. "I hear you are soon to be remarried, Mrs Smith. Please accept my best wishes for your future happiness."

"Th-thank you."

"Now, turn round and let me look at the fit. Oh, yes, excellent! Annie, you're even better than I had thought. No doubt about it, you shall make me some dresses for the spring. A nice fawn, I think, or grey."

Annie, to her own surprise, heard herself daring to contradict her benefactress. "*Not* fawn," she said firmly, "nor grey, either! You should never wear those colours

434

with your colouring, Mrs Hinchcliffe."

"I beg your pardon?" Pauline didn't know whether to be amused or offended.

Annie swallowed. "I said – not fawn or grey. You should wear soft pinks or blues, or even certain greens, though not bright colours. Fawn and grey are the worst possible colours for you!"

A hint of annoyance crept into Pauline's voice. "I *like* fawn and grey. They are particularly suitable for a minister's wife."

In for a penny, in for a pound, thought Annie, who had longed for years to do something about the way Pauline Hinchcliffe dressed. "Well, I'm not making you a dress that won't suit you. If you want me to do it, you'll have to choose a colour that flatters you."

"You can't tell a customer what colour she should choose!" exclaimed Pauline.

Alice stood at the back of the room like one turned to stone. Had Annie gone mad? Here she was, being given a golden opportunity and she was arguing with a customer! Sally, also horrified, tried to catch Annie's eye.

"What's the point in me making dresses for you, if they don't flatter you?" persisted Annie. "You've been on at me for a while to set up as a fashionable ladies' dressmaker. Presumably you'll be kind enough to tell everyone that I make for you. But that won't be much good, unless your dresses look different and better than the ones you've been having made. So I won't make you a dress in a colour or style that doesn't suit you." She folded her arms and nodded her head decisively. Alice's heart sank. She knew how stubborn Annie could be when she set her mind on something.

Pauline decided to be amused. "Annie, I know that you mean well, but you *can't* dictate what a customer should buy or wear! You have to let your customers choose what they want, even if you know it'll look awful. Not that I consider fawn and grey will look awful in my own case!"

"If I set up as a ladies' dressmaker – I say *if*, because I'm still not sure I want to – but *if* I do, then I'm not going to be just any provincial dressmaker," Annie declared, unconsciously using one of Mrs Lewis's favourite phrases. "Every time I go into the town centre, I see ladies wearing things that don't suit them."

"Yes, well, that's their own choice, Annie."

"And," Annie went on, determined to make her point, "Miss Pinkley has been dressmaking in this town for years, but nobody has a good word for her, nobody, and it's partly because she lets her clients choose unsuitable styles and materials. Her sewing's not that bad. The ladies let her make for their daughters – she does Miss Marianne's clothes – and they let her make an occasional everyday dress, but for their best things they always go into Manchester – and they *still* choose wrongly! I worked for Mrs Lewis for years and she has the best dress sense of any woman I've ever seen. You couldn't help learning what looks right with what, if you worked for her. So, if I decide to set up as a proper dressmaker, I'll put what she taught me into practice. I will *not* make up things that I know are *wrong*!"

"Annie, love!" begged Sally.

Pauline looked at Annie challengingly. "All right, then. Make good your boast. I need a new dress for a wedding next month. *You* choose the material, *you* choose the style and if it looks all right, I'll wear it!"

"All right, then, I will! But we'll have to go into Manchester for the material. Hardy's won't have anything nearly good enough for you. And you'll have to be there with me, so that I can see it next to your skin."

"We'll drive over there in my carriage tomorrow," promised Pauline, eyes glittering. She loved a challenge.

So the next day, Annie put on the best of her new dresses, with its skirts supported by every petticoat she owned to give it a fashionable fullness. Over it she wore a matching short jacket and hastily-retrimmed bonnet. They drove into Manchester in Pauline's comfortable carriage, chatting carefully about topics other than dress materials, about which Annie was nervous and Pauline still a little annoyed.

Annie had forgotten how busy the city centre could be. The streets were jammed with vehicles of every description, from private carriages to heavily-laden drays or donkey carts, as well as horses and riders. The crowds of pedestrians all seemed to be walking briskly, as if they had urgent business to attend to and absolutely no time to spare. It reminded her a bit of London.

When they entered the silk warehouse that Pauline always patronised, Annie lost her diffidence in her delight at the beauty of the materials on its shelves. It did not take her long to steer Pauline and the assistant away from the neutral tones and to narrow down her choice to two materials, one a subtle shot silk in delicate shades of lilac and grey, and the other a glacé silk in a pretty blue. Each was draped in turn in front of Pauline and in the end everyone was unanimous in preferring the blue.

Thirty yards of this were carefully measured, folded and wrapped, then the ladies left to visit a bonnetmaker's and a ribbon warehouse that Annie remembered from her days with Mrs Lewis. They followed this by the inevitable call at the Manchester Bazaar, where they were served by a Mr Thomas Kendal, who fussed over Pauline as if she were royalty. The huge shop was now lit by the new Bude gas lighting, which Annie had never seen before.

"Progress," said Pauline complacently, looking round. "Marvellous, isn't it?"

"It certainly makes the inside of the shop brighter," agreed Annie. "Oh, I'll never forget the first time I saw gas lighting in London. I just stood and gaped till Mrs Lewis shouted at me to keep moving. And now Bilsden has its own Private Gas Company and gas lights in all the main streets."

"I wonder how long it'll be before people start installing gas lights in their houses?" wondered Pauline. "I couldn't have it installed in Collett Hall, because we're too far out of town for the pipes. Saul says he's glad and he prefers candles when we're sitting by the fire in the evenings, but I like a well-trimmed oil lamp, so that I can see what I'm embroidering, thank you very much. I don't know about gas, though."

Annie nodded. She knew that Pauline rarely changed anything at Collett Hall, which she regarded as a sacred trust to be passed on to her eldest son. "Things are changing quickly. Too quickly, I think sometimes. And yet my stepmother doesn't even have a proper chimney crane for her cooking pots and she makes do with candles and even tallow dips. She's still living in the Dark Ages in Number Three."

When they had made all their purchases, the parcels were sent round to the livery stables where Mrs Hinchcliffe always left her carriage and the two ladies went for a stroll round the city centre, with Pauline pointing out the places of interest, such as the new Victoria Railway Station, named for the Queen, and the Free Trade Hall. They ended up at a large hotel, which had a room where unattended ladies of respectable appearance could be served with a lavish luncheon for only two shillings and sixpence a head.

Annie, a little nervous in such surroundings, watched carefully what Pauline did and imitated all her actions. She remembered from Park House the array of cutlery and plates that the gentry used and no one, watching her, would have realised that this was the first time she herself had sat down to such a meal. Pauline kept an unobtrusive eye on her and was relieved to see that she had nothing to blush for in her protégée's manners. After a while, however, she noticed that Annie was frowning and realised that she was not getting her full attention.

"My dear Annie, you look as though you have the cares of the world upon your shoulders. I thought we'd agreed that we were going to enjoy ourselves for the rest of the day."

"I was just thinking about your dress."

"And worrying?"

"Yes. I'm afraid of spoiling all that beautiful material. Thirty yards! And the lace alone cost more than I've ever spent on a dress for myself."

"You needn't worry, Annie. I can well afford the loss of a length of silk if things don't work out."

"It's not just a length of silk to me, it's my whole future that's at stake!"

Pauline patted her hand. "My dear, I'm sure you'll manage very well, or I'd not have encouraged you. I *am* a good businesswoman, you know, even if you don't approve of my choice of dress materials. You have a real flair for clothes. Look at the dress you made for Mrs Smith. And look at your own clothes. Even with cheap materials, you always manage to look elegant – or you do lately, since you started taking more care. While we're on the subject, I want you to bear in mind that I would be prepared to help you financially, if there were any difficulties when you decided to expand your business interests." Annie sat

439

toying with her sherry trifle, her thoughts miles away from what she was eating. "It's very kind of you, but I can manage on my own. I have some money put by."

"Now, I'm not having you skimp on things. You'll need to find some good premises and furnish them elegantly, if you want to attract the best clientèle in town."

Annie smiled wryly. "I won't skimp. You needn't worry about that. I know what the London salons look like. I went there with Mrs Lewis once. I've never forgotten and I shall work on similar lines. But . . ." she hesitated, not wanting to offend Pauline, "if I let you advance me money, you'll want, quite rightly, to poke a finger in the pie. Tom's done that with the second-hand business. He's done quite well. We're making more money than ever before. But it's not mine any more. My dressmaking salon is going to be all mine."

"So you *are* going to take the plunge?"

"Oh, yes. You're right. It's more than time I moved. I'll start looking for premises as soon as we get back."

"Just like that?"

"Yes." Annie's voice was quietly confident now that she had come to a decision. "Just like that. I've known for a while that I was ready to do something else, but I had to see how Tom went. So many of the people I know have left Salem Street. Now it's my turn."

But when they got back, all thought of moving was banished from Annie's head, and the parcel of silk lay unheeded in a corner, because William was ill. He'd been off-colour for a few days, but it hadn't seemed much to worry about and he hadn't complained. She'd thought it was just a cold or a chill. She castigated herself afterwards for being so blind, when the influenza was going around and who knew what else. There was always something at the end of the winter. William was now lying on Kathy's old chairbed near the fire in the front room. His face was flushed, yet he was shivering and complaining that he was cold.

"He came home from school," said Kathy. "They sent him home, said he was too sick to study."

"I'm sorry, mother." William tried to smile at her, but was prevented by another fit of shivering. Annie laid a hand on his brow and was alarmed at how hot it felt. "Some of the lads at school have got it," he croaked. "Eddie an' Harry are bad. They've had the doctor in."

"Then I think we'd better have the doctor in, too," she told him quietly, hiding the fear in her heart. "Why didn't you tell me you felt so bad?"

"I thought it was just a cold – and that I'd get better soon. And besides, you've been busy lately." He sighed and huddled down under the blankets, his eyes flickering closed.

"Kathy, go and get Dr Lewis, will you?" Annie asked. She looked across at Alice, not daring to put her fears into words. It looked like – No, she'd not think about it. Best to wait and see what the doctor said.

Kathy was back in twenty minutes, panting from her run across the park. "He's not in, but they'll tell him as soon as he gets back," she gasped. "I wanted to wait, but that maid wouldn't let me. Stuck-up piece, she is! Said she'd deliver my message. But if Dr Lewis don't come soon, I'll go back again and wait on the doorstep, whatever she says." Only for William would timid Kathy have been so brave; for William, she would have bearded a lion in its den barehanded, and won, too.

Two hours dragged past. They lit all the lamps and they tried to make William comfortable. None of them could settle to anything useful, because they all loved the boy too much. Although he was lying in front of the fire, he was still shivering and complaining of being cold. They didn't dare take him upstairs. The bedrooms had no fireplaces and were like iceboxes in winter. William kept muttering to himself and he didn't seem very sure of what was happening. Every now and then he accepted a drink of water, but there was nothing else he wanted, nothing they could do for him. Annie sat by her son as if her very presence would protect him. From time to time she looked at the clock, but said nothing. She knew Jeremy would come as soon as he could.

Finally they heard brisk footsteps along the street, footsteps which stopped at their door.

Alice's "Thank God!" went unheard. Kathy flew to open the door, but she and Alice might just as well not have been there, because Jeremy strode across the room to Annie and William, without even glancing at them.

"I came as soon as I got your message. I've been out at one of the farms."

William roused slightly as the doctor began to examine him and tried to push away the new clinical thermometer which Jeremy had acquired recently, to the immense distrust of his poorer patients. "It hurts," he said fretfully. "My head hurts."

Jeremy finished his examination and turned to Annie. "Do you know what he has?"

"I – I think so." Her beautiful eyes stared at him from a white face. "It's the fever, isn't it?"

"I'm afraid so. It's common name is scarlet fever. I've just come from another case, Edward Farley up at Bridge End Farm." His voice was low, so that Kathy and Alice had to strain to hear him. "It's a bad outbreak, I'm afraid, and this time it's started in the better end of town, not the Rows. And to add to it, we've got the influenza going round as well. It's been a bad winter for illness. I blame the poor summer. It doesn't just give us a bad harvest, but a bad crop of illnesses, as well." He forgot the boy and added indignantly, "And the sanitary conditions in this town are deplorable. I've been telling them for years that the water supply is not satisfactory and that their so-called sanitation scheme is a mockery. No wonder these diseases spread! Well, maybe they'll listen more carefully now!"

Annie wasn't attending to most of this discourse. "You mean – William caught the fever at that fancy school?" She gave a mirthless croak of laughter. "And I was trying to keep him *out* of trouble by sending him there!" Her voice cracked abruptly and she fought back the tears that threatened to overwhelm her. She could not afford to give way to any weakness while William needed her.

Tom came in through the front door, whistling, the sound dying on his lips as he saw the doctor and the flushed child. "What's happened? What's the matter with our William?"

Annie had control of herself again. "It's the fever," she said quietly. "It's going round his school."

Tom looked from one to the other. "Bad?"

It was Jeremy who answered. "It's a very bad outbreak. We usually get it earlier in the winter. We won't know for a while how badly William has it." He turned back to Annie. "He's always been a strong, healthy lad. It's the little ones who succumb most easily." His heart ached at the sight of her pale strained face. He knew how much she loved her son. If only he could have taken her in his arms and comforted her!

"What must we do, doctor?" she asked, still quietly. "How can we best nurse him?"

He forced himself to speak in a businesslike manner. "There's not a lot to be done. You know the course of the illness?"

"Yes. You can't grow up in the Rows and not know about the fever."

"Keep him warm, but not overheated. It's just as bad to get overheated as too cold. He'll shiver, but you must feel his forehead to see if he's too hot or not. As much fluid as he'll take – and boil all your drinking water – for yourselves as well as for him. I think we should always boil our drinking water until we get a better supply, not just leave the cloudiness to settle, and so I've told Mrs Cosden. And keep everything clean – it seems to help – but then, you always do. He's not come out in the rash yet. When he does, leave it alone, though you may sponge him with tepid boiled water. But no poultices or old-fashioned remedies!"

"No, doctor."

"I'll leave you a sleeping draught for him. How long has he been feeling ill?"

"A day or two. We thought it was just a cold." Her voice faltered again for a moment, but she took a deep breath and focused her attention on what the doctor was saying.

"It's best to keep him away from other people. It spreads by touch, we think." He took her hand for a moment, as he would have done with any woman worried about her only child. "Don't wear yourself out nursing him, Annie. It won't do him any good if you fall ill as well. You have Kathy and Alice to help." He let go of the small, firm hand reluctantly and nodded at the other two women. "And afterwards, it could be weeks before he recovers fully. That's when you can do most for him. He'll need plenty of fresh air and plenty of good food if he's to get back to normal again."

Annie nodded. *Afterwards . . . when he gets better . . .* She repeated the words to herself like an incantation against evil. She had to keep on believing that William would recover. For all the doctor's encouraging words, with the fever you could never tell who would succumb. It sometimes took the strong and left the weak.

"I'll come to see him whenever I can." And you, Jeremy added silently. He was unaware that his eyes were betraying his feelings.

Tom, who had not missed the doctor's expression, came and put his arm round his sister. "Thanks, doctor. We'll do what you said. And I'll keep an eye on our Annie."

Jeremy walked slowly back through the Rows, stopping in the park for a few moments of peace. What he hadn't told Annie was that his own daughter had a sore throat and that he was afraid that she too had contracted the scarlet fever. Oh, God, he prayed, let her have it lightly! She's all I've got, all I'm ever likely to have. He had no fears for Annabelle's safety. She was one of the healthiest women he'd ever met, in spite of her protestations of delicate health. She never seemed to catch even a cold. He was quite sure that she'd outlive them all.

When he arrived home, his wife was waiting for him in the hallway. "Don't come any nearer! Just tell me if it's true!" she demanded, before he had even closed the door.

"If what's true?" He shut the door and turned to face her. He hated her most of all when she was in this sort of mood, with that shrill edge to her voice.

"That there's an outbreak of scarlet fever, as well as the influenza, in this godforsaken town. Is it true?"

"We have several cases of scarlet fever, yes, mostly among the boys at the new school. I've just come back from visiting one of them. And there's influenza going round, too, though I wouldn't call it an epidemic. How far they'll both spread, I can't tell at this stage."

He took a step forward and she hastily moved as far away from him as she could, covering her mouth and nose with a perfumed handkerchief, whose cloying sweetness offended him far more than the smells of dirt and humanity he met in the Rows.

He didn't bother to hide his disgust. "You needn't worry. I've no intention of touching you."

"But that's two outbreaks of disease! Even worse than usual. And you'll be visiting the sick and then coming back here. I'm not risking it. My mind's quite made up. I'm going down to Brighton till it's all over, and I'm taking Marianne with me. It'd be foolish to run the risk of staying here when we have somewhere safe to go. We can easily be down there in a day on the train. Just because *you* have to behave like a chivalrous fool, there's no need to expose your family to danger!"

"It's too late to leave. I think it very likely that Marianne has already contracted something. I'm not sure what. Scarlet fever starts a bit like a cold. She was complaining of a sore throat last night."

Annabelle put her hand up to her own throat. "No!"

He was pleased to see that she had at least got some feeling for her daughter, but her next words corrected this misapprehension.

"Well, it's not too late for *me* to go," she said slowly, her brow furrowed in thought. "I haven't actually touched her for a day or two, I think. No, I'm sure I haven't been near her at all today."

"And you'd go away and leave her – with that hanging over her?"

She scowled across at him. "What good could I do by staying? I'm no good with sick people. I loathe illness! And it's Ellie to whom Marianne will turn, anyway. She always does when she's ill. She's far too fond of that woman. She picks up all sorts of coarse mannerisms from her. I've told you so before, but you won't listen to me. She probably caught this fever from her, too."

He looked at her with a loathing so intense that it made him feel physically sick. "I knew you were a cold woman," he said, somehow keeping his voice down. "I knew that I'd made a dreadful mistake in marrying you. But I never realised, no, I never *let* myself realise that you were so monstrous as to desert your own child when she's ill."

"Monstrous!" she threw back at him. "It's you who's monstrous, condemning your wife and child to live in a cesspit like Bilsden. If anything happens to Marianne it'll be your fault for bringing her here!"

He felt nauseated by her very presence. "You are quite at liberty to leave, Annabelle . . ."

"How *very* kind of you!"

". . . but let it be understood that it will be for ever this time. I shall not permit you to return."

Silence stretched between them for a moment, then she shrugged her shoulders. "So be it! You were not the only one who made a mistake." She turned to leave.

"One moment, if you please. I shall make you a small allowance, and you have your house in Brighton, but I have no intention of keeping you in luxury."

She gave a sniff of laughter. "As you please. As you say, I have my house and some small investments from what mama left me. I presume you'll allow me to keep those? I shan't need a fortune to live in modest comfort and enjoy the company of civilised people."

He inclined his head in assent and spoke with a distant courtesy, which irritated her intensely. "I have no fears for you, Annabelle. Your sort always manages. However, I would prefer that you leave my mother's jewellery behind for Marianne and I must warn you not to take anything with you but your clothes and personal possessions. My family silver, for instance. I know every piece of it."

Her mouth dropped open in astonishment, for he had

447

never seemed very aware of material things. She had at that moment been calculating how many of the smaller pieces of household silver she could take with her.

"I've always noticed more than you gave me credit for," he added, as if reading her mind, "but I preferred to live in peace rather than wrangle with you over the housekeeping details. However, I do not wish Marianne to lose what small inheritance she has from my family." He rang the bell. "Ah, Mabel, please tell Cora to pack Mrs Lewis's bags. She has to leave immediately for Brighton."

Mabel dropped a curtsey, surprise in her eyes. "Yes, sir. And sir – there are some urgent messages."

"Thank you, Mabel. I'll attend to them after I've seen Marianne. She didn't look too well this morning."

Mabel bobbed another curtsey and scurried out to pass on the news that the mistress was leaving again, and her only back a few weeks, and that the master was looking furious. This was so unlike him as to cause considerable speculation below stairs.

Jeremy turned to his wife. "Should you disobey my orders and try to take anything extra with you, Annabelle, I shall not only withdraw my financial support, but I shall instruct my lawyer to take over your Brighton interests. As your husband, I would be well within my legal rights to do so."

She inclined her head to signify assent, not trusting herself to speak to him, then she swept out without a word, to vent her anger on the servants as she systematically cleared out all her cupboards and drawers. Cora and Mabel gaped in astonishment as every trunk in the house was brought down from the attics and every single item of their mistress's clothing was removed from its storage place – winter mantles, summer muslins, and even old clothes long discarded.

"I have no intention of ever returning to this town," Annabelle told them. You may come with me to Brighton, Cora, as my maid, or you may stay in Bilsden, but you had better decide quickly."

"You – you're going to live in Brighton – for good, ma'am?"

"Isn't that what I just said? Are you totally stupid, girl?"

Cora goggled for a minute, did a quick calculation that if she stayed her services as a lady's maid wouldn't be required any more, anyway, and said hastily that she'd rather go with her mistress, if that was all right. Mabel just stood and glowered. All her plans, all her waiting had come to nothing, and if Mrs Lewis were leaving, there was no hope of future changes that would give her a chance to become a lady's maid.

"Was you wanting a parlourmaid, Mrs Lewis?" she nerved herself to ask.

Annabelle studied Mabel briefly. "No. You're too fat and ugly! I shall hire my staff in Brighton."

Mabel flushed crimson and turned to leave the room.

Annabelle nodded to Cora, showing no pleasure in her acceptance. "You had better pack your own things, then. But do it rapidly. I'm not staying in Bilsden a minute longer than I have to. We're leaving first thing in the morning, if it takes us all night to pack. Mabel! Oh, you're still there. Good! Please send someone over to the livery stables before you do anything else. I want a carriage first thing in the morning to take me to the station in Manchester. No, they'd better send two vehicles. There'll be all my luggage, too. And send to the carpenter's for boxes. He is to provide them tonight or not at all."

Seething with fury, Mabel turned to obey.

Upstairs in the nursery suite, Jeremy found his daughter to be a bit feverish, but quite cheerful. He sat on her bed and chatted for a few minutes, noting her symptoms, then he tucked her up and asked Ellie to step outside for a moment.

"There's scarlet fever going round," he said abruptly. "I'm not sure whether Marianne has that or the influenza. It's even possible that she has only a cold. Can you keep a closer eye on her than usual and call me if you think she's worse, or if you notice any other symptoms?"

"Yes, sir. Would you want me to move my bed in with her? I could keep an eye on her during the night, then."

"It might be the best thing, if you don't mind."

"She won't like it. Thinks herself too old for that sort of thing." Ellie smiled and then waited, as he still seemed to have something on his mind. The poor doctor was grossly overworked at the moment. Your heart went out to him, sometimes.

Jeremy cleared his throat, finding it hard to continue, so marked was the contrast between the reactions of his wife and of Ellie to his daughter's illness. And Ellie was only a hired servant. "I am – I'm touched by your loyalty, Ellie. I shall not forget it." He cleared his throat again. "I must explain – my wife is leaving for Brighton tomorrow. She dislikes illness."

"Yes, sir, I had heard." Mabel hadn't waited to spread the news around the house.

"She will not be returning."

Ellie's eyes flew to his face in surprise. "Not returning? Not ever?"

"No. I told her that Marianne was possibly very ill, but she still insisted on going, so I told her not to return. I thought *you* ought to know the truth, Ellie. In case Marianne gets upset. But please don't spread the news. I'll see Mrs Cosden later and tell her what she needs to know."

"Yes, sir." Oh, the poor man, she was thinking. As if he

hadn't enough on his plate! He didn't deserve this.

"And I'll tell Marianne myself, when she's better."

"Yes, sir."

"Thank you, Ellie. Thank you for everything. I don't know what I'd have done without you all these years."

Ellie turned bright red with pleasure at this unexpected compliment. "I'm happy to be of service, sir. I'm very fond of Miss Marianne." And of him, she suddenly realised. He was such a nice man and yet he seemed so lonely and unloved. She realised that he was still speaking and forced herself to concentrate.

"And Marianne is fond of you, Ellie. Rightly so. You've been more of a mother to her than my wife has." He sighed and left to attend to his patients and she watched him go sadly. Poor man! Then she brightened up a little. Life would be much more pleasant without Mrs Lewis around.

26

March to April 1845

When Jeremy Lewis visited Salem Street the next day, William was slightly worse and Annie's face was haggard with worry. The other women were not around and he accepted a cup of tea from her, glad to be able to spend a few minutes peacefully.

"You're looking tired, Jeremy," she said, as she handed him the cup. She had not realised that she was using his given name, for although he always called her Annie, she had scrupulously stuck to Dr Lewis.

He had not noticed, either. "I am tired. What with the influenza and now this outbreak of scarlet fever, I'm run off my feet. And it's going to get a lot worse, I fear. I had three new cases of fever today, very young children, not boys from the school. So it's spreading."

"And you the only doctor," she said sympathetically. "There's too much work for one doctor in Bilsden now."

He sighed. "Yes. I've been thinking of getting an assistant, a junior partner whom I could train to my own ways. I should have got one before now, but Annabelle objected to anyone coming to live with us. Well, I have someone in mind, someone I met in London, and I shall send to ask him immediately." He sipped his tea and said abruptly, "I think my daughter may have the influenza."

453

"Oh, no!" She stretched out her hand in sympathy and then was overcome by confusion as he kept hold of it.

"You're a fine person, Annie. I admire you greatly."

"Please, Jeremy – don't..."

"I've got to talk to someone," he begged, clasping her hand in both of his. "And there's no one else. I'm not very good at making friends – too wrapped up in my work, I suppose. And my wife – well, you know what she's been like."

She stopped trying to pull her hand away and let it rest in his, soft and warm, with the fingertips roughened from sewing. "Yes. I know. Is – is Marianne very ill?"

"I don't know yet. You never know with the influenza. She's feverish and complaining that she aches all over. But she's got Ellie, at least she's got Ellie."

Annie thought he put an unexpected emphasis on this statement and looked at him questioningly.

He was silent for a moment, then he began to talk, slowly and painfully. "You might as well know. I expect it'll be all over Bilsden soon. My wife has gone to live in Brighton – permanently. She knew Marianne was ill, but she wouldn't go near her, or even delay her plans to leave. She's afraid of illness, I know. But to abandon her own daughter like that! I was disgusted, sickened by her. So – so I told her – I told her not to come back."

"Never?"

"Never. I can't stomach any more of her shrewishness, Annie. She makes the whole house unhappy. You of all people know what she's like."

"Yes. I know."

"It'll cause talk. I had hoped that she would stay here until Marianne grew up. A girl on the verge of womanhood needs a mother. But a mother who would leave her sick child, refuse even to see her, well, I think we shall be better off without her. When Marianne recovers, I shall see my lawyer and put our separation on a legal footing."

Annie made a sympathetic noise in her throat.

"I must see that Marianne doesn't feel the lack too much," he went on, thinking aloud, rather than talking to her. "She's nearly a young lady now. Perhaps one of my cousins would come and live with us to keep her company. I don't know. I haven't kept in touch with the rest of my family since my parents died." He sighed and let Annie's hand fall. "Thank you for listening to me. I shouldn't have burdened you with my worries when you have enough of your own."

"That's what friends are for," she replied quietly and his face brightened a little at her words. "We all need someone to talk to. I have my brother and several good friends. Sally's almost a mother to me, and there's Bridie, too. I'm luckier than you. I feel honoured by your confidences, Jeremy."

He sighed and stood up. "I must go now. Thank you again, my very dear friend."

When Jeremy came the next day, Annie was asleep and he wouldn't let them wake her. He felt renewed just to visit the house. He hadn't realised how lonely he'd become, how short of real friends.

William's rash came out as expected, but he also developed a raging temperature. As the boy grew worse, Jeremy found it hard to persuade Annie to keep her hopes up. William's face was flushed, his forehead was burning hot and his tongue was heavily furred. He kept complaining that he was choking.

Annie and Kathy shared the nursing, leaving the running of the house and any business matters to Alice, but Annie took the major part in the nursing, spending every minute she could with her son, and only consenting to go and lie down when she was too exhausted to care for him properly.

Night ran into day in a blur of William's delirious ravings. When he burned with fever, they sponged him with boiled water; when he shivered, they covered him carefully. They fed him sips of water as often as he would take them, but he could eat nothing, for his tongue was swollen. He lost weight visibly, his limbs seeming thinner every day. Tom was a tower of strength to the whole household, and Dr Lewis's calls helped Annie, too. Pauline Hinchcliffe sent baskets of hothouse fruits and other delicacies, which were wasted on the patient, but which were a comfort to Annie, as were all the signs of her friends' concern.

Others in the Rows had fallen ill. The Gibson household was the worst affected in Salem Street, perhaps because of Emily's sloppy ways and their poor dietary habits. Little Edward died of the scarlet fever after a very few days and Peggy soon became grievously ill. When Tom brought the news of Edward's death, Annie stared at him glassily through eyes gritty and burning from lack of sleep. She seemed not to understand what he was saying, or not to care.

"Did you hear what I said?" he asked.

"Yes. Edward's dead. I'm sorry. But I can do nothing for them. I must keep my strength up for William. He shan't die, too! He shan't!"

He thought she seemed almost like a mad woman.

Although the rash faded, William didn't get any better. His ears hurt him and his body was still burning hot to the touch. Nothing seemed to reduce his temperature for long and after a while it became obvious that he could not take much more of this. Annie insisted on sitting up with him at night, afraid that he might slip away during the dark hours if she were not with him.

One night, when William was at a very low ebb, she

drove Kathy forcibly up to bed, but allowed Tom to stay with her. They were later joined by Jeremy Lewis, who had come from Number Three. One look at William and he abandoned any idea of telling Annie that her little half-sister was dead and that Emily was now down with the influenza.

"I'll stay," he said abruptly. "I may be of some help to you. The boy can't go on like this. Why don't you go and get some sleep, Tom? You'll be in a better state to help Annie later if you do."

After a bit of persuasion, Tom agreed. "I wouldn't leave you on your own, our Annie," he mumbled apologetically, "but I'm dead on me feet an' as long as you've got the doctor . . ."

"You go."

Annie and Jeremy worked together on the boy, sponging down his burning, emaciated body to try to reduce the fever. In spite of a sleeping draught, he still had bouts of wild delirium, thrashing around and begging them to pull him out of the fire.

A little after midnight, when they had got William temporarily quietened down, Annie suddenly collapsed in tears. "I can't – he's not going to . . ." she sobbed incoherently, feeling that she could not go on any longer like this. Jeremy could not help folding her in his arms and holding her close.

"Shhh, my love, shh!" He rained kisses on her wet cheeks.

She clung to him, forgetting everything in her terror for her son and her need for comfort and reassurance.

"Oh, Jeremy, I can't t-take any more. He'll die and what'll I do without him? I love him so! I don't care how I got him, I love him and I c-can't bear it if he . . ." Her sobs redoubled.

Gradually her hysteria subsided and she relaxed in his arms. "I shouldn't . . ." she whispered.

"We're hurting no one. And as you said the other day, that's what friends are for. You're not alone." She managed the ghost of a smile as he threw her own words back at her. She laid her head against his chest and sighed tiredly, then jerked up.

"It's gone quiet. William . . ."

They turned back to the boy, now lying still and white on the makeshift bed. Jeremy put Annie gently aside and felt for his patient's pulse, more fearful for her than for the boy.

She stood frozen to the spot, hardly able to breathe. After a long-drawn-out moment, when she held on to consciousness only by a last thread of willpower, Jeremy turned to her and smiled. "It's all right," he said, near to tears of joy himself. "He's still very weak, but he's breathing more easily, his pulse is slower and his forehead's cooler. The fever's broken, Annie; William's turned the corner."

She crumpled to the floor as a roaring blackness overwhelmed her and it was several minutes before she regained consciousness.

"William's all right," Jeremy told her gently as soon as he could see that she understood what was happening. "He's weak, he'll need careful nursing, but he has a good chance now. Oh, my love, don't cry!" He held her to him, kissing her hair, murmuring endearments.

After a moment she pushed him away and said in a low voice, "Jeremy, this can't be. You're a married man and anyway, I don't – I can't love you in that way."

He stiffened. "I'm sorry. I shouldn't have lost control like that."

Her heart ached for the loneliness that radiated from him and she put a hand on his shoulder. "Oh, Jeremy, I hope we can stay friends. You've been such a good friend to me, to all my family."

He was staring blindly across the room, but his voice was almost normal. "Yes. Friends it is, Annie."

Neither of them saw Tom pause at the foot of the stairs, then tiptoe quietly back up, stunned by the sight of his sister in Dr Lewis's arms. He'd have sworn that she hated the thought of a man touching her and he wasn't at all sure that he wanted her to get mixed up with anyone. She had enough on her plate with William and the business. Besides, the doctor was married, so nothing good could come of that association. Tom decided to keep his eyes open and step in if necessary. He moved round his bedroom noisily enough to make sure that they heard him coming and then he clumped down the stairs again.

"I thought I heard something, Annie, love. How's our William?"

Annie turned a tear-streaked, but joyful face towards him, so that what she said was unnecessary. "Oh, Tom, Dr Lewis thinks the crisis has passed. William's fever's broken. He's breathing more easily already. He has a chance!" Her voice broke on the words.

Tom moved over and put his arm round her. "That's the best news I've heard in a long while," he said huskily. "I knew our William'd make it." He hugged her and looked so challengingly at the doctor that Jeremy wondered whether he had seen or guessed something. "We're tough stock, us Gibsons, doctor."

Jeremy's face clouded.

"What's up?" Tom asked quickly, as sharp as ever.

Jeremy hesitated.

"What is it?" Annie asked. "You'd better tell us, or we'll be worrying. Is it – someone else at Number Three?"

"I'm afraid so. Your little sister Peggy. She died this

evening just before I came round here. I could do nothing. She wasn't a strong child. And ... and now your stepmother has the influenza. Badly, I'm afraid."

"Oh, no! Poor little Peggy! I'll have to go round there and see what I can do."

"No!" Jeremy and Tom spoke in unison.

"But there's no one else! We can't just leave them. They need help."

'You can't help them *and* nurse William, Annie," said Jeremy. "The influenza seems to pass quickly from one person to another. William isn't out of danger yet. If he caught anything else, he'd surely die. And you're run down yourself. What if you caught it? William has only you." He turned to Tom. "She fainted a little while ago. Don't let her go near the rest of the family. She's in no state to do anything."

"I won't," said Tom firmly. "Annie, you know you can't go round there. Just look at you! You're as white as a winding sheet an' you look ready to drop. Besides, I'm not havin' you riskin' your life for Emily. She's not worth it. If I have to tie you down, you'll stay away from Number Three!"

"But Tom, what will they do?" she protested. "We can't leave them without help. You know what Dad's like."

"We won't. We'll pay someone else to go in and help. I'll see to it first thing in the morning. Trust me!"

She looked at him very seriously, then she nodded.

Tom gave her a little lop-sided smile. "You *can* trust me now, you know, love." Then his tone became brisk. "Right, then, doctor. You're lookin' in need of a rest yourself. If our William doesn't need you any more, I'd suggest you get yourself home. We're more than grateful for your help tonight, but we don't want you killin' yourself. How's your daughter?"

"Oh, I'd forgotten about Marianne!" exclaimed Annie guiltily. "How is she, Jeremy?"

Tom noticed her use of the doctor's first name at once and his lips tightened into a thin line. Oh, no, Dr Lewis, he thought to himself. She's had enough to put up with. You're not going to spoil her life again. You're married an' you've got nothin' to offer her.

"Marianne's much better, thank you," Jeremy said, in his usual quiet voice. "It is the influenza, but it's not a bad attack. Ellie's been a tower of strength. She's like her father. Sam's good with sick people. He seems to calm them down. Ellie has the same touch."

Tom shepherded Jeremy Lewis out, shut the door firmly and came back to stand next to William's bed. "Aye, he does look a bit more like. You can see the difference. Funny, isn't it, how quickly they turn the corner sometimes?"

She nodded, almost too weary to speak, and he put his arm round her and walked her over to the stairs. "You get yourself up to bed, our Annie, and waken Kathy. She can come and sit with William. You look like a bloody ghost! I don't want you collapsing on me!"

"Dad . . ." she begged, in a whisper of a voice.

"Stop worriting! As soon as it's light, I'll go over and sort something out for that feckless lot. I said I would, didn't I? They don't deserve it, but I'll see they're all right. So leave it to me. Go on! Up to bed with you now!" He pushed her gently up the stairs. "We'll look after him properly, you know. We love him, too.

She smiled back at him tiredly. "I know you will. And Tom!"

"Yes?"

"I'm glad you stayed with us."

Then he knew that he was really forgiven.

While the epidemics were raging in Bilsden, taking a heavy toll among the Rows and not sparing the better-off families in their comfortable houses, Tom Gibson came to full maturity. He arranged for the burial of Edward and his little half-sister, Peggy, and supported his father through the ordeal, refusing to let Annie attend or be involved in any way. He also found a woman to nurse Emily and look after the other children, so that his father could continue in employment, for things had not changed since Lucy's death and Hallam's mill stopped for no one. Grief was still considered no excuse for absence from work, once the funeral was over.

The mill did not even close for the death of Frederick Hallam's wife from the influenza which was weeding out the weaker inhabitants of the town, rich and poor alike. And Frederick was back at his desk the day after the funeral. He had not loved Christine, but he was angry that he had been so powerless to help her. He'd have another word with Jeremy Lewis about the town's sanitation and water supplies. Epidemics were bad for business. Why, he'd had nearly a third of his workers laid low by one thing or another this time. Something would have to be done.

It never occurred to Tom that he might catch anything himself and he didn't. He'd had his share of illnesses as a child, including a mild dose of the fever, but he had not had so much as a sniffle since he grew up. Since he'd left the mill, he'd been bursting with vitality. He knew now what he wanted in life and was on the way to getting it. What more could a man ask of fate or fortune, or whatever it was that decided what happened to you?

When Emily died, unvisited by her daughter May, for whom she'd been calling in vain, she was not lamented by Tom. However, he again arranged a funeral and supported his father through it.

"Nay, lad," said John, as they walked away from the chapel graveyard, "that's two wives and four children I've buried. Life's a cruel hard business."

"Aye, well, you've seven children still living and two wives is enough for any man," said Tom unsympathetically. "You've had more than your share."

"What a way to talk, with my Em'ly only just cold!" protested John, shocked.

"It needs saying. You found comfort after our mam died, but you've enough on your plate now, lookin' after what you've got. Don't you go takin' on any more wives!"

John stalked ahead, muttering angrily, but he slowed down again as they turned into Boston Street. "It's all very well you talkin' like that, our Tom, but how am I goin' to look after 'em, that's what I want to know? I can't work in the mill *and* look after the house. I'm no good in a house anyway. What does a man know about cookin' and washin'?"

"Neither was Emily any good in the house, so you won't be missin' much. Rebecca's turned nine. Surely she can do some of it. Our Annie managed the house when she was only ten, and managed it well, too."

John shrugged. "Rebecca's not Annie. Annie allus were as sharp as a needle. And Em'ly – well, she didn't train her lasses like Lucy trained our Annie. Your mam were a rare housewife, as well as the best wife a man could have. Em'ly did her best, but you know how it was. She was a weak reed."

"Aye. We know. But in the meantime, there's still four children left to you, so we'll have to think of somethin', won't we? But no more marryin'!"

The epidemics slowly died down and people began to pick up the pieces of their lives. Then, just as the weather was beginning to warm up a bit and April was blowing gently in, Sally came down with a cold. She laughed at Annie's worries and didn't bother much about herself. She boasted that it'd take more than a cold to keep her in her bed, now that things were going so well for her.

A few days later there was a knock on the door of Number Eight and Annie went to see who was there. "Mr Blunt!" she exclaimed in surprise, seeing Sally's Harry on the doorstep. "Do come in!"

He stepped into the front room, but wouldn't sit down. "I – er – I'm sorry to disturb you, Mrs Ashworth, but its Sally. She's ill."

Annie froze. "Ill?"

"Yes. She seems to have – I think it's the influenza. I don't know what to do."

Annie reached for her shawl. "I'll come over and see if I can do anything to help. Kathy?"

"Yes, Annie?" Kathy peered out of the back room. "Oh, hello, Mr Blunt."

"Kathy, Sally's ill. Mr Blunt is afraid that she has the influenza. I must go to her. Can you see to William?"

"Yes, of course. Annie – take care!"

But Annie was already out of the front door, hurrying along to Number Six. There her worst fears were realised as soon as she saw Sally and heard her laboured breathing.

"Sorry to bother you, Annie, love," croaked Sally.

"Sally, why ever didn't you ask for help sooner? You must have been bad for days. I should have come round myself and checked that you were all right! Why didn't Alice tell me?"

"I wouldn't let her. Didn't want to – to bother you. You had enough on your plate – with your William." Sally's eyes closed and she began to shiver.

Annie tucked the blankets round her and turned to the little man waiting patiently in the doorway. "You'd better go for the doctor, Mr Blunt. Dr Lewis of Park House. Do you know where that is?"

"Yes." His face was quivering, as if he were close to tears. "You – you'll stay with her till I get back?"

"Of course I will!"

When he'd gone, Sally opened her eyes. "I didn't think I'd get it. I don't usually ail. I thought – just a cold, I thought. Eh, I do feel bad. Annie . . . ?"

"Yes?"

"Don't leave me. I'm afraid."

"I won't." Annie tried to speak cheerfully. "I'm an experienced nurse. I know exactly what to do."

She spent the next three days looking after Sally. Harry stayed on in Bilsden and Alice spelled Annie in the nursing, but somehow Sally was always better when Annie was looking after her, and it was Annie she called for when she grew delirious.

Both Tom and Jeremy tried to prevent Annie from wearing herself out, but in vain. Now that she knew that William was out of danger, she didn't even seem to hear their carefully-reasoned arguments as to why she should return to Number Eight for a few hours of uninterrupted rest, or why she should go out for a walk in the fresh air. She would occasionally go as far as the doorway of her own house and talk cheerfully to William from there for a few minutes, but the rest of the time she stayed with Sally.

Towards the end of the week, it became obvious to everyone but Annie that Sally was weakening fast, in spite of all the care she was getting.

"Sally's heart's not strong," Jeremy told Annie, trying to prepare her for the worst.

Annie gazed at him uncomprehendingly, for she was dizzy with fatigue. Then Sally called out and Annie turned back to her. That night, when Annie was alone with Sally, she noticed that there was a change in her friend's breathing. She bent over the bed and Sally's eyes flickered open.

"Annie – love."

"I'm here."

"I'm – so tired."

"Of course you are! You've been very ill. But we'll nurse you back to health."

Sally's head moved from side to side in a feeble gesture of negation. "No, love. Not this time."

Tears filled Annie's eyes. "Don't talk like that, Sally! I won't let you!"

Sally's hand groped for hers and Annie grasped it, her eyes blurred with tears.

The sick woman was silent for a moment, gathering her strength, then she started to speak again. "You've been – like a real daughter – to me."

"Don't tire yourself, Sally!" Annie begged.

"Doesn't – matter. Not now. Pity, though."

"What's a pity?"

"Never got – made respectable – after all."

Annie was sobbing now. "You're as respectable as anyone I know, Sally. And I love you like a mother."

"Annie, I . . ."

Harry appeared at the door. "I heard a noise. Is there – is something . . . ?" He saw Annie's face and rushed over to the bed, but Sally had gone.

They had to take Annie out and lead her home. She seemed stunned and was quite unable to talk or answer their questions. Jeremy shook his head and recommended a week or two's rest in bed and, ideally, a change of scene, a thing usually impossible for his poorer patients.

"Has she – is she – she's not ill too, is she?" Tom asked, with fear in his heart.

"She isn't suffering from any illness, if that's what you mean, not as far as we can tell, anyway, but she's totally exhausted. Isn't there somewhere she could go to get away and give herself a chance to recover? Have you no relatives or acquaintances in the country? She needs a change of scene. That seems to help most of all in this type of case."

Tom stood frowning for a moment, then his face brightened. "I bet Bridie would have her, if you're really sure that's what she needs."

"I am."

"I'll go an' see Bridie today, then."

Bridie not only said yes, but she sent Michael back with Tom to bring Annie and her things in the farm cart. She also insisted that William was to be sent to the farm too, so that Annie would not be worrying about him. It'd do the lad good to run about in the fresh air and she'd soon feed him up on her good eggs and butter. The hens were just starting to lay well, after the winter, and she had a cow just come into milk. The weather was still cold, but there was a promise of spring in the air. William would take no harm, for Bridie would personally see that he wrapped up warmly, and so Tom was to tell Annie.

So it was done, in spite of Annie's cross protests that she didn't want to impose on anyone. What finally persuaded her to agree was Tom's cunning reasoning that it'd be the best thing for William.

Annie asked Michael to stop the cart at the top of the hill and sat looking down into the smoky little valley. "I'd forgotten how ugly Bilsden was," she said dreamily. "You forget about that when you live in the middle of it all." She sighed and closed her eyes. "Thank you, Michael. I'd like to move on now."

467

27

April to May 1845

For the first day or two at Knowle Farm, Annie just sat around in Bridie's best parlour, staring out of the window at the moors which were alternately swept by showers or lit up by the sun. Bridie kept the children quiet and left her guest to herself. Annie was grieving for Sally and was totally worn out by her long spell of nursing. She would come round in her own time.

It was rare that Annie had ever had the chance to be waited on hand and foot like this. The last time she could remember being idle was just before William's birth, and once before that, when she had been ill as a child. But she knew she needed the rest. She had never in all her life felt as deep down exhausted as she did now. For the first few days she just drifted along, listening with mild pleasure to William's excited voice as he explored the mysteries of farm life and smiling vaguely at him when he came to show her some new treasure. Bridie's lilting voice in the kitchen formed a soothing background to the lazy days.

In the bracing moorland air, William's cheeks grew rosy again and he was soon eating as heartily as the other children. It was he who was instrumental in pushing Annie into the next stage of her recovery. He started to drag her out of doors to look at this or that, or simply to listen to the faint calls of birds over the rolling grey-green stretches of moorland above the farm. And now, Bridie made no attempt to keep him away from his mother. She allowed him to drag Annie out to feed the chickens and collect the eggs, to see the new ducklings and to inspect the first shoots of barley and oats.

One morning, Annie was pulled from her bed at dawn by an almost incoherent William, to admire the litter of eight healthy puppies born during the night. He hung over the basket in the shed as if they were the most precious thing on earth. To a boy bred and cloistered in the Rows, the countryside was a treasure-house of delights.

Annie began to wonder why she had not taken more time off to show her son what the world was like outside the smuts and grime of Bilsden. She remembered Brighton and the sea, and vowed that within the year she'd take William to see the sea, too. There was towns on the Fylde coast which were attracting more visitors every year, Blackpool was one, or St Anne's-on-Sea. They could easily afford to spend a few days there. And they would.

After the first week at the farm, Annie began to think about her future, though she still did not feel ready to plunge back into her busy life. There was no longer any need for William to drag her out of doors; of her own accord she began to go for walks across the moors. Sometimes she went with William, more often she went on her own, revelling in the silence and the peace. Even the weather co-operated, for there were very few rainy days and, though it still had not much warmth in it, the sun shone on Annie's peregrinations. She tried several times to help Bridie around the farm, but was shooed away and told to go and enjoy her holiday.

"Get outside, will ye!" Bridie would scold. "I can't do with ye under me feet all day."

470

Annie tried to put her gratitude into words, but was cut short.

Bridie patted her hand. "I know, love. I know exactly how ye feel. An' I'm glad to be able to help ye. I'm that grateful to our Danny for giving us this chance, an' I'm happy to share me good fortune with me friends."

"Where is Danny now?" For once, the thought of him did not fill Annie with apprehension. The real world was still too distant to her.

"He's workin' somewhere called the Cotswold Hills an' he says he's doin' very well for himself, for the whole country's gone wild on building them railways. He writes us letters an' Father Shaughnessy comes and tells us what's in them and writes back for us. Our Danny always asks to be remembered to you." She looked sideways at Annie, trying to see her reaction.

Annie kept her face calm. "That's nice." Danny was so far away that the thought of him had no power to do more than cause a ripple in the surface of her peaceful happiness.

"Ah, he's been a good son to us, that boy. Did you ever see my Michael look so well? And will ye look at the roses in the children's cheeks! Sure, we both hated livin' in the town, for we were brought up in the country, but when they took our fields away from us, what could we do? Ye have to feed your family, don't ye? Ye have to go where the work is. Me sisters've gone to America. 'Tis further away than England, they say. But 'tis a good job they did, because people have been havin' a hard time of it in Ireland lately." She crossed herself.

"What's happened?" Annie felt out of touch with everything.

"The potato harvest has failed and they're starvin'. Folk live on potatoes over there, love. I can't imagine how they'll go on without the crop. We've been collectin' a bit of money at church to send over. The good father's organised it. Me cousins still live there, an' their families, too." She shook her head. "But what am I doin' talkin' to ye about such things. It's cheerin' up ye need, not makin' miserable!"

Pauline came to visit Annie at the farm, but couldn't stay long, for she was nursing Saul back to health. He, too, had had the influenza. She brought several bottles of port wine with her and ordered Annie to drink a large glass of it every night. She brushed aside Annie's apologies for letting her down about the dressmaking. The silk was still there, wasn't it? It could be made up later. And anyway, she wouldn't be able to attend the wedding, because Saul was not well enough yet to leave. Pauline was also looking tired and not her usual self. Every family seemed to have been hit by some form of illness, Annie thought, well, everyone except Bridie's noisy brood.

Jeremy Lewis, when he came over to check on his patients, was astonished at the improvement in them both. "You must be a witch, Mrs O'Connor," he told a delighted Bridie. "I never saw so fast a recovery."

"Ah, well, ye can't beat a breath of fresh air and a bit of good food, can you, now? Will you try one of my potato scones, then, doctor?"

The next time Jeremy had to drive out that way, he brought Ellie and Marianne with him and left them to visit Annie at Knowle Farm while he went on to visit another patient at an outlying farm. Marianne, who was at first on her dignity as an almost-grown-up young lady, was not proof against William's enthusiasm and after a while condescended to allow him and Ben, Bridie's youngest son, to show her round the farm. She fell in love with the puppies and went home with the promise of one for herself, once they were old enough to leave their mother. Now that Annabelle had left, her father had promised her a dog of her own, a thing her mother would never have allowed.

Marianne had also lately started to take an interest in her father's work among the poor of the town and would question him at meal-times about what he had been doing and how she could help. Her mother would never have permitted such unseemly talk. Looking back, Marianne sometimes thought that her mother had not permitted her to do anything interesting. Neither she nor her father had put it into words, but life was a lot pleasanter without her mother. The servants would have heartily endorsed this, even Mabel, who had been very subdued since Mrs Lewis's departure.

Ellie sat and enjoyed a comfortable chat with Annie. She brought her up to date on all the news from Park House. The new junior partner was a very nice young gentleman and a pleasure to have in the house. Always courteous, always ready to lend a hand. With him there, the doctor didn't have to work as hard, and about time, too. And the doctor had had Mrs Lewis's old room redecorated and furnished for his daughter. A proper young lady's room it was now. A cousin of the doctor's was to come and live with them, to teach Miss Marianne how a young lady should behave. But the doctor had told Ellie that it would make no difference to her position as Miss Marianne's personal maid cum family housekeeper. Yes, that's what he'd called her, she giggled. Well, she would personally see that it didn't make any difference! Just let *anyone* even try to come between her and Marianne!

"Don't you ever wish you had children of your own?" asked Annie idly. "You'd have made a marvellous mother."

"Children I'd have liked, but not a husband," declared Ellie without hesitation. "The only sort of man who'd marry

473

me would be too poor to support me in comfort and too rough for me. I've got used to gentlemen's ways and I've been spoiled over the past few years, with Mrs Lewis away so often. I'd hate to have to struggle like my mother did. Look at how it's soured her! We had some bad times before we moved into Salem Street, you know. I haven't forgotten them. I never intend to go hungry again as long as I live. I save most of my wages, and Dr Lewis has been very generous with presents. I expect to have enough saved to keep myself in comfort when I'm too old to work. No, Annie, love, I'm far better off as I am."

"How are they – your parents, I mean?"

"My father's well. I see him often. I don't see my mother."

Annie waited, then, when Ellie didn't say anything, she added in a casual voice, "And Matt?"

"He's as busy as ever. You'd think it was *his* mill, not Hallam's, the work he puts in."

"He was always ambitious."

"Too ambitious!" sniffed Ellie. "An' he's that prim nowadays, you wouldn't believe it. Always talking about the Lord and the Bible – when he's not talking about the cotton market or some stupid lecture he's been to in Manchester. I can't be bothered with him."

After that visit, Annie began to make detailed plans for her return to Bilsden. She scoured Bridie's house for scraps of paper, for although the children could read and write after a fashion, Michael and Bridie were completely illiterate and neither of them had much patience with what Bridie called scornfully, 'the readin' and the writin'. The scraps of paper were soon covered in calculations which made Bridie worry that Annie was addling her brains, but nothing would stop her.

At the end of the third week Annie declared that it was time she returned home again.

William sulked about their coming departure and Bridie protested in vain. "Could ye not stay for another little week, now, Annie, love?"

"No, Bridie, I couldn't. I can't thank you enough for this holiday. It's done me and William a world of good. I'd swear he's grown an inch and he's bursting out of his clothes with all the good food you've been stuffing into us. You really are a marvellous cook!"

Bridie preened herself. "Well, I do have a light hand with the pastry, even if I do say so myself. An' our chickens are as tender as butter. But Annie, love . . ."

"No buts, Bridie! I *must* go back. I'm quite recovered now, you know, and there's a lot to be sorted out – my dad, for one thing. And I want to move out of Salem Street as soon as I can." For she had told Bridie and Michael a little about her plans.

"Annie, me dear, ye can't be takin' everyone else's burdens on your shoulders. Ye've a life of your own to lead an' it's your dad's responsibility to look after his family, not yours."

Annie smiled wryly. "I won't neglect myself, I promise you. But I can't just leave them to struggle along. You know what Dad's like."

"Aye, I do, too. His breeches rule his head, that one. It's to be hoped that he's gettin' past all that now, at his age!"

"Bridie, what a thing to say!"

Bridie blushed a little, but stuck to her guns. "Well, 'tis true! Me an' your mam used to joke about it sometimes, an' look at the number of children he got out of that poor Emily."

"Well, you don't have to worry about me, Bridie. I know exactly what I'm going to do. It's only a question of how best to do it." And how to gain Tom's agreement, she added silently. That'll be the big difficulty.

* * *

Salem Street seemed even more mean and cramped than it had done before. Even William noticed and said, in a tone of great surprise, "How little and dirty it all looks!"

Annie, following Michael and William, who were carrying her luggage, looked around her with the appraising eyes of a stranger. The air smelled sooty, the people seemed pallid and shrunken after Michael and his strapping sons. These weren't her people any more. Even the houses were more dilapidated than she remembered, the window-frames warped, a few panes broken, the doors scratched and scuffed, and the bricks stained a dark reddish-black by the smoke from the big chimney that towered over the street. No, she had no intention of leaving her father to struggle on alone in Number Three. He had helped her in her hour of greatest need, when Mrs Lewis had dismissed her, and she would help him now in return.

She looked at the other houses as they went past, but the people she thought about were those who had been there in her youth. The tenants at Number One had changed several times. The Dykeses were gone from Number Two, the O'Connors from Number Five and Sally from Number Six. The Peters were long gone from Number Seven, though she still thought of it as their house. Only Widow Clegg was left in Number Four. And herself in Number Eight. But now that poor Charlie had died, she would be leaving Number Eight and the street. She had spent most of her twenty-five years there; that was more than enough!

She noted automatically that everything in her own house was clean and shining – trust Kathy for that! – and she was glad of the fire crackling cheerfully in the grate. Kathy rushed to hug her and William, and to exclaim at how well they both looked. Alice followed with a quieter, but no less warm welcome. They hadn't expected her so early and Tom was still out on his rounds, but would be back sooner than usual in honour of the occasion. Sammy nuzzled at her skirts, sniffing delicately at the strange smells and thumping her with his tail.

For a time it seemed that the front room would burst with so many people in it, all trying to talk at once, and William rolling about on the floor with Sammy, telling him about the new puppy who would be coming to live with them. Eventually, however, Michael took his leave, William went out to play and to boast to anyone who would listen about his wonderful holiday, and Alice tactfully took Kathy into the back room, so that Annie could have a rest.

When he came home, Tom found his sister deep in calculations, the bits of paper from the farm piled up at one side of the table and several new pages spread out in front of her, with long columns of figures marching down them.

"It didn't take you long to start workin' again, did it? You'll undo all the good of the holiday!" He pretended to be angry to hide how glad he was to see her.

"Uncle Tom! Uncle Tom!" A small body catapulted into him and he laughed and swung William up in the air, setting the boy shrieking for joy.

"I think you've grown, my lad." Tom pretended to stagger under his nephew's weight.

"I have. I've grown an inch. Michael measured me on their doorpost. I'll soon be as tall as Ben – well, nearly. But he *is* older than me. An' guess what! Michael says he'll give me one of Lady's pups when they're old enough to leave their mother. She's a *very* intelligent dog, so we think the pups'll be clever, too. There's one of them that has one black ear and one white, an' Michael says I can have it. An' Mother says when we move, we can go an' fetch it. It'll be company for Sammy."

477

Tom looked sharply across at Annie. "Hold on a minute, young fellow! Let other people get a word in edgewise, will you? What's this about moving, Annie?"

"I think it's more than time we moved, don't you? Salem Street has had its day."

"Maybe." At least she had said 'we'. She wasn't leaving him behind.

"We'll talk it over later, when this noisy scamp has gone to bed."

So Tom had to contain himself until later, when Kathy and Alice went and sat in the back room, and left him and Annie to talk.

He stretched his legs out in front of the fire. "You look well, Annie. It's good to have you back again."

"It's good to be back, though not so nice to be in the Rows after the farm. It's lovely up there. Why didn't you come to see us?"

"I was too bloody busy. And then there was Dad. He's fretting, doesn't seem his old self."

"Poor Dad! He's had more than his share of troubles."

"I can't get over how well you look," he repeated. "As well as you've ever looked."

"I am well. I haven't felt so good in years, and . . ." She broke off and looked at him.

"And . . . ?" he prompted.

"And I'm ready now to make a move from here. Don't you think it's time we left? I've been making plans during the past week or so," she gestured to the pile of papers, "and I've been trying to calculate what we'll need and how much money I have. I think I've put everything down. Could you just have a look at . . ."

"In a minute. There's something I have to tell you first."

She was instantly alert. "Trouble?"

478

"No! Why should there be trouble?" He scowled at her. "There won't be that sort of trouble again, so you can just stop bringing it up!"

"No. I should know that by now. Sorry."

He smiled, a proud little smile and for a moment, she could see her mother in him. "I told you I could look after things, Annie. It's just – well, there's something we didn't like to tell you before. Dr Lewis thought it might upset you too much at the time."

"Stop trying to prepare me and tell me what it is."

"All right. Sally left everything she owned to you. There was a will, drawn up by a proper lawyer. She said you'd been like a daughter to her and you were to use the money as you saw fit. You've to go and see her lawyer, and he'll explain all the details to you."

She willed herself not to cry; she had done with tears. "But – what about Harry? Shouldn't he have the money? After all, they were going to get married."

"He says he doesn't need it and he wants to do as she would have wished. He's taken her death hard, poor bugger. He gave her a fancy funeral and ordered a headstone made, then he went back to Oldham. He looked older, sort of shrivelled. I felt right sorry for him. We had a bit of a chat before he left. He said to thank you for all you did for her, and not just when she was ill."

"I loved her," Annie said simply. "I didn't do it to get her money. It should be his by right."

"I told you – he doesn't want it, or need it. He's well set up already. He took the locket she used to wear and that was all. I said you wouldn't mind him taking that. He paid the rent till the end of the month. He said he'd take it as a favour if you'd clear the house out for him. He couldn't face goin' through her things. And you're to keep anything you want. Kathy says she'll do that for you, if you like."

Annie took a deep, quivering breath. "I feel funny about it. As if I'm taking something that doesn't belong to me."

He put his arm round her. "You did your best for her, love." Being Tom, he could not resist adding, "Er – have you any idea how much she's left you?"

"A fair idea. She had two or three cottages and a bit of money in the bank. She used to get me to help her with her accounts sometimes."

He whistled in surprise. "That much?"

"She was always very careful with her money." Annie concentrated on the business aspects or she'd have been crying again. "I'll have to see that lawyer, though, to find out exactly what she had."

"Er – you realise what this means, don't you?" Tom started poking the fire, trying to speak casually.

"What?"

"It means that you don't have to work any more if you don't want to."

That explained why he was acting so strangely. "I'd not know what to do with myself if I became a lady of leisure," she mocked. "Goodness, I don't even like to think about it."

"I wondered – there's your doctor friend."

"What do you mean?"

"I saw him kissin' you the night our William turned the corner. You weren't struggling to get away."

She shrugged and leaned back in her chair so that her face was in the shadow. "There's no future for me with Jeremy Lewis. Did you think I'd agree to become his mistress? You should know me better! He's married and we both have our children to think of. Besides, I'm not in love with him. If I was, I'd perhaps think about it. But I'm not. I'm fond of Jeremy. We're friends. But apart from that night, when he was comforting me, there's been nothing like that between us and there won't be! Not on my part, anyway, and I suspect that it was just loneliness, with him." She smiled at her brother. "Is that what's been worrying you, Tom, love?"

"Yes. I wasn't sure whether I'd be included in your future plans. I'd not blame you for tryin' for a bit of happiness for yourself." It cost him a lot to say that.

She looked at him almost blindly. "Happiness? I don't think I was born for that sort of happiness! First Matt, then . . ." She drew a deep breath. "Let's not talk about it any more. That day, when I came home from Manchester and found William so ill, that very day I'd decided to move out of this street and set up as a ladies' dressmaker. Pauline's been at me for a while to do it. I assume that you still want to carry on with the junk business?"

He was grinning at her, reassured, looking like the old Tom again. "Of course I do! But not just carry on – I want to expand, try out a few new things. Did you know that old Mr Thomas had died? It's an ill wind! His widow wants to sell his scrap business. She's given me first refusal. I've got some money saved, but not enough. I wondered – would you like to invest in an up-and-coming young scrap merchant?"

"I might. I'd have to look at the figures carefully. But for Sally, I couldn't have done it; I'd have needed all my money for my dressmaking salon."

"But now . . . ?"

"Now it might well be possible."

He was fiddling with the material of his shirt sleeve. "You wouldn't have to worry about me, Annie. It'd be honest trade. You do believe that, don't you?"

"Yes, love. I know that sort of thing's all in the past now."

"I've grown up a lot lately, Annie." There was silence for a few moments, then he said slowly, "It makes you think, doesn't it, when you see what can happen, when you see how quickly folk can be snuffed out."

"Yes. It's been a bad winter. In fact, I don't know what I'd

481

have done without you since Charlie died last year, Tom."

He pulled a face at her to hide his feelings. "Come on, then. Let's have a look at these calculations of yours. You an' your breakjaw words! You've got *me* talkin' fancy half the time now. What have you decided to do? I suppose we'll be going to live at Netherleigh Cottage?"

"Of course! Where else? You can give Benworth his notice tomorrow. He'll complain, but he's to be out as soon as possible."

"He can complain as much as he wants! It's your house."

"So – the only problem is what to do about Dad and the children."

He looked at her suspiciously. "What do you mean by that?"

She answered him obliquely. "How's he managing?"

"Not so well. You know what he's like. He needs a woman to look after him. Young Rebecca's been doing her best and Mark's got his head screwed on all right, but they'd be in a right old mess if Kathy hadn't helped out. We'll need to sort out something permanent for him before we leave or he'll be getting himself married again."

She smiled. "Bridie says his trousers rule his head."

"I wouldn't have put it so politely myself, but I have to agree."

"Tom – I've already thought out what to do." She took a deep breath, knowing he wouldn't agree with what she was going to say. "They'll have to come and live with us at Netherleigh Cottage." She braced herself to meet his anger.

"*What!* Oh, no! I'm not havin' that! You can just get that idea *right* out of your head, Annie Ashworth!"

"But Tom . . ."

"No! I'm not having it! It's *his* job to provide for his family, not ours! We'll never get rich if we have that lot hangin' round our necks!"

"They need us. We can't let them down. Tom, they're our family."

"Well, *I* don't need *them*! And nor do you! They're not bloody comin' an' that's flat!"

"They are." She spoke quietly, but firmly. "Besides – I think it'll be a good thing."

"A good thing! A *good* thing, she says! A pack of bleedin' kids to feed, that stupid Emily's brats, and you call it a good thing! You've gone mad, Annie! Your brains are addled. You'd better go and spend a few more weeks on the farm and really recover. I never heard of such a stupid idea! Live with us, indeed!"

She took his hand. "Listen, Tom. Just listen for a minute instead of shouting. See if we can't turn the situation to our advantage."

He muttered something, pulled his hand away and leaned back in his chair, his face still hostile.

"You said yourself that Mark's got his head screwed on all right. He has! He's a clever lad. You're going to need people to help you run your business and who better than your own family?"

"It's *men* I'll need, men with muscles, not twelve-year-old lads!"

"You can't see beyond the end of your nose sometimes, Tom Gibson! I'm not talking about now; I'm talking about in a few years' time. He can start learning the trade. He'll do well, will Mark, given a bit of help and encouragement."

"He might," Tom admitted grudgingly, "but Luke's another kettle of fish. I sometimes wonder if he isn't a bit short up top. I'm not having *him* in my business!"

"He's only eleven. We'll have to see. Perhaps he'll need to stay on at school for a bit. I'm sure he'll improve, now he hasn't got Emily nagging at him. She never had a good word to say to him. No wonder he's so nervous!"

"Nervous! He's not nervous; he's downright slow!"

"He's not. He's a nice lad."

"Nice or not, he's another mouth to feed and another body to clothe."

She raised her eyebrows. "Has Dad still got his job at the mill or hasn't he?"

"Yes, of course he has!"

"Then I imagine he'll be bringing in enough money to feed and clothe the children. He doesn't throw his wages away on booze, like some. He hasn't touched a drop of gin since Mam died. All he needs is a bit of baccy for his pipe, an odd glass of ale, and he's happy. You have to admit that!"

. "I suppose so."

"It's not charity I'm offering them, you know. They'll all have to help."

He grunted.

"As for Rebecca, she can help Kathy in the house. Kathy'll train her properly, not like Emily. She can learn to sew, too, perhaps come as an apprentice to me. And I'll make sure she can read and write properly. I know they've all learned their letters at Sunday School, the older ones anyway, but they can hardly string two words together. Emily neglected those children shamefully. They're pig ignorant, poor things. It's more than time someone took them in hand. And they *are* our brothers and sisters, whether you like it or not!"

"*Half*-brothers and sisters. And no doubt Kathy'll be happy to look after little Joan as well? She'll love having a snotty-nosed five-year-old hanging on her skirts. That Joan is a sniveller."

"Only because she's been neglected. Besides, I think Kathy will enjoy looking after her. Kathy loves children. Look how she dotes on William! I do hope she gets married one day. She'd make a wonderful wife and mother."

"You've got it all planned out, haven't you?"

"I told you I had. The only thing I hadn't worked out was how I was going to find the money for everything. And," her voice faltered for a minute, "Sally's solved that problem for me."

He looked at her wonderingly and she could see the first signs that he was beginning to come round. "You're a marvel, our Annie. Doesn't any of this frighten you? You'll be risking everything, taking on heavy responsibilities . . ."

She shook her head, her expression guarded. "No, it doesn't frighten me. I don't really think that there's much risk at all. The junk business is well established. If Mr Thomas is dead, you'll have no competition to worry about when you want to expand. I think, Tom, that if you don't get what you want from life in one way – well, you have to turn elsewhere. I don't think I'm cut out for love and marriage, but I *am* a good businesswoman, and I intend to make the best of that. I shan't let the second-hand clothes business go, either. Every bit of money helps. Alice can supervise that for me, perhaps. I'll work something out."

"Annie, you'll need more than luck to succeed in a high-class business," he warned. "The gentry can be awkward customers. They want value for money, just like anyone else. An' if they take a huff, you're in trouble."

She smiled confidently. "Oh, they'll get good value, never fear. I'm not relying on luck. I'm good at dressmaking, really good. And I'll have several strings to my bow, with the second-hand stuff and your junk yard. No, Tom Gibson, it'll be hard work and clever ideas that'll get us rich, not luck."

"Well, we've never been frightened of hard work, have we?"

"No. And about Dad . . . ?"

He looked at her in exasperation. "You'll do what you

want, whatever I say, so what's the use? Have you – er – told him yet?"

"No."

"You don't think there's a chance that he'll refuse?"

"No. Why should he?"

"Why should he, indeed? No one looks a gift horse in the mouth." He pulled her to her feet. "Come on, then, we might as well go and talk to him now. I want to see his face when you tell him." A grin crept over his face.

"What are you thinking of now, Tom?"

He chuckled. "The poor old sod won't know what's hit him when he comes to live with you after over twelve years of dear Emily!"

She ignored the sarcasm, linked her arm in his and rubbed her cheek against his shoulder. "Thanks, Tom." Then she straightened up and her eyes began to sparkle in a way they hadn't done for years. "And after we've seen Dad, it'll still be light enough to take a stroll into town. I want to have a good look round. I need to find a place for my dressmaking salon, somewhere near the centre, but with a good address."

"Salon, is it? I thought you'd be working from home."

"Not me! I'm going to have the fanciest salon you've ever laid eyes on, just like those that Mrs Lewis took me to in London. I'm going to have the ladies of Bilsden falling over one another to order their dresses from me! I'm going to get really rich, Tom!" And she was going to do it on her own. A picture of Danny crept into her mind, but she pushed it firmly aside. She was an independent woman and would make her own way in life. Just let anyone try to stop her!